Brett Adams • Bryce Anderson • Misha Burnett • Dave Higgins • Karpov Kinrade

Richard Levesque • Russ Linton • Belinda Mellor • Becca Mills • J.S. Morin

Van Allen Plexico • Regina Richards • Christopher Ruz • Graham Storrs

ALL THESE SHINY WORLDS

WORLDS

—— The 2016 ImmerseOrDie Anthology ——

Edited by: JEFFERSON SMITH

creativityhacker.ca

All These Shiny Worlds

Edited by Jefferson Smith
Cover Art by Jefferson Smith
Copyedited by Fleur Macqueen
Published by Creativity Hacker Press (creativityhacker.ca)

First Printing, 2016 (Rev. 2016-02-10 13:10)

Printed in the United States of America

Library and Archives Canada Cataloguing in Publication

All these shiny worlds : the 2016 ImmerseOrDie anthology / Jefferson Smith, editor.

Issued in print and electronic formats. ISBN 978-0-9940795-4-1 (paperback). —ISBN 978-0-9940795-5-8 (epub).— ISBN 978-0-9940795-6-5 (mobi)

1. Fantasy fiction, Canadian (English). 2. Science fiction, Canadian (English). 3. Short stories, Canadian (English). I. Smith, Jefferson, 1964-, editor

PS8323.F3A55 2016 C813'.010806 C2016-900278-0
C2016-900279-9

Acknowledgements

Stories are included in this collection by permission of the authors.

"All the Way," by Graham Storrs. Copyright © 2009 Graham Storrs. First appeared in The Future Fire, vol 18.

"The Ant Tower," by Christopher Ruz. Copyright © 2011 Christopher Ruz.

"Bronwen's Dowry," by Belinda Mellor. Copyright © 1989 Belinda Mellor. First appeared in At The Stroke Of Twelve, from William Collins Sons and Co. Ltd.

"Heft," by Brett Adams. Copyright © 2011 Brett Adams.

"Rolling the Bones," by Richard Levesque. Copyright © 2015 Richard Levesque.

"Scales Fall," by Dave Higgins. Copyright © 2015 Dave Higgins.

"The Blue Breeze," by Regina Richards. Copyright © 2015 Regina Richards.

"The Dowager's Largesse," by Jefferson Smith. Copyright © 2015 Jefferson Smith.

"The First Acolyte of the Upshan Berental," by Bryce Anderson. Copyright © 2013 Bryce Anderson.

"The First Man in the World," by Misha Burnett. Copyright © 2015 Misha Burnett.

"The Rakam," by Karpov Kinrade. Copyright © 2015 Karpov Kinrade. First appeared in The Shattered Islands: Part One: The Rakam, from Daring Books.

"The Red Flame of Death," by Van Allen Plexico. Copyright © 2010 Van Allen Plexico. First appeared in Gideon Cain: Demon Hunter Vol. 1, from Airship 27 Productions.

"The Spider and the Darkness," by Russ Linton. Copyright © 2016 Russ Linton.

"Theriac," by Becca Mills. Copyright © 2014 Becca Mills.

"Three Demon Gambit," by J.S. Morin. Copyright © 2014 J.S. Morin. First published in The Dark Beyond the Door, from Fictiongarden.com.

For every reader who has ever dared the swamps of indie publishing,

And for the indie authors who sweat bullets over every misplaced comma,

We dedicate this collection to all of you.

May we find each other all the sooner.

Contents

Introduction

Okay, by now you've probably heard how ImmerseOrDie works, so you already know that I get on my treadmill every morning and open a new indie novel, hoping it will keep me distracted from the monotony of my daily walk. You've heard that I do my best to stay immersed in the book, but that when my immersion fails, I make notes about what went wrong, and that if it happens three times before my journey is over, I close the book, write up a report about what happened and post it to my website.

But maybe you don't know that ImmerseOrDie is about more than simply pointing out problems in indie books. It's also about celebrating the really good ones. Folks may be drawn in to watch the fun as yet another novel hits a patch of ice and slides into the ditch at the side of my treadmill, but there's another thing I've noticed about the people watching.

They are equally delighted by the books that do make it.

So last year, I started a new component of ImmerseOrDie. Each time a book survived my forty-minute quick sniff test, I put it on a secret pile. Those books were then subjected to a second test: a full-length read. To my surprise, a lot of them went the distance on that round, too. Before I knew it I had nine great survivors, with both great production values *and* a great story.

That's when I approached the folks at StoryBundle and hit them with my proposal. Why not offer a bundle composed entirely of indie books—but ones that had been ruthlessly curated?

And so was born the ImmerseOrDie bundle, which I'm proud to say was so popular the first time we did it, in 2015, that we did again this year, and we'll probably do it again next year as well.

What's so exciting about these StoryBundles is that they don't just help readers find great new authors to fall in love with. They also give those authors a kind of exposure they've never had. For many of them, the three weeks they participate in the bundle brings them more readers (and more income) than any entire year they've experienced before.

And I find it very exciting to be part of that.

But we can do more. The lesson of the bundles is that when authors mingle their audiences, everybody wins. When each of us announces a group project in our newsletters and social media streams, fans who come for one author are suddenly exposed to the work of all the others as well.

Unfortunately, bundles only work for people who can pay a bit of money to buy the collection. It can be as little as just a couple of bucks to get all of them, but you do have to actually buy them, and some people don't want to risk money on a pile of books from nine authors they've never heard of, just to get a book from one who they do know.

Worse, some people may not be willing to tackle an entire novel by a writer they don't know.

So we hit on the idea of creating an anthology. The one you're holding in your hands right now, as a matter of fact. And then we set out to do two things that don't happen very often with indie anthologies. First, we set up a grueling selection process to ensure that only great stories got in. And then we figured out a way to give the whole thing away for free.

To deliver on the first point, we decided to stack the deck, and began by inviting only authors whose books had previously survived the Immerse-OrDie treadmill. Then we figured that strong authors are probably a decent judge of other authors, so we asked each of the survivors to nominate one more author who they thought "had game." This gave us a total of thirty-four authors in our pool, and to them we extended a simple invitation: hit us with your best short story. Not your newest. Not the one you've been having trouble placing elsewhere. Your best.

Some of those authors don't do short stories, some didn't have time, and one or two might have been intimidated by the process. But in the end, we received twenty-five submissions.

Then we gave each of the stories to a panel of three secret judges and told them to be ruthless.

By the time the screams had died away and all the blood rinsed from the upholstery, we were left with fifteen survivors. Just like ImmerseOrDie, but a higher-speed version, played with individual short stories rather than novels or entire collections. And every bit as grueling.

Then we ran the entire collection through two complete rounds of editing with professional editors, and now, at last, we place our polished words into your hot and eager hands.

We hope you like it. And if you do, please point all your friends at it. Why wouldn't you? You'll get all that cred for turning them on to some exciting new authors, and they get a great book absolutely free. Everybody wins: readers and authors alike.

And *that's* what ImmerseOrDie is all about.

So we've done our part. All that's left is for you to do yours. Happy reading.

Jefferson Smith
January 2016, Saskatoon

The First Man in the World

Misha Burnett

Editor's Note: Science fiction likes to forecast the future of some science or technology and then explore the implications for humanity. But it does its job best when those implications are brought into focus for just one person. Or in this case, two.

They killed him for the journey, reduced his body to a handful of genetic material crystallized at 40 degrees Kelvin and his mind to an optical storage rack that took up more space than his DNA and the multiple redundancy freezer unit to keep it frozen for the long years it would take to travel.

His last memory was seeing the bulk of the ship on the horizon.

His first memory was being inside the ship, looking down at a world the color of the filthy dust that collects in air conditioning filters.

He was thirty-eight years old.

He was newborn.

He was one hundred and eighty-four years old.

It was all a matter of perspective.

He was—and numerous court cases back on Earth had verified that he had every right to the name, despite the fact that the body that had held it originally was phosphorus-rich fertilizer by this point—Tomas Kent.

Tomas Kent woke up naked and alone in a metal coffin, skin wet and raw, eyes burning from their first touch of air, and thought, *I've got a world to build.*

The world was dead, sterile, but it had potential. Long range spectrography had confirmed the presence of liquid water and a carbon dioxide atmosphere. The rest was details.

He woke up the ship, booting up systems that had been dormant since they had left Earth. They had been designed to last, and they had. The computer analyzed the world that hung below them, and together they began to plot an act of creation.

Algae was first, bullets of engineered green glop, fired from orbit in shells of ablative resin that, in burning away, would also leave a residue of biodegradable dust to drift slowly to the surface of the sea and provide an additional source of food. The glop would survive on nothing more than sunlight, seawater, and carbon dioxide, but the organics in the burned resin would help.

World building is a game of inches. Any marginal advantage is worth the effort.

Back on Earth Tomas had named his new world Avalon.

It took forty years for Avalon's seas to turn green.

Tomas talked to the computer, and the computer talked back to him, in a voice that was carefully devoid of personality or gender, of anything but meaning. Tomas had grown up with voice-activated equipment—he felt no temptation to personalize it.

Experiments with artificial intelligence had shown that machines were best left as mindless servants for long-term projects. Given too much time to think they became unpredictable, went off in strange directions that their designers could not have foreseen. Jobs that required the flexibility of a human mind required a human body as well.

Tomas would grow lonely, and bored, but the technicians back on Earth were betting that he would stay sane. The odds weren't nearly as good for a mind reduced to digital storage.

He read books, or had the computer read them to him. There were vast libraries of digitized storage. Movies, too, and games.

He had work to do—maintenance on the vast seeder ship. It was designed to be self-repairing, but he could fine tune the systems, keep the parts that fixed the other parts in working order. He spent three years in the system's asteroid belt, picking up raw materials.

He worked out plans to introduce higher forms of life, ran simulations on those plans, and changed the plans based on the simulations.

The computer could synthesize a lover for him and he spent endless hours customizing her, specifying the exact shade of her eyes and the texture of her hair. After a while he found his preferences drifting into areas that disturbed him. Some time after that he stopped being disturbed.

In the oceans of Avalon the patches of green thrived and spread, and Tomas grew old.

To grow an adult human being without the tedious years of childhood required doing some violence to the endocrine system. At forty years of age, or seventy-eight, or two hundred and twenty-four, depending on your frame of reference, Tomas's body ached, and trembled, and could no longer digest solid food. He did some final checks on the ship and told the computer that it was time for him to die again.

His last memory was looking out the window at the sun rising over still green seas.

His first memory was a blue world.

Tomas was four hundred and sixty-three years old.

Or newborn. Or seventy-eight. Take your pick.

The computer had monitored both the ship and the infant world for two centuries, launching regular salvos in its war against the inorganic; more varieties of algae, lichens aggressive enough to suck the nutrients out of the bare rock, slime molds to live on the ground that the lichen had prepared.

It had also recorded incoming messages.

Not from Earth. From Camelot.

Camelot had been launched a few years after Tomas's ship, at a far lower velocity. It held human beings, thousands of them in a cold sleep that would seem identical to death to anyone without very specialized training. Camelot's captain, like Tomas, had died and been brought back to life to tend the machinery and then died again. While she had been alive she had sent a message, long and chatty and rambling, but the gist of it was, "We're fine, we're coming. See you in a thousand years."

Tomas looked down on a world that had both seas and soil. A plowed field, ripe for gardening.

He had work to do before his guests arrived.

The next generation of plants were too delicate to simply drop from orbit. Tomas began growing a fleet of drones: gliders with a single flexible wing, an envelope for the payload, and a microprocessor. They could get from the ship's orbit to the ground mostly intact, and once there the plastic polymer would degrade into a growth medium for the seeds.

He launched thousands of them, aiming their idiot brains for places where the sea met the land, and watched greenbelts slowly appear.

He recorded messages for the computer to encode into lasers aimed at where the Camelot would be when the light reached it. His messages rambled, too, full of the details of his day-to-day life. He'd lost the art of conversation. He included video with his messages, panoramas of Avalon taken from orbit or transmitted from the tiny eyes of the drones.

"I'm getting ready for you," his messages said, "See you in five hundred years."

The captain's name was Sari Vumanipali. Tomas thought that was a pretty name.

For forty years Tomas planted. The computer had mapped the continents—five of them. Three clustered in a rough triangle, one sat by itself surrounded by the open sea, and one straddled the southern pole under a thick cap of ice.

Tomas concentrated his efforts on the more isolated continent, which he named Davidson after his mother's father. It sat nearly on the equator and would make fine farmland once he was done with it.

Sari's passengers would like it there, he thought.

Lichen attacked the bare rock, then fungi settled what the lichen left behind. The fungi contained bacteria to decompose them when they died, leaving behind rich soil for the plague of ferns that came next.

Towards the end of this life Tomas sent down the first of the animals, a dozen species of worms to work the soil, and stingerless bees to spread pollen. He and the computer worked out what was to be done next and he selected seeds to be thawed and grown, and sent down to the surface, along with growing tribes of insects. Most of the tiny larvae would die on the journey, so he told the computer to send them in the tens of thousands.

The next time Tomas was born Davidson was a green jewel in the Avalonian sea. It had been six hundred and thirty-five years since he had been born on Earth. His work was more than halfway done.

There were more messages from Sari. The Camelot was crawling through the sky, and she had been busy keeping everything working. In interstellar space she had no access to raw materials and had to reuse and repair everything on the ship. Nothing critical had failed, but some of the minor problems had required ingenious solutions.

Tomas was looking forward to meeting her in person.

It was time to go down to the surface. The atmosphere was breathable and Davidson was fully forested, although the other continents were still mostly rocky desert. Tomas could only do so much. The grandchildren of Sari's passengers would begin the work of planting forests there; the grandchildren of the grandchildren would walk under the trees.

The majority of Tomas's ship stayed in orbit. The computer set the landing craft down off the shore of Davidson and Thomas piloted it onto the beach in a large natural harbor. *Davidson City*, he thought. *The capital of a new world*.

Tomas had brought two robots with him, dumb things that could respond to simple voice commands. He spent the first week instructing them to carry him while he learned how to walk. His mind remembered walking, and he knew perfectly well how it was done, but these muscles and nerves had never done it. During that week he stayed closed to the landing craft, eating and sleeping inside it, and probing the interior of the continent with the craft's instruments.

Within a month he had the first structure, built from stone and timber. He transferred equipment from the landing craft, then went back up for more. Gene sequencers crafted fish eggs for him to place gently into the tide pools on the beach. First small fish, to eat the algae, then bigger fish to eat the small fish. He set the machines to keep producing pre-fertilized eggs, and every few days took the buckets to the shore.

Meanwhile he was mapping the land with seismic probes. Inside a year he had located veins of iron and copper. He set up automated mines and built more robots.

He sent Sari pictures and video files of the construction. He brought a small fusion reactor down from his ship and used its power to construct and start a large one—one big enough to power a city. He cleared large sections of forest and made fields, seeded them with a grass that would grow and rot and enrich the soil. His own patch of garden was tiny in comparison, but it replaced the synthetics that he had eaten since he left Earth.

He sent Sari a video of the first meal he cooked from Avalonian crops, and another of the first bread he baked.

He built stone walls around the fallow croplands. It was time to introduce vertebrates to the land.

Birds, he thought. *Let's start with birds.*

Gulls and sandpipers to begin, then robins and sparrows and swallows and doves. He raised the birds in cages, feeding them with native vegetation and insects until they could fly, then let them go.

Sari sent him a raft of massive files that turned out to be edited movies. She'd taken films from the Camelot's library and edited herself into them, reacting to the events on-screen as if she were watching the movie with him. It was a thoughtful, touching gift. Nearly the whole library was represented.

She must have spent years on the project.

During the day he bred and raised animals—squirrels and hedgehogs, foxes and feral cats. At night he watched movies with Sari's digitized reflection, and sent his own comments back.

By the time that this body began to ache and reject food, there were herds of sheep and horses running free across the green hills of Davidson's interior.

Camelot was two hundred and seventy years away. Tomas began making plans for their arrival.

He put cameras on some of the robots and set them up to broadcast the feeds to the ship for collection and rebroadcast to Camelot. He wanted Sari to be able to see her destination.

When it was time to die he walked slowly into the forest, lay down at the base of a tree, and took his pills. He made note of landmarks, so that he could find these bones and bury them later. A hundred and fifty years later, he had decided. Davidson could get by without him that long.

His last memory was the sun through the trees, and the wind on his face.

His first memory was looking out a window, trying to find his gravesite from orbit. The control room felt like a steel coffin in the heart of a cage above the world. It was nearly nine hundred years since he had first been born, on a city back on Earth. Sometimes he wondered if that city existed anymore.

He had been alive on Earth for thirty-eight years. He had lived a hundred and twenty years above and on Avalon.

And now he was a newborn again, but he felt very old. As old as the world.

He checked for messages from Sari first. While the computer was sorting through them he checked the ship. It was going to need some work.

The feeds from the robots were all still active, as were the images from orbit. The herds of sheep had grown too large and overgrazed a section of the interior back into desert. He hadn't wanted to introduce any large predators, but he might have to. He told the computer to begin a simulation of how a pack of wolves would impact Davidson.

Life was spreading to the other continents as well, seeds drifting on the ocean tides and winds, or carried by gulls. That was good, and to be expected.

None of the transmissions from the Camelot were marked urgent, so he began to play them in order. Sari had been alive for forty of the hundred and fifty years that Tomas had been dead. He would have plenty of material to occupy him.

He fired reseeding packages into the desert region and hoped for the best. Then he went down to work his mines.

Adjusting to the gravity was easier this time. Camelot, he knew, created its own gravity by spinning on its long axis, and Sari had adjusted the spin to match Avalon's gravity. She would be able to walk as soon as she touched down.

Tomas wanted to walk with her, under the trees that he had grown in this alien soil.

Tomas narrated his own work to send back to her.

He spent five years slagging rocks and separating the molten stone into ingots of pure elements. Sari kept him company, talking about her troubles with the Camelot. The enormous vessel had its own ecology, organic components to produce food and air for her, and on the long voyage they had mutated. It hadn't been a thousand years ship time—time dilatation had helped. Although the acceleration was low, Camelot had spent much of the voyage close to the speed of light.

Still, it had been a very long time—millions of bacterial generations. Sterilizing and regrowing the organics to keep her alive had become an ongoing job.

Nor was the machinery immune to the ravages of time. Everything had to be rebuilt, or re-manufactured, using only the raw materials inside the ship's skin. She had kept busy, but her tone was cheerful. It was a challenge. No one had ever done anything like this before.

The buildings that he had constructed were mostly intact, although they were overgrown. He hadn't wanted to program the robots to cut down plants. He did that himself, shaping paths through the compound and cutting back the brush. The machinery he had mothballed before his last death was still in good repair.

The wolves, he had decided, were necessary. Without them the sheep would breed faster than the pastures could grow. He put off introducing them for as long as he could. First he cleared space for the city, assuming a thousand inhabitants who would want to begin raising families right away, and built a wall around the cleared ground. It was made from stone blocks cut from the ground with a laser, twelve feet high and pierced regularly by steel gates. He never found the bones from his last body. He assumed that the growing tree had buried them and grown fat on their minerals.

He raised three breeding pairs of wolves to young adulthood, then set them free. He couldn't really teach them to hunt, but then, the sheep didn't know how to be hunted, either. Predator and prey could learn together.

The years passed comfortably.

He set up a water treatment plant and a pumping station, laid out networks of pipes for water and sewage, and buried cables for electricity. He set up towers for data transmission. He set down roads and named them after characters from the movies that he and Sari enjoyed. He taught the robots to build simple houses out of stone.

He documented it all for Sari, telling a robot to follow and record him on long rambling walks through the city grounds while he talked about what he'd done, and what he had left to do.

When he felt his body growing old he welcomed it. He told the computer not to bring him back to life until the Camelot entered the Avalon system.

His last memory was lying on damp grass and looking up at the stars.

His first memory was watching a blue-white star that wasn't a star through the window of his ship.

Camelot was ten light-hours away and decelerating, its drive spraying a fan of high energy ions before it like a headlamp.

Sari's recordings were rushed. She was waking up the passengers, a delicate procedure. They took time to convalesce, the newly arisen frozen sleepers. She would have to nursemaid the first dozen until they were well enough to awaken and care for the others.

Tomas was a thousand years old. Tomas was two hundred years old.

Tomas was a teenager, and there was company coming.

He checked the ship only long enough to ensure that no critical systems were in danger of failing, and then he headed for Davidson City. He started instructing his robots on the trip down.

The mild Davidson winter was just ending, and the fields were wet with the last of the melting snow. Tomas started the gene sequencers making seeds. Corn and wheat and vegetables. Despite the wolves the sheep still thrived, covering the hills. Rabbits and squirrels had become a problem, though. *Hawks*, Tomas thought, *I should have introduced hawks before now.*

Suddenly there were a million things to do.

In the months left before Camelot's arrival he worked himself into a happy exhaustion every day. Sari's updates grew more frequent, and the time lag shrunk until they could converse. She had her hands full with the ship and the passengers, who had been silent and still for so long but now suddenly needed managing.

He had his hands full with the land, bringing in the harvest and building silos to store it through the winter.

Still, they had time to talk in the evenings, if only a few words.

"I can't wait to see you."

"Me, too. Soon."

Camelot became the brightest star in the night sky.

And then, quite suddenly, it was there.

One morning Tomas awoke to the knowledge that Camelot was breaking for orbit around Avalon, geosynchronous above Davidson City. Sari's last message was, "I'm bringing the first boat down now."

The boat, like Tomas's landing craft, came to rest in the harbor. It dwarfed the ship that had brought him here from Earth. Once it sat floating gently in the glass-smooth sea it launched its own boats: water boats, inflated bladders of polycarbonate fibers with whining outboard motors.

Sari was piloting the first one to land.

She stepped unsteadily onto the beach and looked around, breathing in the cool, rich air, so ripe with life after so long inside steel corridors. The passengers behind her waited, subdued and still.

Tomas stood. Smiled. Spread his arms to indicate the shore, the continent, the entire world, green and growing all around them.

"Welcome home," he said.

———— • ————

On a world called Avalon, in a place called Founder's Park, at the center of Davidson City, there are two statues. The park is a long quadrangle, with a reflecting pool down the center, and trees arching over it on both sides. The statues are of a man and a woman, one at each end of the park, looking towards each other. The man holds a plow in his hands, of a kind that only historians would recognize. The woman grasps an equally ancient brass spyglass.

There are plaques giving their names at the base of each of the statues, but they are old and worn, in a dialect not read much anymore. Residents just call the statues the captain and the plowman.

No one is quite sure why they were placed so far apart.

About The Author

Misha Burnett draws his stylistic inspiration from the New Wave Science Fiction of the 1960s and 1970s—writers like Phillip Dick, Samuel Delany, and George Alec Effinger. He navigates the internal landscape of his characters, believing that the strangest new worlds are those behind our eyes.

For more information, visit mishaburnett.wordpress.com.

Three Demon Gambit

J.S. Morin

Editor's Note: The "deal with the devil" story has a rich tradition in both fantasy and science fiction. Rich enough that tvtropes.com has an entire page devoted to its usual forms. So imagine my delight at finding a story that puts a new (and humorous) twist on that crowded tradition.

Jaraim's knife bit into ancient wood, following the chalky lines of the glyph. Sweat beaded on his forehead, and as he finished each cut, he gasped from having held his breath as he carved. It had taken him three days of surreptitious work, stealing hours when Faulyr was absent from their shared room. It was nearly finished.

From the top post of the bunk beds, a crow squawked. Jaraim jumped, the knife dropping from his fingers. He aimed a glare at the creature, staring into the black pits of its eyes. "Shut up, Kalab. This is going to work. I can't trust chalked warding circles anymore."

Jaraim regarded himself from Kalab's perspective, through the mental bond shared between master and familiar. He looked haggard, pale, with dark circles beneath bloodshot eyes. Kalab was worried about his health. "I'll be fine. I'll sleep better once I settle this business. Just…don't scare me like that when he gets here."

Jaraim finished his carving, then wiped away the remnants of chalk with a rag. The circle was perfect, and safe from smudges, sneezes, and other hazards of chalk-drawn circles. Waving away the cloud of dust he had added to an already dusty room, Jaraim dug through desk drawers until he found a tallow candle. It was octagonal and violet, with glyphs stamped into each of its sides. As far as Jaraim knew, the glyphs were merely decorative, something to lure more coins from ignorant students. Jaraim was not one of those; he knew he was paying for the appearance of the arcane. Sometimes things needed to appear as they ought to be, and not what they really were.

Setting the candle at the center of the circle of glyphs, Jaraim steadied himself with a deep breath, and with a spark of elemental fire, lit the wick. The tallow gave off a foul odor, some additive in the color burning sour and sulfurous. Jaraim waved away the smoke before beginning his chant.

Dossic was an elder tongue, little used in modern magic except by those who dabbled in demonology. Jaraim had learned it in secret—just enough to practice the summoners' arts. The words were heavy, guttural, each carrying a taint of vulgarity. As he droned on, a pale blue glow formed in the glyphs, growing brighter with each repetition.

Jaraim lost track of time, eyes focused on the candle flame. When the wick flared and the flame burst like a squeezed grape, his guest arrived. The creature in the middle of the circle was no taller than one of Jaraim's shoes measured toe to heel. Its skin was the color of lava and glistened with oil. From its head sprouted a pair of tiny horns, and from its fingers even tinier claws, all ending in needlelike points. Its body was cherubic, with short, pudgy limbs and no defined muscle. Its name was Alkax, and it was a *telik*— a lesser magma demon.

"Greetings, Apprentice Jaraim," said Alkax in a reedy voice that lilted with sarcasm. The demon took in its surroundings, focusing on the circle of glyphs carved into Jaraim's writing desk. Alkax gave a lazy kick in Jaraim's direction and a flash of arcane energy repelled him at the circle's border. "I'm moving up in the world. It's almost as if you're afraid of me. You haven't got a *reason* to be afraid of me, have you, Apprentice Jaraim?"

Despite the barrier protecting him, hearing Alkax speak his name always caused a shiver in Jaraim's soul. Names held power, and the demon had wheedled Jaraim's given name from him when he was still too reckless and inexperienced to know better. Alkax had been the first demon he had ever summoned. He would also be the last, Jaraim had sworn—but not today.

"I require your assistance," said Jaraim. He forced himself to meet the demon's gaze, looking into the black depths that were not so different from Kalab's, now that he thought of it.

Alkax smiled, showing off a mouthful of serrated fangs, lit from within by a furnace glow. "Since when don't you? If you spent half the time studying that you spend pestering me, you'd be the top of your class on your own. I already gave you all the answers you'll need for your final test."

"I've discovered that there will be secret questions at the end, to see who among the students has studied best on their own. It will set the rankings in the event of multiple perfect scores. I stole the questions; I just need the answers from you."

Alkax cackled. "I like you, human. Never satisfied. Never shy about doing what needs doing. Never…afraid to bargain." The demon's smile grew impossibly wide for its face.

"What's it going to cost me?" Jaraim asked. He kept the fear from his voice. It made no difference what the demon asked; he would agree.

"Well, since you already owe me a year of servitude, let's just add a month. Thirteen is a nice number."

"Deal. My service still starts *after* I earn my medallion," said Jaraim. What that service would entail, Jaraim tried not to contemplate. Possession? Enslavement in the nether realm? His imagination had provided nightmares of every description.

Jaraim relaxed as he read the questions from a scribbled list that he kept out of the demon's field of vision. They were a ruse, as was the added portion

12

of the testing. The only answer he wanted was to the last question: "How does one bind a *narvish*?"

"Oh, now that one ought to separate the censer sniffers from the scholars," said Alkax with a giggle. "Nice boy like you shouldn't know such naughty words. I think I'll save you from yourself."

Jaraim knew better than to think the demon had his best interests in mind. It was valuable knowledge, and Alkax would not part with it readily. "So then, our contract is void. And since this was an extension of our original deal, and not a separate one, I am free of obligation to you." Jaraim sat back and crossed his arms, letting a smirk settle across his lips.

Alkax lunged for him. Blue radiance flared at the tip of each of the demon's claws as Alkax tried to scratch his way through the barrier to no avail. "Trickster! You can't worm your way out of a bargain so easily. You belong to me." The demon spoke three words; Jaraim felt sullied by hearing them, but forced himself to echo the chant. "There. Our bargain is complete. I will return in three days' time to collect you, whether you summon me or not."

Jaraim barked a righteous word and forced Alkax back to his own world. The tiny magma demon vanished in a twist of sooty smoke, and the glow faded from the glyphs that bound him to the mortal world. An eerie quiet remained in the room, with Jaraim slumping back in his chair, exhausted. Three days, and it would all be over.

Kalab squawked. There were footsteps in the hall outside.

Jaraim scrambled to clutter his desk, covering the circle of glyphs in books and notes, draping his traveling cloak over the chalk and knife; there was no time to put things away. By the time Faulyr entered, it looked as if Jaraim had been hard at study.

"What's the matter?" Faulyr asked. Jaraim's roommate favored him with a look of concern.

"You startled me. That's all. I've hardly slept, and I was lost in the pages. I didn't hear you sneak in."

"I hardly sneaked," Faulyr replied. "You worry too much; you'll rank as top student, I just know it. Get some sleep." He gave Jaraim a friendly punch in the shoulder.

"Got to be the best," Jaraim muttered as he climbed into the top bunk. *It's the only way I'll survive this mess I've made.*

The next evening, Jaraim cleared his desk and uncovered his summoning circle. A quick inspection revealed that all the glyphs were still intact; no surprise, but it was a sensible precaution when dealing with demons. Feeling at his belt, Jaraim drew out an iron dagger. It was new, but poorly formed

—an apprentice piece, not even cleaned of charcoal from the forge. For two coppers, it was a bargain, considering what Jaraim had in mind for it.

Jaraim took a deep, steadying breath, but his gathering thoughts were scattered by a flapping of wings and a squawk as Kalab landed at the edge of the glyphs. Its black eyes stared up at Jaraim, and it spread its wings to block his view of the circle.

"Shoo! Get off there," said Jaraim. "The circle held Alkax, and he's much stronger than Okaada. You worry like those dusty old masters."

The crow spread its wings and tried to block the summoning circle, but Jaraim brushed his familiar aside. "If you want to help, keep quiet and don't distract me."

Keeping the dagger in plain sight seemed indiscreet. The later Okaada realized her peril, the better. Jaraim placed the weapon in the top drawer and removed a plain wooden bowl, aligning it in the center of the summoning circle. Biting his lip in concentration, he measured out three thimbles of vinegar and six of water. He added a pinch of natron and waited as the mixture frothed.

The summoning chant was different than the one that summoned Alkax. Jaraim wanted Okaada specifically, not just any *narvish*. Though still foul, the words of Okaada's summons were less harsh. They twisted the tongue into unfamiliar shapes, using sounds Jaraim's language had no use for. There was no counting the repetitions as the glyph's glow grew brighter and more insistent. Okaada was resisting him; there could be no other reason for the summoning to take so long. Jaraim fought through the pain as the ancient syllables cramped his tongue.

The mixture in the wooden bowl frothed anew, and with more fervor. It boiled up and over the sides of the bowl, then steamed away as Okaada plopped down in the bowl, ripped unwillingly from her demonic abode. Her body was nearly spherical, with stubby limbs jutting from a bulbous mass that served as both torso and head. Jaraim could see the hints of organs through her translucent blue skin, and fought to keep his dinner inside him; he had never grown accustomed to her appearance.

"What a pleasant surprise," Okaada cooed, her voice sweet and innocent as a young girl's. That voice was the only reason Jaraim had come to think of the demon as female. "What service may I render, mighty one? Or have you finally decided to pay me?"

You wouldn't have resisted coming if you believed that. Even through the protection of the summoning circle, Jaraim could feel the subtle insistence behind the demon's words. Okaada could charm a eunuch, but not Jaraim... not with the glyphs protecting him.

He reached into his pocket and produced a pair of garnets the size of his thumbnail and rolled them across the desk. The gems came to rest just shy of the summoning circle, and Okaada lurched for them reflexively. The demon squashed against the cylindrical barrier the circle provided, causing it to flare a pale blue. "Mine!" Okaada shrieked.

"You can't have them," said Jaraim. Despite his disgust, he could not keep his eyes from the demon. "Zenisha should have been mine by now, but she sees Faulyr most nights, and barely looks at me."

Okaada pulled away from the barrier and threw herself at it again, causing a brighter flare but no better result. Growling, she turned her milky eyes toward Jaraim. "Manless wretch! She'd be swollen with your children by now if you'd listened to me."

"No charms. That was the deal. You're supposed to be a master of manipulating emotions. You could have given better advice if you wanted to."

"You have a soggy mind and a tongue like an axe handle," said Okaada. "Let me possess you, and I'll have her begging to serve you, charms or no charms. You lack the gall to carry out my plans yourself."

"No. We're done."

"Cheat! Liar! You cannot break our deal," said Okaada. She snarled, but the effect would have been more intimidating if the demon had teeth. The wet, mushy gums she bared provoked nausea, not fear.

"I'll make you a deal," said Jaraim. "Tell me the binding chant for a *kiiluut*, and I'll give you your payment and call it even."

A sly smile oozed onto Okaada's face, her demeanor shifting in an instant. "So, looking to settle another deal without paying, is that it?"

"What do you care? You'll have yours."

"Why that girl doesn't love you, I can't imagine," Okaada cooed, her voice sending an unwelcome shiver of pleasure through Jaraim. "You're perfectly devious. Very well, the binding for the gems."

There was no risk to Okaada. The binding for a *kiiluut* would have no effect on her, and she would be cheated of the gems if she refused. She recited the chant and Jaraim echoed her until he had it memorized. Though he tried his best to keep it from showing, the words sent small tremors through his bones and teeth as he spoke them.

"Excellent!" said Okaada. "Spoken like a true demon. Now... my payment, and I should like to be returned to my own realm."

Jaraim held the garnets in his palm and offered them to Okaada, careful not to let his hand cross the barrier. Okaada's fingers drew sparks from the protective circle as she clawed for them. "My father would kill me if he knew I'd borrowed them, let alone bartered them away." He snatched the gems away from the demon.

Jaraim recited the chant that Alkax had given him. The *telik* might drive a spiteful bargain, but he had never led Jaraim astray. Okaada froze, a vile curse choked off mid-word with a squeak. The binding held her tighter than a giant's fist, as still as if she had been encased in stone. The *narvish* twitched and spasmed, fighting the binding. Jaraim felt every movement as if it was his own hand holding her fast.

Keeping the chant at a steady pace, he retrieved the dagger and aimed it for what looked as much like a heart as anything inside the demon. Jaraim put his other hand on the hilt and closed his eyes. Okaada's struggles grew frantic. With a single thrust, Jaraim plunged the dagger into the immobile demon. The summoning circle did nothing to prevent his hand from crossing. The iron hissed as it slid through the demon's flesh, and Jaraim opened his eyes to see smoke pouring from the wound.

In seconds, the demon sloughed away and dissipated, her remains vanishing into the nether regions from which Jaraim had summoned her. Only an odor lingered to prove she had ever been in the room.

"See, Kalab?" said Jaraim, favoring his familiar with a wan smile. "Nothing to it." He slumped back in his chair and let out a shuddering breath.

The bird remained silent, but flapped down to perch on the edge of a bucket by the door. Jaraim sighed. Kalab was right: the room would need a cleaning to be rid of the smell.

One night later, Jaraim found himself back at his desk, which was all clean and smelling faintly of lye. There was no trace of Okaada's odor, nor any evidence that she had been in the room at all. There was only slightly more evidence that Faulyr had been there. Jaraim had fallen into an exhausted sleep before Faulyr had come home and had not awakened all night, his dreams plagued by the chant Okaada had taught him. He had awakened covered in sweat long after sunrise, and Faulyr's blanket had been rumpled sometime in between.

The two roommates had crossed paths in the dining hall just an hour ago, Faulyr looking as if he had been made heir to the king, Jaraim feeling fortunate to keep his feet shuffling beneath him. What had made Faulyr so chipper was also the reason behind his nightly absences: his visits to the girls' wing to be with Zenisha. *I'll have my pick of postings once I'm named First Initiate, and I'll find a better woman than Zenisha,* Jaraim thought.

The bucket sat beside Jaraim's desk, half filled with water. He had refilled it three times in washing up after Okaada's demise, and refreshed it once more afterward. From beneath his mattress, he removed a stoppered vial. Pulling the cork, he took a sniff, inhaling the scent of incense and holy oils. Jaraim poured the contents into the bucket.

"Not even going to try this time?" Jaraim asked. Kalab stood on the window ledge, looking out over the city below. The familiar swiveled its head around and stared at him for a moment, then flew off. "Iogi doesn't much like you, either."

Jaraim rummaged in his chest of clothes until he found his laboratory gloves. While most of his wardrobe was finely made and new, the gloves were scarred, ugly things made purely for function. The leather was worn smooth along the palms and fingertips, and there was a layer of grime that resisted any attempts at cleaning. Jaraim tucked them into his belt before settling in to perform his summoning. He poured a small sack of coal ash into the summoning circle and stuck two bone needles into the pile so that they stood upright, ends dipped in pitch. A flick of Jaraim's magic lit them.

The spell to summon Iogi had always struck Jaraim as whimsical. There was a lilting singsong to it, even if the words themselves were pestilent. The *kiiluut* wasted no time in appearing. Upon completion of the second repetition, Iogi appeared. Or rather, Iogi's essence arrived, and inhabited the ingredients left on the table. The coal ash writhed and formed itself into bones. The flames detached themselves from the needles and rose into newly-formed eye sockets of ash. Out of that amalgam emerged a skeletal gargoyle, bereft of flesh and sinew, with fire for eyes. Shadowy vapors wafted from its bones like steam from a stew.

"Good to see you, master," said Iogi with a bow. The demon had no mouth, nor even a lower jaw. Sound merely emanated from his vicinity. "How do you fare this evening?"

"I have a problem, Iogi," said Jaraim. "Alkax. Time has come to be rid of him." Iogi needed no sugared words, no preamble.

"Of course. Alkax was clever, a good tool for your studies. But he is no threat," said Iogi. "I have given you adequate tools to defend yourself from him, have I not?"

"Perhaps," said Jaraim. "But I prefer overwhelming force. I want him unable to resist as I destroy him."

"Wise. You want the chant to bind him, I assume."

Jaraim smiled. Iogi was devious; he had taught Jaraim all he knew about handling demons. "Yes, Iogi, that's exactly what I want."

Iogi gave him words that rang with power. There was something grand about the chant, as if it was meant for a wizard of great power. Or so Jaraim imagined. At least there was no unpleasant effect merely from speaking them.

"Your enunciation is excellent as always, master," said Iogi. The demon paced in the confines of the circle, his fiery eyes scanning the room. Jaraim pulled out his gloves and put them on slowly. "Ah, I see."

"Sorry Iogi, I'm retiring from demonology. There's no future in it, at least none that I want a part of. I'm getting out while I still have my soul."

"But you don't," said Iogi. "That soul inside you belongs to me. That was our deal."

"I'm breaking it. I'm sure one of *your* kind can understand."

"All too well…" Iogi's voice sounded wistful.

Jaraim began the binding chant and Iogi stiffened. Unlike Okaada, he offered no resistance. When Jaraim picked him up, Iogi's wings crumbled against his body like gossamer. The demon weighed next to nothing, even less than the sack of ash that had spawned him.

"I have so much more I can teach you," Iogi said, his disembodied voice unencumbered by the binding. "And it's not as if you will be free of our bargain if you destroy me. The debt will merely pass on to another."

Jaraim wanted to question him, to object, to deny the claim, but there was no way without ceasing the binding chant. He was committed. There was no turning back. Jaraim dunked Iogi in the bucket of holy water. Just before he hit the water's surface, Iogi gave up his passive mien. The *kiiluut* thrashed and flailed in spite of the binding spell. Without the binding, Jaraim would have had no hope of containing him. The water bubbled and steamed. The bucket shook. Then all went quiet.

The water in the bucket was grey with ash. It was all there was of Iogi in this world, when Jaraim thought about it. Even then, he would dump the bucket in the forest, far from the school's well. It never hurt to be cautious.

A squawk at the window startled Jaraim, causing him to drop the bucket just as he picked it up. The water sloshed up the sides, but did not spill over. "Back, huh? After making me face Iogi alone?"

Kalab extended his wings halfway, and ducked his head. The familiar hobbled along the window ledge, stiff-legged. Jaraim laughed. It was a fair approximation of Iogi's pacing. "You're right, I guess he does look a little like a dead bird. Did, I suppose…there's no Iogi to worry about anymore. It's just Alkax left now."

———— • ————

One night later, Jaraim felt the excitement welling within him. "This is it, Kalab. Last demon I ever summon." The crow cocked its head and stared at Jaraim. "No, I mean it. They've been nothing but trouble. I hardly sleep anymore. I lost any chance I might have had with Zenisha. Faulyr probably hates me for besting him in class; even cheating I've barely come out ahead. What good will that do me out on my own? First Initiate with an education full of holes."

Kalab nodded, bobbing his whole body in the motion, and hopped from the desk, gliding down to alight on the edge of the dry, empty bucket. There was no trace of Iogi left within.

Jaraim went through the arrangements for summoning Alkax once more. He was faced with the prospect of the demon finding his own way into the world if Jaraim did not summon him first. It was difficult for demons to find passage to the mortal realm, but for the collection of a debt such as Jaraim's, Alkax would find a way.

The summoning circle was pristine, the glyphs each intact. Removing evidence of them from the desk surface would be a task for another day. For now, deep, clean cuts were preferable. Jaraim lit the candle and began his chant, a giddy excitement rising inside him. *It's almost over.*

Alkax appeared as the candle flame popped. "My, my, I hadn't expected *you* to have the heart to call me to the mortal realm. Eager to begin your service?" A blackened tongue ran across the demon's lips.

Jaraim reached inside his tunic and pulled out his medallion. The silver was freshly polished, the diamond at it center sparkling, marking his rank. "They named me First Initiate just this morning," said Jaraim. "You kept your end of the bargain."

"I must admit, I had picked you for a whiner and a wheedler. A sniveler, perhaps. I might even see fit to take it easy on you during your indenture-ship." Alkax giggled hysterically.

"Have your fun at my expense once I'm yours," Jaraim scolded him. "First, a toast." He reached to the floor beside his chair, outside the demon's sight, and lifted a goblet. "To bargaining with forces you don't understand."

The giggling stopped instantly. "What's in that?" Alkax hunkered down and backed away from Jaraim until the barrier of the summoning circle stopped him.

"Unfermented wine. Your favorite." Jaraim swirled the goblet under his nose and breathed deeply. There was no acidic tang, just the heavy scent of grape.

"Stupid human. You can't trick me into drinking that," said Alkax with a sneer.

Jaraim smirked. "Who said anything about tricking you? I'm going to force it down your throat. You weakling demons should know better than to bargain with humans."

"I'd like to see you—" Alkax said, but got no further. Jaraim began his chant and the demon's mouth froze mid-sentence.

After pulling on his laboratory gloves, still chanting, Jaraim reached the goblet toward the immobile demon. The bulbous, pudgy magma demon flared red hot, the only act it could manage while held in thrall. Jaraim had only to worry about singeing his gloves. Just as he was about to grab the demon by the neck to tilt its head back, Alkax stepped back.

With one claw of his foot, the demon scratched one of Jaraim's glyphs, and the azure glow of the summoning circle winked out. "I don't think I'll be drinking any of that virgin wine, Jaraim Tenhold, son of Machius Tenhold of Norvern Keep. Your magic can't bind *me*."

He learned my name!

"H—How?" was all Jaraim could manage to utter.

"Your friend Faulyr sold it to me in return for a binding charm for some sorceress whelp he fancied," said Alkax. With a brief flash, a pair of iron man-acles appeared in the demon's hands, barbed and covered in green, burning glyphs. "Time to see your new home."

"No..." Jaraim backed away, unable to take his eyes from the demon. Alkax lunged for him. Jaraim threw up his hands in a feeble attempt to fend the tiny demon off. Despite their difference in size, Jaraim held no illusion that he could fight the creature with his bare hands. He closed his eyes.

Jaraim heard a squawk and a furious rustle of feathers, followed by a string of curses in a demonic tongue he was thankful not to comprehend. Opening his eyes, he saw that Kalab had interposed himself between Jaraim and Alkax, and was struggling to fend off the demon.

"Kalab, no!" Jaraim worked a quick spell, and the crow grew to the size of a hunting dog. Still, it would never be able to harm the inhuman creature. He fended Alkax away with beak and talons, but it was only a matter of time.

Kalab turned toward Jaraim and squawked again. The message was clear: *Run while I hold him off.*

"I'm sorry," Jaraim shouted as he fled for the door.

Jaraim skidded on slippered feet as he bolted into the hallway. Behind him he heard a terrible shriek that could only have come from a giant crow. He put his head down and ran. There was only one hope.

The masters did not sleep in the dormitories, and none of the other students would be of any help. Below, in the basement of the school, there was a door. It was older than the building itself; the school had been built over it. The elder students were told of it, warned that it was only for use in dire emergencies. No one knew where it went, but if an experiment went badly enough, it was a sure escape.

Jaraim tore through the halls, bounded down stairways three steps at a time. He could hear the scrabbling claws as Alkax pursued. He did not spare the breath to scream or cry. Most of his fellow students would wake with no knowledge of what had befallen Jaraim. Except Faulyr. He would know. Would he cover his tracks, or expose Jaraim as a summoner who had met his end by his own vile art?

Jaraim reached the basement level with the sound of Alkax's pursuit fading behind him. His longer legs and panic-stricken energy gave him an edge in speed over the chubby demon, but that only bought him a moment's lead. It ought to have been enough.

When Jaraim rounded the final turn, he stopped short.

"I thought you might be down here tonight," said Faulyr, leaning casually against the ancient door.

"You...you," Jaraim said, short of breath and short of words as well.

"You have three options," said Faulyr. "If you want, I'll let you right through this door. You can send yourself off to who-knows-where, whether that's any better than where Alkax wants to take you or not. Or...you can apologize for cheating me out of First Initiate, confess, and renounce your claim before the whole assembly. I can use the binding chant on Alkax if you tell it to me."

"The third option?" Jaraim asked. Third options left lingering were usually the ones the speaker meant you to take.

"We fight one another right here, and even if you win, that demon will drag you off in servitude."

Jaraim did not even bother with a response to that option. Alkax was growing closer by the second. He told Faulyr the chant.

Hearing the profane words spoken aloud by Faulyr made Jaraim's teeth ache. He backed away, cringing. Alkax fared far worse. The pudgy little demon squealed, his mouth contorted to reveal rows of needle-sharp teeth. His steps faltered and Alkax fell to his hands and feet, his belly too round for his knees to touch the floor.

Faulyr continued the chant, and Jaraim watched in admiration as the rightful First Initiate took control of the demon's body. Alkax drew slowly to his feet, but not of his own volition; he was a puppet, fighting his strings. The demon's movements slowed, his body twitching and spasming under the strain of fighting the binding chant.

Sweat beaded on Faulyr's face. The outstretched hand that pantomimed a crushing grip on Alkax began to quiver with fatigue. He took a quick glance over his shoulder at the shimmering light from the door. Jaraim smirked at the realization that Faulyr was considering jumping through if he lost control.

"Help me, or he'll have us both!"

Faulyr instantly resumed his chant. Even in that brief interruption, Alkax had advanced a step and set his claws grasping at the air toward his captor. The demon's attention had diverted away from Jaraim entirely.

Jaraim circled around, careful to keep out of the demon's reach should Faulyr falter. Though he favored his roommate with a malicious grin, he offered his reassurance. "Keep him under control. We'll get him from both sides. Can't say I'm not enjoying seeing you sweat, though."

"Hurry!"

Jaraim took a long breath and steadied his nerves. Alkax was aligned directly between the two student wizards, hanging mid-leap after his latest brief advance toward Faulyr as the chant was interrupted. The two treacherous creatures were devoting all their power toward each other's destruction—instead of Jaraim's, for once.

Jaraim began a chant of his own, using syllables of the Elementalists' Codex and keeping his voice low. Commanding the four aspects of nature had never been his strongest talent, but he knew enough. Iogi had tutored him on all manner of practical magic. He might not have been Faulyr's equal in history or magical theory, but if Faulyr were as well-versed in demonology as Jaraim, he wouldn't have needed aid to destroy a bound demon.

As Jaraim finished his spell, a gale blew through the basement corridor, more focused and determined than any mundane wind. It caught both traitors in its grasp and hurtled them toward the open door. Faulyr, fool that he was, continued the chant as a scream even as he left first his feet, then the world. Alkax broke free of the binding almost instantly, but it was too late for the demon. Though he managed to twist in mid-air and spit a vile curse, he was swept through to who-knows-where, just as Faulyr had been.

With a flourish of his fingers, Jaraim diverted the last of his gust to catch the door and blow it shut. It slammed with booming finality. His heart pounded in his chest and a giddy laugh escaped him. Slumping against the wall, he found his limbs trembling. Soon there would be questions, demands for answers, a formal inquiry. He didn't have much time to compose himself, but for the moment, he savored the taste of freedom.

———————— • ————————

The following evening, Jaraim sat alone in his room, his desk gone. The masters let Jaraim have Faulyr's, since his unfortunate roommate would no longer require it. There was an emptiness deeper than just the dust-free spot where the desk had been. The masters had ordered it carted away and burned. Jaraim had lost two friends last night—one true and one false. The only tears he shed were for brave, loyal Kalab.

In a contemplative mood, he wandered down to the basement level, spotting Zenisha in the halls. She saw Jaraim and sought him out. "Tell me it isn't true," she said, sniffling. Her eyes were red and swollen.

Jaraim hung his head. "I'm sorry, but I'm afraid it is. It's not your fault. If I had known, I'd have stopped him. Please believe me; I'd never condone using love charms." With no one to gainsay him, Jaraim could spread whatever tales he liked about Faulyr. For all he knew, Faulyr *had* used the charm that Alkax bartered for his name.

Zenisha broke down crying and hurried away. Much as he wished to comfort her, Jaraim knew she did not need *him* right then. Someday, perhaps, he could be that kind of comfort to her. Not today.

When Jaraim reached the door in the basement level, he found it open. Master Orryn stood before it, lost in thought as he gazed into the iridescent light that poured from it. "Where do you think he ended up?" Jaraim asked.

Master Orryn sighed. "One of the great mysteries. Alas, First Initiate, for all that you may ever learn, you will never find the answers to every question."

Jaraim hid his smirk from Master Orryn. "Poor Faulyr. He should have known better than to trifle with forces he didn't understand."

About The Author

J.S. Morin is a creator of worlds and a destroyer of words. As a fantasy writer, his works range from traditional epics to futuristic fantasy with starships. He has worked as an unpaid Little League pitcher, a cashier, a student library aide, a factory grunt, a cubicle drone, and an engineer—there is some overlap in the last two. Through it all, though, he has always been a storyteller. Eventually he started writing books based on the stray stories in his head, and people kept telling him to write more of them. Now that's all he does for a living.

For more information, visit www.jsmorin.com.

Rolling the Bones

Richard Levesque

Editor's Note: If science fiction explores the implications of new technology, then this one might better be called science fiction, despite its magical trappings. Not the darkest story in the collection, but quite possibly the creepiest.

The sedan chair came to a stop, and the bearers lowered it to the ground. It was meant to hold one person only, but today it held two. Inside, Roderick tried his best not to touch the king's body, which was easier now that the chair had stopped rocking with the bearers' gait. Even so, he had pressed himself as far into a corner of the conveyance as was possible. Not for the first time in the last twelve hours he wished himself invisible or far, far away, but his wishes got him nowhere. Without intending it, he had gotten himself into this situation; there was nothing for it now but to let it play out. Old Windhover had rolled the bones, and Roderick realized he was nothing more than one of the pieces the wizard was manipulating on a game board that only he could see.

Old Windhover had pulled the curtains down before sending Roderick and the king on their way. Now, anxious and impatient, Roderick pulled the richly-embroidered fabric aside to peek out. As he had guessed, they were in the marketplace—a bustling cluster of tents and stalls in the castle's main courtyard that was filled with jugglers and minstrels milling about among the shoppers, gawkers, and cutpurses. Everything was brightly colored, lavish, and loud. Roderick stared as a bearded man led a harnessed bear cub past three bawdy women near the castle gate. So busy had Old Windhover kept Roderick since the start of his employment three weeks before that the magician's helper had had little opportunity to visit the marketplace during his time at the castle; now he could not help staring at the people and their behavior.

His eyes were drawn from this bounty when he noticed Old Windhover standing near the gate through which the sedan chair must have just passed. He was speaking with an old woman, her back hunched and gray whiskers sprouting from her chin. Roderick had known her type in the Nevergreen forest where he had grown up—a midwife and healer, a knower of herbs and a whisperer of spells for the times when herbs wouldn't do. The pair approached the palanquin after a few moments, and Old Windhover leaned in through the window, a bony hand pulling back the curtain.

"Help the king out, Roderick," he said. "You're to lead him along behind

Lorentia here. She will pass among the stalls and talk to some of the women. When she finds the one she wants, you're to read this to her, loudly enough for all nearby to hear."

He thrust a rolled and sealed parchment through the window, and Roderick took it without thinking.

"How will I know she's found the one she wants?"

"She'll tell you."

Moments later, Roderick had managed to climb over the king and exit the sedan chair. The monarch, gray haired and doddering, allowed himself to be led out into the sunshine, his pale face tipped up toward the light and a vacant smile on his lips—as though he were a child who had just been allowed outside after a long period indoors. Roderick cringed when he had to touch the king, but there was nothing for it now. The old man would have wandered off without being guided, so Roderick took a deep breath and put his hand on the king's arm so that he could lead His Majesty through the marketplace after Lorentia. Shoppers, merchants, entertainers, and ne'er-do-wells parted for them without a word, and the murmur of the crowd hushed to silence as they passed.

Roderick watched, confused, as Lorentia went into the first stall. She seemed interested only in the women, and the young ones at that. She spoke not a word but checked their fingers. If she found a wedding ring, she moved on to the next. The unmarried women she considered carefully, walking three full circles around each before leaning in to sniff their hair.

Whatever the witch woman was doing, Roderick thought, it couldn't be good for the woman who ended up being the one Old Windhover had described as "the one she wants." Not for the first time since this bizarre affair had begun the night before he thought about bolting, about leaving the king on his own and running for his life. He wouldn't look back until he was in the Nevergreen again.

Appealing as the fantasy was though, his feet stayed right where they were, and his hand did not stray from its place on the king's arm. Old Windhover was powerful. He might appear avuncular and even absentminded at times, but Roderick had heard plenty of stories about the wizard's wrath and the part he had played in the king's court over the years. Stories of palace mice who had once been difficult ministers, and thunderclouds that followed intractable gentry for weeks on end before they acquiesced to the king's wishes. *No*, Roderick thought. If he ran now, he wouldn't make it to the castle walls, at least not in human form.

He remembered one of his first conversations with Old Windhover, the wizard having just hired Roderick as his assistant. "Power," Old Windhover had said then. "It's not in strength, you know. Not always. It's in how you roll the bones." Then the magician had given his new assistant a secret smile and shook the little leather bag full of finger bones that he always kept looped onto his wrist. "Make sure you roll the bones well, boy. Roll 'em well. And always keep your eyes open so you know when someone else is rolling theirs."

It had been both advice and admonition. So he stood still, doing as the wizard had commanded—tending to the king and watching for the old witch woman's signal. After sniffing each woman's hair, Lorentia wrinkled her nose in disgust and started the process all over again. In this way, she examined every woman—merchant and patron alike—in eight different stalls before she found what she was after.

The woman in question was young and comely, with dark hair and wide blue eyes. She appeared to be the daughter of a potato seller, and her mother at first objected to her daughter being so roughly examined. When Lorentia gave her a piercing look, the protest died on the woman's lips. Once she had finished sniffing the daughter's hair, the witch woman said, "Are you betrothed?"

"No," came the meek reply.

"Had a lover in the last two days?"

"No!" said the shop maid, her reply no longer meek and her cheeks red with embarrassment.

Then Lorentia turned toward Roderick and gave a clear nod. She had found the one she wanted.

Nervously, Roderick advanced, keeping hold of one of the king's sleeves. When he had gotten as close as he dared, he stopped. Roderick took a deep breath, fearful that the monarch would flee once his sleeve was released, and then he let the fabric go. The king seemed not to have noticed. Roderick let his breath out and broke the seal on the rolled parchment Old Windhover had given him.

"Be it hereby proclaimed," he said, his voice shaking and barely audible.

"Louder!" he heard Old Windhover say from the edge of the crowd, but when Roderick looked around, the magician was nowhere to be seen. Had he taken a new shape? Or was his voice somehow in Roderick's head? He began again, louder this time so that all who had gathered around the spectacle of the old king and the witch woman could hear.

"Be it hereby proclaimed that His Majesty, King Runnelstone the Grievous of Melincar, having found this woman to be most desirable, fitting of her station, and an example to all, does here in the presence of these witnesses and before any of the gods who may deign to observe such mortal trifles, make known his intention to wed her this very day in the high chapel in the castle of his ancestors."

Another murmur rose up among the onlookers. The young woman's mother gasped, while the king's intended looked taken aback, both frightened and amazed. And Roderick, realizing the import of the words he had just read, felt his cheeks grow red at the lies Old Windhover had just compelled him to read in public. The king hadn't "found" the woman at all. He had no idea what her qualities were, and Roderick well knew that everyone standing in the marketplace had seen the witch woman make her selection for the king. None standing in earshot would dare call it a lie, but Roderick knew they were all thinking it.

Roderick's humiliation was not at an end, however. There was one more sentence, and he read it just as loudly and clearly, despite his consternation. "Let it furthermore be proclaimed that any issue of their union, whether male or female, shall be His Majesty's sole heir and the future ruler of this sovereign land, and that the future monarch's mother shall henceforth be treated with all the respect and dignity as is befitting the mother of such a royal personage."

Amid the further hubbub, he heard the prospective bride's reaction. "Our union?" She looked as though she had just opened a packet of spoiled beef and was now expected to eat of it with glee. Fear and disbelief played across her face; even so, when her gaze shifted from the king's visage to Roderick's, the magician's helper couldn't help but feel drawn to her. Frightened or not, her eyes were blue pools that he felt he had just fallen into.

"Your name, m'lady?" the witch woman asked.

"Jillian," she said, her voice just above a whisper.

"Do you accept your liege's offer of matrimony?"

The potato seller's daughter hesitated. Roderick saw her look at the king, horror in her eyes.

"I cannot," she offered, fear causing her voice to slip out in the tiniest of whispers.

"You can," said the witch woman.

A spark came into the young woman's eyes, and with a bit of hope in her voice, she said, "I *am* betroth—"

Lorentia cut her off. "To a king?"

"No."

"Then His Majesty's betrothal takes precedence." The old woman leaned in closer and spoke quietly, so quietly that Roderick may have been the only other one in the potato stall to hear. "You lie, girl. Accept the king's proposal. It will go hard for you and your mother if you don't."

Further horror played across the young woman's face as she considered the witch woman's cruel smile. For her part, the old midwife merely nodded encouragement.

Finally, the young woman whispered, "I accept."

"Louder."

"I accept." Tears streamed down her cheeks as she spoke the words loud enough for all to hear, and Roderick had to blink back his own tears at the sight of her ruin.

Trembling with anger at the thought of what Old Windhover had manipulated him into doing, he wanted to denounce the magician right there in the marketplace and expose the king for what he was. The memory of the wizard's voice in his head, though, kept him still—along with his knowledge of how terrible the truth of the situation really was. Saying it aloud, here in the marketplace, was too much. No one would believe him, and the plan Old Windhover had set in motion would roll along while Roderick suffered a terrible fate for so publicly slandering the king.

There were other ways of saving the lady, other ways of rolling the bones and getting the upper hand against the magician and his machinations. Maybe he had already found the answers in the weeks of reading Old Windhover's books and just didn't know it yet. And maybe all it was going to take was a sharp eye and a ready hand.

Roderick looked at the lady as she wept on her mother's shoulder. Her sobs were all he heard, even though the muttering of the crowd was loud enough to drown out the sound.

I'll save you, he thought. *I promise.*

Then he led the king back to the sedan chair, trying not to think of all the other promises he'd already failed to keep.

———————— • ————————

What promises? Why just the evening before, he'd been sitting on a high stool in Old Windhover's outer chamber, stacks of books on the floor around him and a heavy copy of *Practical Uses for Mammal Organs* balanced on his knees. A candle guttered on the nearby table, and torches affixed to the walls threw light and shadow across the quiet room, littered with books that the old wizard had charged him with sorting and cleaning. The books were tempting, crying out not only to be dusted and shelved but to be read. And even though Roderick had promised himself many times that he would not let the books' contents distract him from his purpose, the pages were just so tempting… Promises made to himself were easy to break, but there were still more to come. Darker promises.

When the door burst open and the wizard blustered in, Roderick almost fell off the stool. The old man moved quickly into the chamber, faster than Roderick would have thought him capable, a flurry of billowing cloak and flying gray hair. He went straight to one of the piles of books that Roderick should have finished sorting days ago and pointed at one with a black cover. "That one," he said, his voice conveying urgency but not panic.

"Yes, sir," Roderick croaked as he set *Practical Uses* on top of another pile and hurried to do his master's bidding. Moments later, he had rescued the book from its stack and handed it to the magician, stealing a glance at the spine as he did so but finding himself disappointed. The title, had it ever been printed there, was long worn away, and the plain black cover offered no hint of its contents.

Old Windhover took the book with only a cursory glance. Then he said, "There are three parchments hidden in the bust of Mediger the Mild. Bring them to the king's chambers at once." And without another word, he turned with one more flurry of cloak and hair, leaving the room, raising a cloud of dust as he went.

The king's chambers? Roderick thought, his mind racing. *Why on earth would you want* me *in the king's chambers?*

Pushing his questions aside, he ran his fingers over the bust of Mediger the Mild, found the secret spring in its base, and pulled the scrolls from inside it. Each was sealed with black ribbon, and he felt his curiosity rising again. He could peek at one of the parchments, just for a second or two, if only to make sure he had the right ones... But he knew where that line of thinking would lead him. The unsorted books all around were evidence aplenty, and something told him that Old Windhover was not in a trifling mood this evening. The urgency Roderick had heard in the wizard's voice—it had not been anything he'd heard before.

Soon after, the parchments held carefully in his hands, he arrived outside the king's chambers. Two guards stood at either side of the door, their faces doleful. Farther along the hallway, Roderick saw several noblemen huddled together. The king's council, he assumed. One or two looked his way as he approached, their expressions blank.

"Old Windhover sent for me," Roderick said to one of the guards. "I'm his... assistant."

He held up the rolled parchments as though they were some sort of authentication. The guard made no move to inspect the documents, just opened the door to admit the magician's helper.

The chamber was large and ornately appointed, but the young man barely glanced at the embroidered wall hangings and jewel-encrusted cups laid out at the bedside; his eyes instead were drawn to the sight of the magician at the head of the old king's bed and a priest in high ceremonial robes at the foot. The priest was muttering a prayer in a language Roderick did not understand while Old Windhover stared impatiently at the king stretched out on the bed before him. The old king looked gaunt, his papery skin all yellow and his long white hair tangled around his head.

"Oh, *do* get on with it!" Old Windhover said to the priest, who paid him no mind and kept muttering. The magician shook his head and motioned Roderick over. He took the parchments, giving them a quick glance before saying, "What you're seeing or are about to see must never be spoken of. Not to your family, not to a bride should you ever find one, and not even to me unless I speak of it first. Do you understand?"

"Yes, sir," Roderick answered, his voice barely audible.

When the priest had finished, the magician ordered him out. The priest's protest died on his lips when the old man shot him a look.

"Your job," Old Windhover said once the priest was gone, "will be to restrain His Majesty."

"Restrain?" his helper asked.

"Kindly do your job, Roderick," was the only reply. Hesitantly, the magician's helper knelt upon the bed, his legs as close as he could get them to the king's body without actually touching the royal torso. Then he took a deep breath, leaned over, and put a hand on each bony shoulder.

Beside the bed, the magician began reading from the parchments, unintelligible words similar to those the recently removed priest had used. Nothing happened at first, but when Old Windhover rubbed an ointment on the king's forehead and placed a leaf in the king's mouth, Roderick felt the king's cold skin grow a little bit warmer. When the magician had finished with the second parchment, he put his ear to the king's chest, nodded, and started reading the third. And when the last incantations from the final parchment had echoed off the high ceiling of the chamber, Roderick felt a tremor in the king's shoulders. Looking down at the body in fear and fascination, he saw the chest rise almost imperceptibly and then fall again. There was a rattle in the king's throat and then a full exhalation into Roderick's face. Then the king opened his eyes, locking his gaze onto the eyes of the magician's assistant...

Roderick stared back. He saw confusion in the king's eyes—along with fear, torment, and loss, all followed quickly by anger. But then, most profoundly, there followed looks of shame and embarrassment. Roderick could not have guessed why the king was so upset; all he knew for certain was that the old king was not happy about being revived.

That was when the king began his inhuman howling. Tears streamed from his eyes—eyes that darted in their sockets, focusing on nothing—and the panic in those eyes only seemed to make the wailing worse.

Old Windhover shouted, "Hold him! Hold him tight!" This struck Roderick as strange since the king was offering no resistance, but after a few more seconds of howling, the king tried sitting up. It was all Roderick could do to hold his shoulders still. When the king started thrashing his arms around, trying to dislodge the magician's helper, Roderick had to bear down harder and feared he might break the king's bones.

And then, mercifully, Old Windhover was leaning forward and inserting the end of a dropper into the king's mouth. Seconds later, the wailing and thrashing ceased. The king lay quietly on the bed, his eyes still darting in panic, but he gave no other sign of resistance, or even awareness of the other men's presence.

The breath that escaped the king's mouth felt cold on Roderick's cheeks, raising gooseflesh on his arms and neck. And when he looked into the king's eyes, he realized that the old man wasn't really looking back. Rather, he looked but seemed incapable of understanding anything he saw. Realization crept into Roderick's mind like the slow understanding he gained from reading the wizard's books.

"You didn't just cure him, did you?" Roderick asked.

"Cure?" Old Windhover said, half chuckling. "I didn't cure him at all. He's beyond curing."

"He was...dead then?" Roderick asked.

The wizard nodded.

"And...now?"

Old Windhover leaned in, his fingers on the king's throat, looking for his pulse. "The basic facts remain unchanged."

"But...how? He's...alive, isn't he?"

"Put your ear to his heart."

Roderick hesitated. Not only was the magician asking him to be even more familiar with the person of the king than he already had dared, he also felt too frightened to lower his ear, fearful of what he might—or might *not*—hear. The wizard's gaze compelled him, though, and so he dipped his head down and put his ear to the old man's chest. He heard nothing.

When he sat up again and looked at Old Windhover with awe, the magician chuckled. "It's not a trick, Roderick. A different force flows through his veins now, not blood. He will appear as one alive for a short time, time enough for us to complete the task that's been set for us by the council."

"Task?" Roderick said, his voice quavering.

"The king in his youth paid little attention to his advisors, and in his old age the habit was cemented. When the council bade him take a wife and produce an heir, he always claimed there would be time for that another day. And now the king has run out of time."

"I...still don't understand," Roderick said.

"Do you have any idea what will happen if the king dies without an heir?" Old Windhover said, his tone condescending.

"No, sir."

"Every shirttail relative going back ten generations will descend on this castle, from minor nobles within our own borders to pig farmers three king-doms away, all with a claim to the throne. And it won't likely be settled without a skirmish or two, if not an all-out war. When the dust settles, do you know where the old king's allies and advisors will end up?"

Roderick swallowed. "Not...in good places?"

"To put it mildly. I have talent and persuasiveness enough to keep my head from ending up on a pike, but the same is not true of the men on whom my continued comfort depends. The deaths of those on the king's council will mean changes in my situation that I do not care to endure." The magician paused and gave his helper a long, cold stare. "Do I need to explain to you how your fate is tied to mine, young Roderick? How a change in my station will mean an even greater change in yours?"

Roderick's ears buzzed at the thought. "No, sir," he said.

"Good." The wizard rubbed his hands together and turned his attention to the living corpse. "Your job will be to keep the king under control. In his current state, His Majesty could do damage to others and himself. He could wander off. He has no idea who or what he is. He functions on the lowest of instincts now. He will eat and drink and sleep. I'm trusting at least one other base instinct will remain fully functional, or else this whole effort is for naught."

Roderick nodded without fully understanding. And then he watched in horror as Old Windhover began gathering up his things, clearly intending to leave his assistant alone with the dead king.

"What do I do if he begins to yell and thrash around again?" he asked, panic in his voice.

The magician paused and thought about it. "He should get more used to his new state. The docility he exhibits now should remain after the drug has worn off. If it doesn't, though..." He handed Roderick a sealed phial and a dropper. "Two drops on the tongue should do it. No more or you'll undo my earlier work, and then there'll be no reviving him again."

He turned away, ready to leave.

"Sir?" Roderick asked.

He looked back, a raised eyebrow his only response.

"For how long do you expect this...job to last?"

"As long as the king does. He's already started to decay. Before long, the body won't be viable. If we want to keep our positions in this castle, we'd better hope we've achieved all our goals by then."

"Yes, sir."

The wizard leaned forward, staring into Roderick's eyes. "The king must have an heir, Roderick. I am doing my part to ensure the outcome, but you must do yours as well."

"I understand. I'll do what I must," Roderick said, and when the magician failed to look away, he added, "I promise."

Old Windhover stared a moment longer, as though prying into Roderick's soul to see the truth behind his words. Then he nodded, almost imperceptibly, and left.

Roderick stared down at the witless creature on the bed. For the first time since coming to the castle, he regretted that he had ever left his home in the Nevergreen. He could have gotten along there just fine for the rest of his life, could have found a buxom forest girl to grow gray with. But the castle had lured him with all its promises of secrets and fine things. Now he found himself surrounded by more fine things than he'd ever imagined and secrets so great that the truths behind them made him shiver.

He sat up with the animated corpse, too frightened of it to sleep. In the morning, Old Windhover returned with two trays of food, one for Roderick and one for the dead king. The magician's prediction had been accurate— when the potion had worn off, the king had remained docile. He sat up in his bed now and let the magician's helper feed him. He did not howl again, nor did he thrash about, and Roderick was glad to note that the dead king had no interest in biting at his fingers when he placed food between the corpse's lips.

The job disgusted him, though, in part because the living corpse had started to smell. Though he didn't seem to take regular breaths, a foul smell poured from his mouth each time he opened it to take an offered bite.

When the meals were finished, Old Windhover said, "Get him dressed, Roderick. His sedan chair awaits at the bottom of the stairs. There's no time to waste."

The wedding was quick and quiet. Roderick stood beside the king, holding his hand throughout the ceremony lest he begin wandering around the chapel or accosting the handful of wedding guests. The king moaned or whimpered on occasion, and Roderick guessed that all in attendance, the Lady Jillian foremost among them, knew that the old king had no concept of what was taking place. But with Old Windhover standing to the far side of the altar, no one dared question the validity of the ceremony.

When it was time for the king to make his vows, the best Roderick could elicit from him was a grunt, achieved by giving the dead man a subtle poke in the ribs. This was sufficient, as the high priest declared the union eternal and retired to his chambers, probably to weep over the abomination he had just presided over. There was no kiss at the ceremony's conclusion. When the Lady Jillian turned her face from the altar at the ceremony's end, she looked first at her lord and then at Roderick, horror and confusion still registering in her eyes. Roderick managed a sympathetic nod and then forced himself to look away; her eyes were too beautiful, too plaintive to be gazed into for any length of time. Instead of drinking in her beauty, he steered the king out of the chapel, through an arched doorway, and straight back to his chambers.

Old Windhover waited there. "Prepare the king for his wedding night," he said without ceremony.

"Prepare...?"

"Gods, man," he said with disgust. "Time is of the essence. His body won't last but a few hours more. If there's to be an heir, it has to be tonight."

"And you think the lady will..."

Roderick had wanted to say "be willing" but was unable to get the words out.

Old Windhover must have misread his helper, as he said, "Yes, yes. She'll conceive tonight. I charged Lorentia with finding a bride who was ripe and ready. If there's no child in nine months, I'll have her head." Then he gave Roderick a piercing look and added, "Or yours. Maybe both."

He turned to exit, adding, "Make haste. The lady comes within the hour. I'm afraid you will need to remain present. If only for the lady's safety."

"Sir?"

"We wouldn't want the king biting his bride, or anything else untoward."

Bile in his throat, Roderick undressed the dead king and forced his spongy body down onto the bed, covering it with a downy quilt. Then he waited for the king's bride, the living corpse making mewling noises and threatening to rise from the bed every few minutes. Roderick considered using another drop from Old Windhover's phial to make the dead man more docile, but he refrained. There was a chance he might give the king too much of the potion, and the result would be disastrous. The king might die outright, ruining Old Windhover's plans and jeopardizing the lives of everyone in the old king's court, Roderick's included. And if he didn't die, if he was only left completely incapacitated…there would still be no heir, and the result would be the same.

When the Lady Jillian entered—a guard at either elbow, Old Windhover at her back, and tears dampening her cheeks—Roderick stood and felt tears of rage in his own eyes at the sight of her distress. He caught another meaningful look from the magician and forced his emotions into check. Moments later, the door had shut, and he heard it being locked from without. They were alone with the dead king.

The Lady Jillian fell to her knees, weeping inconsolably.

Roderick kept a respectful distance, his gaze shifting from the weeping woman to the living corpse on the bed. His mind raced as it had done since he'd read the proclamation in the marketplace, but he could see no way out of the situation. There was nothing in the old books, no knowledge he had gained through reading or observation that could possibly be of help to either himself or the corpse's beautiful bride. Stepping forward, he knelt beside the lady, and though he knew it was not his place, he put a hand on her shuddering shoulder.

"It need only be once, my lady," he said. "And then all will be over. We can put out the candles to keep you from having to see. And to keep myself from witnessing as well."

Still sobbing, she managed to say, "I cannot. I cannot. Let me die first."

He felt as though the thick walls of the castle had been built around him, the stones and mortar all meant to keep him entombed. Old Windhover had set the walls in place, and the lady's refusal now amounted to the last space in the wall being filled in with the tightest-fitting stone to seal him in forever.

"We shall both die then," he said quietly.

"You?" she said, lifting her face from her hands. "But why?"

"For failing in my duties, my lady."

"Your duties?"

"To ensure that an heir to the throne is produced this very night."

She screamed then, a look of greater horror on her face than she had had before. It took Roderick a second to realize that the Lady Jillian was not reacting to his words but rather to the figure of the dead king on the bed behind him. He turned and felt horror himself at seeing the king squirming out from beneath the quilt to rise naked from the bed. It was a frightening sight, the dead man's eyes darting in their sockets and the whimpering starting up in his throat again.

Without thinking, Roderick stood and turned, pushing the king back onto the bed, but the monster struggled to rise again immediately. Glancing at the corpse's bride, Roderick saw that she had retreated to the farthest corner of the room and crouched there, cowering.

All fear of Old Windhover left him then, along with all fear of what would happen if the king's relatives learned that he had died without an heir. The pitiful sight of the crouching, crying woman filled Roderick with loathing for the magician and for the king's council—fat and cowardly men who would see this woman suffer that they might retain their plush lives. He felt loathing for himself as well, for the role he had played in the lady's transformation from potato seller's daughter to dead king's unwilling bride. And as loathing replaced fear, he felt moved to act.

He removed the phial from the pouch at his side. Holding it up, he said, "There is another way."

"What?" the Lady Jillian managed to say. "Poison?" And in her terror he saw hope in her eyes, and relief in the knowledge that death would at least give her respite from her fears.

"Yes, my lady. Of a kind."

In the morning, the guards unbolted the door and let Old Windhover in. Members of the king's esteemed council crowded into the hallway beyond. They looked in but did not dare follow the wizard. The king's chamber was as silent as the tomb it had become. The magician found the king truly dead on his bed. He lay dignified atop the quilt, fully clothed with his eyes closed and his arms folded across his chest. Beside the king lay the Lady Jillian. Old Windhover found Roderick on the floor in a far corner of the room.

The wizard ignored his helper and the woman on the bed, examining the king for a moment before turning to the council members.

"The king is dead," he said with great severity.

Though the council members had known this to be true for at least a day and had kept quiet as the corpse had walked among them, they now made a great show of exhibiting their grief and lamentation at the loss of their sovereign. Several rushed in to gather round the bed, and ladies-in-waiting were called in to remove the Lady Jillian, who had awoken during the hubbub and appeared as grief stricken at her husband's death as any new bride ever was.

In all the confusion, Old Windhover came to the corner from which Roderick had yet to move. The magician waited until he rose before him. Then, quite quietly, he said, "I trust our efforts of the last two days were not in vain."

Roderick nodded. "Yes, sir. All appears to have come to fruition."

The wizard raised one eyebrow at his helper's choice of words.

"We'll have an heir, then."

His eyes seemed to burrow into Roderick's.

"Yes, sir," Roderick said after only a moment's hesitation. "I have every confidence."

"Good man." Giving his bag of finger bones a little shake, Old Windhover added, "You're finally learning to roll the bones well, I see."

"Yes, sir," Roderick said, aware of the color rushing to his cheeks as he recalled the previous night, conscious that his face might betray his secrets to the shrewd old man. He wanted to put a hand into his pocket so he could finger the empty phial to know it was still there, to be sure it hadn't slipped out in the night and ended up in some spot where Old Windhover or one of the council would find it. He kept his hands where they were, though, folded before him. Putting them in his pockets would only draw the wizard's eyes that way.

He wondered if the night's outcome had been the thing Old Windhover had intended all along. Knowing how to roll the bones was important, just as important—Old Windhover always told him—as knowing when others were rolling their own. Looking at the kingly bed, the tranquil corpse still upon it, Roderick allowed himself to wonder how long it would be until he could safely see the Lady Jillian again. He imagined himself putting his hands on her belly again, imagined the next monarch growing there already. Then he looked Old Windhover in the eye and said, "I rolled the bones very well, indeed."

About The Author

Richard Levesque writes books that are hard to categorize: from cyberpunk dystopias to hard-boiled time travel novels set in the 1940s, paranormal mysteries, historical fiction blended with contemporary literary mystery...If he was smart, he'd pick a genre and stick with it, but he's having too much fun writing things he feels inspired by. When he's not writing, he's teaching other people how to write, as well as teaching them all about the history of science fiction. He also collects old science fiction pulps and tries to be better than a mediocre guitar player.

For more information, visit www.richardlevesqueauthor.com.

All The Way

Graham Storrs

Editor's Note: All progress comes with costs. Some great, others small. One of the jobs of science fiction is to remind us of these, inviting us to consider whether those costs are justified. In the end, it turns out that the smaller costs might be the hardest to bear.

"Someone's on the down-wire," the supervisor told me over the link. I looked up from what I was doing, bolting a bracket the size of a house onto the end of T15. "She says she wants to see you."

"Who is it?"

"Eden, she says."

I looked out at the stars all around me and the thick trunk of the tether climbing up to vanish into the Moon above. "ETA?"

"Bit more'n a day."

In the distance I could see the bright slash of the supply tether that would bring the gondola and my granddaughter down the wire to meet me.

The two-tier space elevator was invented because people aren't really designed for living in zero-G. After a while they get sick and die. So you take a standard space elevator—which is a space station in geosynchronous orbit with a tether down to the planet's surface—and you extend the tether way, way beyond the station and tie on a second station. This second station is now swinging 'round the planet like a bucket on a string and people can live there quite happily, feeling the force as if they had real gravity.

So it's sort of ironic that, by the time the first two-tier el was being built, there were hardly any standard humans left in space to enjoy it. People I met these days just weren't standard anymore.

Take me, for instance. This is my fifth deathday. Five years now since my old blood-and-bone body lay down and died and I was uploaded into a little box about the size of one of those thumb drives I had when I was a kid. It took me a while to work out what to do with myself, now that I was immortal and all, but, like most scans these days—the ones who don't want to live in VR—I chose a career in space.

My deathday party was a quiet affair. Just me and a bottle of scotch. I drank to the old bastard who died and bequeathed me himself. The alcohol had no effect on me, of course, but I've got a nice little add-on I found on the grid that simulates getting hammered almost perfectly. Doug Cameron was his name, and I will be, quite literally, eternally grateful for what he gave me.

Here's to you, Doug! And to me too, I suppose, since I took his name along with the rest of his personality.

———————— • ————————

"Granddad?"

You couldn't blame Eden for being unsure. Last time she saw her grand-dad, he was a shrivelled thing lying in a hospital bed, ninety-five and riddled with cancer. She was a scared-looking kid back then, genemodded in the fashions of the time, trying to look cool, or hot, or something, with leopardskin fur growing on her upper arms, and her eyes and hair bright violet. Fifteen and trying not to retch at the sight of old Doug's decaying body, hanging back behind the other visitors so she wouldn't have to talk to him. I remember seeing her through old man's eyes, looking for her mother's face and not finding it. Her grandmother, my own dear Penny, didn't go to see the old man. Not even once.

"My you've grown, Eden. I suppose I should get Earthside more often. Keep in touch more." It felt funny to say words out loud instead of just thinking them into the link, but Eden wasn't auged like that. She wore her linknode as a facial tattoo—a pretty one, all flowers and birds—and talked to people with her mouth when they were right there with her.

She ran her eyes up and down me. "You look…"

"Different?"

"…imposing."

I smiled. I supposed I must. Three metres tall and almost as broad, the macrobot my brainbox rode around in was built for strength. My hands, with a span as wide as Eden was tall, could wrestle multi-tonne masses in free-fall, and my feet and tail were designed for gripping onto things while I worked. "I was out on the wire when you arrived. I didn't think to change into something less…functional."

"It's OK. I sort of knew what to expect."

"It's good to see you," I ventured, although it wasn't, particularly. The old man had seen her a dozen times, maybe, when she was growing up. I didn't know her at all, really.

She nodded. A silence fell. I dredged up another platitude to fill it but she didn't let me.

"Grandma's dying," she blurted. "We need you to come and talk to her. She's being so…she won't listen to anyone."

I looked into her distressed face. In the old man's time, I'd have got up and paced around in agitation, but my hormones weren't like that now. There was a module in my software that simulated them and I'd tuned the responses way down. Who needs agitation when you can have inner peace?

"Penny doesn't want to talk to me either," I said. "She hasn't wanted to for many years now." The fact still filled me with bitterness. It made me mean. "You've wasted your trip. This was your mum's idea, I suppose." My daughter, Terri, had always been romantic like that.

Eden steadied her gaze, tilting up her chin defiantly. Now I saw Terri in her! "Mum asked if you'd come. I said you'd only upset Gran, but Mum asked me if I'd come and get you."

———————— • ————————

We rode the wire up to Partway Station, neither of us talking much on the long journey. It would be another six years before Alltheway Station was complete. Until then, the best way to leave the Moon was from the Partway Shuttleport at the zero-G point. We exchanged the gondola for the shuttle, I took Eden to visit the observation lounge. We hung in the webbing and admired the massive disc of the Moon, and I pointed out several of the hundred-plus settlements down there.

I shed most of my mass before we set off, storing all those litres of nanites away in their vats in my quarters. After that, my body was as near standard as it could be. I was even wearing clothes, although it was pretty obvious I wasn't exactly human any more. Eden seemed much more comfortable with me now. Looking human wasn't a big deal here at Partway but I knew it would be down on Earth.

The shuttle took almost a day to get us to Earth orbit and we spent yet another day crawling down the old Florida Spacebridge. Blue ocean and brown land rose to meet us, and when we finally hit atmosphere and the sky started turning blue, I felt my mood lifting. Whatever the beauty and grandeur of space, there's nothing like that feeling of being home when you go back down.

By the time we reached the ground, Eden had been out of Earth's gravity for about a week, and it took her most of the four-hour hop to London Heathrow to get her land-legs back. Me, I just let my body automatically adjust—strengthening its endoskeletal matrix and amping up its muscles—and I didn't even notice the change.

"You're quite a lot like him," Eden said in the taxi out to the hospital, "but not in some ways."

"What?" I'd been gazing through the windows, readjusting to the scale of it all. Ten billion people squeezed into one tiny planet! It was something I'd just taken for granted before.

"I mean, I remember him as grumpy and sarcastic. I never dared talk to him. You're sort of calm, peaceful."

"You only knew me when I was sick."

"Grandma's sick. She's still nice."

———————— • ————————

The hospital was just another hospital, with its wide, bright corridors full of bustling robots. I linked to the local grid as we entered the building and asked for Penny. A simulated nurse appeared in my sensorium and led us along the route to my ex-wife's room. Eden said she was going to the café and left me to gather my courage outside the door.

"I wondered how long it would be before they sent you to see me," she said, scowling at me.

She looked tired and worn—every year of her very long life. I wanted to weep for her all over again.

"They think I can talk you into being uploaded."

A tiny smile appeared on her thin lips. "Go on then."

I smiled back and sat down beside her. "I think I will. You know my views on the matter. There are people who love you and don't want to lose you."

"They're going to lose me whatever I do, only, if I have myself uploaded, there'll be a copy of me hanging around that thinks it *is* me, like some kind of animated holograph. It's too damned creepy."

"You could come out to the Moon with me. I'm working on Alltheway. When the station is built, we'll start on the starship. Ten years from now, I plan to be in the crew that takes her out."

"A crew that's all uploads and AIs, I hear. No people."

"I'm still people, Penny. I'm still Doug Cameron. Everything about him that mattered, anyway." She shook her head, looking sad. "And I still love you. When they copied Doug into here—" I tapped my head as if that's where my processor was. "—they copied everything: every memory, every thought, every feeling. I was there the day we met. I was there the first time we made love, when Terri was born, when we paid off the mortgage... I sat up all night with you and watched the first Mars landings. I held you when your sister died."

"Stop it!"

I closed my eyes and looked away, all the old pain flooding back. The silence dragged out until she spoke again.

"We went through all this when Doug made his decision. You were there that day too, right? I told him if he did the upload, I didn't want anything to do with whatever they copied out of him. With you. There was only one Doug Cameron, only one man I loved and wanted to spend my life with. That man wasn't a piece of software running in a fancy robot body. He was a unique and fragile accident of evolution, the product of a time and place we grew up in together, before cognitive augmentations and cyborgs and space elevators and genemodded teenagers. Do you know there is a gang of wolf-kids in New York who have been killing and eating rival gang members?"

She fell silent again, and I absorbed the fact that in her mind I was the same kind of abomination as those kids with their illegal mods. I'd known it would be impossible to reach her, but I'd known I would try anyway. I gave it another shot.

"What harm would it do you, to be uploaded? As you say, when you die, you die. But an upload would mean you were still around for your family. Eden tells me she has a partner and they're thinking of contracting to have kids one day. Wouldn't you like to know that something of you would still be around for your great grandchildren? I know Terri would like that, and Eden. And maybe... Maybe if you were uploaded, you'd see things differently. I'd like to take you out there, show you some of the things I've seen these past few years. We're going to the stars, Penny. Can you believe that? I'm going. And you could come too. We could start again, you and me. It would be like..."

I stopped talking. The tears running down her face were eating into me like acid.

"I'm sorry," I said. "I didn't mean to..."

"But you did. That's why I didn't ever want to see you. You're too like him. It's horrible. And I know how you must feel—about me—and I always hated the thought that I'd have to reject you again, because I know what it's like to be in love like that and see the person you love pull away from you and go somewhere you don't want to follow."

"I–I was dying, Penny. I had no choice."

"Rubbish! You could have chosen to go on living. You might have had another five years, ten even. We could have had those years! Me and Doug. You stole them, so the cancer wouldn't get to your precious brain, so they'd get a clean upload. You could have had more treatments but you thought you could live forever, you stupid, selfish man!"

I stood up, horrified at what she was saying, aware that she wasn't even railing at me but at the old man, that I was just a reminder of her pain, not in any way a substitute for what she'd lost. I stumbled through an apology and fled the room. I ran down the corridors and out of the hospital and I kept running until I was off-planet and headed for home.

———— • ————

The big platform for Alltheway Station was being spun up. A whole comet, rubble and ice inside a tough polymer bag, was being warmed by the sun at the aphelion of its tight, elliptical orbit, and whirled around so fast it would flatten into a gigantic plate, two kilometres across. By the time it reached us here at the Moon, it would have refrozen, the tethers would all be in place and the platform could be guided in and attached. We were building the biggest space station ever. A whole city, with one-sixth gravity and a spaceport on its outer face that, one day, would fling the first starships out into interstellar space.

I had a message from Eden when Penny finally passed away. It was there in my mail one day when I got off my shift. It was short and to the point and it thanked me "for trying to help Grandma." It made me laugh and rage both at the same time. So I wasted another bottle of scotch on my unresponsive system and let my illegal software extension keep me drunk for three days before I went back to work.

I hung by my feet on T17 and watched the tugs nudging a freighter into the dock on T2. From her markings she was carrying nanite paste from the new factory on Ceres. Behind her, the Earth was a blue crescent, dazzling and remote.

Another world.

About The Author

Graham Storrs is a former research scientist who now lives in the Australian bush and writes science fiction. He has published short stories and eleven novels, covering all the major sci-fi themes, including time travel, dystopian futures, transhumanity, alien invasion and space opera and, within each theme, he likes to mix it up, writing thrillers, adventure and comedy. Keeping the science real is as important to him as keeping his characters real, and his books and stories are heavily researched. He does most of his writing outdoors, in the mountains and gum forests that surround his home.

For more information, visit grahamstorrs.cantalibre.com.

Scales Fall

Dave Higgins

Editor's Note: Fantasy spends a lot of time in quasi-Arthurian worlds, but magic has flowered in many human cultures beyond Medieval Europe. Take ancient Egypt for example. If your taste is for dark magic, I'd go with mummies every time.

Philip Luttman ticked the final item. "Well, the crates are all present and undamaged. The contents are another matter."

"It's Dyer's first big find, dear." Anna placed Dyer's telegram on a bench and picked up a crowbar. The scent of dry straw cut the air of the museum as she eased the top from a small crate. "If anything, he'll have packed everything too well. There's space for twice as much in this crate. I don't know why he didn't use the opportunity to come back with them, though. Especially with the problems."

"You mean that guide trying to steal some of the grave goods? You have to expect the odd bad apple with native workers. But it's all petty crime, no planning. I mean, trying to carry a five-foot-tall brass mirror through the camp. No wonder he was caught. No, Dyer might be a little slack on details, but he's right about doing a survey of the rest of the valley. No sane archaeologist gives that up to shepherd crates."

"I didn't just mean that. Egypt closed the Suez Canal. Do you read the newspaper or just use it to hide the toast?"

"President Nasser gives a good speech, but he's not got the stomach to take on Great Britain." Philip picked up the second crowbar and worked the nails out of Crate 42. "And his people certainly don't. Scratch most Egyptians, you'll find they're scared of devils hiding in the sand. Take Dyer's diggers; one look at the inside of the tomb and they're babbling about ancient curses. And the ones who aren't superstitious are all trying to buy civilisation. Worst Dyer might face is some little Egyptian bureaucrat asking for more *baksheesh*."

Anna reached into the straw. "Hopefully. Small bowl, dark glaze with traces of an unidentified substance in the bottom. I'd say Naqada III." She glanced at the manifest. "And, Dyer says Naqada. So, that's one detail right."

"Well, pottery's a beginner's topic anyway." Philip ducked as his wife reached for the crowbar. "Although, there might be subtleties. The electrum dagger is the critical find. Dyer describes the mummy as crude, and you, the most skilled and beautiful of all pot experts, agree with his dating of the bowl.

43

Suggests Third Dynasty. But, an ibis-headed dagger doesn't fit the rituals of the Third Dynasty. We should start there."

"Only last month, you said knives weren't worth considering." Anna lifted a cracked jar from its bed of straw and turned it in the light. "Mrs. Hadsall hasn't forgiven you for spreading butter with her best ladle."

"I can't be held accountable for that: I was sleepwalking. It's your fault. You know it happens occasionally when I can't relax, so if you did your wifely duty…"

"Wifely duty? You convinced me to marry you, not support your theory about a missing Pharaoh."

"Not missing; excised from the record for unspeakable blasphemies. You agree placing an unsheathed dagger between the mummy's hands is unusual?"

"Yes, dear." Anna settled the jar back in the crate. "Play with your knife. I'll finish cataloguing the pottery."

Philip kissed her on the cheek. It was fortunate they had the museum to themselves tonight. The last thing he needed was someone making a joke about how his theories were so mad even his own wife wouldn't support them.

After picking up the dagger, he strolled to the photography lab. He shouldn't get ahead of himself: a single artefact didn't prove the gap in Egypt's dynastic record was deliberate. But a crude mummy entombed miles from any others with the trappings of immense power and riches meant something. And the placement of the dagger screamed divergent rites to anyone who wasn't too tied up in the past to consider the evidence.

Not that he was free of the past himself. The museum's camera might be older than him. With a firm kick, he got the tripod to lock. After fighting the same war with the swivels on the lighting stands, he took a series of close shots. As he lined the lens up for a shot of the whole dagger, an odd glint caught his eye. He tilted his head, hoping to see it again.

There was a subtle pattern or carving on the blade. Dyer's notes hadn't mentioned that. It could be the turning point. Camera stable enough to release, he picked up the knife and angled it back and forth. Something. He brought it even closer.

The slight shift in angle revealed two lines of early hieroglyphics. *Kheft-ek…en…Seba'u…*

Kheft-ek ertaw en set/Seba'u Kher. Thine enemy is given to the fire; The Evil One has fallen.

From *The Book of Coming Forth By Day.* Which suggested the New Kingdom, Eighteenth Dynasty at the earliest. The hieroglyphics were in the oldest format, though, in use from the Second Dynasty onwards. The Book had to be based on older rituals. He might be on the verge of—

The sound of pottery shattering interrupted his racing thoughts. Before he could gather them, a scream echoed. Anna!

Philip sprinted for the storeroom. From around the corner, he heard someone shouting for Clegg to leave it. He saw four men heading away as he turned the corner. On instinct, he raced after them, only to collide with a fifth man emerging from the doorway.

Shoulder bouncing off the wall, the stranger fell, knocking Philip down too. Philip's vision blurred as the fall slammed his head against the hard floor.

By the time Philip's senses returned, his attacker had left. He eased himself upright. Anna!

Despite his throbbing head, he staggered into the storeroom. His wife's legs stuck out from behind a pile of crates. Fragments of pottery crunched under his feet as he rushed forward. He knelt beside her. Moist stickiness oozed through the knees of his trousers, but all he noticed was the absence in her eyes.

———— • ————

Amber liquid sloshes from a dirty bottle, the flicker of a gas mantle casting golden pools across a rough table.

Filthy curtains twitch over a rain-spattered window.

Stubby fingers, nails hacked square, lift a glass.

The shadows stretch, metal glinting.

Gold and crystal explode.

A gaping mouth pushes against the night.

Flabby guts tear.

An impassive face stands in a pool of whiskey and blood.

———— • ————

Philip's elbow struck the bedroom wall, sending a jolt of pain along his arm. Fragments of his nightmare sank back into the darkness.

Gentle tapping came from the door. "Professor? Are you all right?"

He untangled the blankets and staggered to the door, an erratic throb stabbing at his temples.

"You shouted fit to wake the—" His housekeeper pressed one hand over her mouth. Eyes wide, she clutched at her worsted dressing gown. "Oh, sir. I didn't think."

"I'm fine, Mrs. Hadsall. Sorry for waking you."

"Can I bring you anything? Some warm milk? Or cocoa?"

Philip's stomach roiled. "No, thank you. I'll ring if I need you." Closing the door on her frown, he headed for the bed. Something tangled around his feet.

He reached down and picked up a pair of trousers, still damp to the touch. A darker patch next to them proved to be his jacket, also damp. How had they ended up on the floor? He'd poured a generous tot to fill the space after dinner. The vase in the drawing room had been empty, so he'd gone into the garden to cut a few roses. After that, the evening slipped into darkness. He must have had a few more tots, then stumbled up to bed. That explained the nightmares and going three rounds with the blankets.

Philip slumped onto the bed, reality fleeing before he could pull the blankets across.

———— • ————

Philip strode through the back entrance of the museum, neutral expression gripped in place. The remains of the night hadn't overcome the excess of whisky, but he needed to do something. Mrs. Hadsall kept lurking on the edges of the room, gaze like limp rags; and when she wasn't there, the house was so empty.

"Professor Luttman." The assistant curator gaped at him from ahead. "We didn't expect... That is, I'm sure I speak for everyone when I say—"

"Anna wouldn't want me moping around, Mr. Chivers." Philip nodded as he marched past. "She'd want us to finish the cataloguing. Get a full list of what's missing for the police."

Chivers scurried after him. "Already in hand, professor. I had the porters call around all the staff so we could—"

"Well?" Philip spun and thrust his face at Chivers. "How much did we lose?"

"Most of the crates are still sealed. Crates 45 and 47 have a few fresh marks near the nails, so the police think that your wife... That is the thieves ran off when they were disturbed. Two jars were broken during the theft. Crates 39 and 42 were empty. So, four canopic jars, a bowl, several items of jewellery, and an ibis-headed dagger."

The dagger? He was holding it when he heard the scream. He must not have put it down, and the thief grabbed it after he fell. "Photographs. Has anyone...? The police will want them."

Leaving Chivers to flap like a fish, Philip marched towards the lab.

Three hours later, two copies of his photographs hung on the drying line. After slipping the first set into an envelope, he scrawled *For the Police* on the front and dropped it at the porter's lodge. He snatched up the negatives for comparison, grabbed the second set of pictures and hurried to his office. Keep busy. That was the best remedy for it all. Like at university. Just work through the hangover.

He ran his magnifying glass across the images of the blade. The hieroglyphics stood out even clearer in the photographs. He'd need a second opinion on the translation, but they were there.

If Dyer had missed something that obvious, what else had he missed? Philip dumped all the other papers from his desk onto the floor and spread the pictures out. An hour slipped by unnoticed as he inched the magnifying glass across the images.

There! What seemed, at a casual glance, poor carving or wear on one feather, on closer inspection took on a sense of purpose. Caught at the right angle, it was tiny hieroglyphics, "Place of Judgement." He squeezed the bridge of his nose. His eyes were too old for this. Anna's eyes were sharper, and she'd want to— Already halfway out of his chair, he collapsed back down. Magnifier creeping across the photographs, he struggled to separate tiny pictures from chance patterns.

He'd found what might be "no rest" when a voice broke his concentration.

"You didn't hear me knocking." Chivers breezed to the desk, holding a tea tray. "Thought a cup of tea—"

"What? No time." Philip stood, chair thudding against the wall. "Take it away."

Chivers staggered back. His left foot landed on the pile of papers and slid sideways. Arms shooting out to catch his balance, he upturned the tray. Amber liquid spewed from the spout as the pot struck the centre of the desk. A lake of shards and boiling water washed over the photographs. "Good God, man!" Philip shoved Chivers away. "You're worse than those bloody thieves." Grabbing his coat, he strode out of his office. It was clear he wouldn't get anything done here. Mrs. Hadsall loomed, but at least she let him work. He needed to refer to Culp's notes on the "Parchment of Sobek" anyway. And the mummy; there might be something on the wrappings. He whirled on his heel in the corridor and fixed Chivers with a glare. "Crate 45. Have it sent to the house." With Chivers still mopping at the ruined images, Philip marched out into the storm.

———————— • ————————

Rain gusts down an alley, spreading the shadows.
  Hunched shoulders bend over cheap boots.
  Shadow lashes out, exposing a cruel beak.
  Hands clasp the wine-dark mess of a shirt.
  Grey feathers cut the gloom.
  Fingers drop from a torn stomach.
  A falcon soars into the rain, bloody flesh trailing.

———————— • ————————

Philip awoke, chest tight. While wrestling himself free of the nightmare, his arm struck something. A stack of books cascaded off the table. He was in his study. He must have dozed off after lunch.

Six o'clock. Why hadn't Mrs. Hadsall woken him for tea? Well, he'd have it now. A cup might clear his head. He'd better tidy his papers first, though. The last thing he needed was someone else causing an accident.

His coat lay on the floor near the French windows, dark patches on the carpet surrounding it. He dumped his books on the desk and snatched the coat up. Soaking wet. Coat tails dragging behind him, he stormed to the bell pull.

The pad of heels marked Mrs. Hadsall's approach. Too impatient to wait for her, Philip yanked the study door open and thrust the coat at her. "I told you to hang this to dry. And where do I find it…?"

"I did, sir." Mrs. Hadsall's shoulders drew back. "If it's moved, then it wasn't me that moved it."

"And what about afternoon tea? I requested it at—"

"I brought it at four." She gazed up at him, concern warring with anger. "You didn't answer when I knocked, so I left it beside the door. Knocked again at five when some porters turned up with a crate. You hadn't said where you'd want it, and it had such a funny smell, so I told them to put it in the garden shed."

Crate? The mummy. Philip looked past her. A tray of sandwiches and tea languished on the hall table next to the telephone. "Sorry for snapping. I…"

Mrs. Hadsall patted him on the elbow. "I'll hang this up, then bring you a fresh pot."

As soon as she was out of sight, he raised one leg. His trouser cuff was damp, and he was in his socks. A few steps took him to the French doors, and he peered around. A pair of brogues, droplets of water clinging to the leather, lay behind the curtain as if kicked off. Now that he thought to look for it, the damp patches on the carpet bore a resemblance to footprints.

He'd been sleepwalking again. Only one thing for it: he'd have to tie his ankle to the bed tonight, as his mother had done when he was little.

———— • ————

Moonlight creeps through curtains, slashing across the barrel of a revolver.

Thin blankets mummify the legs of a sleeping man.

A plain gold band glints as a hand wraps around his throat.

Eyes gape as a revolver spins to the floor.

An ibis tears at a man's chest.

Familiar fingers reach into the wound.

Plumage shining silver, an ibis-headed dagger slashes twice.

The hand withdraws, dropping its bloody prize into the mouth of a jackal.

———————— • ————————

Philip snapped awake. A third nightmare filled with murder. This time containing the missing dagger. As he attempted to sit up, dull pain yanked at his ankle.

The cord. Sliding down the bed to ease the tension, he threw back the covers. The knot, somehow having twisted in the night, resisted his fingers. He scrunched further down the bed. Even with both hands, it was too dark to see what he was doing. Not that there was much point in untying it until morning anyway.

Caught on the edge of sleep, fragments of the nightmare rose. Ambivalence filled him: decent horror at the brutality of the dreams; and pleasure at seeing murderers suffer. And something else: familiarity.

The attacks were vicious, but the cuts—at least the ones in the latest dream —had been precise, and focused on the abdomen. Like the evisceration of a mummy.

Eyes gritty, he shuffled back up the bed and tugged the blankets over himself. Egyptian funeral rites on filthy louts. Perhaps there was something in that psychotherapy the Americans were so set on. There was nothing he could do to the thieves in real life, so he was taking revenge in his dreams. Still uncomfortable with how brutal his unconscious was, he slipped into a troubled sleep.

———————— • ————————

Philip dropped the lid back on the salver and swallowed hard. "Mrs. Hadsall. No more devilled kidneys for breakfast."

"Certainly, sir. I'll take that away now. Will you be requiring—?"

The doorbell interrupted her attempt to fill the void in his day with kedgeree, or eggs, or whatnot. Philip poured himself another cup of tea and moved over to the window. The roses Anna had planted next to the pergola had bedded in; he'd have to... He sighed. Would that be his life now? Would he pretend the projects she had started still meant something without her? At least the Egyptians believed their rituals helped the deceased; all an Englishman would get is a vicar blathering on about the consolation of grace.

Two sets of footsteps padded along the corridor. He placed his cup on the table with a clatter. Who called before ten and then entered without being invited?

Mrs. Hadsall pushed open the dining room door. "Detective Inspector Stevens."

As she ducked back, a man in his late forties stepped past. One side of his tweed jacket bulged. Shifting an unlit pipe to his left hand, he strode forward and stuck out his right. "Professor Luttman. Sorry to bother you so early."

Philip shook the outstretched hand. He vaguely remembered the inspector from the museum, but most of the night was a blur. "Can I offer you tea? Or perhaps some...toast."

The inspector grimaced. "Most kind. Expect you don't want me eating when I could be out there searching, though. Two reasons for coming. I'll get right to it. Not sure how it happened. You might want to sit down, sir. There's been a problem at the mortuary..."

Something about misfiled paperwork, apologies from the highest level, and heads rolling washed over Philip. They'd lost the body. How would Anna find peace without her body? He broke a piece of toast in half, then paused. It had been their little joke: I'd share my last piece of toast with you. Who was he going to share toast with now?

China rattled, then a blurred cup of tea appeared. He should—

"Take your time, sir." The inspector rested a hand on his arm. "I'll ask your housekeeper to bring something for the shock."

"No." Philip turned his head away and dabbed at his eyes with a handkerchief. "I'd prefer to keep my faculties sharp. If I don't, I might forget she's gone, and the remembering..."

"Quite understand. Felt the same when my mother passed on."

"Thank you, Inspector. You said there were two things?"

"Does the name Matt Timmins mean anything to you?"

Philip racked his brains. Had he heard the name before, or did it just seem familiar because it was a common name? "I don't think so. I know most of the museum staff but I might not recall a cleaner or delivery driver. Does this mean you've found the thieves?"

"We recovered this from Mr. Timmins' room. Unfortunately, we didn't find anything else." The inspector pulled a bundled handkerchief from the pocket of his tweeds. Holding it in the palm of his left hand, he eased back the corners. "If you could not touch. Do you recognise it?"

Philip lowered his half-raised right hand and gazed at the arcs of ceramic beads interspersed with polished metal. "It's a *wesekh*. A necklace indicating power or honour. If you're asking whether it's one of the stolen items, I'm afraid I don't know. The manifest listed a *wesekh*, but we'd only opened a few of the crates when..."

"...when you went to photograph the dagger." The inspector wrapped the necklace up. "Thank you, sir. And sorry again for the mistake."

Inspector Steven's mouth creased. After a half step toward the door, he swung back, then drew a deep breath. He stared at Philip for a moment, then turned back to the door. "I'll show myself out."

Before Philip could respond, Inspector Stevens was gone. Found in the room of? The inspector hadn't said whether they'd arrested Mr. Timmins, or anyone else. So the thieves must still be out there. But then, why didn't he say they were pursuing leads? And why did Timmins sound familiar? It wasn't anyone from the museum. And if there had been a connection, the inspector would have mentioned it.

The cold dregs of his tea swallowed, Philip moved over to the bookshelves. A Reverend Timothy, but no Timmins. Someone Anna knew? He pulled open her top desk drawer.

No address book. He checked the other drawers, but it wasn't there. He frowned. Timmins still felt familiar. It would just be a random coincidence —if he even had seen the name before—but he wouldn't be able to shake it until he found out. And he hadn't told everyone she was... had passed away. He'd need Anna's address book to make sure he missed no one.

Letting people know! She'd called her cousin about something on Tuesday. The sense of familiarity grew as he strode into the corridor and snatched up her address book from next to the telephone. No Timmins. He flicked through again to be sure. Nothing even close. As he turned towards his study, the notepad caught his eye. The top sheet was blank, but he had the strongest feeling that was where he'd seen the name. He tilted it back and forth. There were indentations in the paper, too shallow to read. Maybe in a better light.

He rushed into his study to find a pencil. Even with the desk light and a magnifying glass, the pencil rubbings were too faint to make out clearly. Abandoning his project, he realised he couldn't face calling casual friends and distant relatives. Address book and notepad back in their normal places, he buried himself in Culp's notes.

———— • ————

Philip blinked at his steak pudding. Apart from the two forkfuls he'd forced down to stop Mrs. Hadsall lurking in the doorway, it was the same as when she brought it half an hour ago. He'd barely touched breakfast and missed lunch. He should eat, but those mouthfuls had tasted like dust. Defeated, he headed for the sideboard. A little whisky would take the edge off. And if his appetite came back, he'd ask Mrs. Hadsall to bring something.

After the second tot, the pudding smelled more appetising. Fork clutched in his right hand, he alternated between scoops of meaty filling and sips of whisky until only fragments of pastry remained. Rich food and poor sleep dragging at his eyelids, he dozed. The image of the telephone pad drifted up. Timmins, 14 Langdon Road—

His head thudded against the back of his chair as he jerked awake. He remembered. Not just Timmins, but three other names and addresses. The steak pudding and whisky twisted in his stomach and a drumming filled his ears.

His sleepwalking was worse. Three dreams about horrible murder. Timmins had been the third. The inspector hadn't said why they had searched Timmins' room, but he had called at breakfast; if someone had reported a disturbance in the night, the time was right for Stevens to have come straight here. Or was this his mind putting random pieces together?

The fourth address. Simon, 67B Cardew Street. Not the best area; exactly where he expected a thief to live. Did that make it more or less likely? If one of the thieves lived there, then…then what? He should tell the police. But how would he explain knowing?

It was better to be sure. Even if he knew the addresses, it didn't mean he'd killed anyone. He headed for the front door.

"Professor? You're going out in this weather?" Mrs. Hadsall frowned at him from partway along the hall.

Philip realised the drumming was rain hammering against the windows. "An urgent errand."

"Well, at least let me call you a taxi."

"No." He yanked the door open. "Need to clear my head." One shoulder of his jacket already sodden, he scurried down the path, still pulling his coat on.

———————————— • ————————————

Hair flattened and coat defeated, Philip stumbled into Cardew Street. His shoes squelched each time he took a step. If it were possible to feel less like a brutal killer on a relentless hunt, he didn't know how. Grief made people do odd things, and this was one of them. He should—

The entrance to 67B gaped, rain driving into the gloomy hallway. He stepped in, wondering whether to call out.

A door swung open at the far end, revealing a hunched figure lurking behind something.

Philip flattened himself against the wall. The man slipped out of sight.

Before Philip could decide what to do, a flash of lightning lit the hallway, flaring off glass. A mirror over the fireplace. Not a lurking figure, but his own reflection, soaked to the skin. As he crept to the end room, an acrid smell wafted out, raising memories of the War.

A small man, apparently unconscious, lay next to an overturned chair. Dark stains further marred his already-tattered shirt.

Gaze flicking around the room, Philip moved closer. A flash of lightning caught the mirror over the mantle, drawing his eye. For an instant, the after-images made his reflection appear to twist in pain. He squeezed his eyes shut and opened them again. What was—?

With a crunch, the man's chest tore open, exposing his lungs.

Acid boiling up his throat, Philip sprinted from the room.

---•---

Rain battered Philip's face. He lay on wet soil. Thorns tugged at his sleeve. Anna's rose bushes. He was in his own garden.

Another burst of nausea surged as he remembered the graunch of ribs opening. He rolled over and vomited thin matter. Eyes tearing from the bitter stench, he pushed himself upright. Dark stains coated his hands. He'd run. He hadn't touched the man. How did he have blood...?

What if it was hysteria? Had he killed the thief and then imagined he'd only witnessed it because he couldn't cope? Were the dreams memories? He needed to call the police.

As he shoved the front door open, his feet slipped on the wet step, pitching him to the floor. In the light of the hall, the backs of his hands looked more brown than red. The dark stains were soil. He hadn't killed anyone. Had it even happened, or had he been sleepwalking and dreamt it?

Coat dripping on the carpet, he headed up to the bathroom. Wash his hands, pour a stiff drink, then decide what to do. Mud, a reassuring dark-coffee tone, swirled away. He reached for the tap to wash the residue away, pausing for a moment as a dragging sound came from above him. Strange time for Mrs. Hadsall to be in the attic. Steering the large drifts of dirt into the drain, he swilled his fingers under the running water and twisted the tap off.

Calmer now, he realised his trousers clung to his legs. Change first, then have a drink. As he squelched along the landing, he heard an incoherent muttering coming from above. What was Mrs. Hadsall doing?

He headed up the attic stairs and pushed the door open. The scent of natron and cinnamon filled the room. Philip stumbled to a halt. Candlelight spilled from an old full-length dressing mirror, falling on bare boards edged with boxes and dust-sheeted piles, yet there were no candles in the room.

It must be a trick of perspective; the candles must be behind a pile of boxes. Taking a few steps forward, he looked for the source of the light. Only bare boards met his gaze. Even more confusingly, the mirror reflected the boxes but not him.

Instead, four canopic jars stood in a square, and within them Anna's body. Before he could reconcile the image with reality, the back of a man came into view, almost against the frame.

Philip rubbed his eyes. The man wore the same suit as Philip did, but the stains on his fingers were too red to be mud.

Dagger raised in his left hand, the man paced towards the falcon-headed jar. His body shifted for a moment, seeming shorter and broader. He crouched and ran the dagger around the base of the lid. The light glinted from a plain gold band as he twisted the lid free with his right hand.

Faint vapour rose from the jar and drifted over Anna's body.

The man moved to the human-headed jar. As he crouched, his jacket fell back, revealing a bloodstained rip in the side of a crumpled shirt. Why would he wear such a cheap shirt with an expensive suit? Then the figure looked up.

Philip's breath stuttered. The man could be his twin. Except for the eyes: the man's eyes were so sunken they seemed almost black.

When Philip's double rose, the image tore apart, stretching and thinning to reveal another man within: his attacker from the museum. A breath later, the two figures snapped back together.

Continuing his widdershins circle, the re-merged figure opened the jackal-headed jar, then moved to the last lid. But—unlike at the other three—Philip's almost-twin removed it without cutting around it first. Of course! The jar of Hapi contained the lungs. They'd only been taken this evening, so the killer wouldn't have needed to seal the jar to keep them fresh.

Arms spread, Philip's almost-duplicate shouted, "*Kn'a ron ngthrod uaaah chafh'drn shagg!*" Left arm sweeping in, he collapsed backwards. The mirror juddered in its frame as he slid until only the top of his head was visible.

Philip shuffled a few steps closer. The flickering light fell on untidy curls, not Philip's short-back-and-sides. As Philip inched closer, a stocky body in an old shirt came into view. He moved nearer still. The dagger jutted from the side of the man's abdomen. Exactly the height Philip's hand would have been when they collided in the corridor.

One body with the face of another. How could the thief have Philip's own face? It didn't make sense. And yet, the Egyptians had believed the personality, the *ba*, could interact with the world after death, could leave the corpse at night and return at dawn. Egyptian funerary practices were supposed to send the *ba* into the afterlife, to stop it merging with the corpse, prevent the shambling, bandaged monster of cheap novels. If the *ba* separated from the body but the rituals to release it weren't performed, it would have no rest; just as the dagger said.

The Book of Going Forth By Day spoke of it happening after death. What if there were a way to separate it before death? Didn't fakirs and mystics claim they could send their spirit out of their bodies?

The dagger was more than a way to free the soul before death. It destroyed the victim's *ba*, replacing it with the wielder's, consigning an enemy to the flames. Egyptian religion was half cursing enemies and half buying power in the afterlife. A weapon to punish the enemies not with mere death, but with becoming your slave fitted both.

His dreams of vengeance were so vivid because he had been there, in spirit if not body. And he knew the addresses because the thief did; like a spiritual palimpsest, some knowledge from the previous occupant had remained. There must be more to it, though. The ritual had only been visible in the mirror. Mirrors. The odd reflections when the thief had been killed. Dyer's guide had tried to steal a mirror, too. The hieroglyphics on the dagger meant

"Place of Judgement" but they could also mean "Gateway." To a primitive desert culture a mirror would be the work of a skilled craftsman, but even a pauper could afford pure glass in England. Locked doors would be no barrier and witnesses no risk if you could pass through any reflective surface, kill a man not in this world but in its reflection. But why a reversed mummification ritual?

"Philip." Philip stared into his wife's eyes as she beckoned him closer. Of course! Resurrection. The highest goal of all Egyptian magic. He merely needed to pass through the gate.

He reached for Anna's hand, only to stop as his fingers struck the glass. It didn't make sense. The thief's body was in the mirror, and must have passed through it several times to gather the organs for the ritual and to take Anna's body. Why couldn't Philip pass through? "How do I pass through?"

"I don't know." Anna reached toward him, but had no more luck than he. The tips of their fingers turned white as they each strove to bridge the thin gap between them.

After a moment longer, Philip drew his hand back. How could a thief do it when Philip couldn't? Even after it all, that thug was with Anna while Philip couldn't reach her.

But the thief hadn't done it. The idea of a thug like that performing magic, knowing even one word of it, was ridiculous. Words. That had to be it. Egyptian magic was based on words. Not wanting things but demanding them, stating them so forcibly they became truth.

Philip drew himself up and spread his arms wide. "I am Philip Algenon Luttman. It is I who performed this ritual, not another. The mirror does not reflect me because I do not stand before it. It shows my enemy, for he lies here dead. Philip Algenon Luttman passed through the gate. Let he who denies it be cast into the flames. Let—"

Pain lanced into Philip's side. Vision blurring, he struggled for balance.

Warm arms and the gentle scent of roses enveloped him.

About The Author

Dave Higgins writes speculative fiction, often with a dark edge. Despite forays into the mundane worlds of law and IT, he was unable to escape the liminal zone between mystery and horror. A creature of contradictions, he also co-writes comic sci-fi with Simon Cantan. Born in the least mystically significant part of Wiltshire, England, and raised by a librarian, he started reading shortly after birth and hasn't stopped since. He lives with his wife, two cats, a plush altar to Lord Cthulhu, and many shelves of books. It's rumoured he writes out of fear he will otherwise run out of books to read.

For more information, visit davidjhiggins.wordpress.com.

The Ant Tower

Christopher Ruz

Editor's Note: A grown man may not believe in bogeymen, but let him travel alone awhile through strange and foreign lands, then ask him again what he fears.

The sandstorm wails and scratches and tries to tug away the kaffiyeh pulled tight over my face. The soldier ahead is a dim silhouette behind the howl. I hear nothing but the wind; not the slap of my sword against my leg, nor Officer Slopes shouting at me from behind. I ache through and through, all the way down to the ends of my fingers. They throb with my heartbeat. I can't stop to rest. If I tire I'll lose sight of the line, and the desert will dry me out until I'm shrunken and empty, sightless sockets forever staring at the sky.

There are five of us.

The magician leads the procession. How he picks his path I do not know; the sand comes up early most days and blots out the horizon. We walk bent over against the wind, eyes open only to slits. We each wear a white burnouse in the style of the Moors to hide our armour, but it does nothing to stop the heat. I can smell my sweat, and the leather is glued to my skin. I'd shuck it off but there are raiders in the dunes, and we have learned they aren't above attacking their own.

I follow Corm. He follows the captain. The captain follows the magician, and the magician leads us to the Ant Tower.

I speak to the magician some nights. Things are different between us now, since the night in Gail.

I remember when he inspected us on the Lontoa parade ground. We were a full century then, half retired soldiers and half farmboys. Shoulder to shoulder, whispering, jostling. The magician walked the line with Captain Brales, whispering in his ear, desperate to win the commission. I didn't know he was a magician, then. Just a dusky man in a workman's tunic, nails crusted with dirt. I straightened up as he passed, staring straight ahead. Half a year since we last fought, and we were all hungry.

At the end of the row the magician said, "They'll do. We leave in three days for Amir." All along the line I could hear the relief. Corm nudged me. "Just in time, Parkin?"

"Always a saviour when we need it most."

"True." He shivered, and I knew he was remembering the walls of Tinnarim. "True enough."

Yussef took with spotted fever halfway to Amir. There was no cure. I cradled Yussef's head as he spat his guts over my tunic. He told me not to weep. I prayed that the night would stretch on forever, but dawn came much too soon.

We buried Yussef and ten others with their swords clasped to their chests, points down, brothers fallen on the march. Our century was now eighty-nine. Captain Brales blamed bad provisions, and we marched on hungry.

———————— • ————————

The storms have stolen away the horizon and the wind smells of sulphur. Corm Swift is stopped up ahead, shapeless under the flapping burnouse. I wave. "Corm."

"Parkin." He holds up a hand. "Listen."

The magician and Captain Brales are just ahead, shouting to be heard over the storm. Their voices carry. "What?" says Brales. "What?" The wind changes direction and sand spatters against my hood; the weave stops the spray but not the sound. It rattles in my skull. "You never paid us for that!"

"I haven't paid you at all yet," says the magician, and I know he meant for us to hear. Then he tugs up his kaffiyeh and advances into the cacophony, guided by some compass far beyond the reckoning of little men like me. I watch him go and feel a burning in my gut, in my groin.

The captain comes to us. Officer Slopes is caught up now as well, and we huddle in a square, shoulder to shoulder. "He wants us to climb it," says Brales. "Climb the damned Ant Tower." A second of silence. "I'm no climber."

"Nor I, sir."

"Well," he says. "Better learn fast. And you." He prods Corm in the chest. "We'll be there by noon."

We march.

Even under the robes it's clear how thin we've all become. When we left Lontoa Captain Brales was a stocky man, stomping about the parade ground. Now when he points to some feature on the horizon I see the bones of his wrist jutting, knuckles almost arthritic. I know I look the same.

Corm tugs my sleeve. "Is that it?"

"Looks like."

A finger of shadow in the distance. Some in Pushka said it was a thousand feet high, that when the sun dipped below the dunes the shadow of the tower was the shadow of God's hand. They said a man who slept in those shadows would dream his own end.

It's not a thousand feet tall. I'm no surveyor but I see that much. Maybe a hundred and fifty, two hundred at most. Not even the softest sands will cradle a man who falls from the top. I imagine the fall, the tatter of wind. It makes me shiver. "We can't climb it," says Corm. "He's insane."

I shake my head. "You underestimate him."

"You love him too much," says Corm, and spits into the sand.

It's almost noon and the Ant Tower is close enough that I can see the spires running up towards the sun, the pits and scars where termites scurry from daylight to darkness. I squint and see the Cathedral of Saint Ramona, arches and pointed peaks, the sun making the stained glass maquette of the Risen Daughter glow from within. But this cathedral is built from sand and spit, and its hollows are black as night.

The closer we get the greater it grows. When I imagine climbing it my hands tremble.

We march with our heads down and suddenly we are at the base. The magician presses his ear against the mud while I circle the tower: forty paces around makes it about thirty feet wide. I look up. The sun sits just behind the peak as a fiery halo but the tower itself is all shadow. I feel a child again, tiny before my father, waiting for the swing of his fist.

A whistling of sand in the distance. Another storm. The magician gently pats the slope of the tower like the flank of a horse. "Let's not waste time."

Slopes leads us in stripping off our greaves, our swords, our gauntlets. "What do you think?" he asks the captain. "Boots or no?"

"Better the boots," says the captain. "Termites might mistake your pale little toes for their own. Carry 'em right off." He laughs, but his eyes are cold. I don't blame him. The tower scares me too.

We line up at the base. The mud writhes as a million million termites wriggle blind across the shell of the tower. They build even as we watch, all the tiny rivulets and hidden chambers weaving upwards from the dunes. It is pockmarked and scabbed by tunnels. Those will be our handholds. The thought of digging my fingers into those pits and feeling termites squirm and pop...

The magician dusts his palms. He looks back at me and grins, and my breath sticks in my throat. "Catch me if I fall."

———— • ————

A dark-eyed woman with silks draped around her hips and ribbons through her hair beckoned from a doorway. "Corm," I whispered. "What do you know of women in Amir?"

"They'll bite unless you soften them with coin." He grinned. "You owe me."

"You're sending me bankrupt, you know?"

The woman led Corm into a shadowed doorway and I went back to the campground to take the night guard. The magician's tent stood silent at the back of the grounds. Three days in Amir and the flaps of his tent were still shut. Corm said that the magician was a demon, that he'd burst into flame if he stepped into the sun. Sometimes I suspected Corm was right.

My companion for the night was a skinny-faced boy called Dory, flinching and scrabbling for the hilt of his sword every time a bird called in the darkness. He whispered that it was his first time on the road with a real captain. I told him to hush. The Amir nights were warm, pleasant on the skin, and I set my feet so I wouldn't stumble if I fell asleep.

Dory tugged on my sleeve. "Parkin! Look! Is it on fire?" I turned to watch the sputter and flash behind the cloth of the magician's tent, like a dying gas lamp.

"Stay." I slid my sword free and took slow, careful steps towards the tent. The flickers behind the canvas grew to yellow flashes, like bursts of daylight. A long wedge of light trembled through a gap in the tent flap and across the campground. In that sliver was a silhouette.

"Sir?" No reply. I pushed the tent-flap aside.

He was on his knees, hands cupped around something shimmering like dawnlight on water, head bowed as if to kiss it, or whisper to it like a lover. It spat light in stutters and fits. "Sir?"

The magician clapped his hands shut. The tent went dark. Bright spots danced across my vision. "Why are you here?"

"The lights..." I swallowed. His eyes were still alight, as if a tiny fire burned inside his skull. "I was worried for you. Sir."

"Well. Thank you. But don't bother me again when the tent is closed."

"Sir." Shapes swam into focus. A chest with brass locks. Scrolls with wooden handles bound tight in leather. "Would you be alone?"

"Yes," he said. "Please. And do mind. When the tent is closed..."

"Sir."

I pulled the flap down and returned to the watch. Dory asked me questions I couldn't answer.

Two men deserted in the night between Amir and Pushka. Captain Brales didn't fuss. There'd been worse before, and there would be worse again. Corm spent the march telling me of the girl in silk. "Young, but the things she knew, Parkin! You should have joined us. Might have cured you. Will they have such girls in Pushka?"

"Better, perhaps. If you know where to look."

Pushka was the last great city before the desert nations. We climbed the walls at the southern gates and pointed out the line where the grass died, and was consumed by rock and sand and bone. Brales gave us three days' leave. Our employer had business to attend to.

I hadn't told Corm what I saw in the tent. Not yet.

I spent my days in the souk, crushing spices between my fingertips, breathing in cinnamon and cumin and long pepper. Men in tall headdresses babbled from street corners. Some knew my language. They thrust curiosities at me: ivory daggers, sashes woven with gold thread, a shard of crystal as big as my palm. Some men kept their daughters on leashes of red string and proffered them to me when I passed. Some did the same with their sons.

There was a low stink hanging over Pushka that made my stomach coil like a cat in a basket. I would call it heathenism but for the temples, the *masjid*, golden minarets twisting high over the rooftops, prayers ringing from a thousand tongues. No land with such temples could be a land of heathens. And children were often sold on the streets of my own city, years ago. I was one of them.

When the men left the grounds to find company for the night I waved them off and stalked the courtyard, staving off sleep. My boots pinched my feet. I wished for home.

The flap of the magician's tent was pinned open.

"Come in." His voice was low and soft. He sat on his trunk, papers curling at his feet. The candles flickered, scented with turmeric. He tweaked his beard, grown since Lontoa, long enough to twine around one finger. "You're alone for the night?"

"Sir," I said. "The city by night is the same to me as the city by day."

"But this is Pushka! Good coin buys anyone a good night."

"I'm saving my coin."

"For? A farm?" He grinned. "A wife?"

Did he see my hands twitch? "Sir."

"Well." He looked back to his papers. "Do you know where we go next?"

"I don't, sir."

He flattened a map across the floor, furrowing his brow. "I need you to do something for me. Parkin, yes?"

"Sir."

"I need you to tell everyone where we're going. It's a hard trip, and a man unprepared will die. I'm telling you this because I don't need eighty-seven men. I need fifteen. Maybe ten. A good small bodyguard is better than a hundred, but the only way to find a good small bodyguard is to cull them from a hundred. Besides…a crowd attracts attention. Yes?"

"Sir."

"Good. Tell them where we're going, and those that would leave may leave. I'll pay them out."

"Sir." I paused. "Where are we going?"

Candlelight flashed in his eyes.

———————— • ————————

I can't tell how long we've been climbing. The rock flakes away beneath my boots. We're about halfway up. It was easy to begin with. Many handholds, many ledges. The tunnels were wide enough for me to jam in my arm and catch my breath. The handholds are small now, big enough for a finger and no more. They will only grow smaller.

The termites are albino white, their bodies swollen, legs thick as match-sticks. They crawl over my hands and between my fingers, leaving sticky trails. It makes my stomach roil as they march up the sleeve of my burnouse and along my arm, catching in my hairs. I slap at one in disgust and its body breaks against my skin.

The wind squeals in the distance like a petulant child. The stirring of the sand is a cloud hanging low over the desert. It could be morning mist, if mists were ever so dark and furious. The magician is somewhere far above, burnouse snapping in the breeze. "Parkin! Are you safe?"

"Sir! I am!" My cheeks burn with embarrassment. Did he have to single me out?

"Good," he says, and pushes on. I hear Corm snicker below and I blush harder.

Further and further. We're closing on the peak. The wind rises to a ban-shee howl. Not long now. I free one hand long enough to pull my kaffiyeh back over my face.

Captain Brales yells, "Dig in, men!" and the storm pounces with claws bared.

It's impossible. There's no way the storm could move so fast. I twist my fingertips into the fluting as the sand whips my hands, my face. The burnouse cracks around my cheeks and the sandstorm shrieks like a man on the rack.

Corm calls to me from below but his words are snatched away. There is nothing but the tumble and the screams. I crane upwards and open my eyes to slits. The magician is still there, a few feet above Officer Slopes. I can't see his face but I feel the echoes through my fingers as the wind slams him into the side of the tower over and over. He clings on despite it all, and I am so proud.

The wind is so loud it aches in my skull. All I can smell is the sourness of my own breath and sweat. I grit my teeth and endure. It's been too long to let myself fall.

Slopes shouts from overhead but I can't make anything out... His kaf-fiyeh flaps free like a flag of surrender. His eyes are squeezed shut tight against the storm and he shakes with the effort of keeping his hold on the tower.

No. Something worse.

Slopes arches his spine and throws his head back like he's been speared through the middle, and he claws at his face with one hand, shoving fingers into his mouth. I know what's happening. The sand is in his lungs and he's trying to dig it from his throat. I turn away.

He doesn't scream as he falls. Instead he makes a guttural choking sound, like a man drowning in hot oil, the same sound I heard on the battlements of Tinnarim. Somehow it carries through the storm, and that chills most of all.

Corm and Captain Brales pull into the tower as Slopes tumbles past. They press their faces against the mud and let the termites crawl through their hair. I watch him hit the ground. A cloud rises around him and then settles, and before I can take another breath Slopes is swallowed by the sand.

I shut my eyes. "He won't let me fall," I whisper. "He won't."

The sands whirl around me, cackling, triumphant.

———— • ————

People in Pushka knew the Ant Tower. They didn't speak of it in the alleys or temples, but there were places. I found a bazaar where men draped in silk crowded around a hookah, smoke bubbling against the glass. They tweaked their moustaches and I thought of the magician, and how he twined his beard. The men told stories, hushed and hesitant.

They said the Ant Tower had existed five or six generations now, growing year after year by inches and hands and feet. Traders never stop there, and when a caravan passes they make sure to stay on the east side in morning and the west side in afternoon, so its long finger-shadow will never cross their path. I offered coin to the men crouched around the hookah, smoke roiling in the shadows of the tent. "Why would anyone visit it?"

"There is no reason," they said. "It is cursed."

"The tower is evil?"

Silence. Then a young man dressed in scholar's robes leaned forward. He spat his words, like my language tasted foul. "The tower is not evil," he said. "Something evil lives inside. There are many mounds in the desert. They are as tall as a man." He waved above his head, to demonstrate. "No taller. Or they would fall over."

"But this one is different?"

He shook his head dismissively. "The mound is no different. It is the insects. They build up and up. There is no reason for it. Something makes them crazy. They build forever, I think. Until they reach the sky."

"And how high is it?"

He shrugged. "Two hundred, three hundred hands. I saw it years ago. It will be taller now. It will grow forever."

Two hundred hands? Just over a hundred feet. Impossible. Superstition and heathen tales. But I knew better than to say so. "So it *houses* something evil."

He shrugged again. "Maybe not evil. But powerful, yes. It is building a monument to itself, I think. It is vain. It uses the insects, the termites, for its own pride. That is what I think."

I slept badly that night, but I didn't expect otherwise.

I wasn't the only one to ask after the tower in the dark corridors of the bazaar. By the time we left Pushka there were only eight men left besides myself. We looked at each other as we advanced into the wastes. I walked slumped, like a man crushed beneath his regret. There was no reason for me to press on. Better money elsewhere, and every city housed a mercenary captain hoping to fill his ranks.

Perhaps it was Corm that put it best. We made camp one night by a tributary to burn the nightly offerings and he leaned over the fire to take the smoke into his lungs. "Parkin. Try it. You'll like it."

"Will I?"

He coughed, then laughed. "No. But you'll keep coming back."

Even the tributary died, in the end. The grasses became hard-packed dirt, the earth cracking underfoot like pottery forgotten in the kiln. Captain Brales let us rest one night in Recca, a small town glad to see foreign gold. Beyond Recca the earth became sand.

The magician left his tent open at night. I sat, cross legged and wide eyed, watching him dabble with elixirs and wortroots and beakers filled with light. I didn't speak unless he asked me a question. His hands were quick and deft, measuring boiling liquids between vials with uncanny precision. Dark hairs curled out from his sleeves, up the length of his wrists.

"I'm crafting a spell," he told me one night. "I'll use it at the tower. It'll see us through safely." He cocked his head towards me. My signal to speak.

"It's a termite mound...but they call it the Ant Tower?"

"Old names and superstition are stronger than facts."

I recalled the words of the old swami in Pushka. "Why are we going if it's so dangerous?"

The magician lifted a beaker, examined the colours silting inside, set it down. "Don't put trust in men with heads full of grass-smoke. I admit, the tower is strange. Maybe powerful. Not dangerous. It's the trek that will cause us trouble."

"And this..." I motioned towards the scrolls covered from end to end in tiny chicken scratch script. "This will keep us safe?"

"Yes. Old magic, but the old stuff is best." He smiled again. "Don't worry, Parkin. You worry too much."

"But why are we going?"

He stared at me for a moment, lips pursed. Then back to his potions. "There was something buried long ago that our king wants retrieved. Something stolen."

"Valuable?"

"Yes," he says. "To some. To others, not at all."

"What is it?"

He shook his head. "Not for you to know, Parkin. Not tonight."

————————— • —————————

"Keep going!" shouts Captain Brales. "If you stop I'll throw you off myself!" So I climb on.

Handholds are getting rare. The termite tunnels are now too thin for me to jam even my little finger inside. I wedge myself between two buttresses and shake out my hands. Sharp rock has peeled away the skin of my right hand, the flesh beneath spongy and soft. Blood runs down my wrist in streams and dries in the folds of my elbow. I barely feel the pain.

Corm taps me on the heel. "Are you alright?"

I show him my hand. He secures himself against one of the buttresses and pulls a knotted strip of linen from his robes. "Wrap it up before the ants get at you."

I bind my hand tight; the sting fades into a dull, distant heat. "Did you see Slopes?"

"I saw. Shame. Better him than us. How much farther?"

"Far enough."

He shakes his head. "Just don't fall. If you do, Brales will climb all the way down just to piss on your corpse. And besides, your magician would be heartbroken."

I duck away. Sometimes Corm says too much.

The wind is picking up again. The magician calls faintly from overhead. "Listen. Listen to it!" Then the sands are back, and my burnouse flaps against my skinny legs. The rock is so hot it burns. I press close to the tower and wish I could just let go.

I understand the magician now. I heard it faintly when I first started climbing and thought it was an echo of myself, but since Slopes fell it has grown. When I push my ear against the dried mud-brick of the tower it's as loud as a war drum, rumbling up my arms and into my ribcage.

The tower has a heartbeat.

"Parkin! Don't stop!"

I'm past the point where Slopes fell. I keep my eyes on the next handhold, trying not to look up. The sky is hidden behind a sheet of spinning sand, so thick I can't tell the difference between it and the desert below. It doesn't feel like climbing, but rather crawling head first down a precipice. My guts are a tangle.

We pass the vertical buttresses. Now we must climb ridges like the threads of a screw. Close to the top. Twenty feet to go, maybe less. My arms are lead. When I reach upwards for the next termite hole my right shoulder screams. I can't ignore it much longer.

The magician's words somehow slice through the storm, clearer than Corm's or the captain's. "Parkin! Trust! We're almost there!"

Then, below me, a shout. Even though the words are fuzzed by wind I recognise the voice. I press against the face of the tower, the heartbeat that should not exist buzzing against my chest.

Corm is only a body-length below me. I see where he should go next: one hand right, towards a thin shelf, his left foot sideways into a crack just wide enough for the toe of his boot. He sees this too. "Parkin! How much farther? I can't see through your flapping dress."

If it were Slopes or Brales making the joke it would have ended in blood, but because it's Corm I laugh. "Not much. It's easy from here."

"Maybe I should race you to the top!"

"Would you wager?"

"If I win, you buy the whores!" he says, and reaches for that little shelf of rock.

The crack is sharp and high. He stares, eyes wide, refusing to believe. The nubbin of stone is loose in his hand. "Merciful..." Then he swings free, wind-tossed, his left hand gripping white-knuckled to a ledge barely a finger wide, both feet dangling in the air. It is a hundred feet to the dunes, maybe more.

"Merciful Daughter!" he says. "Help, Parkin, help!" I want to move but my arms are frozen. I can barely breathe. The beat of the tower grows louder. "Help!" He kicks for purchase but his boots only gouge out strips and stones that rattle down in the captain's face. "Grab me, damn you!" I stare, slack jawed. "Parkin!"

I start to move, then stop. I look to the magician. His eyes catch the light even in the shadow of his cowl. Very slowly, he shakes his head. First to one side, then the other.

"Come on, Parkin!" says Corm, and that is when the little hook of stone snaps. My throat starts working again. I scream his name.

I had no love for Slopes, but watching Corm going end over end brings bile to the back of my throat. I choke it back and wait, eyes squeezed tight enough to hurt, the sand slapping at the hood of my robe. It echoes like applause.

———————— • ————————

We'd been riding four days through sand and heat haze when Dory tumbled backwards off his horse. He hit the ground headfirst with a brittle snap, like dried twigs. The dark feathers of arrow fletching hung from his throat.

"Raiders! Get down!"

The sleeve of my tunic tugged as an arrow ripped through close enough to score the skin, and I threw myself off the horse, sand spraying up in my face. I spat it out and clawed for my sword as the horses bolted. Someone screamed. I prayed it wasn't Corm.

I couldn't see anything but the roll of dunes, gentle crests like a woman's belly as far as the horizon, the great desert, the oldest desert. A heat shimmer hung over the sands. I wiped sweat from my eyes and tried to calm the hammering of my heart. All I could hear was wailing as one of our men bubbled out the last of his strength.

Please, I thought, *not Corm, or the magician. Anyone but them.*

Shapes rose from the sand. Men in long dusky robes the colour of earth, shadows under their cowls, curved blades flashing. Seven, eight, more. The morning sun threw wavering shadows across the dunes, so long I could almost touch them, and I shied away, remembering tales of the Ant Tower.

These are only men. They'll fight like any other.

They charged, howling, scimitars above their heads, and suddenly I was back on the battlements of Tinnarim with the hordes battering at the gates. I felt the weight of the oil pots as I tipped them over the edge and watched the flesh fall from the faces of those below. The deep satisfaction in my gut as they screamed.

They'll fight like any other, I thought again, and picked my man.

Our blades hit so hard that I tumbled backwards in the sand, rolling and coming up on my knees, and only luck brought my sword up in time to meet his second swing. It glanced off and the ring of steel on steel was so sharp it stung my ears. Then I was on my feet, sword up, trying to stop fear from catching my breath. The man grinned, teeth shining gold in the tangle of his beard. Then he moved too fast to judge and I lashed out with my eyes closed.

I opened my eyes. The man thrashed with his guts coiled on the sand, flies already settling on the ropes of his intestines. The sound of clashing steel was ending.

Three of ours dead to four of theirs. Dory was the first. There was sand in his eyes that we couldn't brush free. The second was a man called Yurik. He spoke often of children scattered throughout the five duchies, born of as many as eleven mistresses. He had an arrow through his liver and died a day later, whispering his daughters' names.

The third was Antony, a boy whose voice still cracked when he sang on the march. He was back-to-back with Corm when a scimitar caught him across the thigh. He bled out on the sands, still slashing at the raiders, never screaming or crying. Corm said he didn't realise Antony was hurt until he went limp.

We buried them side by side, swords on their chest, points up. Brothers fallen in battle.

Corm was very quiet the nights that followed.

———— • ————

The tower has hushed with Corm gone. I can hear it if I press my ear hard against the mud and let the termites crawl over my cheek and tangle through my hair. Otherwise it is silent.

Every time I shift handholds I wait for the splintering sound that will send me flailing, robes beating around my ears. The tip of the tower will shoot upwards towards the sun. Will I feel the impact? Not from this height.

But they don't break. The outcroppings are secure.

The world becomes quieter without warning and sunlight brings tears to my eyes. I blink stupidly. The sands whirl and eddy below. I've climbed out of the storm.

Four, five, six more long stretches, nooks just large enough for me to jam in my fingers, the palm of my left hand blistered and weeping, my right hand painted with blood, legs no longer hurting but simply dead weight. The tower is levelling off. I'm at the summit. The magician kneels on the plateau. "Parkin! Grab hold!"

He hauls me up as if I weigh no more than a child. My lungs feel torn. Breathing is like swallowing knives. Behind me I hear the captain dragging himself over the edge. "Damned close thing," he puffs. "Damned close."

"Imagine," says the magician. "The first to stand here in near three hundred years. Pilgrims in a foreign land."

I spit. The metallic taste at the back of my throat is blood. I look at the cloth wrapped around my right hand. Thin chequered cotton. I recognise it now. Corm's old handkerchief.

I didn't cry for Yussef. I won't cry for Corm.

It's easy to make promises.

The magician had a burnouse for each of us in his chest. "I brought these to keep us safe from the storms," he said. "If I'd given them to you earlier, perhaps those raiders..." He trailed off. I slipped the burnouse over my armour, scratchy against the nape of my neck. The magician closed his chest. In the moment before the lid slammed down I saw inside. Empty but for velvet lining and ribbon-bound scrolls.

He sat us down in a valley between two dunes. The sky was clear and blinding. There were no birds. Perhaps they were northward, scratching at the graves of Yurik and Antony and poor nervous Dory. The magician pulled a map from his robe and spread it flat.

"That's the tower." He pointed to a black square. "We're here. We'll pass through Gail and Kurnsk. A week's march, or less."

"Are you sure?" Captain Brales' eyes were dark and sunken. He stared with the same weary finality I saw at Tinnarim, when two centuries of men armed with arrows and oil peered over the walls at two thousand file-toothed fanatics.

"One week," he said. "Watch for raiders. Watch for shadows."

Corm and I walked at the back of the line. Sweat ran into my eyes until my feet and the sands blurred into one. "Did you see?" Corm whispered so the captain and Officer Slopes couldn't hear. "In his chest?"

I shook my head.

"The chest," he said again. "He only brought five of these damned robes."

"Luck."

"No! I don't trust him. He's too strange."

"He's a magician."

"You have eyes for him."

I shrugged. "You know I don't hide it. Not from you."

"Pfeh." He kicked at the sand. "Yussef was a better man than him. I don't trust anyone who doesn't carry a sword. He won't fight for you, Parkin." Again he lashed out, and sand sprayed in both our faces. Corm wiped his eyes. "Damn this place. Damn this desert. Damn you for telling me to come."

Gail was thinned by plague. The corpse pit just north of the gates was close to overflowing, bare legs jutting skywards, shrivelled by desert sun. I pulled the hood of my burnouse tight over my nose.

We lodged in a tumble-down boarding house owned by a squat Moor woman, eyes milky with cataracts. Captain Brales waited for the magician to leave before calling everybody into his chambers and locking the door.

"Officer Slopes," he said. "Men. We have five days march left, if what our employer tells me is correct." His upper lip curled in distaste. "Our employer...is not forthcoming about certain details." He leaned in close. "If the bastard tries to run, cut him down."

Corm and I explored the streets at night, faces hidden in the shadows of our cowls, peering in the windows of empty houses. Shutters swung limp in the wind. Some still stank of the dead. "Plague comes to all places," said Corm, in the low voice he reserved for when something weighed heavy on his mind. "Are we safe here?"

"As safe as on the plains."

"Think there are any whores to be bought?"

"None that would suit me."

He laughed. Then, without warning: "The sword was meant for me, not for Antony."

I stopped. Dust settled around my boots. "What do you mean?"

"The raider was swinging for me."

"Antony got in the way?"

"I *pushed* Antony into the way," he said. "I grabbed him. Around the neck, like this." He demonstrated in the air, hooking one arm around an invisible foe. "He didn't fight. I don't think he knew what was happening. Then..." His other hand chopped down.

I licked around my teeth. "Did...did the captain see you?"

"What?" His hands dropped and curled into fists. "I killed him, Parkin. I think he had a girl."

"Then he was a fool. If you keep a woman, plan to leave her a widow. I'd rather you alive than Antony a hundred times over."

"Why?" His voice echoed in the laneway. "Am I so special to you? Do you love me like Yussef? Or like that damned conjurer? You want this?" He grabbed his crotch. "Is that it?"

"No! You hurt me, Corm."

"I killed him."

"Yes. You did."

He hunched his shoulders and turned away. For a moment he was silent and I saw his shoulders shake. Then he walked away, footsteps ringing. Something fell away inside my chest and left an aching hunger.

I took the long route back to the lodgings, half hoping Corm would be out buying company for the night, half hoping to run into him on the steps so I could apologise. When I closed my eyes I saw him squeezing his crotch. It made me ill.

There was a figure on the steps. I didn't know whether I was glad to see him or terrified.

"Parkin," said the magician.

———— • ————

The peak of the Ant Tower is a plateau of sand ten paces across but the outer edge is solid as brick. Even so, we cower in the centre, where the sand is softer. Not even Captain Brales dares stand at the edge. I feel like I should be shouting our triumph, planting a flag in the sand. Perhaps if Corm were here I would. Instead I feel old and brittle. There's no victory here.

The storm still thrashes below. Looking over the edge is like standing above a whirlpool, the waters beating into foam, tunnelling down into darkness. The skin along my arms goose-bumps despite the heat.

The magician pulls an endless succession of vials and scraps of paper from inside his burnouse. The captain stands over him. "I don't want to be up here come night. Those birds..." The buzzards are black specks against afternoon sun. "How long will this take?"

"Don't worry," says the magician. "They won't attack. They prefer meals that don't move." I think of Corm. We were only paces apart. Had I been following him instead...

The magician pours two vials on to the sand in the very centre of the plateau. They hiss. Bile-green steam rises in a plume. "Hold your breath."

The captain leans over. "What's this? Tricks? I thought we'd be digging."

"Quiet."

"Sir," Brales growls, "nobody tells me when and when not to speak."

The magician ignores him. He takes a handful of sand and crushes it in his palm, sifting it through the gaps between his fingers. It seems to shimmer and evaporate in the air. "You know what I'm here for," he whispers. "You know what it takes to unlock. Leave me."

Brales sits beside me, head in hands. He pulls back the hood of his robe. The desert has aged him. He is dry and shrunken. I see my father in his face. Rotten gaps in his gums, hair falling away in silver wisps. The man who raised and sold me.

"Did you ever think you'd come here?"

I wet my lips. "No."

"Nor I." He lets out a long, shuddering sigh. "And then we have to climb back down. I don't know if I can do it. You might have to carry me."

"Sir."

"He was your friend, wasn't he?"

I flinch. It seems hours ago I watched him fall. "Corm. Yes."

"Mm." Brales traces a circle in the sands. "I'll have a lot of pension slips to sign when we get back. Perhaps you can help me with that."

"Sir." The lump in my throat is painful. "I can do that."

The magician stands. The skin around his eyes is dark and sagging. Raising his arms seems to take a terrible effort. "Almost done. One more step."

Captain Brales walks to his side. "And?"

The flash of steel is almost too quick to see. Captain Brales's head snaps back. Blood floats on the air like morning mist. Then he slumps, boneless, and the magician toes his body over the edge.

I fumble for my sword but my fingers are clumsy and slow. The magician is mouthing something that I can't hear over the heartbeat of the tower. It swells, shaking my teeth, rattling my eyes so the whole world blurs. I try to stand but my legs are numb. The magician says the word again, but all sound is blotted out. The storm is roaring.

I think he is saying *sacrifice*.

———————— • ————————

Dawn light broke through the magician's tent in mosaic patterns of gold and burgundy. I collected my tunic, my armour, my sword. "You won't tell Captain Brales."

"No." He stretched and smiled. "And neither will you."

They were waiting for me at the steps of the lodging house, packed and ready. Captain Brales led us out the gates and into the desert and the people of Gail watched from the windows, thin brown faces hidden in shadow. The magician waited until we were well past the city walls before calling for a stop.

"Headcloths," he said, holding up fistfuls of patterned fabric. "Or, as the Moors say, *kaffiyeh*. There are storms this time of year." He gave us one each and kept the last for himself. When he reached me he brushed my hand. "Tie them tight. Don't breathe in the sand."

The captain waited till he was done before calling us to attention. "Small century that we are, you are still soldiers. Let's finish this march well. Slopes!"

Officer Slopes was bent with exhaustion, as if he had to carry all of us instead of just himself. Captain Brales was the same. Corm dragged his feet, leaving long snake-trails in the sand. The only one walking upright was the magician.

He glanced back at me, grinned and winked. A little spark of warmth flared inside. *He'll keep me safe. He watches for me.*

Three nights into the desert he came to me.

He told me of being a child. His first book; leather bound, creaking with age. The crack of a staff across his knuckles when he mispronounced a spell. The ache he held long into the night. Kneeling before the king at fourteen. The war. He was not trapped at Tinnarim through the long siege with Corm and me, but two hundred miles distant, ambushed, screaming with an arrow in his guts. A fellow soldier snapped off the tail and yanked it through the hole in his back, and then the magician sprinkled the wound with one of his own potions and waited to heal or to die.

"The Ant Tower is the very end," he said. "It took near two years to find that what the king wanted was hidden there. Two years is a long time to wander."

My hands twisted in my lap. "Can you just walk away from the king?"

"He may grant me some lenience."

"If you succeed."

"Yes. There is that." He twined his moustache. "You're a good man, Parkin. I would see you, after this is done."

I started. Memories of the night in Gail were still fresh. The strength in his hands as he pressed me down, and then the softness in the small of his back as I did the same to him. "I... I understand."

He shook his head. "You don't." Then he smoothed the sand from his robe and returned to his tent.

———— • ————

I stagger to my feet. My hand trembles on the hilt of my sword. "Why?"

He spreads his hands, smiles. "Parkin. I didn't craft these locks. I'm only here to break them."

"Is it worth it?"

"To me, no. To our king, yes. It's worth all our lives."

"So kill yourself!"

His eyes are hard. "Blood sacrifice, taken unwillingly. I didn't write the terms. Don't blame me."

"So who did?"

"A man and his mistress. Sorcerers. Both long dead. They had a fondness for spells demanding a blood price. You wouldn't know their names." He stirs the sands in the centre of the plateau with one long finger. "Almost done."

"You only brought five robes. Did you know?"

He ducks his head. "Yes. I knew everything as far as now."

"What happens next, then?"

"I claim the prize." Then he plunges both hands into the sand, burrowing down until he is elbow deep. *Now! Cut his head off and climb down and go home!*

But I can't move. I want to but I don't have the strength.

The sand is up to his shoulders. No. Not just sand but termites, white as drowned flesh. They crawl over his neck and into his clothes, exploring his hair. They skitter across his lips. The drumming of the tower is so loud that the ground pitches back and forth, trying to buck me off.

Do it! Kill him!

I can't.

The magician crows in triumph and jerks back. Termites fall away, kicking at the air, dying before they touch the sands like his skin is poison. He clasps something to his chest like one would an infant.

"Is that it?"

"This is it. Not for you to see." He tucks his prize away beneath his robes. I swear there is a fluttering under his burnouse. Whatever is hidden there is pulsing, breathing. He stands, swaying with the wind. Or is it the tower swaying beneath him? "One last thing to do," he says. "Do you think it'll let us climb back down, Parkin? Or do you think the tower is vengeful?"

"I don't know. I don't know why you're asking."

"Because I value your opinion. Come over here." And, even though I resist, even though just to look at him makes me ill, I go to him. We stand together in the epicentre of the plateau, and the winds shriek around us.

"The final step," he says, and takes my hand. His touch is cool and soothing and I feel the ache in my chest fall away. "Parkin. I'm sorry. This isn't my choice. It's the tower." Then, before I can move, he brings his hands together. The clap echoes through the storm.

"Don't—" I stumble. The sands have turned soft beneath me like molasses, creeping up my legs to the knee. My hands hit and are sucked beneath the surface. I rear back, yank hard. It's as heavy as stone.

"Damn you!" I pull until spots of light burst before my eyes. One arm comes free but the sand is already up to my waist. It isn't just heavy. It squeezes me like a living thing.

The magician stands before the sun, his shadow long and spider-thin. "The first sacrifice," he says. "Betrayal of a brother. That wasn't easy." He crouches, close enough for me to feel his breath against my face. I grab for him and he jerks back; my fingers brush his nose. The sand is over my hips.

"Damn you! I'll kill you!"

He closes his eyes and whispers, and there is sadness in his words. "The second sacrifice. Not to break the spell, but to placate the tower. Love lost."

It's up to my neck. Something is tugging and pinching at my feet. One boot comes free. All I can see is the hem of his burnouse, slashed and spattered with Brales' blood. I open my mouth to scream and the sand rushes in.

The storm slows, the howl fading to a pleased whisper. The magician lowers himself over the side of the tower. The last thing I know is his face, lined with what I hope is guilt. Then the sand closes over and all is darkness, and the heartbeat thrums through my bones.

It drums and drums and drums.

I open my eyes.

There is nothing. The blackness is absolute in all directions. The air scratches my throat. Something tickles in my hair. I stretch out blindly. Space enough to move my arms, but only just. My knuckles crack against stone. I'm in the Ant Tower.

That thought sends me screaming. I drag my fingers through my hair and termites wriggle between my fingers, gnawing and building their nests.

Above all of this is the heartbeat, ceaseless and deafening, the drum roll of an army on the march. It rattles my lungs inside my ribcage. Sand drifts down from above as the walls shake.

Do you hate him?

It's a voice scratching inside my head and the answer comes fast. *Yes. I hate him.*

Would you kill him?

"Yes!" The howl echoes off the walls. "Yes!"

Would you kill him would you kill would you revenge would you kill him for me

I recognise it now. It's the tower, or whatever lives inside. I don't care which. I remember the night in Gail. That wink. I see the snag of rock breaking in Corm's hand, and his eyes, wide, disbelieving.

Kill him. Bring it back.

"I'll kill him." The voice in my head becomes a low buzz, like a child humming a tune. It sounds pleased.

I see light.

———————— • ————————

Desert under my hands. I squeeze my eyes shut against the sunlight reflecting off the sand. Slowly, very slowly, I reach out. The sand burns my palms. Wind is a cool finger against my cheek. I'm outside.

I open my eyes. The dunes are white under the dawn. I smell my own sweat and piss. Behind me is the Ant Tower, pitted and twisting. At its base is a fluttering cloth that marks the spot where we piled our armour. There is water in there, and bread, and my sword.

The voice in my head again. *Kill him. Revenge.*

I spit. My mouth is dry as coffinwood. I have a long way to walk before night.

About The Author

Christopher Ruz is an Australian author, teacher and stuntman raised on Moorcock, Zelazny and King. He writes across genres, self publishing the fantasy trilogy Century of Sand, the small-town horror serial Rust, and the Olesia Anderson spy thriller series under the pseudonym D.D. Marks. Ruz has too many ideas to fit in his head. He writes most days, and writes most nights, and generally gets on everyone's nerves because he won't put that goddamn notebook down. He's currently working on five books, which is four too many.

For more information, visit www.ruzkin.com.

Heft

Brett Adams

Editor's Note: Science fiction is not always about exploring the implications of new technologies. In some rare cases, it can show us troubling new uses for tech that already exists.

The sex snail.

Meetings with Walt always ended with the sex snail.

To this day, I don't know if he was just odd or clinically insane.

We met every morning I was downtown at Café Le Labyrinthe, and had done so for seven years. Inside if it was raining, otherwise outside at tables that rocked on the fake-cobblestone verge and spilled our lattes.

It's not that Walt was a scintillating conversationalist. To be honest, most days he bored me to tears. But every so often, maybe once a month, he brought something with him. An item that marked the day as magic. Like a talisman fallen from another world.

I hungered for those magic days.

Our final meeting was one such magic day.

The item that always turned my day from lead to gold was an envelope. A commonplace, yellow envelope. He would place it on the table and slide it toward me, end-on between the sugar tray and our foamy teaspoons.

He always used the same envelope, and I was careful to return it the next day, when I had digested its contents. By then, it had become creased and tatty, like an old dollar bill, but one that had only known two owners. He'd tap it once, wink, sip, and scowl. If his first sip hadn't done it, the second would leave a wisp of foam on his upper lip, caught on the tufts of stubble missed by his razor.

On the last day, it occurred to me as I took it from his hand that his skin was like that envelope, as if it had adapted to its texture, chameleon-like, through frequent contact.

Once I knew, I got restless. It was as if I'd stolen a cookie from under Mom's nose and had to escape to the long grass beneath my mulberry tree.

I gulped my coffee, which made my eyes water, and sat up straight. He seemed to sense I wanted to go. He shook my hand and took his leave by telling me the story about the sex snail.

It is the story of a man who takes a pretty shell home and places it in an aquarium with his tropical fish. It fits right in and he admires it over the course of a year or so, until one day his wife returns home to find the top

75

off the tank and the cleaning apparatus out. And beside the aquarium, her husband's dead body.

The pretty shell, it turns out, is a cone snail, a little harpoon-shooting mollusc dubbed the cigarette-snail for the time it takes to kill a man. (Biologists, no sense of humor. A historian would have called it a sex snail. I do.)

I think Walt meant for the story to be a reminder of the need for vigilance or a work-a-day attitude. In the days leading up to our last meeting, his eyes would light up before he told it, as if it had just occurred to him, as though it really *was* fresh. I didn't let on he'd told it before. But it did worry me that the CIA chose Walt to courier sensitive information.

With the envelope secreted in the inner pocket of my coat, I hurried away. I rode the cable car to Fisherman's Wharf, and drifted through the markets, pretending to hunt for a souvenir. The place was swarming with tourists, and the air was heavy with the scent of salt and clam chowder.

When I was certain no one had followed me, I escaped back up the hill and into the quiet gloom of dead hour at McAughney's—my mulberry tree.

I ordered a tall black and hunkered down in a booth in back, facing the street, which blazed through the doorway in an over-exposed rectangle. The booth afforded me a good view of the whole bar, and to my right was a hall that led to the restrooms and escape. It was all very *Don Corleone*, I thought, just wrong city, wrong parents.

I slipped the yellow envelope—a fortune cookie, it occurs to me now—from the folds of my coat, which was just light enough to be inconspicuous in the weather, and laid it on the table. Inside was a dossier. On the cover of the dossier were stamped the words, *Top Secret: C-level 6.*

My breath caught.

A six! Highest I'd had yet.

The classification made the dossier feel heavy, as if it held sheets of lead. Which, as it turned out, was not so far from the truth.

Under the classification was a list of names, people I'd never met, and at the bottom Yours Truly, under the field name Cuckoo. No matter how many of those dossiers I'd received, seeing my name always thrilled me.

I ordered a brandy, pushing the coffee aside. It was poor form at eleven in the morning, but I couldn't help it. A six! There aren't many jobs where one can plot one's progress as simply as by the numbers. In my mind's eye, my currency was snaking upward like the post-crash Dow.

The brandy came, and as it bit and swirled over my tongue, it bore a memory. The memory was seven years old, from my last year as a professor of history, and the night I met a man named Nathan Blaylock.

We met at one of those university-industry mixers that must exist for some reason not visible to my naive eye. Nathan was dumped on me by a passing colleague—I forget who—like train trash, smelling of booze and smiling. He wasn't drunk though. Someone has spilled brandy on his suit.

I was barely polite. It was end of semester and my brain was groping after complete sentences like a grizzly after the first salmon. End of semester had felt like a preview of Alzheimer's for years.

He didn't seem to take offence, and before long had manoeuvred me onto my soapbox, whereupon my synapses began firing. I told him I was a history lecturer, and was encouraged when he didn't grimace. My specialty was the lives of great men, guys whose legacies endured. I offered what I liked to call my "Movers and Shakers" lecture series, about the men and women whose corpses are dragged out every few years to be pumped full of the latest ideology and sent shambling onto our screens: Joan of Arc, the Liberated Woman; Genghis Khan, paragon of supply chain logisticians and Sensitive New Age Moghul; and so on.

This happened about the time the university began calling students "customers." Nathan seemed to pick up on my disgust.

"Seemed to" nothing: he plucked me like a ripe tomato.

You see, "Nathan Blaylock" wasn't his real name. And he had the solution to my problem. He offered me a career change.

How would I like to work for the CIA, he said, as a Non-Official agent. NOs are the guys who don't technically exist. They are ghost operatives, working without schedules, bureaucracy, and, above all, students. NOs have all the fun of the case research without the term papers.

Two weeks later I'd resigned and met Walt for my first mission.

When, seven years later, I opened The Six, I was pleased to notice the job was local, just a shuttle down the coast to L.A. The shine of paid-for travel had long since been dulled by jobs all over the States, and to be tackling my first six on the West Coast gave my confidence a shot in the arm.

The mission's target was a German visiting L.A. under the cover of a burgeoning acting career. For Germans, acting usually means *voice* acting. They have a dubbing industry as big as Hollywood, and those who fancy their chances at the real thing are drawn to California like bimbos to a casting couch. So the cover was plausible.

The tricky thing about the assignment, what made it a six, no doubt, was that the mission's window was a single night—five days hence. Which did *not* seem so plausible, and I briefly wondered if Langley had that right. They'd been wrong before. But it was not my place to question. In fact, it was not even possible to question. Communication with NOs was a mostly one-way street.

I left McAughney's, coffee undrunk, and made arrangements for the mission that afternoon. The envelope had not contained a plane ticket or a fake driver's license. That's all movie fluff. I had a passable cover as a Time-Life library salesman in semi-retirement. I had the pamphlets, and supposedly got the leads for the distributors to go in with the real materials, lovely hardcover kids books. I'd have bought a set myself if I had kids.

Four days later I was sitting in the departure lounge of Gate 17, San Francisco Airport. I would arrive in L.A. with a day of ballast, but was antsy to scope out the location before the target arrived. I plugged the guy's name —Erhard Thait, a Finnish-born German—into my Blackberry and seeded a bunch of sticky internet searches with it. If anything came up on Herr Thait —anything at all on the *entire web*—my searches would shunt it instantly into my Blackberry's inbox.

A straight-out search turned up nothing, but that didn't surprise me. The target probably wasn't using that name yet.

I touched down in L.A. early afternoon on the Friday, and booked into a rat hole. (Time-Life wasn't doing so well anymore. The internet probably had something to do with that too.) By 1600 hours I was dragging the froth off my first latte at the *Bourgeois Pig*, and staring across Hollywood's Franklin Avenue at Château Élysée, also known as Celebrity Centre, Church of Scientology.

I was casing the joint, as much as you can case something the size of Madison Square Gardens. The building is a monolith, desecrated and re-sanctified to the great L. Ron Hubbard, and reminds one of a Norman-revival castle, complete with turrets and hundreds of delicious nooks and crannies. It also looks like a theme park, and at any moment I expected to see Tinkerbell splash its roof with scintillating colour. This was going to be easy.

Stealth, contrary to popular thought, is not so much about hugging shadows as being invisible in plain sight. I'd had to learn that on the job, being an NO, and I guess that's why I'd been given missions on a gentle curve.

You see, visibility is relative. A CEO can't see the bum begging for money; the bum might as well be a lamp post. Unless the bum is the CEO's brother. Or his business. The only reason Mayor Giuliani could see the bums messing up Manhattan was because it was *his* Manhattan—right before he pest-awayed them to the boroughs.

The trick to stealth is to find a niche, a fold in space, where, for the folks you want to elude, the photons just flow on around you and go their merry way. That's real magic, and I used that afternoon to collect the ingredients to invoke it. Simple reagents, easily collected.

When I crashed the party the following evening I made sure the first guy I bumped into was a security guard. My stint at the *Bourgeois Pig* had told me two things: first, the location of the service entry, which was opposite the cafe; and second, the dress standard of the delivery men for the hotel restaurant, *The Renaissance*. The restaurant was a snooty affair, and as I'd suspected, its staff were neat bordering on chic. In contrast, I was wearing a kitchen hand's whites, none too clean. I held a milk crate pilfered from the alley behind a lunch bar—most smoker's haunts have one—laden with fifteen of the most expensive TV dinners I could find, with their outer packaging removed.

Then came the magic.

When the guard pinned me with his flashlight as I angled out of the garden's gloom and onto the service road, he didn't see a failed academic running a job for the CIA. He saw a dinner with his name on it.

He knew, I reasoned, there was no way he, along with the dozen other extra security guards contracted for the night's event, were getting rations from the five-star hotel restaurant. Rent-a-guards are used to rent-a-dinner. And I was the supply wagon.

But to make sure he didn't baulk at the lack of a company insignia on my whites, I added a final touch. I mentioned the reason I was coming from the gardens was that I'd just puked all over a potted ficus. Last night had been my cousin's wedding, a big Catholic affair with an open bar. I was feeling seedy—not smelling of drink, mind you—and had been playing catch-up all day. I'm not much of an actor, but if there was an Oscar for best portrayal of embarrassment, I'd be on the short list.

This generated the quantum of sympathy I needed. The guy had been there too. He shone the torch into the milk crate, perhaps checking I hadn't also puked on the dinners, and then gestured for me to follow him.

When that transaction was complete, I knew I was in. He walked me to within sight of the kitchen entry, in view of the two guards lolling at the door, and then returned to his patrol. But he'd already given me what I needed: association with someone within the invisible envelope that shrouded the Château. The two guards had seen us, breaking conversation for a second only, and in that moment had pinned me with a mental green flag. The fold in space opened and I stepped in, vanishing from sight, and walked through the door into the kitchens.

I dumped the crate of dinners out of sight, beneath a bench that had the look of not clearly being anyone's responsibility, and walked to the staff toilet I knew to be off a connecting corridor. The floor plan of the Château is available on the internet, if you know where to look, courtesy of a disgruntled ex-Scientologist—no kidding.

In a toilet stall, I shed my white cocoon, doing my best to bust a hole in the laminated chipboard walls with my elbows, and emerged in my academic garb, a mauve shirt, mismatched with a red tie, and thin grey slacks that had fit under the baggy kitchen-hand pants. Like I said, I'm not much of an actor, and all my reflexes fire in the pattern of an itinerant lecturer.

I needed to drop my first disguise because a kitchen hand would have no business wandering around the guest floors, which was where I was headed. The target, Herr Thait, was billeted up there and, with luck, he'd left some tasty crumbs incriminating himself in a Middle Eastern intelligence racket for me to find while he put in an appearance at the Chamber of Commerce mixer.

That was Plan A. It had been impossible to secure a ticket to the event, so I was sketchy on its timing.

I found the elevator with no problem. My hand shook as I pressed the call button, and I knew it came from more than the adrenaline fizzing in my veins. This mission, if I managed a scoop, would have a rare payoff, because attached to the German were some high-profile names, some *Hollywood* names. And if I could nail some celebrities, it would make the news.

Maybe that sounds arrogant, but I'm not one to blow my own trumpet. I'm not. I had no problem when Nathan told me up-front that NOs toil in the shadows and only rarely see the fruits of their labor, let alone get to touch it and taste it. But I've since learned that although I can do without recognition, a sense of contribution and completion turns out to be vital. Like air in your lungs, or blood in your veins.

This shouldn't have been surprising. I've lectured on the human animal's need to work.

While researching my Movers and Shakers lecture on Hitler—he moved and shook, for the Devil—I came across the account of a cohort of concentration camp POWs who were subjected to a peculiar kind of torture. Already starved of food and warmth, they were made to dig a vast hole. The twist came when the following day they were ordered to fill it in and dig another. They had survived work on roads and train lines, and even knitted socks for Nazi toes, I guess. But this final deprivation was of *meaningful* labor: The dirt they were told to shift served absolutely no purpose in all the universe, not even to ease the way of an enemy battalion. So they began dropping like flies.

Purpose is a basic human need. I would put it before food and shelter.

So when the doors slid open on the elevator, I was relishing the hope of one day seeing on my TV screen, back home in Berkeley, a scandal I had helped unearth. I could hear myself in that future, wagging a finger at the TV:

"Yes, Mr. Cruise, freaking Oprah out is cute, but putting guns in the hands of jihadists is not."

I exited the lift on the sixth floor, an admin level, and made for my first soft target. I had no idea which room was Thait's, but finding out would be a piece of cake. You don't lock your door in Fort Knox, so I was betting that Celebrity Centre admins didn't either. The admin, a Ms. Graver, didn't let me down. Her door was not only unlocked but open. I entered, eased the door shut and sat in front of her computer.

Two minutes later I had her PC out of standby and was scrolling through the Château's occupant listing thanks to the password her browser had helpfully saved for her. Laziness greases the wheels of espionage the world over. (No need for my skeleton key, a thumb-drive filled with the PC-equivalent of the Ebola virus. One minute with Mr. Key and PCs spit their organs all over the screen. It's quite therapeutic.)

Then I encountered my first major hiccup, followed three seconds later by my second: the register had no Erhard Thait; and a guard picked that minute to do his job by investigating the door that had been open and was now shut.

The handle turned and I had a split second to take evasive action. I could make the blind side of the door, but I'd leave the chair spinning. I could fall back on the lost, preoccupied academic, but what on earth was he doing shut in an office? My mind juggled this hot coal in time lapse while I sat motionless and gaping...

Until inspiration burst over me like a summer shower. I swivelled to face the screen as the door opened, laid my hands on the keyboard, and began to punch up something—anything—in the browser.

The scuff of the guard's feet fell silent as he entered the room.

"Yep?" I said, my attention absorbed by the screen.

I would have laughed if I wasn't so damn scared. I fancied his thoughts were spilling out over the floor: "What the hell do you think you're doing?" —or maybe—"How much of the briefing did I doze for?"

The seed of inspiration for this piece of Invisibility In Plain Sight (TM) was a memory of the time a projector had failed during a lecture. The IT contractor on call who had come to fix it had been dressed like me. Academics can wear whatever they like—'cause it's all about the grey matter, right?—and IT contractors, those modern day troubadours, can be quite colorful too. On top of that, the IT crew work their magic at all hours, and, the icing, I was working on security. Me and the guard were on the same gig.

He found his voice eventually. "What are you doing?"

"Plugging a hole in the firewall. These guys are paranoid. Always getting hacked." I mopped the sweat off my brow with a sleeve. "Failing that, working out where I'll sleep tonight."

"Hacked," the guard said, and made a chopping gesture with one arm. "Yeah, that's right." He laughed at some private joke, and left without shutting the door.

I was alone again. But this was bad. No German, and the Château felt like it was closing over me like a stabbed bouncy castle. The guard had been too close, and soon I would start sticking to the radar.

The only solution I could see was to find Erhard and learn what name he was using, which meant venturing into the star-studded mixer on the ground floor.

I took the elevator down, my nostrils smelling carpet cleaner, and my gaze on a faux-18th century print of a violin. I braced myself to enter the fray, where a thousand barbed or hopeful glances were cast every second, with me wearing a disguise that already felt worn and showing.

I exited the elevator into a corridor and headed in the direction of *The Renaissance*. I rounded a corner, and when I pushed open a glass door, noise hit me like an ocean wave—the sounds of ringing glass, and raised voices, and eruptions of laughter.

And this was just the restaurant lobby.

Through an enormous set of French doors cast open on the cool night, I could see that clots of guests had swirled out onto the terrace and beyond to the gardens. I snatched a drink from a passing waiter and surveyed the scene.

At the second mouthful, I found who I was looking for: Messrs. Cruise and Travolta clumped with half a dozen shining-eyed hangers-on at the lip of the terrace. Among them was a tall, fair-haired man with his back to me.

I felt a thrill of excitement. That man had to be Erhard. I'd found my target.

I drifted toward him. All I needed was to get within earshot. To hear him called by his name.

I felt naked crossing the terrace, and glanced about desperately for someone to rope into conversation, for an excuse to skulk near Erhard so I could steal his name. But I fortified myself with the thought that one name was all I needed, and then I'd be back ravishing Ms. Graver's PC for Erhard's hotel room. And from there it was connect-the-dots back to my hotel and the drop-off.

Child's play, really, I thought.

Which was the last coherent thought I had for some time.

It's funny how your ears can detect a step with *purpose* in it.

Just as I got within feet of Erhard's group, a hand clamped onto my shoulder. A voice spoke to me, and I recognised the owner to be the guard who had found me in the admin office.

His fingers felt like a vice, and I knew the mission was slewing off the rails. It was about to wreck in flames.

I was desperate to retrieve something. Anything. This was my first *six*!

I plunged one hand into a coat pocket, hunting for my Blackberry, and in the same moment stretched with the other to cuff Erhard on the back. I wanted him to turn, to see his face. If I could just get a photo…

But that was the last cast of the net on storm-threatened waters when all the smart fishermen had turned for port.

The storm hit with unexpected ferocity.

It's all jumbled in my head. I know Erhard turned and said, "What gives, buddy?" with a flawless American accent. Then the guard kneed me in a kidney and tackled me to the tiles…and somehow Tom Cruise had rammed his shoulder into my guts, too. I retched, and a girl screamed a Hollywood-hopeful scream.

I guess someone called the cops, because when I was bundled out the front gate, there were red and blue lights strobing the darkness. Camera flashes punctuated the night.

When my mind stopped reeling, I decided it all seemed a bit overboard. I said as much to the cops on the way to the station. Turns out the Sunday before a man—Meyerski? Majorski?—had been shot dead on the Château's front steps as he came at the guards with a samurai sword in each hand. Talk about bad timing.

They let me go the next afternoon. The Celebrity Centre was keen to appear beneficent, especially when it came out I'd been gang-mugged for wanting nothing more than a photo.

I was gathering my belongings from the station registrar when the email that changed my life pinged my Blackberry.

I waited until I had found a sidewalk cafe and ordered a tall black before opening it. I was hoping, maybe, to salvage some intel from this debacle.

The email had been automatically generated. It was an alert from one of my internet sticky searches watching for the search term: Erhard Thait. Google had found the first and only matching page among the web's billions of pages.

I clicked the link and loaded it up.

A photo filled my Blackberry's screen, and my brain had a little brownout.

Have you ever looked in a mirror so long you become a stranger to yourself? Kept staring until you don't know the guy staring back? That's how it was looking at the photo, only in reverse.

It captured a typical night-scene police bust. In the foreground was the perpetrator restrained by two burly cops. His eyes were averted, or perhaps hunting for the source of a flash that had fired from somewhere else only a second before. Then with a jolt of recognition, I realized "the perpetrator" was me. The photo was from the L.A. Daily, which had run the previous night's debacle at the Celebrity Centre as breaking news. The photo had probably earned $10,000 for the dark but unmistakable profile of Mr. Cruise, seen in the background returning to the party, having busted my ass.

Now that was embarrassing, but embarrassment never stopped the sun in its arc.

No, *that* happened when I took a closer look at the web page, wondering how my photo and the name Erhard Thait had surfaced on the same webpage.

The page was part of a blog—a personal journal.

And the blog's title read: Operation *Erhard Thait*, aka *Hit the Radar*, outs the Cuckoo.

The Cuckoo? My secret, known-only-to-the-CIA, codename?

I'd been set up.

By a philologist with a penchant for anagrams, apparently. Cute.

But who was publishing this in a blog, and why? I scrolled down the blog, going back in time, scanning its articles.

Here's what I discovered: a complete list of my missions for the last three years. Wire taps and mail surveillance on a Detroit insurance broker the previous winter. Before that, my hound dog work on a Westchester family that daily scattered beneath the fall colors like hide-'n'-seekers when the counting starts. All the way back to the pretend break-and-enters I'd done on my home turf, UC Berkeley, on two professors suspected of running an immigration racket.

This blogger, whoever he was, was in deep doodoo.

I scrolled back to the top of the blog and looked for a link to the author's profile, not expecting much. Even a moron would know that spewing the operation history of a CIA NO into the public malls of the internet was illegal, however he'd come by the information.

The blogger's alias was Langley. Even cuter than the Erhard anagram.

The author had neglected to provide a real name, but had included a photo. It framed a young woman, and I knew instantly she had to be the daughter of Nathan Blaylock, the man who'd launched my career with the CIA.

I returned to the blog articles and scrutinized them carefully—and realized my first interpretation had been wrong. Radically, cataclysmically wrong.

The blog was not describing the work of a CIA field agent. It was *prescribing* it. The author, alias Langley, claimed to have conceived each mission, issued it, and monitored its outcome.

And I knew without a doubt it was true.

Which is when the whole world seemed to turn upside down in an instant.

Everything felt suddenly weightless—the folk on the sidewalk, the cup in my hand—without heft.

But to my surprise, the revelation that I had been playing a game for seven years didn't leave me feeling anger or sorrow. It left me feeling *powerful*. Potent with the pointless power of a Greek god, those destroyers and debauchers, unfettered by the fear of consequence. I was brim full of a numbing power.

After my epiphany, it didn't take long to assemble the complete picture as I have it today.

Nathan Blaylock, now deceased, was in fact the multi-millionaire Lionel Meyer, the original creative force behind "Project Sandbox" and its principal player in the early days. His son, Timothy Meyer, now deceased, took the reins from his father, and in turn gave them to Laurel Meyer, also deceased.

The seed of Project Sandbox, I can only imagine, was a simple observation: rich men control the lives of less-rich men. They do it in their factories and firms through the armature of the *wage*. But factories and firms are only the most conventional forms of this dominion. Money can buy more than car parts and happy clientele. Entertainment, education, and countless other items wear a price tag.

Nathan—I should say Lionel—probably woke one day to find boredom had leaked in through his dollar-bought defences. Perhaps he grew tired of ordering employees about, lavishing rewards on the good ones, firing others. What's the point of being a little-g god when you're bound by the same rules that bind your servants?—minimum wage this, severance pay that, social mores the-other. And besides, he knew anyone with half a brain could work their way to his net worth. That's the seduction of the American dream.

So he looked outside the box. And found me, a 40-something academic with a barely-veiled repugnance for life; a historian of the great men, not so much standing on the shoulders of giants as pimpling them.

He took me into his employ, pretending to be an agent of the CIA, to be his own little plaything, and through me, through the missions he created for me, played at being spy vicariously.

My pay arrived every week, and Lionel's father, Walt, was my only contact. (Lionel must have thought himself so clever to find company for his father into the bargain. Poor Walt. To have lost his whole family beneath him.) I honed my spy-craft, threw myself into the increasingly complex tasks assigned to me, heaped up a mountain of material evidence for cases beyond recalling. And all for nothing but the amusement of an idly rich man with a bout of ennui.

The irony is not lost on me.

In time I guess he grew bored of me, but by then he'd realized the worth of his sandbox and toy spy. His children were growing up and I offered a unique opportunity to educate them in the skills of management. First Timothy, then Laurel were apprenticed in conceiving realistic missions, communicating them, and analysing their outcomes, all the while husbanding me and my own foibles carefully and sustainably.

As each child matured, their father gave them greater challenges. The missions became more complex, varied, and like the creations of a blossoming writer, the effects achieved became more subtle, or comedic, or tragic. I found myself spying on colleagues in the very halls of academia I'd forsworn; and assembling materials on spider biology—me, the arachnophobe!; and, yet more cruel, surveilling targets in the building where my ex-wife works, slinking about equally horrified and yearning.

Laurel, a writer at heart, had scarcely begun her apprenticeship when she hit upon the idea of anonymously blogging her exploits. Her most recent concoction, *Operation Erhard*, was her magnum opus, and perhaps her graduation project. Set by Lionel no doubt, its goal was a novelty: to make Cuckoo appear in the media. What a thrill it must have been! To fire off a document to old Walt and days later see my mug in the news, like flicking the switch on a dynamited building and watching it crumble. To *also* capture Tom Cruise, her favourite actor and a dollop of pure pop culture, was the artist in her. His presence had dismissed any doubt of a paper running with the story.

And I'll give it to Laurel, it was pure genius to drop me in the Château just days after a mad samurai was killed on its steps. He had blooded the guards, leaving them alert for the faintest whiff of a strange scent—which I was bound to give, poor little lamb me, looking for a man who didn't exist.

Gosh, I do mix my metaphors when I'm tired.

Still, I can be philosophic about my time as a CIA Non-Official agent, a ghost operative. It taught me many skills.

The lawyers want to give me the needle. But I tell you a higher court has examined my actions and pronounced justice done. You should have seen Nathan Blaylock's face in its last moments of animation.

Do you have a watch? They don't let me have one in here. I have an appointment with a lady from CNN next and wouldn't want to keep her waiting.

But before you go: have you heard the story about the man who took a pretty shell home and put it in his tank?

About The Author

Brett Adams grew up knowing two worlds—country Western Australia, and Middle Earth. One was vast, bright, and dry. The other had elves. Somewhere between one world and the other writing became a joy with this challenge: to create stories that invite scratching below the surface. Stories with skin, organs, bones. Stories that might walk. Later he circumnavigated the continent by caravan. He now enjoys being able to step sideways, and the blurred boundary at the edge of dreams. He lives with his wife and children in Perth, Western Australia.

For more information, visit dweomingwell.blogspot.com.au.

The First Acolyte of the Upshan Berental

Bryce Anderson

Editor's Note: Fantasy often gets criticized for having a predilection toward male heroes surrounded by weak women, but the indie world has no problem giving us strong and courageous females. Even if they can't always see their own strength.

"Don't make it more complicated than it needs to be."—The final words of revered founder Dorica Longmire, as inscribed above the entrance to the Temple of the Upshan Berental

The same dream had come for her every night this week: Reesa stood tongue-tied as the sphere of the Upshan Berental grew larger and brighter. Flames poured out of it, closing in around her and incinerating her instantly. Bodiless, she floated there, listening to High Priest Ragnar. "Poor girl, she should have practiced her enunciation." Then he would hobble down the marble steps to fetch the dustpan, muttering, "Well, if she couldn't get a few simple words right, what use was she?"

Now the thirteen year-old girl stood upon those same steps, feeling the gaze of hundreds of pairs of eyes upon her back. Four girls had already taken their vows and come back down the stairs unincinerated. In fact, in the nearly nine hundred years since the Founding, zero initiates had caught fire. She'd asked. *Stop imagining things that never could happen,* she chided herself. *You're making it more complicated than it needs to be.*

High Priest Ragnar motioned for her to approach. She climbed, feeling naked and exposed in her simple white robes. She knelt before the priest, who splashed water on her forehead. As she opened her mouth to speak, she froze. How did the chant begin? "I..." she sputtered.

"Vin virimas..." the priest whispered, an indulgent smile on his face.

She gasped with relief as the words began to pour out of her. "Vin virimas wolda, chomaskli," she called out, speaking with phonetic precision the long string of words whose meaning had been lost to antiquity. The priest responded with a few words of his own. She would respond at the proper moments by raising her hands above her head and shouting, "Tah kali! Upshan!" During her instructions, she'd asked three different priests what the phrase meant. Only handsome young Brother Uther had had the humility to admit that nobody knew.

The ritual continued with two more unintelligible exchanges and a notoriously difficult bit involving three candles. The knot in her stomach released as the high priest nodded in approval, then sent her back to stand in the line.

Finally, in the climax of the ceremony, the high priest turned to a marble pedestal behind him, pulling a cloth away and revealing the sacred Upshan Berental. The translucent, glowing ball hovered about a handspan above the altar. But in the minds of the gathered worshippers, the ball was no mere parlor trick. It was an object of reverence and devotion. It was a conduit linking their minds to the minds of the gods. It was glowing green today.

According to the teachings, the Upshan Berental protected the temple and the whole village. From what, Reesa wasn't sure. Maybe from the Bad Place, the place the Founders had been fleeing when they came to this tiny, fertile valley surrounded by impassable mountains. No one knew how they'd come here or why the Founders had fled. In the nine hundred years since, nobody had entered or departed the valley.

The ball made for an odd, inscrutable protector. It glowed, it hovered, it frequently changed color, and from time to time stray cats would wander in and take great fascination in it. She'd once overheard a priest call it "The Sacred Thingy," which had seemed blasphemous but also accurate.

Nervously, the five inductees stepped forward and placed their hands upon the sphere. Giving it all her focus, Reesa struggled to feel the monumental significance of this moment. It wasn't easy. She'd half expected the touch to bring some flash of revelation, some deeper understanding of the universe and her place in it, or maybe the flames would come to punish her for some past transgression. But no, it was just a warm, glowing rock. Once the smell of incense washed out of her hair, Reesa's life would be unchanged save for one new obligation. As an acolyte, she would be required to stand watch over the ball for eight hours twice a week. Though the Upshan Berental—Conduit to the Mind of Heaven—was admittedly very pretty, the older children had warned her that long hours of boredom and drudgery lay ahead.

The ceremony switched back to their native tongue and Reesa spoke the solemn vows, promising to guard the ball with her very life, wax and polish it whenever necessary, and keep herself undefiled by men. *No problem there*, she thought. Conversations with boys inevitably left her pondering why the gods had created such hopelessly stupid creatures.

The high priest spoke a few words, praising the girls for their willingness to make the required covenants, which made Reesa flush with pride. He followed his praise with a rather long-winded speech, starting out as a parable about virgins and lamp oil, but soon drifting off into a story about a beautiful woman he'd met before joining the order. Before the old man could say anything too incriminating, one of his assistants whispered something in his ear, and he wrapped it up.

Their rite of passage over, the girls made their way back down the stairs and began filing toward the entrance. Soon the last few months of fasting and study, separated from their parents, would be a fading memory. Reesa gave a backward glance to the Upshan Berental. *Silly, overgrown marble*, she thought.

I heard that, said a voice in her head. Her face went pale; she spun around to face the shining sphere. She stared at it, then heard the congregation muttering in confusion. Finally, in embarrassment, she turned and started walking quickly. *Just my imagination*, she thought.

Just your imagination, the voice agreed. Reesa broke into a sprint, nearly toppling the girl in front of her.

———————— • ————————

For three days, Reesa dreaded her upcoming communion with the Upshan Berental, when she would spend eight hours alone guarding the sphere. But what could she do? Ask one of the priests to guard her as she guarded it? Tell people she'd been hearing voices? Fake an illness? Her fear of the Upshan Berental was exceeded only by her fear of embarrassment. She resolved to pretend nothing had happened, and hoped nothing would.

The hour of reckoning was at hand. She entered the temple as the sun set, finding her friend Arkit standing watch at the pedestal. Arkit, though only a year older than Reesa, stood a full head taller and was as self-confident as any adult in the village. And she was beautiful. They would laugh together about the way boys salivated over Arkit, about the foolish ways they tried to impress her. Secretly, Reesa wished she could inspire even a tenth as much foolishness.

Arkit waved her over. As they embraced, her friend said, "Hey, Ree. I have to run. I'm supposed to meet Jedoan down by the lake. I know, you think he's too old for me," she chattered as she headed for the entrance, "and of course he doesn't have a single thought in his head. But I can overlook that, since he's so pretty. Try not to get caught sleeping!"

Arkit was sprinting toward the door. "Wait!" Reesa yelled.

The older girl hurried back. "What's wrong?"

"What if it..." Reesa swallowed hard, staring at the ball. "What if it does something?"

"Oh, Ree. The Upshan Berental doesn't *do* anything! It just floats there." She gave it a demonstrative shove. The sphere was nudged slightly off its center, then slowly floated back into place. "I once saw it change color. Red to blue."

"Can it...can it get angry? Do you think?"

"You've just got jitters. The ball won't do anything, and if anybody comes in, there's a dozen priests quartered upstairs." She leaned in and whispered conspiratorially, "I hear that some of them are warrior monks. They know secret fighting arts and could punch a brick in half."

She squeezed Reesa's hand, and then she was gone. The heavy temple doors thundered closed, leaving Reesa alone with the suddenly menacing orb. The girl stood in the appointed spot, apprehensive eyes fixed on it. Its unblinking gaze met hers, and the hours began to pass. Eventually her resolve waned and the discomfort in her back and shoulders waxed. She sat down, hoping none of the priests would catch her.

The priests had warned her to be vigilant and always remain standing, meditating on the glow of the orb, divining hidden wisdom from its slow flicker. But Arkit swore she'd never gotten in trouble for sitting down, or even sleeping. More than a couple of the boys claimed that they could skip out for hours at a time unnoticed. Reckless, stupid boys.

Ree. Sa.

The voice entered her mind, frigid and sharp. Reesa yelped, jumping to her feet and spinning to face the orb. "Who's there?"

Ree. Sa.

It had heard her thoughts before. She was sure of it. *Just stop it!* She flung the thought back viciously. *Whoever you are, leave me alone!*

The orb grew brighter, its pale cream color melting away as a furious crimson arose. *Ree. Sa. Come. To. Me.*

Controlling her breathing, she stepped closer to the pedestal. Every muscle in her body was primed and desperate to flee, but she'd been given a command, a test of her faith. Fighting down her rising panic, she reached out toward its warm, glowing surface with a single finger.

Right as she touched it, the light extinguished and the orb dropped, crashing to the pedestal. As it clattered down the steps, making a *bang bang bang* noise that only the dead could sleep through, Reesa screamed at the top of her lungs.

The acoustics of the temple were really quite remarkable.

———————— • ————————

The rumor spread like a brushfire as the town awoke: how Reesa had burst in on half a dozen unconscious priests in their nightrobes, sobbing as she screamed, "I broke it! I broke it!" How they'd all rushed down the stairs to find the Upshan Berental burning quietly in its proper place. How the poor, crazy girl had hurled venomous accusations at the ball, using such language as had not defiled the temple in centuries.

Not centuries, some listeners reminded them, for three weeks ago Brother Ralsam had dropped that marble idol of Kunush the Preserver on his own foot.

For her ungodly behavior, she was banned from Watch for a full month, confined to the temple's kitchens when she wasn't at studies. Washing dishes was dull, humid drudgery, but it made Reesa happy. Plates never whispered to her brain.

The month passed too quickly, and her embarrassment soon faded. When it came time to return, she was given the coveted morning shift, when the body was fresh and people sometimes came by to break the monotony. This would be easier, she figured.

But it wasn't. By the end of her first hour, her nerves were worn raw from the constant tension. Any second now, the voice would come to her again. It would be inside her head, saying… saying… saying…

Just say something! She shouted the thought into the gaping silence where the voice should have been.

I'm sorry. I didn't mean to scare you. The voice was a young boy's, serious and apologetic. Reesa tried to keep her face neutral as she looked around. A few elderly worshippers milled around the periphery of the room, offering up prayers, or maybe just gossiping to pass the time. They certainly weren't paying the girl any notice.

Who are you?

My name was Kyron. But that was a long time ago.

Are you a god?

No. I was…a boy. An acolyte like you.

Curiosity almost overcame the girl's resentment. But not quite. *So, I probably won't burn in the Blackfire if I tell you to leave me alone?*

Probably not. I doubt I have any say in the fate of your eternal soul.

Good. She turned her back on the pedestal, staring determinedly towards the vaulted ceiling.

I really am sorry, the voice spoke. Reesa didn't reply. They waited out the remainder of the shift in silence.

Finally, Arkit arrived to replace her. "Did you have fun?"

"More than you can imagine."

Arkit wrinkled her nose, like she found the sarcasm unbecoming. "Rile asked if you'd be at the festival this evening," Arkit nearly squeaked the good news. "I think he fancies you." The sphere flared red again, but only Reesa noticed.

"It'll be good to be away from here," Reesa said. "This overgrown marble is starting to get on my nerves." She turned and bounded down the stairs to the awaiting entrance. Someone let out a shriek; Reesa spun around.

The Upshan Berental was following her.

———— • ————

Four priests stood in a circle around Reesa and her unwanted companion, studying the pair like a new kind of insect. The aged High Priest Ragnar was the first to give his professional evaluation. "She's bewitched it! The girl is an evil sorceress!"

"That may not be the case, your excellency," said Brother Uther. "It may be that the gods have chosen this girl for some special purpose." He gave Reesa a wary, apologetic smile, and the girl felt her pulse quicken.

"Most irregular, most irregular," the high priest muttered. Then he rapped the orb with his cane, shouting, "Speak up!"

Brother Uther cast him a worried look, then turned to the girl. "I'm not sure how to ask this," he said, "but have the gods tried to...contact you?"

"No." It was truthful enough. Kyron said he wasn't one of the gods.

"But you've seen some unusual behavior from The Sacred Thing—I mean, from the Upshan Berental, correct?"

"I wasn't lying. The first night, when I touched it, it turned off and rolled down the stairs."

"Unnecessary complications," the high priest muttered. "We were warned, you know."

Brother Uther nodded. "Before that? Before you touched it, I mean."

"It was red."

"I see. You recall nothing else?"

"Nothing," she lied. What was she supposed to say? *There's a boy in your ball, and we're having a quarrel?*

She snapped back to reality a moment too late. "What?"

Brother Uther repeated, "Until the Conduit stops following you, we can't allow you to leave the temple."

———— • ————

Reesa was beginning to suspect that the priesthood actually enjoyed waiting on her. They'd rigged up a tent and some bedding behind the pedestal, giving her a private place to sleep. One of the older priests taught her how to repair the temple's books, then set up a work bench near the pedestal. The priests took turns bringing her meals, and released her and the other acolytes from their vows of silence as they stood watch. And once every waking hour, they would escort her to the temple's entrance to see if the Upshan Berental would follow. It always did, like an eager puppy looking for a walk.

Occasionally she would try and strike up a conversation with her captor, but without success. Sometimes it seemed like Kyron was stubbornly refusing to respond. Other times, it was like he wasn't there to answer. But whatever the reason, it was almost a week before she heard from him again.

The silence was broken after the third visit from her parents. Their meeting had gone poorly. Her father had yelled at her, as though the whole thing was something she'd made up to get out of chores. As usual, mother seemed to disagree, but her objections were timid and muted. When her parents left, Reesa burst into sobs.

Reesa?

The girl's temper flared for a second, but she fought it down. As much as she disliked the boy, she would never be free without his cooperation. *What can I do for you, Kyron of the Glowing Marble?*

He laughed. *I'm in an awkward position. I have many strange and fantastic stories to tell, and some secrets of the universe to reveal. But the only one I can tell them to is angry and cannot forgive me.*

Of course I'm angry! You're keeping me prisoner!

You were ignoring me!

You humiliated me in front of everybody! Why don't you bother someone else?

Like I said. You're the only one I can talk to.

Reesa was taken aback. *Not even the other acolytes?* There was only silence. "You're alone in there, aren't you?" she whispered aloud.

Not exactly. Sometimes I can sense others, but they're impossible to really talk to, and they never stay long.

Reesa wasn't quite sure she understood, but she got the sense that he was lonely.

So, if I forgive you, you'll tell me the mysteries of the universe?

Yes.

Then I forgive you. But let me ask for ink and paper. Mysteries of the universe ought to be written down.

———————————— • ————————————

Nearly seventy years ago, Kyron had watched over the Upshan Berental, as so many had before him. He had been fascinated with it, maybe even obsessed. He found that when he was completely calm and relaxed, he could feel the orb as a distinct, textured warmth in his mind. He'd meditated upon it for years, becoming familiar with its shifting patterns. Late one night, he found something deep inside. It was a way in.

It was open.

The moment his mind entered it, the door slammed shut. Kyron watched in horror from inside the sphere as his body stood up and shambled away, eyes unfocused. For years, he could do nothing but watch, the temple's weekly services punctuating the monotony.

Every week, his parents would dress his walking corpse, comb its hair, guide it to services, and seat it next to them. His mother would stand in front of the congregation sometimes, weeping openly as she spoke to the congregation of the difficulties they were having raising their suddenly silent, mindless child.

Those years of imprisonment had felt like the Blackfire. But after exhausting himself with pounding on the walls, screaming to get out, Kyron gave up. He began to explore in earnest. With careful focus, he could look up and down or side to side. After getting bored with spinning himself dizzy, he explored further. He found another direction to move, one which he couldn't reconcile with the physical space he was familiar with. A small twist in one "direction" and he found himself looking out over a gleaming metal city at sunset. Another twist put him face to face with strange and frightening creatures, all feathers and tentacles, squawking at the sphere in either outrage or lust.

He quickly became lost, and his attempts to retrace his steps only led him further afield. When his panicked dash through the sphere had exhausted itself, he found himself staring at the surrounding ruins of an abandoned temple, half collapsed and covered with jungle life. Two creatures that looked like shriveled people with extra arms were beating the sphere with sticks, howling at it.

It seemed as good a place to stop as any.

The creatures eventually got bored and left. Kyron also got bored and began fumbling around, looking for other controls. He found one, which he explored for the longest time before giving it the most tentative twist he could manage. Time froze. Emboldened, he twisted it further. The shriveled humans returned, walking backwards. Another turn, and time moved much faster; the jungle life started retreating from the ruins, which were stacking themselves back up into a fully-constructed temple. Kyron recognized the temple he'd stared out at for so many years. He was home.

He went forward in time, briefly, watched as the Temple of the Upshan Berental was sacked and burned by a pack of angry, fuzz-faced creatures.

It must have been awful, Reesa whispered.

She felt his muted agreement more than heard it. *Imagine cute, fuzzy stuffed animals slaughtering each other. Better yet, don't. It's not pleasant.*

When he couldn't bear to watch anymore, he fled backwards in time, watching the great hall undergo hundreds of sudden redecorations. Time ground to a halt, putting Kyron face-to-face with a girl his own age, her face scrunched in concentration as she pressed her hands against the sphere.

I've probably left thousands of times since then. I still don't know my way around, but it always draws me back to that point when you're making your vows to the Upshan Berental. I think it wanted me to meet you.

After vainly trying to grapple with the enormity of that statement, Reesa gave up. *When you leave,* she asked instead, *where do you go?*

That's hard to explain. It's like I'm always in the same place, but looking in different directions. At first I thought I was moving between different spheres, but I'm not. This sphere is the only one there is, but it looks out upon millions of worlds. This is just one.

"Millions?" Reesa wondered aloud, then she clamped her hand over her mouth. She'd never had any real use for that number before. After several minutes of clumsy explanations, Kyron gave up. *I'm not making sense. I can't explain what it's like to live in an all-seeing sphere that permeates the fabric of reality, and you look tired.* Reesa only nodded in befuddled agreement. *I'll let you go, if you like. But I have other things to tell you, so promise you'll come back.*

The next time the priests came to escort Reesa to the front door, the sacred orb didn't follow. She went home and, after reuniting with her parents, stole off to the barn to find a secure hiding spot for the mysteries of the universe.

---------•---------

Five years later, another dreaded day had come. Upon reaching her eighteenth year, Reesa had been expected to take up new vows, which would induct her into the ranks of the town's adults and its marriageable women. Thus would she be freed from the duties of guarding the Upshan Berental —or, as she now thought of it, story time. Reesa had stalled as long as she could, making every possible excuse. Her dowry was poor. She could offer guidance and moral support to younger acolytes. She'd lied to the Brethren, swearing she'd been warned away from the rites by a soothsayer.

The dreaded day had already arrived once before, but she'd cheated adulthood by faking an upset stomach. Her efforts were making her the subject of gossip and ridicule, but Reesa didn't care.

She tried not to care.

Now, as she walked next to the now-High Priest Uther, she knew her excuses were at an end. He would ask her to take the vows, and because it was Father Uther doing the asking, she knew she would relent.

"Reesa," the high priest's kind voice carried only a small hint of his frustration. "I suppose I must pull it up by the roots. The guarding rites are for the benefit of those who guard. They instill physical and mental discipline, to prepare you for your life as an adult in our community. The Glowing Marble—and I truly wish you'd stop calling it that—doesn't require anyone's protection." He looked at her expectantly, and she realized with a start that he thought he was telling her something she didn't know already.

"I... I understand." She tried to summon up a thoughtful look, as though it came as a revelation. She wasn't sure she'd succeeded, but the conversation flowed on.

"You've always impressed me as an intelligent, deliberate young woman. From the beginning, you've had more discipline than most of your peers would ever develop. The whole village is waiting for you to take the last step into adulthood, and I wish I understood why you're hesitating."

Reesa mulled this over for the longest time as she walked with the high priest through the town square. Father Uther, infinitely patient, allowed her the time to think.

Reesa hazarded a glance at his handsome features, deciding to trust him with a small part of the truth. "I guess I enjoy the time I spend with The Sacred Thingy. It's a quiet place where I can live in my head, where I can ponder—" she hesitated, then added, "the infinite variety of the universe."

Father Uther made a thoughtful noise. "If you enjoy it that much, I suppose some arrangement could be made." He thought quickly. "Perhaps you could become a special advisor to the acolytes. The younger ones practically worship you already, though I've warned them it's kin to idolatry. But from such a lofty position you could still guard the sphere yourself from time to time."

"Really?" Reesa tempered her initial rush of excitement. She poked and prodded at the idea, as though it might be booby-trapped, then felt her eyes well up. "That would be nice," she concluded. "But people would find it a bit strange."

"Strange? Who knows? I minister to a widow on the edge of the village who keeps thirty cats. She insists that I treat them as full participants in our conversations."

Reesa laughed. Uther smiled and continued. "Nobody is without their eccentricities. I would be disappointed if you were the only exception. Is there anything else bothering you?"

"When I think of marrying, the idea overwhelms me. That is, even if I could find a man who would be tempted by the dowry my family could offer."

The high priest nodded. "Your family is poor, true. But only a truly stupid man would need a bribe to marry you."

Something in his tone gave her pause. "Why do you say that?" she asked. She slowed her steps noticeably.

He glanced at her, looking nervous. "You have a keen mind and a gentle wit. You desire to honor the gods in all things. You're beautiful."

"Nobody would call me beautiful."

"I would," Uther said, a little too sincerely. "But I cannot speak for other men," he added quickly, then winced as he stumbled over the subtext of what he'd just said.

"But, speaking only for yourself," Reesa said, trying not to laugh, "you think I would make a good wife?"

Reesa caught the frown of concentration that crossed the young priest's face. She stopped walking, grabbed his hand, and pulled him to a halt. The question spilled out of her before she could stop it. "Uther, do you love me?"

His response was simple, with only a hint of hesitation. "I believe I do, yes." Reesa had expected him to be flustered, to stammer, to perhaps deny that any such thought had ever crossed his mind. "You seem disappointed," he continued. "I promise that we need never speak of—"

"No, no. Uther, I'm not. I feel the..." she faltered. "I love you. I think I have for a while now. But they made you the high priest, the youngest ever. That is such an accomplishment, how can I ask you to throw it all away for me?"

Uther smiled. "I know marriage is...discouraged. I'd probably be asked to let someone else take over the duties of high priest, and I would not protest. But I would remain a priest still; taking you as a wife would not break any sacred vows. The gods won't hold me in contempt for it, so I don't care if the priesthood does. I only fear that you might."

"No, never!"

The priest laughed with relief, his eyes joyous. "Then the day you take your vows, I'll go to your father and ask for your hand."

"Only my hand?"

"Only your hand. I could never convince him to part with eyes as green as yours."

Reesa smiled graciously. "Are priests allowed to flatter innocent maidens so?"

"Tell me you'll say yes when the time comes."

A thought came to her, one that both thrilled and frightened her. "Before you ask for my hand, I have to tell you..." she trailed off. "I wouldn't want to keep secrets from my husband."

"What is it?" He squeezed her hand, looking concerned. "What sort of secrets?"

She laughed. "The secrets of the universe."

———— • ————

Trapped, deeply shamed, physically and emotionally spent, Reesa watched the eyes of the priests as they pored over the notes she'd gathered over the last five years. From time to time, one of them would glance up at her, each look accusing her of the most vile blasphemies. Except High Priest Uther, who seemed unable to look at her at all. She kept looking, hoping for a compassionate glance, a word from him in her defense. But no, she only saw the chasm between them and the betrayal and despair on his face.

They had been in council for six exhausting hours. Reesa was desperately thirsty, but didn't ask for water. If her throat was dry, then so were her eyes, and at the moment her only solace was that she had no more tears left in her.

"Now, child," Brother Nolhein's high, cutting voice bored into her. "Are we to understand that, on one of these... *other worlds*," he spat the phrase in disgust, "there is a race of lizard men named the Tarktok?"

"Yes, Brother," she whispered, without a shred of resistance.

"And they have another sex which is neither man nor woman? And fly about in these metal birds?"

"Yes, Father."

"And these orgies you describe…" As he spoke, Reesa sank lower in her chair. "They're part of the religious rites of these demons?"

Reesa only whispered, "I don't think they're dem—"

The priest cut her off. "Clearly, they are. Blasphemous, low creatures who mock the gods with their disgusting rites. Others here have encouraged you to recant. I disagree; you should stand by these tales, pretend the gods whispered them to you. Far better than admitting you could invent such vileness." Some of his peers nodded.

Father Uther addressed her for the first time in several hours. "What disappoints me most, my child…" *My child.* The cold formality of the phrase shook the girl to her core. "…is the absence of piety in your imaginings. You don't even tell lies about the gods. It's as though they don't even exist in this world you've invented. All these years, I saw you as an impossibly devout young woman, who loved the gods and was beloved of them in turn." He stood, turning away from her. "All those long nights you spent with the Upshan Berental, you weren't worshipping the gods. You were *mocking* them."

Reesa realized that she'd still clung to a shred of hope; that was the moment it was torn away from her. Head hung in shame, tears flowing, she whispered, "Burn them. They're all lies."

Uther gave a nod, then strode from the room. The other priests gathered up the tattered papers with their delicate writing, then began to feed them one by one into a blazing cistern in the middle of the table. Reesa hid her eyes.

———————— • ————————

The priests escorted her down the stairs and out into the main tabernacle. She passed the altar without looking at the orb, her eyes fixed dully ahead.

Reesa? What happened? The words whispered in her mind. Kyron asked her again. She tried to keep her mind silent and empty, but she couldn't conceal the depths of her humiliation from him. She stared at her feet, kept walking. The marble tiles brightened to an angry red.

She exited through the front door. "Reesa Calvaugh," Brother Ralsam spoke behind her. She turned, barely able to meet his gaze. "You are convicted of blasphemy and sentenced to one year's banishment. You are not to approach these doors—"

His words were lost in a crack of thunder. The priests turned. The Upshan Berental floated like a flame amid a rising cloud of dust, above the rubble that used to be its pedestal.

As the priests exchanged wide-eyed glances, Reesa turned away and began her long walk home.

———————————•———————————

At the end of her year's banishment, followed by three days of fasting, Reesa returned to the temple. She feigned penitence as she asked Father Uther's permission to perform the rites which would reunite her with her village. Their meeting was brief and cordial. They did not discuss marriage, and Reesa did not regret that they never would.

When the time came, the doors to the main hall opened to grant her entrance. She marched to the front of the hall, where Brother Nolhein was waiting. She knelt before him and offered her penitence. The priest poured water over her head, then bid her to stand.

She closed the ceremony by placing her hands on the Upshan Berental.

Hello, stranger, Kyron said.

I've missed you, Reesa thought, smiling.

Me too.

Then she turned to the assembly, and Brother Nolhein presented her as a full member of the congregation. She took her seat next to Arkit, and caressed the tiny hand of her friend's new infant. "You did great," Arkit whispered. Reesa tried to smile at the encouragement.

Can we talk? Kyron asked as Reesa's mind drifted away from the services.

Certainly.

I've been exploring, studying the door that brought me here. I think I can open it.

You can get out?

No. When you're in here, you're in for forever. But I think I could open it wide enough to bring you in.

What? I couldn't!

You always told me how much you wanted to see the screaming turnip people. At this, Reesa laughed aloud, drawing some indignant looks. She couldn't deny it; she really *did* want to see the screaming turnip people.

There's so much to see in here. More than that, there are people in here, others like me. I'm learning to talk to them. Every one of them used to live in one of the places I've told you about.

Really?

I think they found their way here, found a way through the door. We're working together, trying to figure out how it all works. Will you join us?

Kyron, please. I just want my old life back.

We both know that's not true.

She glanced at Arkit and her baby, then stole a glance at her parents before turning back to the Upshan Berental. She closed her eyes, squeezing tears from them. *Kyron?*

Yes?

Tell me a story.

The services concluded and the congregation began filing out. Reesa sat staring forward in her seat, unmoving but for shallow breaths and the occasional eyeblink. Father Uther watched her from the temple's entrance, first with sadness and then with annoyance. When Reesa's mother grabbed her shoulders and began to wail as she shook her daughter, he rushed back inside.

Reesa's mother was sobbing uncontrollably, clutching the girl's head to her chest as she cried, "No, please, please come back." Arkit's arms were around them both, trying to offer comfort. Her father stood beside them, one hand on his wife's shoulder, his face stoic as plaster.

Father Uther's heart sank. Like all the priests, he knew the legend of the empty boy. "Did she say anything to you before—?" Uther tried to summon a word for it, but came up blank.

Arkit nodded. "She said she was sorry, and she asked me to look after her parents."

"Is that all?"

Arkit gave a choked laugh. "I don't know what she... She said, 'The secrets of the universe are mine.'"

About The Author

Bryce Anderson, author, programmer, and part-time underworld lich king, resides in Salt Lake City, a real, not-made-up place that exists. A cat named Zoidberg lives in his apartment and frequently gets all up in his grill. Bryce would be a political revolutionary if he had any real ambition at all, but since he doesn't, curmudgeonly will have to suffice. His writing advice is simple, and also applies to jump-starting a beleaguered national economy: persistent, bold experimentation.

For more information, visit bannedsorcery.com.

Bronwen's Dowry

Belinda Mellor

Editor's Note: Nobility looms large in fantasy stories. Heroes and their honor, kings and their duty, good vs. evil, etc. But nobility is not limited to such grand stages. Sometimes it plays out in a single heart.

The journeymen shearers called at the farms in early summer to clip the flocks of their winter wool and barter a few wares on the side. At Olber Stoson's farm the shearer had arrived with only a few tunes to trade, and those from poor pipes. He was a sparely built man; young yet weathered, with few words and fewer smiles. He was good at his craft and not a single sheep shorn was bloodied. Olber Stoson was impressed.

The price for the shearing was a small percentage of the fleeces. Pawl earned his supper with a few simple tunes. Olber Stoson was not impressed by those. Olber was a widower, recently bereaved, soon to be wed again. He had found a new wife on the far side of the Hill, a woman somewhat younger than he, once wed but now widowed like himself, and possessing a fine piece of land. That was her only quality it was said, but it was quality enough for Olber, for his flock grazed land that was not his and the roof over his head belonged to another, and they were required back.

Olber had but one problem, one possible snag in his plans: as a young man with a young wife he had hoped for a son who would work alongside him, support he and his wife in their old age. His wife had provided him with a child, but it was a girl, and she never bore another. They had struggled on but the harvests were bad and the winters were worse; the lambs died and the family had nothing like enough to eat, even after The Finder had visited the Hill one spring. When a local gentlewoman offered to take the child and raise her as her own, Olber and his wife had readily agreed.

That had been fourteen years ago. Then his wife had died. Alone, with nothing but sixty sheep to his name, Olber could not have hoped to find a new wife, so, to his present regret, he had gone to the fine house and demanded the return of his girl. There had been shouting and some swearing on his part, but eventually he had his way and took her off to keep house for him and help on the farm.

Then the farmer over the Hill had died, out riding one day in a storm, and his plain and argumentative wife had been left a farm she could not manage, and Olber had moved fast and should have moved in, but for his daughter.

Bronwen was a pretty girl, even though she had lost a lot of weight since coming home and her hands were now chapped and her cheeks pinched. She would not be welcome at the farm over the Hill. The big house had made it quite clear that she was now her father's responsibility so he could not take her back there, and how could he marry her off? He could ill afford to part with any of his sheep and, even if he could, what sort of dowry would a few sheep be? Yet until she was gone he could not go.

"Have you a wife, Pawl?" Olber asked, after Bronwen had served up a mean supper of cabbage and wheat stew.

The journeyman laughed, slightly, mockingly. "Do I look wed?"

"You would like a wife though? Or are you content to be your own man?" the farmer persisted.

Pawl looked at his hands, thin, supple with lanolin from the fleeces. "Aye —and what man would not? But I can ill support myself, let alone another, and if there were little ones..." The statement hung in the air, and Olber knew the scene all too well.

Bronwen was brewing a nettle tea in the lean-to area where the cooking and the washing took place.

"My daughter needs a husband, and I have found no one to take her. She is a good lass..."

"But she has no dowry," Pawl finished.

"And you have nothing to offer, so no other father would even let you look at his girl," Olber countered.

And so the deal was done. When Pawl the journeyman shearer left that side of the Hill he took with him not only three fine fleeces and his sorry pipes but also a pretty wife, with a small satchel of threads and needles under her arm.

Bronwen did not look back, nor could she bring herself to look at the stranger walking beside her who was her husband. She was not afraid of him for he was not a man who caused those around him to fear, rather she was shy and bewildered, and somewhat surprised at the turn her life had taken. He was no less surprised than she; he had not intended to look for a wife and in his experience of life up until this point nothing was found unless it was looked for, and even then there was no certainty. It was not that he had no wish to marry someday, rather that he had a more immediate priority, an event in the late autumn, which for him marked the finishing of the old year and the start of the new. That event was the Piper's Quest.

Nightfall found them on the far side of the Hill, knocking at the solid door of a solid farmhouse. The woman who opened the door was as sturdily built as her home, and she looked appraisingly at Bronwen's thin face and Pawl's bony hands and might have taken them for vagrants but that she caught sight of the shearing blades in Pawl's belt.

"About time too," she grumbled, and directed them to the barn where they could sleep. "I suppose you haven't eaten?" she added, as an afterthought, and fetched them some bread and some broth, with which they celebrated their wedding feast.

Pawl woke early, as was his wont, yet Bronwen was up and gone before him. When he had worked and washed and evening was closing in, he returned to the loft and Bronwen smiled her welcome.

"We're to eat in the house," she told him.

He frowned. "How come the invitation?"

"I, too, have worked today," she said. "I have cooked and I have mended. The woman is to marry again soon, she told me. There is a lot to do; I helped, she said to eat in."

Bronwen's dress was plain but it hung well on her, it even suited her.

Pawl knew he did not look so well in his clothes. "I have only two shirts, the other is more worn than this—"

"It is mended now."

And so it was. Mended and decorated with an intertwining pattern in green and red, gold and blue.

"The Dancing Serpents," Pawl muttered approvingly, recognising the design. At least that problem was solved for the Piper's Quest. Maybe old Stoson had done him a favour greater than he had guessed.

Feeling less discomfited than he would have thought possible, Pawl, with Bronwen, ate supper in the cool of the farmhouse. When they had finished, the woman asked if the journeyman could do more than shear sheep—could he perhaps mend fences?

And so they stayed. Not too many days, not too many tasks—there were others waiting on Pawl's arrival and a journey to be made, a place to be when the year ended.

They ate in, daily, and sometimes the woman of the house smiled and hummed along with Pawl's piping and sometimes she scowled and her eyes burnt with a hunger, a desire, and she would not talk. On those evenings they left early for their straw-filled loft, where they slept as secure as wintered stock.

"What does she want?" Pawl asked his wife one morning.

"Morning and evening—the promise of long-life and security."

"Meaning what?" he insisted, but she smiled and made no other reply so he shrugged and went out to secure the roof of the hen coop as he had promised, while Bronwen opened her satchel and took out her needles and threads and some fine linen that had once been a nightgown when she had lived a gentler life.

"We must be on our way soon," Pawl said that night at supper. He was, in a way, sorry to leave. He had put on some weight in just the few days since they came here, and Bronwen looked better than when he had first seen her.

"Just one more task, then I'll not keep you." The woman was relaxed, happy even. Her hunger gone, satisfied. "A simple task—it shall not take you long."

She spoke truly. By noon the following day he had finished the black-wood frame and Bronwen had collected their few belongings together and was ready to go. They ate a noon meal alone and, when they were done, the woman appeared, radiant with pleasure and with pride.

"It looks just so," she declared, fetching down a faded dried posy from a nail in the wall and hanging in its place the blackwood frame, within which the Arc of Dawn and the River of Dusk sparkled and flowed in an almost perceivable pattern of silk threads against a milk-pale cloth. Pawl gaped and Bronwen hid a smile behind her napkin.

The woman misunderstood his expression and a guilty glimmer lit her eyes. "I know, I know," she soothed. "Yet you have no home, and you will get better use from the price I paid."

"Yes," Bronwen said quickly. "We will."

"Of course," Pawl agreed, wondering what it was he was agreeing to, recalling the only other time he had seen the great symbols of home and life— a tapestry in a crowded hall, a wedding gift to the Master of Myron, where the Piper's Quest would be resolved, this year as always.

She gave them a horse, instead of fleeces, for the shearing and the work he had done. It was not a particularly good horse, nor a young one, but it was the first Pawl had owned and he was pleased with the bargain. They still had two of the fleeces Bronwen's father had paid; the third was spun already. Pawl felt richer than he had for many years. They even had food for a day or two. Nevertheless he was not relaxed.

"Where did you get that embroidery?" he asked urgently, as soon as they were away.

She laughed lightly; the horse pricked its ears.

"I sewed it—I made it myself. Once I lived in gentle company. I learnt many things."

"Obviously," he muttered. "That was what she was so anxious about." It was a statement, not a question. She answered nevertheless; she felt she owed him that.

"She is to marry soon. She saw my design, I was working on it and she saw it. I told her it was for us, but she wanted it. Eventually I agreed." She made a little, dismissive, apologetic gesture.

"What did she offer in exchange?" Why did he feel so angry? What, he reasoned, could they have done with the embroidery if she had kept it? Hung it about the horse's neck?

"I can make another," she said contritely, though she knew it was not so, not really. The Arc of Dawn was the symbol of life and of a marriage; the River of Dusk was the symbol of security and the home. These things came into the pictures once, perfectly; after that they were copies only. "Materials, threads, clothes from her past to cut and remake," she answered his question. "She has much, we have little. Now she has something she could not have otherwise had, and we have more than before. She also let me keep the spindles I borrowed. Now I can spin the fleeces. I shall make you a tunic."

Pawl, strolling beside the horse, smiled slightly, despite himself. Then he raised his arm in salute to a figure in the distance, a shepherd driving a flock of sheep towards the place they had just left, and Bronwen laughed and waved too.

"That was your father!" Pawl exclaimed.

"It was," Bronwen agreed. "I wonder where he is going."

Summer passed and, as the days shortened, the distance to Myron shortened too. They left in their wake a trail of shorn sheep, mended fences, cleared ditches and gentle music. Bronwen spun and sewed and was content. Pawl was growing restless. He cut himself wood for new pipes and spent long hours whittling and paring, and made music that hung mistlike on the early autumn air, blending harmoniously with the melody of the woodland birds and the breezes and the streams. Music that would be lost amid the high rafters of the great hall of Myron, would be muted by the tapestries that hung about its walls, would be dismissed as mere pleasant tunings from a wandering shearer and would fail, as ever, the Piper's Quest.

Bronwen listened to his playing with joy and to his misgivings with sorrow. He was committed to the Quest; each year it drew him back to Myron and each year it sent him out again to search for better tunes, to hone his skills, to long for a finer set of pipes that were far beyond his reach.

On the morning when the outline of Myron crenelated the horizon, Pawl sat by their campfire and traced the intertwined shapes of the Dancing Serpents that adorned his wrists.

"They chase each other endlessly. No escape. So the pattern continues and the seasons follow in their rightful order. I am the winter snake." He sighed, fingering the blue serpent, "Chasing the Piper's Quest like winter follows autumn's tail."

Bronwen nodded, understanding. "Chase on," she told him. "I shall follow you meanwhile, as spring follows winter. The cold is forgotten then."

He smiled wistfully. "What are you making?"

The cloth in her hands was cut small, jade green and shot through with threads of cherry red.

"A gown," she replied. "From an old skirt given me by that farm woman. Green for happiness, red for good health."

"It is a child's gown," he stated tonelessly.

"Indeed. A mother's twofold wish for her child." She held up the tiny garment for his inspection. "Of course, it is not finished yet."

Pawl looked aghast. "We have no money, little food. I am going there"—he pointed vehemently towards their destination—"on a fool's errand."

She packed her handwork away. "I said it was a child's gown, not that we are having a child. Most of the skirt was badly worn; the good cloth was too small to do much else with."

"I am sorry," he muttered, after a heartbeat's silence.

"For what?" she asked mildly.

He rose to his feet and kicked the fire to ashes, saddled the horse and lifted her onto its broad back. "Sorry I can offer you no more than a fool's dreams."

———————— • ————————

The Piper's Quest lasted a moonphase, marking the end of autumn, when the harvests were gathered in and the animals brought off the high pastures to the valleys and farm barns, and the earth lay dormant, waiting. Then the pipers of Eral gathered at Myron and made music that would seep through the frost-hardened ground and touch the seeds of new life, bring ships safely home, and warm cold hearts and cold hearths.

Eventually they would be judged, and from their number one would be chosen and named The Finder. For The Finder, life would never again be the same.

———————— • ————————

Even Bronwen, used as she had been to genteel living before her return to her father's house, was overwhelmed by the splendour that was Myron. Yet, before long, the architectural grandeur and the ostentatious wealth of the city paled beside the beauty of the gathered pipers' music. It soared to the rafters, carrying its listeners' hearts. It soothed their cares and worries as it settled into alcoves and recesses. It elevated the lowly and reduced the mighty, so that all seemed in harmony. And Bronwen wept for the loveliness around her and for her husband, whose misgivings and premature sense of loss she at last understood.

Whilst Pawl renewed old acquaintances and practiced for his first recital, Bronwen began to learn her way around the maze of inner corridors and outer paths, and listened as much to what was said as to what was played, and watched.

There were many like Pawl amid the contenders—skilled but ill-equipped—and many others who but for their fine pipes would not have been there at all. Bronwen was not surprised by that discovery. She had learnt that life was ever thus.

Yet, there were some present who had the good fortune to be both skilled and wealthy, and it was from these that the final selection would be made, according to Pawl's somewhat gloomy predictions; those who had been there before would have been inclined to agree with him.

One such contender was Marika. She might have taken the title last year but for a spell of poor health which took the edge off her performance. The year before that she had taken part, but with low expectations, having just given birth to her baby daughter. This was her year, of that she was certain. She stood aloof from the crowd and practiced only in private—this year everything was going her way.

Bronwen watched the women pipers with interest, and the elegant Marika especially. She had thought at first that Marika, with her young daughter clinging to her skirts, was merely accompanying one of the contenders, like she was; some subtle quizzing had corrected that mistake: Marika was the likely Finder for the year to come, so the rumours suggested.

"Her music is her life," said one.

"She can afford for it to be," grumbled another.

"Always the most beautiful pipes—and new ones each year," sighed a third.

Bronwen smiled, hopeful, an idea forming. "She likes the best?" she suggested.

"She tolerates nothing less," was the reply.

No one would see Marika's new pipes until the Quest reached its climax, but Bronwen had seen the set Pawl coveted: blackwood and silver, smooth with age, bright in tone and not for sale, even if they could have afforded them. They belonged to Gloran Smithson, had been his father's and grandfather's, and on the first day of the Quest they put their owner into prime position and won for him the blue sash of First Quest Leader. Pawl played well; he was not placed. Marika was elected fourth and seemed unconcerned.

"Not her best pipes," whispered an admirer.

"Not her best playing," scorned a detractor.

Bronwen heard the exchange but took little notice, she needed to be with her husband.

"Tell me about Marika," she suggested, when he had come out of the dark mood she had found him in and was prepared to eat and speak again.

"Marika? She is very wealthy. She lives nearby, I think. Certainly her music master comes from the city; her pipes are made here. What do you want to know?"

His tone said *Why do you want to know?*

She answered the question he had asked aloud. "Was she rich before she wed?"

He laughed, and she wished that someday he would laugh, or even smile, simply with pleasure. "You of all people should know that without asking! Of course she was rich." He turned away.

"As rich as she is now?"

"No!" he snarled, and rubbed his face distractedly. "I'm tired—can we talk of something else?"

———————— • ————————

The air was cold but the sun shone brightly in a clear sky and Bronwen, well wrapped in a thick woolen shawl, sat outside in the garden, sewing. The child's gown was finished, all but for the design over the heart square. The other three quarters of the breast panel held minute representations of the Bird of Joy, the Tree of Learning and the Lake of Tranquility. Bronwen heard footsteps approaching and started to wrap her few remaining threads to pack them away.

"Surely you are not leaving the heart square!"

Bronwen glanced up with a slight smile. Marika was standing behind her, looking over her shoulder, uncertainty in her eyes, and admiration. Bronwen ignored the gown but left it in her lap. Marika was alone, giving Bronwen a subject for conversation where she had feared she might have none.

"Where is your little girl?" The child was always at her mother's side except during performances, and mother and daughter walked in the garden daily.

"With her aunt. She has a slight fever."

"I am sorry," Bronwen said sincerely, sensing the mother's concern. "It must be worrying; she is very young, I think."

"Two years. She is not very strong," Marika replied.

Bronwen could see she had spent a sleepless night, and moved her satchel to give the other room. Marika sat down beside her while Bronwen absently fingered the cherry-red lights in the gown.

"Red for good health," Marika said ruefully. "Who is it for? Why have you left it unfinished?" She reached over and smoothed the fine cloth, and Bronwen, who had been waiting for that moment, turned her head away to brush an unbidden tear from her cheek. She knew what she had planned to say, planned to do. Everything had fallen into place as if it were meant to be: she had traded her marriage picture for the materials to make this gown, and she knew that she could persuade Marika to trade a set of pipes for it, pipes Pawl could make real music with. Yet parting with a marriage picture was one thing—she was not searching for security, Pawl had no home, had promised her none—but to give a heart gown away, that was something else again. Pawl may have reacted with horror when he thought she might be having a child, but one day she would need more than a wandering shearer's life and a yearly pilgrimage to Myron. Even with good pipes, how many years might it take him to achieve the Quest? The best pipes in the world could be no guarantee. Bronwen knew that, of all the many things she wanted, what she desired most was a child of her own. She was prepared to wait but when the time came she wanted it to have the robe she had just made: the Robe of Life.

"It is for no one as yet, thus it cannot be finished."

Bronwen's heart sank as she recognised the expression that stole over Marika's face, she had seen it in the farmer's widow over the Hill when that woman had first seen the marriage token Bronwen sewed.

"Not for a child of yours, then? Do you mean to sell it?"

'Yes—for the right price,' Bronwen meant to say. Instead she said, "I think not. I hope to have need of it one day. May your little girl be better soon."

And she left the garden, and Marika sitting alone on a stone bench wanting a baby's dress as dearly as she wanted the Piper's Quest.

———— • ————

Pawl played even better that day and won some favourable comment, though nothing else. Marika was distracted and fell from her high placing. The black-smith's son regained the prime position and earned a purse of silver coins. The contest was into its eighth day.

Marika approached Bronwen that evening after supper. They were in the great hall and Bronwen was studying the tapestry hanging over the doorway —the wedding gift to the Master of Myron and his new wife, from their over-lord, the Ruler of All Eral, who would attend the final days of the Quest.

Bronwen would rather have continued with her appraisal than deal with Marika's need. She turned down the offer of a bolt of sky-blue silk imported from Tesk, a second horse, a purse of silver. The child's gown was beyond price. Finally Marika bowed her head slightly, seemingly acquiescent, obviously disappointed.

"Is that your husband?" she asked, watching Pawl approach and be way-laid by a heavily-built, bearded man. "He has much talent," she continued casually, when Bronwen indicated that he was. "A pity he has only inferior pipes. Should you desire it I will trade you a set of mine for the gown. If your answer is still no, I will not raise the matter again, but maybe you would con-sider it?"

Bronwen closed her eyes. She had resolved not to ask. But to refuse the offer—how, in good conscience, could she do that? Opening her eyes she saw Pawl's strained expression across the hall; he wanted to be away, alone with his frustration.

"Maybe," she whispered. "Let me think on it."

"Tomorrow morning?" Marika pleaded.

Bronwen hesitated just for a moment. "All right. You will have an answer in the morning."

———————— • ————————

Pawl was quiet that night. He lay down on the thin mattress provided by their host and pulled a woollen blanket, which Bronwen had woven, over himself. He pretended to sleep.

Bronwen unwrapped her sewing and conjured a vision of Marika's little daughter, Rosa. Not focussing her attention, she let her hands select threads without reason, and worked the first image that came to mind, surprised at her choice, for the child was delicate and quiet.

Beyond their window the broad crescent of the moon hung amid pale stars, muted by wispy clouds. Bronwen sat, cross-legged, beneath the casement and doubted her decision. The lightning flash filling the heart square was surely not for Rosa. Had she been untrue when she assured Pawl they were not expecting a child? She looked at him and allowed herself a faint smile. He had relaxed and was actually sleeping.

———————— • ————————

Bronwen assumed she would meet Marika in the garden, as before. She waited in the bower, sheltered from the driving rain, and steeled herself to say, that, despite Marika's kind offer, the answer had to be no. To bolster her resolve, she had gone empty-handed, leaving the little garment in her sewing bag under the bedcover.

Time passed, the contest was about to resume and Marika had still not shown. Almost relieved, Bronwen rubbed the cold from her hands and rose, intending to go to the hall and listen to the playing. Only when her hand was on the latch did she realise that she was at Marika's door instead.

The room beyond the door was rather different than the one she shared with Pawl, which was little more than a sleeping alcove with a small window. There were servants, dressed better than she, attending to their duties with quiet competence and barely suppressed concern. Bronwen guessed the cause of their unease and her resolve crumbled. Recalling the days when she, too, had servants to command—though admittedly far fewer than Marika—she gave directions to her room, a description of the garment to be collected, and where it was to be found. She left without seeing Marika.

———————— • ————————

Pawl had gone to the hall without waiting for Bronwen to return. He listened with admiration to Sareb Delver, the bearded man with whom he had spoken the day previous. A mood of resignation stole over him and he felt better for

110

it. There was no reason to think this year might be different from any other, and he knew from past experience that when he accepted that fact he could begin to enjoy the music for its own sake.

He felt better still when he saw Bronwen walking across the room towards him.

"Each day I wonder if you will still be here."

They were the first words he had spoken to her since the competition yesterday.

She was glad he did not take it for granted that she would be.

Three pipers performed before she felt something being pressed into her hands. Marika, smiling, moved away. It was her turn to play next and murmurs of inquiry were already circulating as to her whereabouts.

The pipes Bronwen held were in no wood she recognised. Honey-red and hard as iron, they were bound not with reed, as were Pawl's, nor with leather or bronze, as was common, nor with silver, as were the smith's son's, but with gold—or so she took it to be, for she had never seen gold before, only heard tell of the precious metal found far beyond their shores.

They did not hear Marika play. Bronwen pulled Pawl away, took him outside to give him the pipes.

"What did you give for these?" The question was ungracious but his smile, for once, was genuine.

"Nothing—they are a gift freely given," she replied, with mock severity. "Go away and learn to play them. The noon break is soon; you have little time."

Pawl returned just as the afternoon session began. Marika had played brilliantly—Rosa was over the worst of her illness. Come the final days, according to her admirers, she would astound all with an even greater performance, from even more exquisite pipes. Bronwen had no opinion on the first matter and knew better on the second. She knew something else—the symbol of the lightning was for little Rosa, after all: two years ago, at the time of Rosa's birth, autumn in Myron had reluctantly given way to winter after days of furious storms. Bronwen felt unaccountably relieved and, as she told Marika later, if lightning was the symbol of tempestuous character it was also the sign of genius. Marika was not unduly troubled as to what it indicated; only one thing mattered: Rosa was going to be well.

Marika took the third sash, her playing inspired by her daughter's recovery and her wish fulfilled, but among the leading contenders was Pawl, playing pipes he had never held before that morning, feeling the stir of a genuine hope in place of an unobtainable dream.

Pawl's elevation improved his mood and secured him a place in the last stage as the moon reached three-quarters full. Most of those passed over stayed at Myron to listen, nowhere else to go. As the year turned to its coldest it seemed that life was centred around the Piper's Quest.

On the night of the full moon, Bronwen dreamt of a great forest of huge honey-red trees, tall and straight, rising higher than the eye could see. Trees with gold-green leaves, hard and pointed, like spearheads. Trees with amber, clear as sunlight, seeping from their bark. All was gold and green, bright as morning.

The next day, while the rivers of Myron lay under a solid layer of ice, Pawl took the sash of seventh Quest Leader. It occurred to him that he almost wished Olber Stoson were there.

Three more times in the course of the competition, Pawl regained the prime position and earned more silver than he had ever seen. If he was even more single-minded than before Bronwen did not blame him, yet she looked forward to the spring, whatever that might hold.

By the time the Ruler of All Eral arrived at Myron, the moon was in decline, and the tensions among the remaining contestants were almost palpable. There were twelve left in the Quest and, of those, six were considered likely candidates for the title of Finder. Marika seemed to harbour no regrets in having parted with her best pipes, nor in having given them to a man who now posed a real threat to her ambitions.

Bronwen, caught up in the excitement, began to wonder what life would be like in Eral's seaport capital, where the Finder would go after the Quest was achieved. By night the trees in her dreams grew broader and taller—she feared they were telling her that she really wanted to be in the forest, not at the coast. Awake she had no firm opinion on the matter.

Pawl, meanwhile, tried just to live from day to day, tried not to speculate on a future still so tenuous, tried not to grasp at hopes too fragile to hold. Not that he could imagine what life would be like if he were to prove successful in the Quest. He had never met the Finder of any previous year once they had left Myron, no one spoke of what befell them once the year of their victory was over, maybe no one knew. One thing seemed certain: they would not return to the life they had left.

———————— • ————————

The final day of the competition seemed the coldest day of the year. Pawl, unable to sleep, rose long before the feeble winter sun. The water in the wash bowl was crusted over with ice but he washed as well as he could, shivering.

"Come back to bed!" Bronwen scolded. "It's dark yet."

"I was concerned I would disturb you."

"You have disturbed me, now come back to bed."

He needed no more encouragement than that and stayed there, glad of her warmth, until the low, sullen gong sounded: in the dining hall the morning meal was prepared.

Pawl refused to go near the laden food trestles, taking only a cup of hot milk. Time hung heavy. He knew he had to be patient. The twelve remaining contestants had to play before the final decision was made. He would be fifth to perform. Already his heart beat faster than normal.

Marika had drawn to play first, a position she relished, which Pawl would have loathed. She played with the same pipes she had used throughout the contest, yet her recital that day surpassed all her previous performances, holding her audience spellbound.

Bronwen thought it sang of winds billowing in sails, of seabirds soaring effortlessly over the waves. She felt an ache when the music faded, and a pang of guilt.

Gloran, the blacksmith's son, had taken the place immediately prior to Pawl's and, unlike the three before him, gave a performance to rival Marika's. Bronwen was reminded of her early childhood, when the Finder had come to their farm and played for their harvests. The memory warmed her but, unskilled in music as she was, she would not have presumed to choose between Marika and the smith's son.

Pawl could not consider the merits of others' performances either, if for reasons other than his wife's. Gloran's final notes signalled the start of his trial. Moments later he was stepping up onto the dais and moistening dry lips. Just as he could not afford to think of those who had gone before, neither could he think of those who were judging. He stared into the middle distance, at a memory of grassy banks and fruit-laden trees, and played as if he were alone in the sheep pastures of his youth, before he had ever heard of the Piper's Quest.

Bronwen knew that it was not merely biased pride that told her Pawl's playing transcended anything she had ever heard before, for it could have quickened the buds on the trees and the seeds in the ground long before their appointed time. It sang of the great trees of her dreams, the trees from whose wood his pipes had been cut, and it sung of the spring she yearned after, for, while he played, spring slipped into the winterbound halls of Myron.

The Ruler of All Eral smiled as the Master of Myron leant over and whispered something to him. Bronwen saw the exchange and saw also the rapt expressions about her.

Pawl finished.

For an instant there was total silence, and then cheering such as Bronwen had never heard, led by none other than Marika. Bronwen frowned, puzzled, but put the matter aside to congratulate her husband.

"That was for you," he told her, as he held her briefly.

There were still seven to play.

"Fourth place–Sareb Delver." They had come back into the hall, the judging complete. The moment of truth had arrived. Sareb Delver a silver miner from the south coast, was cheered onto the dais.

"In third place–Gloran Smithson." A not unexpected result, and well received.

"In second place–Pawl Shearer, and–The Finder–Marika of Myron!"

Bronwen's heart missed a beat. She glanced quickly over to Pawl, but his face was unreadable. Whatever he felt, he composed himself enough to take Marika's hand in a gesture of goodwill before joining Sareb and Gloran on the dais. Marika followed him to take her place, amid the applause of the gathered company.

———————— • ————————

The Piper's Quest was not a competition to discover the most talented musician in all Eral. If it had been, it could have been decided in a day. Rather it was exactly what it claimed to be–a Quest–undertaken by the pipers of Eral, one of whom would be successful, would be named The Finder. The greatest obstacle facing the contestants at the outset of the Quest was the fact that they had no idea what it was that they were searching for.

Pawl walked alone, alongside one of Myron's twin rivers, absorbing the truth regarding the nature of the Quest–and the reality of his failure.

He had left the celebrations taking only a question with him, a question put to him by Bronwen: had he wanted to be the best piper in Eral, or had he wanted to be The Finder?

Until that day he had assumed that the two were actually one and the same. The Ruler of All Eral himself, had dispelled that misunderstanding, had given him a gold ring of High Favour, and had caused Bronwen to ask the question that was now troubling him. He understood, as well as one who was not chosen as Finder could, that the Quest that year had been for one in tune with the sea: with the tides and the fish shoals, the ocean winds and currents–that was Eral's need. His music was that of the forest and the field. "Losing" in the Piper's Quest meant failing to find rather than being bettered, and he had not found the songs of the ocean in his music.

When Pawl returned to the hall, he found Bronwen speaking quietly with Marika, in whose arms was little Rosa, dressed in a green and cherry-red gown. As Marika turned to accept congratulations from the Mistress of Myron, Pawl presented Bronwen with two tiny white flowers.

"I discovered them by the river, struggling through the ice. Too soon–they came to their fullness too soon."

She breathed in the delicate perfume of the blossoms, "Yet their roots remain. They can flower again next year. It may be that the climate will be kinder then," she suggested.

"Yes, it may be," he agreed. "Though we shall not be here to see if it is so."

Bronwen felt the relief flooding through her; she linked her arm through his. "And where shall we be?" Not that it really mattered.

"North of here, the Kauri grow." He smoothed the honey-red wood of the pipes hung about his neck. "I thought we might buy a few sheep, build a house, settle there, at least for a while. We shall still be poor, yet with time, who knows? The timber there is the best in the land, the ground beneath the trees rich in amber. The grazing is good. We have a horse, you have your spindles, and perhaps I can make you a spinning wheel. It will not be an easy life—"

"Can we go straight away?" she interrupted him.

"Tonight?"

"Well, in the morning."

———— • ————

They travelled all day, eventually finding shelter in an abandoned cottage. Myron was behind them, out of sight.

"What are you making?" Pawl asked, coming in with his arms full of firewood.

Bronwen glanced up from the small pieces of sky-blue silk on her lap. "A gown," she said. "In blue for safety; sky hues for broad vision."

"A child's gown," he stated, in tones that clearly said: *Another child's gown!*

"Yes." She waited. He put more wood on the fire. "Are you not supposed to remind me that we are still poor, our future still uncertain?" she asked mildly.

"Why? You know all that. Anyway, I have learnt a lot since last time, including the folly of jumping too quickly to conclusions."

"Last time was different," she pointed out.

"How so?"

"That time I was merely using up old material, I was not preparing for the birth of our own child."

And the evening rang with the pure sound of joyous laughter.

About The Author

Belinda Mellor describes her work as mythopoeic-fantasy. She has two novels published, which explore the relationship between humanity and nature, and is working on a folklore-inspired YA novel about faerie changelings. When she is not writing, or editing other people's writing, she is to be found pottering about her lifestyle block (mini farm) or else planning something sociable, as she lives in an area where people still "make their own entertainment." English by birth, Irish by choice and a Kiwi by adoption, Belinda and her family are currently happily settled in New Zealand.

For more information, visit silvana.belindamellor.com.

The Spider and the Darkness

Russ Linton

Editor's Note: Is there anything more inspiring than a young woman mired in a hopeless situation who takes charge of her own destiny rather than waiting for help? Chalk this up as another victory for the self-rescuing princess society.

"*Things* live down there." Blind Old Jai wagged a finger directly in front of Kaaliya's face as if he knew right where her nose was. "Terrible things the ancient priests, the Murti, were waiting on to come and fill their empty altar. You mustn't seek that place."

Could she really be the only one that wondered what the darkness was like? Daylight from the surface world could only penetrate so far and the deeper one went into the Pit, the closer one felt to slipping under that smothering cloak. Sometimes, she wanted nothing more.

She looked up from the rope bridge where the two of them sat, up through the opening of the Pit many spans above her. Light burned in like their own personal sun, netted by a crisscross of bridges. It was a clear day. No mist, no curtains of water from rainy season floods pouring over the lip. The cave mouths and decorated facades of the cliff dwellings surrounding them stood out as empty voids against gray walls. The clamor of busy households was a hushed whisper echoing strangely from the depths.

"I've seen the empty altar," Kaaliya whispered. "It's a stone dish, polished and smooth, with a hole in the center. The hole runs down into the pedestal, down past where anyone can see. And there are paintings on the walls. Old and peeling like dead skin, but you can still see them. Mountains growing on the clouds and blue people without faces."

Normally she wouldn't have told anyone about her exploration of the forbidden ruins, but Old Jai was different. Before he'd lost his sight he'd seen more of the world than anyone in the Pit. They'd come to an agreement of sorts where they traded story for story—a kind of currency she didn't mind, and an escape from the dreary confines of her world.

Rarely were these trades even, for she never felt she had good stories to share. She'd been saving the one about the temple, unsure how he'd react. He had yet to answer and she wondered if she'd gone too far.

Old Jai's pearly eyes widened. "You know the temple is a taboo place," he stated.

"I know," she said, avoiding those eyes.

Carved into the far cliff side, the dilapidated temple's imperfections were hidden at this distance. Cracks in the aging relief melted away and only the standing pillars were visible, not the toppled ones that littered the ground. Those priests had been the first to live here ages ago. Worshippers of a forgotten god. Or a dead one, Kaaliya wasn't sure. She'd broken taboo and climbed through their lost sanctuary. Seen that empty altar.

She'd seen every habitable part of the Pit though she'd never fully explored the surface world. Her father forbade her from wandering too far. He often visited the towns and villages outside but rarely returned with anything except the men he traded her time with.

"Don't you tell anyone," Old Jai finally said, "but I've seen a taboo place or two myself." Kaaliya couldn't help but smile. "You've seen trees, haven't you?" he asked.

Though she'd only ever seen them in her imagination, she nodded, then remembered to say, "Yes."

She always had to remind herself the old man was blind. His tales of the outside were so vivid, so real. Jai had only been forced to seek the sanctuary of the Pit after an illness cost him his status and his sight. A giant sinkhole in the lush pastures north of the hill-covered Paharibhumi, the Pit housed the dregs of society. Their human cast-offs and trash and those, like her, unfortunate enough to be born here.

"Around the mountain city of Cerudell," Jai continued, "the trees grow so straight and tall they brush the bottoms of the clouds. So close together, they clap their trunks in the slightest breeze." Old Jai raised his arms, rigid, and slapped them together in lazy motions. "There, on the edge of that frontier city, is a troll hut."

"Troll hut?"

"It is a dome, like the great rooftop porches of Stronghold or the mud dwellings of the Ek'Kiru, only this dome is woven from the roots of the earth."

"You mean roots of the trees?" Kaaliya had only imagined what trees were like, but she knew they were plants. Plants had roots, not the earth.

Old Jai wagged his finger again. "The earth," he said decisively. "The troll hut, Redburl's Realm, is taboo. Many fear the trolls, a mystery of the wild spaces of the world beyond."

"What are these trolls?"

"Harmless creatures who speak in riddles and take the form of plants. They keep to their own domains and are nothing to be feared."

"Domains? Like the troll hut?"

Old Jai nodded.

"So, you've seen a troll before?"

"Kaaliya!" A voice broke the spell of Jai's story and she tensed, her eyes darting toward the opposite cliff. She knew the small, irregular doorway that was her home—the lintel slanted at an off-angle she'd long since memorized. Her father stood there, calling. She hopped to her feet and the bridge shook.

"Thank you, Jai," she said and hurried across the bridge.

"Take care of yourself, Spider," called Jai, watching her, she knew, with those all-seeing eyes.

She made it to the path quickly and turned toward her home. Her father stood there, arms folded and a satisfied look on his face that she knew meant work. Her stomach fluttered and she steeled herself.

"Go fetch some water. We have a visitor tonight."

"Yes Father," she whispered. She hurried down the path and her mind wandered into the darkness again as she ran.

Even this far away the defect was obvious. How far down did she need to be before the doorway to her home became just another hole in the rocks? She dangled her feet over the ledge into inky darkness and the promise of one last place to explore or escape.

Lost ages ago, a priest had rigged an old winch and bucket to collect water from a spring that fed into the black. No one else came here anymore. Too far out of the way along unmaintained paths of soft boards and frayed bridges. When her father sent her for water, this is where she came.

Usually she came here alone. This time she'd brought a friend. Or rather, been followed by one. She didn't want him here right now, but she couldn't find the words to explain why he should've gone home.

"Damn, it's stuck!" Shailen stood behind her at the winch which was spooled with a worn rope, swollen and fuzzy like a caterpillar.

"Well, fix it," she called.

He leaned on the winch, stringy muscles hardening under his skin. Before long his arms went slack. "No use. We should try another."

If Shailen lived in one of the surface cities from Old Jai's stories, like Stronghold or Cerudell, he'd be swollen and fat like the old rope. He was lazy, always trying to find a shortcut. Today he'd followed her to the bottommost spring bucket only because he liked to walk behind her. When they were younger, he'd been a loyal companion, but since they'd both come of age she could sense there was something else keeping him at her heels.

She wished he didn't have to change like that.

Kaaliya rose and stretched, her toes gripping the edge. The complex mix of alarm, indecision, and enjoyment in Shailen's face was at least entertaining. If he had to change, no reason she couldn't have her fun.

"You should get away from the edge," he said. She could tell he wanted desperately to move to her but was too scared.

"What kind of a Pit dweller are you?" she chided.

"One who isn't a spider," he replied.

Spider. She'd always liked the nickname. As a child, she'd drop in on neighbors in the most unsuspecting ways—showing up on their porches by hopping down from above, or scaling sheer faces and scrambling over the edge like a beast clawing its way up from the depths. The women would scream in mock surprise, "Look! Look at the size of that vicious spider." They'd point to the weave of bridges above and below. "I should've known better than to make a home in your web," they'd say. They'd call to their husbands to squish her and instead, they'd bring her a treat. A bowl of goat's milk or piece of candied ginger if she was lucky.

Like with Shailen, things had changed. The women no longer called to their husbands. Instead, her father called to the men and she, she dreamed of what lay in the black.

"I think I can see where it's wedged," she lied.

Shailen inched toward her. "Leave it and we'll get water elsewhere."

"Pretty sure I can reach it."

"Come on, there are better places to get water. Safer," called Shailen.

Kaaliya left the ledge and walked over to Shailen. "Don't worry about me." She kissed his cheek and his eyes glowed in the dim light. "Just be ready to pull me up." Then she disappeared over the side. How hard could following a rope be?

She'd made her way down several body lengths before Shailen's face appeared close to the ground, one hand gripping the rope. "Be careful," was all he could manage to say.

She looked at the smooth spot on his cheek where she'd kissed him and where blood still flushed his sandalwood skin. She hadn't minded it. So different from the scratchy faces of the men her father brought home. She cast her eyes down into the dark and didn't look up again.

Before long she reached the bucket. The rope handle had hooked on a chunk of stone jutting out from the wall right along the bucket's path. She could hear the spring trickling from the wall only a span below her. Odd that the bucket had never caught here before. Shailen's luck, she supposed.

A few quick tugs on the winch, maybe a re-positioning of the guide rope, and he could've reeled the bucket in. She clicked her tongue and slid the handle free. Water sloshed inside.

Only half full, the Pit's window to the surface world was reflected as a small white disk floating on the satin surface. She stared into it, an odd symmetry against the walls of the bucket. A crisp blackness floated over the disk and she felt sure a lid had settled over the Pit. She almost gazed into the light above to check.

But the floating shape was too real, too substantial. Closer than the reflection of the opening. She steadied herself against the wall and reached into the bucket.

Between her fingers she held the stem of a leaf. Shaped like a spade, she could see green in the meager light. She twirled it from side to side in wonder.

It was common for surrounding villages to leave things at the Pit's rim or toss them into the black. Many things cluttered the upper ledges, beautiful and vile, useful and wrecked. Some were offerings from an aging group of believers. Some were secrets never meant to be found. The worst she'd seen was a broken form no bigger than her forearm. Rotted flesh around thin bones.

One thing she knew for certain the open pastures around the Pit didn't have was trees. She ran the stem between her fingers.

"Are you okay?" Shailen called from the ledge, his shout thin and distant.

"The bucket's free," she replied, her eyes on the leaf.

Water trickled down her arm where she gripped the cliff face. That was strange. She probed the edges of her handhold. More water trickled out.

"Grab on, I'm going to pull you up," he shouted.

The crevice where she'd wedged her hand began to spray. The rock that had blocked the bucket's ascent shot from the wall, a geyser behind it.

She clawed with her hands and set her feet. The leaf plunged into the depths, snatched by the cascading water. She'd be fine as long as the footholds stayed stable. Hands were for balance, she told herself. More water gushed down her arm and she pressed against the wall in the chilly eruption of the spring.

She tucked her chin to her chest. Her heart hammered and with every breath she fought to swallow only air. She needed to move. It was the worst thing she could do, her hands still searching for that balance.

She squinted into the spray and saw the bucket creeping out of her reach. She could yell for Shailen to lower it.

Far above, she could just make out the crooked lintel of her home. She still wasn't deep enough. She stared into the dark and lunged.

———— • ————

The darkness didn't swallow her alive. It scraped and slapped and arrested her with bony arms until she slammed into a deep cushion that enveloped her in a choking cloud.

She sat up and sputtered. Gagged.

"Shit."

"Yes, that's right, Cave Daughter," said the darkness above the rush of water.

"Who's there?" Kaaliya called.

She inched forward, feeling with her toes. She'd fallen on a slope of some kind, the ground made of loamy packed earth. No, not earth. She knew the smell from the meager gardens grown in the upper houses of the Pit. It was guano. Shit.

"Very funny," she said, trying to sound brave. "Who are you?"

Even the opening to the Pit was blotted out in a darkness so pure it settled like a film on her skin and eyes. Slowly, a subtle buildup of light burned away the murk. Separate from the rush of flowing water, she heard a sound like the scuttling of feet. Shadows flickered overhead. Insects, maybe, or bats. She continued scooting down the slope.

Stark points of light winked into existence ahead of her, the source of the changing illumination. The points formed a loose cloud billowing out of a tunnel in the cliff wall. Water, which must have been from the spring, spilled into a stone gutter over the tunnel and diverted toward the base of the mound where she'd fallen.

She looked overhead where the shadows flickered. Not bats or insects, but leaves. A tree grew behind her, straight and tall, with a trunk that looked like it was made of bundled limbs.

At the heart of the glowing cloud forming in the tunnel, a figure emerged. It was short and broad, dwarfed under the high roof of the tunnel. Strange, sinewy gaps allowed the illumination to shine through where flesh and bone should have met.

The cloud coalesced and draped the creature, and in the brilliance she could see a face. Twisted branches formed the outline of a head. Gaps suggested where eyes should be and in them she caught a gleam of spotted amber, each black spot contracting under the glare. The branches tapered together at the crown and pushed upward to form spiraled antlers.

"So this is how we meet, Cave Daughter."

Her stomach clenched and she held her breath. The voice could've been an echo from the Pit, and the rumbling tone reminded her of Old Jai's warning of the things that lived here. But far from terrible, this creature appeared regal, robed in light and crowned by horns that rivaled the beauty of a moonstrider's.

"My name is Kaaliya, not Cave Daughter," she said.

"You are embraced by the bones of the earth." It tilted its head up. "And very fortunate."

She followed its gaze and saw the battered limbs of the tree reaching out over her. Picking out the path of her fall brought back each stinging slap and jarring crack of the branches. Fear tossed aside and her adrenaline sapped, her back and neck began to ache. Open cuts on her arms and legs burned.

"Who are you?" she asked.

"I am the root who pierces stone, watcher of the Elder's passing, who runs deep and forever in the void."

"You must be a troll," she replied.

"I am the Hollow One, if lies are to be spoken."

"Lies?" She stood slowly, groaning with the effort. "What lie?"

"Names. Words that seek to make us different."

She thought for a moment. "Some people call me Spider because I can climb better than most anyone. Maybe I *am* different."

The Hollow One raised its chin and gave a broken growl. It was laughing...she hoped. "Maybe you are. We are not."

"We? You don't look like me." Her bravery recovered, she moved toward the troll. "We're very different."

It reached out a hand. Clad in the shimmering light to its wrist, the palm and fingers were a twist of bare wood the color of bone. She searched for her fear deep inside, but it had completely vanished. She'd known rough hands. Dangerous ones she needed to guide with subtlety and distraction, counting the time until the knock on the door. Despite the harsh appearance, these were not those hands. She took it.

The troll traced her knuckles with a sharp finger. "Are these the hands that grip the walls when you climb, Spider?"

She nodded.

"Are they yours?" it asked.

"Of course."

"Where did you get them?"

"I was born with them."

"Ah, and they were spider hands then?"

"No, I learned to climb."

"So you are only what you become?"

"No... I mean, I don't know."

"You are what you were when you came here and before." It walked away from the tunnel, past the tree, and she followed, her hand clutched in the root-like grip. "The well is deep and you are always a part of her. There is no escape—only surrender."

She could see its eyes, sap in constant motion dotted with irregular spots, clenching and relaxing. It watched her and let go.

They were on another ledge, not at the bottom. She and the tree and the troll occupied a large shelf with more darkness below.

She stood at the precipice like she had so many times before. There were no shadows cast by the troll's light, only smothering emptiness. The troll and the light moved away and those depths stayed the same.

All she needed to do was to step forward. Surrender. It would work this time. She'd never have to leave her sanctuary.

"You will follow us," came the troll's eerie voice. "But you will wash first in the water." It said this not as a demand but a statement of fact.

Why should she listen to that strange little thing? She'd be happier in the dark. She thought of Shailen above and hoped he didn't follow. This was Shailen though. Fearful, cautious, he'd never come for her. He'd assume as she had when she let go that she'd been lost. Even Blind Old Jai, with all the things he'd seen and could still see, would think the same.

Yet she'd explored everywhere in the Pit, and the tunnel beckoned. She walked to the entrance and watched the clear water trickle down either side, diverted by the stone gutter. She cupped her hands under the stream and rinsed her scrapes and cuts. When she was done, she looked up. The opening to the Pit was no bigger than her palm, and the dwellings tiny blemishes on the rock.

She stepped into the tunnel and ran her hand along the smooth rock where the passing of the troll had left a luminescent coating. Light broke free from the wall under her fingers and floated toward her, condensing into a cloud. She opened her palm and let it cover her arm. A thousand tiny hairs prickled her skin, and the illumination bloomed.

She squinted into the gauntlet of light. Countless eyes stared back. Miniature crystalline spiders coated her arm, their bodies glowing brighter than the cave walls.

"Spiders," she said aloud.

Her voice filled the empty tunnel and even the splashing water behind her sounded far away. She half-expected the Hollow One to respond, but it was nowhere in sight. She raised her arm and made her way deeper into the tunnel.

The sides narrowed, the ceiling dropped, and soon she was stooping but she pressed on, feeling more liberated than confined. Deeper she went until the tunnel opened into a tall, domed chamber. There, the Hollow One sat in the center on a carpet of moss.

"Come."

She stepped lightly, feeling the soft squish of the ocher moss between her toes. Tentatively, she took another step. Her footing held, despite the constant sensation that she was walking on mist. The tiny spiders on her arm leapt into the air and floated toward the walls on hastily-spun strands of silk.

"Is this your troll hut?" she asked.

The Hollow One shrugged. "This is a hole in the earth. My hut. Yours." It gestured to the sparkling walls. "Home to the spiders as you call them." Amusement overtook its reedy voice. "They know you. This is good."

She rubbed her arm where the tiny feet had touched her. "What exactly do they know?"

"That you are indeed a spider. You may catch many flies. Though one may prove too large for your web." It patted the moss next to it.

Kaaliya sighed and sat. "So many riddles. Why is that?"

"Only truth is spoken here."

She settled into the moss and fell back without knowing she'd done so. Aching muscles uncoiled as she sank into the surface.

"I'm so tired."

"See? Only truth," laughed The Hollow One. It rose and moved toward the tunnel. She followed it with her eyes but couldn't find the strength to do more. "Rest. You have a long journey ahead of you."

"Mhmmm..."

The spiders scattered across the ceiling and dimmed. They did know her. In some strange way, they were connected. Like her and Old Jai, connected by stories. Or her and Shailen, connected by dual natures, like fire and water. Maybe she should have listened to his caution and not climbed down?

So far under the earth, her clothes soaked through, she should've been cold, but she wasn't. She felt...embraced. That was the right word. Isn't that what the Hollow One had said? She'd been embraced by the bones of the earth? It was a strange feeling, but she couldn't keep her eyes open long enough to worry about it.

———————— • ————————

"Kaaliya?" She heard her name whispered and a hand touched her shoulder. Her name came again and someone shook her. Shailen. "Are you okay?"

"You came?" she asked. She scrunched her eyes and rubbed her forearm across them. "How?"

"I'm sorry it took us so long," he said. "I tried to climb down..."

She looked at the dirt on his hands and saw the deep earthy stain on his thighs where he must have clung to the rope for dear life.

"But the rope, the bucket, it doesn't reach down here," she said.

"We had to borrow more rope."

We. Of course he'd run to the village and gotten others. There weren't many Pit dwellers who would bother tracking down a reckless girl lost so far below the inhabited ledges. She was surprised by the gesture, and amazed at Shailen's bravery. She started to thank him but then her heart dropped.

"Who did you get to help?"

She hoped it was Old Jai. What better person to lead her out of the darkness?

Shailen's eyes weren't on her but on the effusive glow of the ceiling. "Your father."

She sat up.

A torch lit the narrow tunnel into the chamber. She heard a thud, followed by cursing. Her father squeezed in through the gap and the constellation of spiders above retreated ahead of the greasy torchlight. Shailen shrank away, distracted as he watched the ceiling move.

The gap had been much too small, and she wasn't sure how her father had managed to get inside. A welt was already forming on his forehead. Dirt and grime skinned his hands and knees, and she realized how out of place that was on him. His smile, supposedly of joy and relief, was a leering glare in the dancing orange fire of the torch.

"My dear Kaaliya!"

The cushion of moss under her felt like guilt and she avoided his eyes. His hand reached out to pull her to her feet. She stood without his assistance and gritted her teeth at the pain.

"I'm so happy to have found you." He pulled her close with his free hand and she flinched. She kept her hands at her side and her head down, waiting. He moved her to arm's length. "I was worried I'd lost you like your mother. You can't leave me like her, dear girl."

Shailen tore his eyes away from the ceiling where shadow and smoke had replaced the glowing spiders. His curiosity shifted to concern as he read her expression. There were things about her she'd never meant for him to know.

"Are you hurt?" her father asked. He bent, inspecting her closely, the heat of the torch biting and the smoke stinging her eyes. Kaaliya looked away from Shailen as her father took inventory of the bruises and scrapes on her legs, then lifted her ragged shirt to inspect, finally ended with her hand in his, turning it over and over. "So much climbing has made your hands rough." He sighed in dismay. "Come, let's get you home."

Her father dragged her out toward the tunnel, the torch held before them. He continued to talk but she didn't hear. Her feet left the moss and fell on the cold and uneven stone. Her father had blundered ahead without noticing the change, but she saw Shailen pause and press his foot deep into the carpet one last time.

The tunnel, the ledge, they were both different in the fire's unsteady glow. Darkness hunted them from the fringes. When they exited the tunnel the tree looked sinister, clawing up from the guano mound like a hand from a grave.

"...firewood so close." Her father looked past her to Shailen. "A healthy young man like yourself, you should be able to gather it?"

Kaaliya stopped. Her father, still moving, yanked her arm and she stumbled out of the tunnel. His grip tightened.

"What's wrong?" He waved the torch toward where a fresh rope hung. Shadow crawled across his face. "Come, let's go home."

She shook her head.

He smiled, the corner of his mouth sharp points and his eyes flicking to Shailen. "You can't stay here, dear."

Shailen watched mutely.

"The boy will go first, eh?" Her father directed Shailen to the rope with a hard stare. "He'll then pull us up with the winch. No problem."

Kaaliya looked at Shailen and his indecisive hold on the rope.

"He can't do it alone. Maybe you should go first," she mumbled.

"The boy has help, dear. We had a visitor waiting for you. He's been very patient."

She shot Shailen a glance and he winced. He'd only mentioned bringing her father. Shaking her head, she swallowed back tears and understanding dawned on Shailen's features. She'd kept her business to herself all the years she'd known him. Never had she invited him beyond that off-kilter lintel.

"Maybe we should wait," Shailen offered. "Let her rest."

Her father dropped her hand and spun to face Shailen. "We have no time for rest. It's been one wasted night already, I *won't* lose another."

She tried to hide from Shailen's astonished look.

"M-m-maybe she's hurt?" More unexpected bravery from her friend, but he was pushing into depths he didn't fully comprehend.

Her father advanced and Shailen shuffled away from him further out onto the open shelf that held the tree. "She's made of sterner stuff than you, boy. She's fine, aren't you?"

Kaaliya nodded meekly.

"I don't—" Shailen's words were cut short. The slap was sharp, a crack that lingered in the impenetrable depths. The boy staggered and raised his hands as darkness welled up behind him.

"Don't talk back to me. Climb the rope."

"Please sir," Shailen wailed. "I mean no disrespect."

"You..." her father kicked the crouching boy and Shailen scooted away. Away from the tunnel. Away from the rope. "...are talking..." The man unleashed another vicious kick and Kaaliya stepped toward them, her tears flowing freely. "...not climbing."

"Stop!" she yelled.

She withdrew as her father eyed her with suspicion.

"Has he spoiled you?"

The absurdity of the question shocked her and she couldn't answer at first. "No! He's a friend."

"Well?" he demanded, turning to Shailen.

Any answer the boy might have given trailed off as he jerked violently backward, barely catching his balance. His groping hands, feeling their way along the ground as he scuttled away, had found where the shelf dropped into nothing.

"Tell me!"

Shailen's wide eyes moved frantically between the edge and her father. Unintelligible sounds choked from his mouth. The bravery that had escorted him down the rope was lost and his old fear gripped him.

"Please, no," she whispered, creeping toward the two, scared that her presence might upset the deadly balance.

Her father reached for the boy. Desperate, Shailen lunged for the outstretched arm. The two collided and her father swiped with the torch, battering Shailen's forearm and releasing a spray of orange sparks. The boy gasped, his attention focused on the yawning void behind him.

Kaaliya quickened her pace and the struggle continued, her father swatting and Shailen fighting madly to move away from the edge. The torch tumbled. Orange shadow dropped into the Pit like a dying sun.

"You little bastard!"

With the torch lost, the sounds were her only beacon. Muffled cries and grunts, rock scraping rock, wordless rage and protests.

Then a noise reached her she'd heard a hundred times before while scaling the sheer walls of the Pit. Instinctively, she froze as though she were the one perched on the wall and the foothold she thought secure had loosened.

A choked cry of alarm sounded and dissipated, like the retreating glow of the torch.

She couldn't move. Deep, solitary panting continued somewhere ahead of her.

"Shailen?" she called.

"This is your fault," her father's voice crept out of the black. "Now get up that damn rope."

Kaaliya turned and ran. She honed in on the sound of the spring that straddled the tunnel entrance and slowed, feeling her way around the corner.

"Kaaliya!" her father shouted. "Come back here!"

She moved faster. Behind her her father stumbled and cursed.

"Hollow One!" she shouted.

White light seared the walls. The only darkness was her own shadow made black and monstrous by the sudden flare. Spiders streamed along the ceiling and walls. She raised her arm and they spiraled down to sheath it, but they didn't stop there. Tiny legs tickled her shoulders and face. They cascaded down her chest and legs. Soon they'd covered her from head to toe.

Her father stood propped against the tunnel entrance, dazzled by the display. As his vision returned his mouth dropped open and his eyes shone like two swollen moons. She pointed a finger toward him.

"You killed him, didn't you."

"Kaaliya? Is...is that you?" he stammered, his false bravado born of cruelty shriveling. "He fell—it was an accident."

"Only truth is spoken here," she whispered.

"Come," he said, backing away. "We must leave this place."

She didn't answer. Instead, she reached toward him with an upturned palm. The spiders leapt at him in a coruscating arc.

Screams erupted from within the glowing mass where her father once stood. She shielded her eyes to see the spiders enshroud her father's face, burning brighter than she'd seen before, so bright the tree beyond the tunnel opening shone its bone white palm. She fled down the tunnel.

When she reached the domed chamber she collapsed on the moss, tears streaming down her cheeks. Her father's screams echoed from the tunnel.

"I want it to go away," she pleaded into the mossy patch.

"What, Cave Daughter?" The Hollow One rose from the moss next to her, the tiny fibers boiling like maggots around its bare form. "What do you wish to go away?"

"All of this. I should be the one in the Pit. Not Shailen."

"You will see beyond the darkness one day. Today is not that day."

Another scream echoed through the chamber.

"Are they hurting him? The spiders?"

"They know him for what he is, but the only wounds he suffers are his own fear."

"Make it go away."

"We will do more than that."

She began to sit up but it knelt and placed a hand on her shoulder. Knotted fingers pressed her into the moss. Fibers began to writhe and squirm along her flesh and she sank. Alarmed, she stared into the Hollow One's eyes—eyes she couldn't read. An expressionless mask. Eyes somehow like Old Jai's, in that they saw more than what this moment in time would allow. Into the ground she sank until the wriggling moss crawled along her cheek. She wanted to scream but could only hear her father's cries fading away, like Shailen's.

Soon, everything was dark. She could stay here, she thought. This was what she'd sought when she leapt from her precarious position. Nothing was lost or cast off in this place. Everything that was here, belonged.

———— • ————

Kaaliya came to under the sheltering boughs of a tree. In her wildest imaginings, she'd never conjured a tree like this. Thin, whip-like branches draped the ground on all sides. Beside her sat a leaf from the Hollow One's tree piled with edible roots. Next to this was a gourd. She picked it up and sniffed the contents—water from the spring.

She crawled forward and parted the branches of the sheltering tree. A blue sky bound by open plains greeted her. More of the tendriled trees dotted the horizon, and a road ribboned its way between them and off into the distance. A bird squalled, proud and powerful, and she squinted into the sun.

Returning to the protective canopy, she took up the gourd and drank then she nibbled at the roots until she'd cleared the leaf which held them. Picking the leaf up by the stem, she stepped out onto the road.

She took a few steps, those turning into long strides. Cerudell, Stronghold, all the cities and hidden places from Old Jai's stories awaited her. Taboo or not, she'd see them all and more. One day she'd return, rich beyond wealth, ready to repay Old Jai. Or at least offer a fair trade.

About The Author

In the fourth grade, Russ Linton wrote down the vague goal of becoming a "writer and an artist" when he grew up. After a journey that led him from philosopher to graphic designer to stay-at-home parent and even a stint as an Investigative Specialist with the FBI, he finally got around to that "writing" part, which he now pursues full time. Russ creates character-driven fantasy about unlikely heroes. He writes for adults who are young at heart and youngsters who are old souls.

For more information, visit www.russlinton.com.

The Dowager's Largesse

Jefferson Smith

Editor's Note: Adventure is a young man's game—or so you might believe if you let fiction be your guide. But the truth is, adventure can come to us at any age. And the older you are, the more annoyed you are likely to be when it does.

"Better grab your man there, before he chokes himself to death." Karsten nodded toward the back of the shed where another man lay sprawled against the wall. His unconscious form had slumped down lower on the slippery straw and the chains at his wrists were now wrapped precariously around his neck.

DaGuss turned to look and then nodded to the servant at his side. "Take our friend out to the wagon," he said. Then he turned back to Karsten as his tidyman dragged the captured thief out into the sunlight. "Can't allow him to escape us that easily," the fat merchant said with a chuckle as they passed. "Certainly not before I find out where he's taken my merchandise."

Karsten shrugged. "That's none of my concern. I've delivered him, as agreed. I'll be paid what I'm owed now and leave you to your...reunion."

The two men were sitting across from each other on musty bales of sawgrass in the middle of a small cow shed. Bright blades of light sliced down through the air around them, swirling with the dusts of mildew and rotting fodder. It had been a number of seasons since any cattle had sheltered there, which was why Karsten had chosen it for the exchange. A quiet location beyond the walls of Ruheen, sheltered against both weather and prying eyes. As a bounty hunter, he preferred to keep his face anonymous. You never knew when being recognized might spoil an otherwise easy warrant.

DaGuss sighed. "Why must you always be in such haste? Won't you at least join me in a little refreshment? There is another matter I wish to discuss, and business goes so much more pleasantly over a meal, don't you find?"

"What I'm owed," the bounty hunter repeated. "We'll finish the first job before there's talk of a second."

The merchant's gaze flicked briefly to a spot above Karsten's eyes and he licked his lips uncertainly. Men like DaGuss always seemed unnerved by the gallows mark on the bounty hunter's forehead. The noose-shaped brand was an all-too-real reminder of the Emperor's intolerance of those who danced within the shadows of his laws. As for Karsten himself, the scar was nothing more than a souvenir of his ill-spent youth, but that didn't keep him from taking full advantage of the effect it had on others.

Like now.

With a nod, the merchant reached inside the folds of his kaftan and withdrew a small box, offering it to Karsten with a flourish of his hands. "In payment of the debt that stands between us," he intoned formally. "Do you accept?"

Karsten took the box and flipped it open. Two jewels gleamed up at him, shimmering their yellowish light against the dark velvet lining. Phoenix stones, as they'd agreed. Karsten poured them into his hand and hefted them for a moment, then returned them to the box, closing it with a tight snap.

"I accept your payment," he said. "The debt between us is balanced."

DaGuss bowed his head once in solemn acceptance, and then broke into a smile. "Now, to other matters. Haroon! The food!"

Karsten watched in silence as the tidyman came back in bearing a wide tray laden with cakes and meats and cheeses. Why DaGuss had bothered to bring all that out here on horseback was something of a mystery, but if there was one thing about powerful men that never failed to amuse him, it was their perpetual need to drape themselves in theater.

As DaGuss helped himself to a handful of dainties, he began to talk. Typical grease words about how Karsten's reputation was known throughout the region. How often they had worked together. How rare a thing it was to find dependability among hired agents. How singularly talented DaGuss was at spotting it—and rewarding it. Wouldn't Karsten like to arrange an easier life for himself? It couldn't all be phoenix stones of course, not if he was on a full retainer, but he'd be well paid and...

The merchant interrupted himself in mid-sentence, his eyes shifting across the tray that had been set on a spare bale between them. Then he looked up.

"You've touched nothing," he said, a strained note edging into his voice. "Do you mean to refuse my hospitality?"

The bounty hunter sighed. Men like DaGuss lived on the veneer of delicate manners that they conjured around themselves, like a painted eggshell wrapped around the brutal core of their truer nature. To insult that shell would almost certainly be taken disproportionately, and to spill truth upon it, Karsten *had* been wondering lately about just how long he would be able to stay in this game. Wiliness and a reputation for ferocity would only protect a man so far. Sooner or later he'd run up against a hard enough case— or young enough—and he'd take his retirement on the end of a blade. He wasn't quite ready to hang up his own and take suck from the teat just yet, but it couldn't hurt to start listening more closely to the offers.

"I ate before you arrived," he said. "But I'll take the Empress if you've got any." That was safe enough. The merchant had more faces and angles than a cut gem and Karsten wouldn't trust the man to fall if he jumped from a ledge, but not even DaGuss would risk the Emperor's wrath by tampering with a bottle of the Dowager's famous brew.

The merchant smiled indulgently. "You're a careful one," he said. "I'll give you that." With a quick nod he sent his tidyman scurrying out to the supplies. "Happily, I anticipated your caution. So what will you have? The green?" Then he his eyes twinkled darkly. "Or will you try the gold?"

Karsten couldn't keep a look of surprise from his face as the servant came back in bearing two bottles on a tray, one of dark green, the other a smoky amber. Both were marked with the sigil of the Emperor, surmounted by the bird-in-flight emblem of his mother, known across the empire simply as "The Dowager."

He'd seen the green bottles before, of course. They were a common enough sight in way stations and kherabats—any place that might attract the poorer folks who could not afford a pint, or the braver ones who enjoyed the thrill of the old woman's gamble. He'd even chanced a taste of the green himself, on occasion, but the other bottle was little more than a rumor. Karsten had never even seen one before.

"The gold," he said, quickly, before his nerves could betray him.

For years afterward, Karsten would wonder what had made him choose as he did that day. Wanting to parade his courage in front of a liverless whelp like DaGuss was his usual conclusion, but the truth was that he'd chosen the gold because he thought he'd never have another chance to try it. Simple as that.

If DaGuss was surprised by his choice, he hid it well. "To the Dowager," the merchant prompted, raising his goblet and pausing.

Easy for him, Karsten thought. The man was drinking some fruity spirit or other. He'd never be fool enough to risk everything he'd made of his life on the Dowager's lottery. Still, at least he was gracious enough to salute a man who was.

"The Dowager," Karsten agreed. Then he snapped the fastener from the top of the bottle, matched DaGuss's salute with it, and raised it to his lips.

It was the last thing he knew.

———————— • ————————

A rough curry brush of hot, wet bristles scraped across his cheek and Karsten sat up.

"I'm awake," he said, as much to announce his own surprise as to fend off the creature that loomed over him. The shafts of light were slanting low now, almost horizontal, and they'd lost their earlier brilliance, which explained the poxing llama. With darkfall almost upon them, Babette had come in to see why they hadn't departed yet. She'd been with Karsten for many years and had proven herself dependable in all manner of weather and terrain, but she had one infuriating weakness.

"Still afraid of the dark, huh?" He reached up and scratched at the usual spot on the underside of her chin while she pretended to only tolerate it.

After a minute or so of llama maintenance, Karsten's head had cleared and he pushed her away gently to look around. DaGuss and his men were long gone, and no wonder. Karsten had seen a man lose the Dowager's dice-roll once. It had been an impressive display, with the unlucky sod flopping and jerking across the floor as the magery took hold. The band of cutthroats he'd been with at the time—hardened men each and every one—had all taken a measured pace back to watch in silent horror, each of them sharing the same thought: Could just as easily be me down there, performing that unexpected fish dance.

For Karsten though, it hadn't been the play of lights sizzling and sparking across Quinsha Half-Lip's agonized face that had left the biggest impression that day. It had been the unmistakable odor of magery lingering in the air afterward. The twin stenches of lightning and scorched meat, all for having picked the unlucky bottle from the pile. And that had all been for a green. No telling what horror steps he himself had just danced upon losing to the gold. By all chances, the merchant and his tidyman had been back on their horses and heading for the High Way before Karsten had even hit the straw.

Following her chin scratch, Babette quickly turned to her other great fascination: looking for food. She nuzzled hopefully about through the moldering floor sweepings and soon chirruped with delight. Apparently their host had not paused to pack up the victuals on his way out. When the llama's head came up, it was to show Karsten the unblemished pear she'd found. With a quick toss of her head, she sucked her prize in and began to chew noisily. But the fact that DaGuss was gone now didn't mean his larder was any safer than it had been earlier.

"Spit that out," Karsten said. The llama looked him straight in the eye. Then she swallowed. The bounty hunter merely shook his head. "Your burial," he said.

With the pear debate now concluded, Babette returned to her search of the floor, pushing past Karsten as she worked her way further into the shed. That brought her saddle bags forward, which reminded him of the disquiet in his own belly. It was an ache that had been gnawing at him since before DaGuss had arrived, but it wasn't pangs of hunger that drew him now to his feet. It was an emptiness of a different kind.

Her saddle bags did not seem to have been touched, but there was only one way to be sure. With a flick of his hand, Karsten twitched aside the old blanket that lay draped over the leather cases. Only then did he let out the breath he had not realized he'd been holding. The Sisters were still there, gleaming in their custom saddle sheaths. Of all the bad things that had ever happened to him—and being a bounty hunter, there had been more of those than he cared to count—the worst had always come when he had been parted from his Sisters. There had been no avoiding it this time—DaGuss would not have even set foot in the shed if he'd seen Karsten wearing steel, so he'd had to set them aside. But all that was done now and he slipped them easily out of their hiding place and back into the matching sheaths he wore on each hip. Much better. Of course, retiring the Sisters didn't mean he'd faced his employer unarmed.

Shooing Babette further into the shed to give himself room, the old bounty hunter knelt down between the straw bales. Three times he jammed a hand into the one he'd been sitting on, and each time it came out holding another of his smaller blades. Then he turned to DaGuss's bale, and then to two more, each time increasing his bright-edged collection. These were the Cousins, and he spent the next few minutes returning them to the various places on his person—and on Babette—where they would be most ready to hand if needed.

Only after he had completed the ritual and felt fully himself again did he finally raise his hand to his lip. The flesh there still burned and throbbed like a banked fire. He could remember taking that first pull. There had been a snapping tingle and a flash that had seared him like the sting of a drunken scorpion...and then darkness. Now the entire flap of meat below his nose screamed in protest at his probing finger, as though it had been flayed open to the air, although he knew it had not. He needed no vanity glass to tell him that a new brand now stood on his lip to match the gallows mark on his forehead. The Dowager's bird-in-flight. If the stories were true, it would remain etched there on his face until she herself removed it. Assuming he actually presented himself, of course, but that was a question for later.

Right now, he wanted a taste of the storied concoction that had cost him so dearly, and for that, he would need the bottle. His search, however, turned up nothing. He knew there was no chance that DaGuss or his men would have touched it. Not and risk a marked lip for themselves. Even so, it was not among the bits of cheese and meat scattered across the straw, nor wedged between any of the bales.

It was Babette who finally found it. As Karsten finished searching through the hayforks and scythes that lay in a jumble by the door, he looked around in frustration, only to see the llama tipping her head back, sucking hungrily at the upturned amber bottle.

"Here! Drop that!"

The llama's eyes rolled around to look at him, but she continued sucking greedily, daring him to do something about it.

Old straw is slippery, and it took him a moment or two to make his way to her, but that was all the time Babette had needed, and with a happy chirrup, she dropped the bottle at his feet just as he was reaching for it. Empty. Then she belched in his face.

Karsten glared at her. "Stupid beast," he growled, but no fish dance or lightning show followed, so he shoved the llama back toward the door and snatched the bottle up from the straw.

She'd found it at the very back of the shed, where it must have dropped down between the rotting straw and the rough boards of the wall. It had almost certainly lain there, undisturbed by DaGuss's men, exactly where he'd flung it when the magestorm had taken him.

"Woulda liked to have seen that," he muttered to himself. It seemed a shame to have endured one of the rarest—and most painful—spectacles in the modern world, yet not have even a hazy recollection of the experience as compensation. Now, thanks to Babette, he wouldn't even have a taste to remember it by. The green was widely regarded as one of the better ales anywhere in the Empire, but the gold was rumored to be a honeywine that surpassed even the rare elixirs served to Emperor Marghul himself.

Except the stupid llama had drunk it all, leaving Karsten nothing to enjoy but the price.

With the green, the Dowager's gambit was simple enough. Take one of the freely offered bottles, which were available nearly anywhere, and if you escaped her magecrafted summons, you could drink it down. No fee, no encumbrances. It was essentially free ale. Fewer than one of every ten thousand bottles was said to carry her price, so most folks were happy to take the risk.

For those unfortunates who did lose, the cost was a year in the Dowager's service at her villa by the sea, after which you'd return home and be immune to any further risk. So the beer would be free for the rest of your life. Not a bad proposition at all, which was why so many people risked it.

The gold, however, was a gamble of a different order. Nobody knew for certain how the rules changed, and the rumors about it were wild and varied, but two stories seemed consistent among them. There was no single-year limit to the time of service, and not one of the gold-bitten had ever come back.

Quite a price to pay for not even having had a taste.

Karsten raised the empty bottle now, and held it above his mouth, giving it a shake in the hope he might catch a last solitary drip, but it was as dry as winter air. Of course it was. Well, no use weeping over what the llama drank. Might as well get on with it. He now had one week to present himself at the Dowager's villa.

Karsten turned to throw the empty vessel back into the corner of the shed, but then he checked the movement, and after a moment to consider its dull yellow-brown shine and the face of the old woman molded into it, he stooped over instead and set the bottle on the bale. Leave it for the next visitor who found this shed. Let him see it and wonder who it was who had lost the Dowager's wager in this unlikely station.

"Damn me for three kinds of fool!" Karsten muttered as he backed the llama out of the shed. A trip to the Dowager had not been part of his plan. He cast a seasoned eye at the darkening horizon and took up the heavy travel staff he favored.

"Moon'll be up shortly," he said. "If the stories are true, I'd best make use of every hour." Babette turned her head to look at him and Karsten sighed. "Still, that don't mean you have to," he said. "Same offer as always. Come or stay. As you like."

Then he turned his back on the llama—and on all his supplies—and set out across the scrubby field toward the trail proper, leaving Babette to decide for herself.

A moment later, he heard the frantic swishing of her split-toed feet twitching through the grass behind him.

"Good decision," he called out. Then he dodged hastily to one side, narrowly avoiding the wad of llama spit that was her only reply.

Once again, they had an understanding.

———— • ————

For two days they journeyed along the wider roads and High Ways that laced the empire together like rivers of packed dirt, heading steadily south, toward the storied villa at the edge of the world. There were other travelers of course. Merchants and farmers mostly, taking goods and foodstuffs to one place or another, but folks tended to respect each other's space, so for the most part, Karsten and Babette managed to keep a stretch of roadway to themselves.

Privacy of the road, however, did not extend to the villages. Karsten had little patience for idle talk, but he purely loathed the inane chattermongers who seemed to hang from the doors and windows of every town he'd ever set foot in. Wizened little spiders waiting to spin news into power. A gold-marked pilgrim bound for the Dowager would bring them like a plague, quickly ensnaring him in their sticky little webs of gossip. So whenever a town or village loomed ahead, he would step down from the Emperor's road and strike out across whatever field path or cartway looked to steer the widest berth, and so far, Babette had always followed.

It was on one of those detours, after they had skirted past the broad sprawl of a fair-sized village, that Babette halted at his side and raised her nose to sniff at the air.

"We're not stopping for more stinkberries," Karsten muttered, which was the usual reason for these stops, but his senses were on alert now just the same. The field to either side of the path they were following was tall with wild grasses, but that wasn't where Babette was looking. Instead she was staring at the small grove of shrubs and low trees up ahead. The path vanished into its depths before emerging on the other side and climbing a small rise to rejoin the High Way.

"Bandits?" Karsten asked. He rattled the Sisters in their sheaths, primping them for the dance in case they were invited. But Babette trilled a low gargle in her throat that Karsten had always interpreted as "No, and you're an idiot for asking." With a grunt of irritation, she shoved past him, moving forward with her ears perked up. Karsten shook his head. She'd always been that way with him. Impatient. As though she had more important things to be doing and it was *he* who kept getting in *her* way. Stupid llama. He set off after her.

A few strides later, he caught the sound for himself. Cursing. It sounded like an angry woman. Karsten walked forward slowly toward the trees until he drew even with Babette. Man and beast shared a curious look for a moment, and then they continued forward together to investigate.

"Hello the cart!" Karsten called as they entered the little wood and the scene was revealed. It really was an old woman, apparently in some minor distress.

"Hello, yourself," she spat irritably as she wrestled with a large box. It was lashed to the bed of her cart, which was tilted wildly to one side, owing to the shattered axle. Two halves of a broken wheel lay in the leaves beside her. Beyond the cart, an old draft pony with a deeply swayed back stood in its traces, munching on the few shrubs it could reach.

Karsten scanned the scene cautiously. It wouldn't be the first time brigands had tried to waylay him with the hapless traveler trick, but he sensed nothing around them save for the regular hum of a thicket in summer, and now that they'd arrived, Babette seemed more interested in joining the pony at her shrubbery than anything else. She certainly wasn't staring toward any brigands hiding among the trees. Karsten turned his attention back to the old woman.

"Lend you aid, Mother?"

At that, the old woman turned a frustrated glare on him. She had a familiar look to her, the way all women of a certain age began to look alike, but this one's tongue was sharper than most.

"Ain't your mother, am I?" she barked, but then she seemed to catch herself and quickly ducked her head. "Apologies," she said. "I'd be obliged of another hand."

Trusting the llama to keep watch, Karsten went over to the shattered cart. It had seen its last journey, that was certain. By working together, he and the old woman were soon able to release the bindings and lower the box to the ground, but Karsten couldn't help noticing the agitated buzz that emanated from it whenever it shifted.

"Bees?"

"Ayup. Hospitality gift, I s'pose ye'd call it."

To Karsten, that sounded like a daft idea. A beehive? Then the old woman leaned into a dapple of light and he got his first clear look at her. He laughed, and the woman looked up at him quickly in irritation.

"You as well?" he said, tapping his lip. Like him, the old woman bore the Dowager's bird-in-flight below her nose, although hers was green. Rather than share his humor though, she grimaced unhappily.

"So she's caught herself two old fools then. Least I weren't fool enough to risk the gold."

Karsten shrugged. "If she wants an open-ended contract from a man with little end left to give, she's welcome to it."

"That's fine for you," the woman said, "but I've got plans for my days and I can't say I like having 'em interrupted. Not even for the likes of her." Then she seemed to remember her courtesies and gave the bounty hunter a curt nod.

"Pardon my troubles. Folks call me Gramma Wax," she said, nodding toward the beehive by way of explaining. "I thank ye for the loan of yer hand, but you've got the Dowager waitin' on ye. Best get on now, while the light's still good. Don't want to risk her lash catching up with ye before you reach her."

Karsten frowned. "I'm well ahead of that, Mother, but what about you? It seems you've been some time on your own trail and now you'll be set back even more. We can stay long enough to help unhitch your pony and get you up on her. You'll reach the villa in three more days."

The old woman shook her head in refusal. "Bees have got to come," she said. "It ain't proper to show up in a woman's home without some token for the hostess."

That gave Karsten pause. She was being indentured into a year of service and wanted to bring a gift for her new master? "But, Mother—"

"And there's to be no more 'Mother' talk. If you won't call me Gramma Wax, you can call me Meerah."

"Alright, 'Meerah' it is, but surely you see that your pony can't carry both the hive and yourself?"

The old woman nodded. "Ayup. Don't expect her to. She'll bring the bees and sundries. I can bring m'self."

"That's madness, woman! You'd be a full seven days getting there, and judging by your look, that'd put you under her lash for three. Am I right?"

Meerah looked away grumpily. "A whole week, you reckon?" Then she sighed. "That'd make it closer to five days o' the damned lash."

"That many?" Karsten said. "Surely you don't..."

"Don't what?" Meerah spat. "Don't have enough years left in me to be giving up five?"

"Better to live them, however many there are, rather than have them torn from you unspent. It'd be a damn piece more sensible to set the hive by and get yourself there the sooner."

The old woman set herself unhappily down on the crooked cart bed and let out a sigh. "No use in that," she said. "What difference losing a year to the lash or ten? Without my bees, I won't last even the one year of service." Then she looked at him slyly. "Truth to say, they's more'n just a gift. Runnin' a meadery as big as all that? That much honey needs bees, and any keeper'll tell you, ye can't never have enough different kinds of bees. So if I brings a donor colony with me, mayhap she'll let me tend 'em as my service for the year. That much I *can* do, and will do. Gladly. But without 'em? She'll set me to some unfamiliar work, and that'll be the end of me. So it don't matter how many years I give up to the lash. If the hive don't get there, I won't never leave."

Karsten could see the truth of her words written on her tired face. No matter which way he left her, he'd be consigning her to an early grave. Not really his problem, of course, but it didn't sit right just the same.

"Well, Babette? What do you think?"

The llama looked around at him from the elkshrub she'd been sampling and then stamped her feet. She was as eager to get moving as he was.

"I guess that settles the question," he said. "We'll just have to get you on your pony in short order then, Meerah."

"I told you—" she began, but Karsten cut her off.

"And I heard you," he said, enjoying the look of surprise on her face as she clopped her mouth closed. "Now, as I was saying, you'll ride the pony." Then he grinned. "Babette here will bring the bees."

The llama's head whipped up at that, her surprise a perfect mirror of the old woman's, and Karsten felt a warm glow bubble up inside. For the first time in a long while, he'd spoken the last word against two women in the same conversation.

———————— • ————————

Fortunately, Meerah turned out to be more capable than Karsten had feared, and so long as she stayed atop her bedraggled pony, she proved no more hindrance to their progress than Babette was with her willful sidetrips every time she caught the scent of stinkberry on the breeze.

For two full days they proceeded in a companionable fashion, sharing their provisions freely at meal stops, each growing a little easier with the other as their journey wore on. To pass the hours, Meerah told stories of her life as a bee granny, and even risked a few rather bawdy tales as she grew to trust him. By listening between her words, Karsten knew that there had been a husband some time back, and a child, but most of her anecdotes were from her life after that and he saw no point in digging into her pain.

Meerah, however, had no such misgivings, and asked him constantly about what she saw as the dangerous and exciting life he led. "Nearly as exciting as the tales of heroes."

That had caught Karsten unawares and he snorted in disagreement. "Only in the seeming," he said. "Most days are filled with waiting. Or walking, like we're doing now." Then he chuckled. "By that measure, you're as much in a tale of heroes as I've ever been. Can you feel the glory?"

Meerah laughed. "Depends," she said. "That what you call all this numbness in my tail feathers?"

"Ayup. That'd be it."

And so their conversation flowed, like two chance-met warriors in the common battle against time, touching on everything and nothing, but humorful just the same.

By the morning of that third day, the road had begun its long, slow climb toward the bluffs of the coast, and shortly after high sun—a full day ahead of the lash for Karsten, although Meerah would not say how long it had been for her—the bounty hunter and his companions found themselves approaching a well-kept villa overlooking the sea.

All day their road had wended its way between the endless fields, each another square in the enormous quilt that sprawled across the countryside for miles in every direction. There was a pattern to it all; one that drew you in, and up, toward the great villa that now stood before them, and then swept away beyond that to vanish at an abrupt line, leaving nothing in the distance except gulls wheeling in a sea-colored sky. Rumor said that the Dowager dwelt in beauty, drawing her power from the very edge of the world, but Karsten had always thought that to be just fanciful talk. Seeing this place though, he could see that it might be true, with both the beauty of the land and the power of the sea in perfect balance.

Power, however, made the bounty hunter uneasy, and he called to Babette, who reluctantly abandoned a clump of melonsuckle at the edge of the road and rejoined the rest of the party.

"Now, for one time in your miserable life," Karsten said, "you be quiet here. Keep that disrespectful tongue of yours inside your head."

In response, Babette stuck the tongue in question out at him and gargled some insult or other in llamish. Meerah laughed, having seen the two of them like this many times already, but Karsten could only shake his head.

"Be that way if you like," he growled, "but I can't shield you from the Dowager. If she orders you chopped for her breakfast pot, I'll ask for nothing save that she spare my saddlebags and the Cousins. I won't be able to protect your sorry carcass in a place like this, so I won't be trying."

Meerah raised an eyebrow at that, but if Babette was in any way offended, she gave no sign and strode confidently along the roadway beside him. The pony took no notice.

To either side, the fields that flanked them now on this final approach were bursting with flowers set in alternating rows. Mareslip, evening lily, melonsuckle, lovers' knot, all known for their honey production, according to Meerah. Karsten had never had much interest in decoration and ornament and wouldn't know a cactus from a cucumber, so he took her word as truth. Between the rows, at scattered intervals, laborers knelt or squatted in the soil. Some looked up as the foursome passed, but seemed entirely disinterested and after a casual glance, bent quickly back to their work.

"Probably get a few like us each week," Karsten muttered. "We're hardly worth a spit, I'd wager."

For some time now, he'd expected to be halted by the Dowager's guards, who would demand to know his purpose and probably wouldn't believe even the evidence tattooed to his lip when it was pointed out. At the very least, he would be disarmed, so he'd spent some time earlier that morning, rearranging the Cousins until he was confident that a few would be left undiscovered.

In the end though, there had been no sign of even a token force anywhere along their path, and to his utter surprise, they walked straight up the last stretch of road and right to the front of the villa itself, without so much as a grumbling nanny to stop them.

The old bounty hunter looked around, more out of curiosity than trepidation. What now? Meerah just blinked at him from the pony's back, clearly leaving the next move to him. With still no sign of anyone paying them even the least mind, Karsten shrugged and strode up to the large door, knocking on it loudly with his staff.

"Just a moment," called out a young voice from within. He could hear the shuffling of feet and the sound of something being shoved across the floor. Then a heartbeat later, the great doors swung out and a young farmwife appeared between them. Pushing a wisp of sweaty hair back up under her kerchief, she cast a quick eye over him, and then she looked up at Meerah.

"Found him then, did you, my Zah?"

That's when Karsten realized why Meerah had looked so familiar. He *had* seen her face before, or at least, a much younger version of it. Formed in the amber glass of the bottle that had brought him here.

Meerah was the Dowager herself.

———— • ————

"Come, let me show you my estate."

A stable boy had come and taken the pony away, although Babette had refused to be treated like simple livestock and now followed along behind them. The old woman led the way out from the main building and onto the field of flower beds. Karsten followed, as instructed, but he was still trying to reassemble the world and silence weighed heavily between them. The carefree conversation of previous days was now gone. Eventually though, even he could sense the strain of his silence.

"The Dowager's name is not Meerah," he said. Everyone knew that the wife of the previous Emperor had been Empress Ayini.

By this time, the three of them were standing in the shade of a dapple tree, looking out over the riotous color of the fields. Her fields. The old woman sighed.

"A travel name," she said. "Since the beginning, it has been my custom to observe each gold-bitten pilgrim unawares, though that is not possible if I am known. So when I sense the flare of a new mark being made, I make haste toward it, and seek to meet the pilgrim on the road, to be encountered just as you did. An old woman in some minor distress." Even the coarse speech of Gramma Wax was gone, replaced now by the measured cadence and tone of a woman long used to power.

"So it was a test then."

She shrugged. "A necessary one."

Karsten was still not sure what to make of the new situation, so he lapsed once again into the silence of his thoughts. Meanwhile the Dowager Empress walked him around the grounds. They took in the hives, the orchards, the brewhouse, the carpentary, even the stables. It was a complex and bustling operation, all centered around the production and distribution of the Dowager's famous libations. And everywhere they went, the faces of the workers bore her distinctive bird-in-flight mark upon their upper lip. For the most part, green birds, but one or two showed gold.

"Why necessary?" he asked, picking up the thread of her earlier comment. The tour had concluded and they were seated on a row of low crates behind the coldhouse, where Babette had found an unpillaged stinkberry shrub and was busy nipping its tasty prizes out from between the dagger-like thorns.

"What do you think the Largesse is for?" the Dowager asked.

There had been a time not too long past when Karsten would have felt he'd known the answer to that question. An old woman, deprived of the power she'd once enjoyed, had found a way to build an army of servants around her, once again ruling the lives of commoners. Maybe even having a bit of sport at their expense. But now he wasn't so sure. "Meerah" might not have been a real person, but she'd seemed a fairly earnest one, and his memory of that woman did not match the power-addicted old crone he'd always imagined.

"Servants?" he guessed.

The Dowager shook her head. "Independence, to begin with. My son was most generous when I first retired to this place, permitting me a large and capable household."

"But they were *his* servants," he said, and she nodded.

"Right, but there's more to it than just that." Across from where they sat, a field of blue-green shrubs that Karsten didn't recognize stretched into the distance. Among them, several heads could be seen bobbing up and down where green-bitten laborers worked their way along the rows. The Dowager waved a hand toward them.

"What sort of people take up my offer?"

That was easy. He didn't know any of the people here at the villa, but he'd seen plenty take the Dowager's wager over the years. "The desperate and the foolhardy," he said. "Present company included."

The Dowager smiled. "Perhaps it would be more generous to say that my gamble appeals most to those who have the least," she said. "Only, when they leave here, they do so after having spent a year learning new skills, new techniques, maybe even a new trade. They've been clothed and fed, tended if they're sick, they've met new people and been exposed to new ideas. Most return to their homes as very different people from the ones who left. Wiser, I hope. Healthier. Certainly more capable."

"Perhaps," Karsten conceded. "But that's only the greens. Some never go home." He meant the golds, of course. Like himself.

The old woman frowned. "True enough, but who is it who risks the gold?"

Karsten shrugged. "Adventurers, gamblers, and boasters, so far as I've ever heard."

"Just so. Most often it's the ones least inclined to work for their keep or contribute to their fellows. The leeches and wastrels. The cheats and charlatans." Then she cast a narrower eye over Karsten, taking him in from toes to eyebrows. "But sometimes," she said, "it's the brave."

Karsten barked a hoarse laugh. "Brave? Not me," he said. "I took a gamble and lost, simple as dirt. No bravery about it."

"You did not do it for brave reasons perhaps, but there is bravery in you. Along with other qualities I have seen. Qualities that I have been seeking, hidden among the foolhardy, for a very long time."

"And what, you think you've found them in this ribbon-winning specimen?" Karsten thumped his chest to emphasize his point, but he was still coated in dust from the road, and it rose up in clouds around him, making him cough. It was a deep, painful sound. An old man's cough. When it had passed, it took a moment for him to catch his breath, which left him feeling humiliated as well as old.

The Dowager, however, seemed undeterred. "Disbelieve me if you will, but I have taken your measure these past days and I believe you to be the man that all of this"—she waved her hand at the entire villa around them—"was created to find." Her eyes shone with the thrill of a long-awaited accomplishment.

"Once found, I had always meant to charge that man with a particular task, and by that mark on your lip you *are* mine to command..." Then the thrill in her eyes softened. "But having known you a little, I find myself uncertain. I must know that you will honor the task once I give it. I need more than simple coerced obedience. I would like your word."

Karsten had never wanted to spit more intensely in his life than he did now. Truth was, she was beginning to sound like a tinkerman pitching ill-gotten wares under a shine of talk. A man who tells you how special you are usually believes the opposite, and that probably served doubly for empresses. Still, how do you cry false on the Emperor's own mother? So Karsten kept his skepticism to himself. And his spit.

"What task would that be, my Zah?"

It was the first time he had referred to her by her proper form of address, and she frowned at the sudden change. "Actually, it is not so very much different from your chosen profession," she said. "Let us say that I would have you ride circuit in my name."

Karsten looked at her evenly. "Never heard of it."

The Dowager nodded. "There is no reason you might have. Not by that name. It is a very old custom. From the earliest days of the Empire. A singular honor for the courageous and the just. In those days, a few such men were appointed to ride about the land, empowered by the Emperor to hear disputes in his stead and to settle them, to seek out perfidies and abuses and stop them, to mete out imperial justice to any and all who deserved it, wherever they be found. Any place. Any person." She'd emphasized that last bit, but then her face grew somber. "Sadly, that tradition has fallen into ill repute in modern days, and for good reason."

"Yet now you think the Emperor would vest such power in me? On your word alone?"

The Dowager shook her head. "No. He would not. Although you've seen for yourself how badly it goes for the common man. They have no recourse, no court, no champion. It is I who would have you change that."

"Just without the Emperor's patent or power."

"Now that is an interesting point," she said. "Even as a young woman newly married to the throne, I had some talent for magery, and with little else to do between imperial beddings, I bent my curiosity to its study in my husband's private library. There I learned much that has stood me well in the years that followed, but there was one particular record that told of the founding magics of the Empire itself, from which even the Emperor's own powers flow, and in that record I discovered a most curious wrinkle."

The former Empress paused and looked up at Karsten, fixing him with her gaze as though peering into his secret self. After a long moment, she nodded to herself.

"You see, the mageries needed to consecrate a... 'circuit rider,' are granted only to one who sits the throne." Then her eyes began to sparkle and she leaned in close to whisper.

"It seems, however, that they are not rescinded when one steps down from it."

She might have said more, but at that point, the young woman who had greeted them when they'd first arrived came scampering around the corner.

"There you are, my Zah! Come quickly! There are visitors approaching up the avenue."

The Dowager frowned in irritation. "Not now, Seelia! This is impor—"

To his surprise, the younger woman actually interrupted her.

"I know that, my Zah, but the visitor... It's an Advocate!"

The Dowager's face ran cold. "What? Now? How could he possibly know?" She sat there for a moment, her gaze darting about as a hundred thoughts seemed to race through her mind. After a moment, she drew a deep breath, settling herself, and then she climbed to her feet.

"No," she said. "I will not be denied. Not after waiting for so long." She turned her defiant gaze on Karsten. "Choose now. Will you take this task if I give it? Once the bolt is loosed, my son and his mages will move quickly to smooth out the wrinkle that permits it. There will be no second chances."

"I hardly..." Karsten began, but the Dowager shook her head.

"Tell me yes or tell me no. Right now." Her voice was steel. The Empress herself. Ayini Zah, accustomed to unquestioning obedience. But there was something else. In her eyes. There he saw the Meerah he knew.

And she was afraid.

Karsten nodded. "Then I will serve," he said. What choice did he have?

———— • ————

"The candidate may approach."

After the Dowager's sudden departure the previous day, things had taken an unexpected turn. No sooner had she stormed off on the arm of her housewoman than a burly yard foreman had arrived in their wake to take Karsten under charge, putting him to work in what had seemed to be a series of pointless chores. Nothing more had been said about riding circuit or indeed about any official duties, so Karsten had simply held his tongue and done as he was told.

He did so again now and took a cautious step forward into the great hall, his eyes sweeping the scene around him. The Dowager was at the center of the room, lounging on a low divan, although this was an older, more severe-looking version of the woman Karsten knew. At the end of her bench, a fiercely orange-red cockatrice screeched once and then began to pick at a gobbet of meat gripped firmly between its talons. This was certain to be Vagesh, the Dowager's famed familiar and the model for her bird-in-flight crest. Of all the magical creatures that a mage could bind with to gain access to the mageries, the cockatrice was said to be the most powerful. Yet in all the Empire, Vagesh was the only one of his kind ever to have allowed himself to be bound.

If there was a focal point of the scenario however, it was neither the Dowager nor her familiar. Instead, it was the tall figure standing before them, dressed in robes of silk. He had been gesturing to punctuate some flowery pronouncement or other when Karsten had been marched in, but at the Dowager's interruption, the man's arms had folded curiously over his chest as he'd turned to see who it was she had summoned. Now his dark eyes locked onto the bounty hunter, like those of a raptor onto a hare, and a sinuous head covered in bright blue scales peered out from behind him with exactly the same expression. A wyvern, which signified that the man was powerful in the blood as well. The newly arrived Advocate, perhaps?

"I'd heard rumors that a pilgrim of gold had been seen upon the High Way," the man said with a sniff. "He doesn't look like much." The wyvern punctuated his declaration with a hiss of its own.

"You think not?" the Dowager replied casually from her divan. "I thought I might make a gift of him to Marghul. He's always going on about the constant drain of deserters in his army. Would an experienced bounty hunter not be of some use there?"

Karsten blinked. That sounded a long way from circuit rider, but he held his tongue.

"Bounty hunter?" the man brayed. "This one?" His face creased into a sneer of contempt as he peered more closely at Karsten. Then he turned back to the divan. "He looks a bit long in the lobes to be bringing trained soldiers to heel. Even runaways and cowards."

The Dowager smirked. "Is it really so hard to imagine, Xihara Baj? I'm more than twice *your* age and I brought *you* to heel." Beside her, Vagesh puffed out his chest and ruffled his feathers in defiance.

So, it *was* the Advocate. "Baj" was a title given only to those twelve powerful men appointed by the Emperor himself. And the crazy old woman was actually baiting one like he was some kind of carnival bear. If the man took offense though, he hid it well.

"Come now, Ayini Zah. We both know that with your mageries, this is not an apt comparison."

"Ah, but it is," she replied. "For I have sensed some small bloodtalent in the pilgrim as well." The Advocate raised an eyebrow at that, but Karsten went one better.

"That's poxing ridiculous," he muttered. Him? With mageblood?

Unfortunately, the Advocate must have heard, because the man whirled in a sudden fury, reaching back toward the wyvern with one hand and forward toward Karsten with the other.

"Silence!" he roared as a rope of brilliant light leapt from his outstretched hand. The end uncoiled in the air and wrapped itself tight around Karsten's throat.

Instinctively, the bounty hunter reached for the noose that now pulled tight around his neck, but his hands passed through it as though it weren't even there. The smell of lightning and singed leather enveloped him. Karsten quickly sagged to his knees, feigning weakness as he reached around to the back of his belt. The foreman had confiscated the Sisters of course, but he hadn't spotted the Cousins. Finding one of his steely teeth with a fingertip, Karsten plucked it from its slumber and drew back his arm, ready to let fly. Maybe he could cut the rope at its source.

"Hold!" the Dowager said, calmly, as Vagesh pierced the great hall with his cry, underscoring the authority of her command. The air of the room crackled with barely restrained power and Karsten felt his arm lock rigidly in place.

The Dowager turned to the Baj. "Release him, Xihara."

Feigning deference, the Advocate turned to face her, but Karsten couldn't help noticing that the magerope was still in place. Worse, the scene was beginning to sparkle with flashes of light and dark bubbles around the edges of his vision.

"But Ayini Zah," the Advocate implored, "this filthy pilgrim has dared impugn the House of the Emperor! He must die! And judging by the mark on his brow, it is a job long in need of completion."

The Dowager laughed. "He does no harm by expressing his surprise, Xihara Baj. After all, I had not yet told even him of what I had sensed."

Still the Advocate held his arm stretched out, fingers wrapped tightly around his rope of light.

The Dowager continued. "Imagine it, Xihara. See how resourceful he is. How determined. Even when facing those with power. Imagine what he will become when he is bonded to a creature of power. And how much more terrifying for that mark of the gallows he bears. Not just a Truant Hunter, nor even a Truant Hunter mage, but a Truant Hunter mage reclaimed from the gallows. An agent of Death himself! My gift to the Emperor. To be delivered to him by his most loyal Advocate of course."

At that, the Advocate's expression shifted, and the wrinkles of his fury narrowed into cold calculation.

"That would indeed be a gift of a different station," he said thoughtfully.

Karsten could actually feel the cold blackness seeping into him now, as well as see it, and he was glad he was already down on his knees. His hands kept clawing at the light around his throat, but he still could catch hold of nothing. Neither rope nor air.

Then suddenly, the one was gone, and Karsten felt the other screaming its way back into him. He heaved his lungs wider than he had ever stretched them before and pitched forward onto all fours, sucking air like a newborn babe first pressed to mother's milk.

Ignoring him, the Advocate lowered his arms and turned back to the woman on the divan, stroking the head of the wyvern at his side. "How soon will he be ready to travel?"

The Dowager gave a dry laugh. "So quickly you change your song, Xihara. No doubt the pilgrim would say he is ready to travel this very day, but we cannot send a mage to the palace unbound, can we? If he is to be my gift, he must bear a familiar of suitable breeding. Can you picture a mage at my son's Court with a hedge-pixie on his shoulder? Or dragging some mange-inflicted brownie behind on a length of rope?"

The Advocate's face blanched at the very thought. "N-no. Of course not, my Zah."

"Good. Then it is agreed. The pilgrim will be taken to my menagerie where he will bind a familiar appropriate to my House—a creature of suitable magic and stature for Court. Once it is done, you will then go to the palace, as my ambassador, and present him as a gift to my son."

"It will be done this very hour, my Zah."

The Dowager frowned. "You would have him face the menagerie so soon, Xihara? After nearly killing him? Do you really value the Emperor's property so poorly that you would let it die in the pens before the Emperor has even seen it?"

"No, my Zah."

"Good. Then let's give him till high sun to recover, shall we?"

"As you say, Ayini Zah." The Advocate bowed then, touching his brow to his fists in the formal manner. The wyvern, however, reared up behind him, as though to claim back any stature the Advocate might have lost by the gesture.

The Dowager chose to ignore the haughty familiar and addressed herself to the man. "Now that we have concluded our business, Xihara Baj, allow me to show you my private cellars. We have produced a most delicious arak that I believe you will enjoy."

With that, she stood up from her divan and hung a hand in the air, which the Advocate took in his own, and the two of them went out of the room together, chatting like old friends, each of them followed by their creatures, both magical and human.

Karsten felt a tugging at his elbow as the foreman tried to pull him to his feet, but he responded only sluggishly, still light headed and more than a little bewildered.

Mageblood? Familiars? What was that woman playing at now?

———————— • ————————

Following his audience, Karsten had not been assigned any further work, allowing him to "build up his blood for the coming ordeal," as the foreman had put it. Instead, he spent the morning at the stable, repairing his packs and giving Babette a good brushing down. So high sun found him—and Babette—standing at the fence of the Dowager's menagerie, discussing his options with the sun-darkened man who ran this part of her operation. A cheerful little fellow named Kimma.

"Dangerous? Ayuh, that's a certainty. Seen 'em take a man's arm off more'n once."

Even the wisps of Kimma's eyebrows seemed to know more about what was about to happen than Karsten did. They stood there waving and flailing in the air, just above the menagerie master's forehead, as though signaling to the helpless bounty hunter in some secret language of hair.

Together, the two men leaned against the fence of the creature pens, looking out over an odd assortment of animals that were all steadfastly ignoring them. A wyvern, two griffons, a unicorn foal with no mother at hand, and a dozen smaller creatures that he'd only glimpsed in the shadowed recesses of a small wooden structure, taking shelter from the bright morning sun. These were the seldom-seen creatures of whisper and legend, most of which Karsten had always believed to be more fanciful exaggeration than reality. Yet here they all were, gathered together for the Dowager's amusement. He watched as the wyvern arched its long tail up and over, almost touching its own head like a scorpion. Then it squawked a cry of defiance and squeezed out a massive rope of dung.

Yup. They seemed pretty real.

"So what am I supposed to do? Just go in there and try to ride one?"

Kimma laughed. "You could do. Save me the trouble of having to feed 'em today."

Even Babette seemed to find that funny, and she looked up from her effort to reach clumps of hay inside a rabbit hutch to give Karsten a mocking thump with her hindquarters. Had he not been ready for it, her shove might have actually launched him through the bars of the pen, but as it was, he merely staggered a half step forward.

"Well, maybe I should send you in there for me," he said, giving her lead a sharp tug.

"Not the stupidest plan," Kimma said, nodding thoughtfully. "They's pretty sniffy creatures at heart. Wyverns especially. Always willing to accept tribute. Shows 'em you see 'em as yer betters. Been one or two taken that way as I recall."

Karsten shook his head grimly. "That's all I need," he said, flicking a sidelong glance at the llama. "Exchange one creature who thinks she's my equal for one who thinks she's my master? Don't see how that improves my position."

Kimma shrugged. "Probably for the best. You let one of these beauties get airs in her head, won't be long afore you been demoted to food."

"Right. So now that we've settled how I'm *not* going to do this, any suggestions for how I *should* do it?"

The old man laughed while his eyebrows waved hello, goodbye, and how's your mother. "Musta seen a hundred fellas standin' where you be now an' I ain't never seen two of 'em try it the same."

"I'll not be getting much help from you then, is that what you're saying?"

"Ain't that I don't want to," the master said. "Could tell ya all kindsa things, make you think ye know exactly what to do, how to stand and whatnot." Then he shook his head. "But truth be that's the surest way I know to get ye killed—send ye in there all cocky like, s'if ye got a plan. Best thing is to tell ye the truth. Go slow, stay careful, and seize the moment what feels best."

Karsten stared out over the pens. "Any suggestion about which one I should choose then?"

Kimma looked him over. "Well now," he said. "Bein' a goldie, and bound fer Court, you'll want sommat grand. Pixies and mage-hens'd give ye the magery, but you'll be wantin' something fierce enough to cow even powerful folks. A beast that can look both generals and viziers in the eye and make 'em take a step back. Anything less and ye'll not reflect well on the Zah."

"So none of the timid ones hiding in the shadows, huh?"

"Right. One of the big'uns is all I can tell ye. Rest is up to you. So what'll you try?"

Karsten sighed and shook his head. This was utter madness, but what choice did he have? Better to get it over with now than to stand here and let the water take his belly.

"The wyvern," he said, handing Babette's lead to the smaller man. Then he climbed up over the fence rail and dropped neatly down inside the pen to face his blue-green adversary. She turned her horned head briefly to blink at him twice, and then looked away with complete disinterest.

Karsten took a step forward, feeling out the situation with a fighter's instincts. Then he paused and looked back toward the fence.

"If I get eaten," he said, thrusting his chin at the llama, "send her in after me, would you? I'd hate for her to end her days pining away all alone." Then he turned back to his business and stalked cautiously forward.

Behind him the creature master and his eyebrows laughed merrily.

———— • ————

"Hold still, dammit!"

Karsten put the needle between his teeth and reached out to adjust the saddle bag, realigning the polished glass that hung from it so he could see what he was doing. Babette belched her amusement, but this time she held still and Karsten was able to return to the task at hand, stitching the small gash below his eye.

"Stupid beast," he muttered, but even he wasn't sure which animal he meant.

"That goes double for you," Kimma said from where he'd been leaning against the stable wall. "Pure foolishness to tend your own wounds like that. Especially a face gash. That'll scar on ye, no doubt, so's you'll frighten little children in the middle of the day. Not to mention ruin what little chance ye ever had with ladyfolk."

"It's a test," the bounty hunter said as he continued to draw needle and thread through the torn flesh. "Of a sort. The day I'm conscious and can't pull my own stitch is the day I'll retire." In the glass he could see the little man shaking his head. "So what do you suggest now?"

Kimma shrugged. "Wanna try that griffon again? The second one? She seemed to almost tolerate ye there for a while."

In answer, Karsten turned and extended both his bared arms to show the network of cuts, bruises, nips, gouges and tears that he now sported. "It was that second griffon did most of this," he said. "And you think I should try her again?"

"Well, that was later. After she figgered out you didn't have enough mage-blood to hold 'er to yer will."

"Is that what happened?"

"I reckon. Never had a speck of it m'self, so I couldn't say for sure, but the Zah says ye got it, so I suppose ye must do. Some, anyrate."

"So I'm supposed to just whittle myself down to the bone on griffon beaks to prove her right?"

"Here, now!" Kimma growled. "Ye'll mind yer tongue about Her Lady-ship in my presence, or ye can do this by yer own self."

Karsten sighed and gave the last stitch under his eye a careful tug. Satisfied that the repair was clean and tight, he started gathering his supplies and pushing them back into the side bag.

"My apologies," he said. "I know even less about mage things than you do, but it doesn't seem like I can have much in me, does it? After what happened out there?"

The little man sucked air slowly through his teeth before nodding. "Ayup. I'll give ye that. Ain't never seen a man of the blood stood down by a glimmer bunny before. Not even a thinblood apprentice. Rabbits is the most timid creature goin'—even the magical ones. That's why they use 'em to train the littlest magelets when they blooms early. Harmless puffballs and full incapable of resistin' the bind, so long as ye've got even a hint of the blood."

"Then why did she say I have it?"

Kimma shrugged. "Who can say what she's anglin'? But she said it yest'day, did she? In the great hall?" Karsten nodded. "Am I right in guessin' it was her Dark self?"

"Dark self?"

The creature master glanced around the stable to be sure they were alone, but there had been nobody else through since they'd come in and the space was utterly empty. Even so, he took a step closer and lowered his head.

"You know. Dark an' powerful. Mean-tempered. More like the Emperor than her usual way. Ye follow?"

Karsten nodded. "Yes. Like that."

"Thought so," Kimma said. "It's on accounta the Baj bein' here. Xihara. Whenever there's folks come from Court, she puts on that... Well, not my place to be sayin', but ye seem honestly gold-bitten, no mistake. Ye'll either find out soon enough or ye'll be dead, so ain't no harm in telling, I s'pose..."

"Telling what?"

Kimma shrugged. "Well now, ye've seen two different Zahs, am I right? One spry and happy, t'other grim and frightful?"

"Exactly!" Karsten agreed. "What are—?"

"I'm gettin' to that," Kimma replied. "The spry one, that's our true Ayini Zah. The Bright Lady. Only, for reasons she ain't never set out, she don't want folks at Court knowing 'bout that side. So when they pays a visit, she puts on all manner of grim and queenly. The Dark Lady. A right bitchhound, ain't she? Wouldn't sit proper, though, her doin' that to an Advocate and him seein' her treat the rest of the household all friendly. So we go along. It's important to her, so it's important to us."

"What about making a gift of me to the Emperor? That part of her game too then? A feint of some kind?"

"Well, that I can't rightly say, but feint or no, one thing's for certain."

"What's that?"

Kimma shrugged. "Don't matter what she was planning to do with ye now. There ain't a speck of mageblood in ye to be doin' it with."

To that, Karsten had no rebuttal.

———— • ————

Following his total failure with the animals, Karsten didn't even get a second audience. There had seemed no point in belaboring a proven fact by trying again, so Kimma had sent a stable boy to the Dowager with the news while the two men went back out to await her summons by the pens. The bounty hunter was trying to coax Babette away from the wyvern's bedding straw when a cloud of curses and shouts went up from the villa. A moment later, the Advocate stormed out, surrounded by his attendants, clearly enraged by the lost opportunity to curry favor at Court. By the time the cloud of his road dust was halfway to the horizon, the yard foreman appeared at Karsten's side.

"You're to report to the bilgeworks at Qintarrah," the man said, handing the bounty hunter a small lacquered tube. "Give this to the yardmaster there and he'll fill some hole with you." He eyed Karsten narrowly. "Try to give her *some* value before you drown." Then he turned on his heels and stalked off to other more important errands.

"The great dam," Kimma said, drawing a hiss of breath through his teeth at Karsten's side. "That's a blow for certain. Don't often see a goldie sent there." For once, even the little man's eyebrows seemed unhappy, and they hung limply forward over his face like a pair of weeping mothers.

Karsten looked down at the tube in his hand, then he glanced over toward the villa. Maybe he should go have a word.

"Nay, there's no use in that," the creature master said, guessing the direction of his thoughts. "Once ye've been given yer task, talkin's done and it's time to get on it."

A sudden dull throb brought Karsten's hand up to probe at his lip.

"Right," Kimma said. "That'll be the new lash taking hold of ye. Ye'll have three days now to get up to the damworks, or start payin' the price for dawdlin', by the year. Best you see the kitchenwife fer yer victuals and get movin', while there's still light."

Karsten thanked the little man for his help and then turned to the llama. "Not much point in you coming on this one," he said, placing her lead in Kimma's hand. "The master here'll find you a good—"

But before he could finish, Babette lowered her head and plucked the end of her tether neatly out of Kimma's hand with her teeth. Then she dropped it over Karsten's arm.

Something heavy caught in the bounty hunter's chest for a moment, rising into his throat. He coughed. When it was gone, he put a weary hand on the llama's stupid, fuzzy neck.

"Still just as pigheaded as usual, are you?" She belched her reply and then nudged him toward the road with her head. Then she trotted past him and set off in that direction herself.

"Guess she's right," Karsten said to the little man at his elbow. "We've got plenty of supplies. No need to waste time in the kitchens."

Then, with a quick salute of his staff, he set off after his damn fool companion.

———— • ————

They made camp that night in a circle of old waystones. Karsten had set a small fire to heat their soup while Babette settled herself down beside it to be closer to the light. He had just pulled the kettle from the flames and set it aside to cool when Babette lifted her head and turned to peer into the darkness. A moment later, something stepped into view.

It was the sway-backed pony.

"Hello the fire," called a voice from the darkness.

"Hello the traveler," Karsten replied in the usual manner, but his heart was little for it.

The pony moved to one side and the Dowager stepped past, firelight dancing on her face.

"You travel quickly for a spurned pilgrim," she said as she lowered herself to the dirt at Babette's side. Correction. It was not the Dowager after all. This was Meerah again. Karsten dipped his mug into the soup and handed it to her.

"And you travel quickly for an old Empress," he replied.

They were quiet then for a time, each regarding the fire while flicking side-long glances at the other. Eventually, Babette looked back and forth between them as though urging one or the other to say something.

"I apologize for the deception," Meerah said. "But it was necessary."

Karsten nodded. "Can't say I know the first thing about courtly intrigues," he said. "Baj this and Zah that. Scraping, bowing, feints and double bluffs. Get's so a man's got to keep so many lenses, mirrors and lanterns hung about himself to let him peer in a thousand directions at once, that he can't just look at a thing straight anymore. So no harm. I'd've made a poor showing at Court anyway. Even if I had held a touch of the blood."

"It was never my intention to send you there," she said. "But make no mistake, you do have the blood. I can hear it even now."

Karsten snorted. "Did you bring another griffon to try me on? Maybe if you watch this time you'll believe." He jabbed his stick into the coals of his dinner fire and watched as it stirred fresh sparks up into the air.

"Give me your hand," Meerah said, reaching her own out toward him.

Karsten looked at her doubtfully for a moment and then shrugged. Setting his poker aside, he extended his arm and put his hand in hers. Her skin was dry and papery, but warm too. She ran her fingers over the rough calluses of his palm for a moment, then slid over to his thumb, wrapping her entire hand around it as she folded her other around his littlest finger. With a brief half-smile of apology she looked down. Karsten was just beginning to wonder what she was sorry about when white-hot pain lanced up his arm. With a cry, he jerked away, leaping to his feet. By the fire, Babette bleated in pain too, and struggled to get up to her own feet beside him.

"What did you just—?"

Meerah rose stiffly and stood in front him, catching his eye with her own.

"I told you," she said. "The deception was necessary. Xihara came upon us at an entirely ruinous time. I had to convince him that you were absolutely worthless, or he would have found some way to take you for his own. Even my own household had to believe it, because I cannot know for certain that he does not have a spy among them."

"Fine!" Karsten spat, as he tried to flex the tingles out of his arm. "But what did you just do to me now? I can barely feel…" Rage boiled inside him. "Corpses take me! This is my *throwing* hand, woman!"

Meerah clucked at him, dismissing him as a matron dismisses a boy with a scraped knee. "The feeling will pass," she said. "Though now that you have been sparked, you may find you have less need of a 'throwing hand.' "

"Sparked? What's that mean? Some kind of mage attack?"

"It means, you cantankerous old goat, that you *do* have the blood, and that I have just ignited it. For both of you."

Karsten looked at Babette, who was curling and twisting her upper lip as though she'd been stung. The old bounty hunter reached out to help her, thinking she must have caught a cinder from the fire, but the moment he touched her, the world around him hummed.

"What in the seven devils...?"

"Good. You can hear the Song," Meerah said. "Do you still insist that the magefire does not flow in your veins?"

Karsten lowered his hand, breaking contact with the llama, and the sound died away.

"For now, it will only come when you touch her," the Dowager said. "In time though, you will learn to sing even at a distance. As Hassep and I do." From the edge of the firelight, the pony whickered softly.

"The sway?" Karsten asked, and Meerah nodded.

"Like Babette to you, Hassep is my familiar."

Karsten raised an eyebrow. "What about the cockatrice?"

Meerah laughed. "Vagesh is an ornament," she said. With a flicker of light, the fiery bird was suddenly there, clutching at the old woman's shoulder with its powerful talons and preening, ignoring everyone and everything but itself.

"She is a glamor," the Dowager said. "A convenience for when I must play at being Empress." With a twitch of her shoulder, the bird of power vanished. "Can you imagine the scandal? The Emperor's mother bound to a common nag?" At her side, Hassep stamped a foot, affronted by the term, and Meerah reached out to stroke her neck in silent apology.

"But why me? Why now?" Karsten sputtered. "I'm too old for this. Bloodkin are found as children, raised with a lifetime of training, and you would put that saber in the hands of a monkey. An *old* monkey. No good will come of it."

"You've seen what comes of the usual training," she said. Xihara is known by his brother Advocates as 'the Soft Baj.' For what I intend, I chose a man, not a monkey—one of proven mettle—but sparking you was merely the first step. If you'll abide it, I intend now to set an even greater sword in that hand. One that has been needed in this land for a very long time. But I must know now. Will you still take up the task, as you agreed before Xihara's untimely intrusion¿'

Karsten was not fond of hasty decisions, but this required no decision. Even buffeted by all that was changing around him, he knew where his honor resided. "I've given my word," he said. "It is no longer mine to retract, even if I wanted to."

"Spoken like a man of honor," she said. "Now take Babette's halter."

Karsten grabbed at the lead that trailed below the llama's head. "So I'm supposed to bind her? How do I do that?"

To his surprise, it was Babette who answered, letting loose with the growl-throated yawn that llamas save for only the funniest situations. The Dowager laughed with her.

"Bind her?" she asked. "Are you really that dim?"

Karsten just stared at her as he reached up to rub Babette's muzzle with his free hand.

"Why do you suppose a full-blooded mage like yourself was unable to bind even a glimmer bunny?" Meerah's eyes twinkled with delight. "It was because you were already bound, and you have been for years. To her. It's not the mage who does the binding, you know."

While Karsten was busy puzzling that out, the Dowager reached up to place one hand on him and the other on Babette, and the Song erupted once more in his head.

"Hold fast now," she said. "I don't know what will happen when I do this." Then she closed her eyes. A moment later, they flew open again and she threw back her head, stretched tight by some unseen power as the sky shot through with arcs of color behind her. Karsten could feel the ground melt beneath his feet and flow upward through him, entwining itself into his bowels and around the vessels of his heart and setting fire to his hair. For a moment, he could even feel it coursing through his hooves and tail.

Then it was over. The colors faded from the sky, the roaring in his ears abated, and the tingling in his skin died away. With a solemn face, the Dowager released them both and stepped back.

"I name you Karsten, and consecrate you Baj, 13th Advocate to the Emperor Marghul III, and Singer of His Divine Song."

Karsten could only gape. "Baj?" he sputtered. "*That* is the circuit you would have me ride? You name me Advocate in some mocking jape, to be flung into the teeth of the most powerful men in the Empire?"

Even as he spoke the words though, he could feel the untruth of them. In the marrow of his bones and the fibers of his hair, something stirred. Not just a hum now, but a full-throated song. Rich and deep. Powerful.

It was the Might of the Empire itself, stirring within him, and the bounty hunter was humbled by it.

"I cannot do what you ask of me," he said. "Surely there must be another…" But the Dowager shook her head.

"It is done and done," she replied. "You heard my offer and accepted, twice over. What has been given now cannot be undone. You will ride the land and bring justice to those who seek it. Wherever they might be and against whatever foe."

"Whose justice?"

"Your own, of course, as was intended by the First Emperor himself."

Beside her, the pony whickered softly, and Meerah nodded. "Now you must go. My son will have felt this. His Advocates as well. They will be shocked for a time, uncomprehending, but by morning they will be here, and you must be gone."

Karsten gazed at her for a long beat, but eventually his shoulders slumped in submission. This was simply more than he could master. "Where would you have me go?"

"For now, anywhere but here. You and Babette need time to explore what has been given you. But then? Wherever your conscience takes you. You are Karsten Baj. You answer to no one. Not even to me."

"Just the Emperor," he said, but the Dowager shook her head.

"Nor him either," she replied, her eyes glittering with fervor. "I sparked you in the original way—not in the cowardly manner practiced by my son and his more recent fathers. In the days of the Empire's beginning, Advocates were true circuit riders, *selected* by the Emperor, true, but *empowered* by the Empire itself, with power even over him, if need be. It was the failsafe conceived by the First Emperor to ensure that even a corruption in himself could be cut from the world by any of the twelve honorable men he had appointed. His later sons, it seems, were not so noble of spirit and they soon broke faith with his intent, creating their own Advocates in shallow mockery of their original stature."

Still unable to accept the scope of what had been done to him, Karsten turned to his one last hope. The llama. If anyone knew him, she did. Babette knew him for the wretch of a man he truly was, and not the "noble spirit" that the Dowager had woven into her dream of justice. If he could get the llama to testify to the truth, then perhaps the old woman would listen.

"What about you then?" he said, looking at his fuzzy companion in the flickering light. "Stay or come, as you will."

Babette fixed him with her gaze and he thought she was getting ready to spit her opinion at him, but then, to his utter astonishment, she did the damnedest thing he had ever seen. Kneeling her forelegs low, she presented her flank to him.

Babette was inviting him to ride.

Karsten was utterly undone by the gesture and knew at last that he had been beaten. By both of them. There was simply no fight left within him. Unsure what else to do, he stepped forward and threw a leg over Babette's back, clenching his fists into her coarse wool to steady himself as she rose up. Even if he didn't agree with what had been done to him, the old woman was right about one thing. The Emperor and his Advocates could not have mistaken the ripple of what she had done here this night, and they would arrive by first light. Perhaps sooner. Along with half a dozen generals and no telling how many companies of Imperial Guards. Karsten no longer cared much for his own neck, but if the stupid llama was to survive the coming day, he would have to get her as far away from this place as he could.

Despair bubbled up within him as he looked down at the Dowager, her face shining up at him with a hope he did not share. "What have you done to me, you crazy old witch?"

The Dowager shook her head. "It is not what I've done *to* that matters," she replied. "It's what I've done *for*. For the people. For the future. For the Empire. In time, you will understand this. I hope." Then she stepped aside and Babette lurched forward, away from the campfire and its ring of protective stones, and carried them both out into the dark unknown.

The last sound Karsten heard behind him was a whicker from the sway-backed pony, to which Babette called back a curious reply—a sound that he had never heard her make in all the years they had been together.

It sounded like gratitude.

About The Author

Jefferson Smith is a liar of the first order. He has lied to kings and queens; he has lied to hobos and urchins. He has lied to the mightiest of the mighty and to the lowest of the low. He is probably lying to you now. But in every lie there is a grain of truth, and in every telling a bewitchment. So it should come as no surprise that Jefferson bends his talents to the one craft that reveres both the liar and the lie, weaving entire worlds out of falsity and invention, raveled up in strands of guile. He is an author, and you will not find his equal in any other sphere. Or so he keeps telling us.

For more information, visit creativityhacker.ca.

Theriac

Becca Mills

Editor's Note: Genre fiction often presents us with big evil and climactic confrontations, but in real life, the hardest battles are often the ones we fight with ourselves against our own beliefs and prejudices.

Callie wanted to wipe away the drip on the end of her nose, but Suzanne was right there—only two steps away. If Callie wiped, Suzanne would see. If she didn't wipe, Suzanne might not notice. Surely she was talking too fast to notice.

"Now, you may not know that Archie Davidman's been plowing Pastor Ezra's driveway since before Kingston was born," Suzanne was saying. "As a courtesy, you understand—Archie never would take a cent for it. But now that Kingston has the new business, Pastor Ezra says we should all be supporting him. He told the Interfaith Reading Group—d'you go to that? No? Well, he told them they should all be supporting Kingston. But here's the thing, the pastor himself never..."

The drip fell. There was no break in Suzanne's rapid-fire patter, but Callie saw her eyes dart down, following its progress.

"But then again," Suzanne continued, "there's the baby to consider. I know the pastor..."

Callie's eyes suddenly felt wet, despite the dry air. She blinked hard. How silly to cry over such a small embarrassment.

I'm just tired, she thought.

She went ahead and wiped her nose on the back of one of her thick wool gloves. That was better.

"And do you know," Suzanne was saying, "that Carly never stopped smoking the entire time? Why, in this day and age..."

Callie saw movement behind Suzanne. It was Twanda Sullivan, and she was headed toward the movie return slot. Callie murmured an apology to Suzanne and hurried over to intercept the other woman.

"Hi, Twanda."

Twanda startled. "Oh. Callie. Hi." She stopped, but her eyes strayed over Callie's left shoulder. She wanted that return slot.

Callie glanced down at the DVD box Twanda was holding. *Bride Wars.* She hadn't seen it, but that was no surprise. Most of the movies she watched were older ones.

She nodded at the box. "Did you like it?"

Twanda shrugged. "It was okay. Hey, listen Callie—"

"I know Big Screen is a great resource for the community," Callie cut in, "with a lot of great movies like *Bride Wars,* but I really think they should be a little more selective about the movies they carry. Don't you?"

"I guess, but—"

"People bring their children here. I don't think there should be smut on the shelves where children might pick it up."

"Well, sure, but—"

Twanda's body language was now trending significantly to the left. Callie could tell the other woman was about to make a break for the slot, so she rushed through the end of her spiel.

"I think the community should send a clear message that pornographic movies are not welcome in Dorf. Would you please consider signing this postcard and sending it to the owner? It says you'll boycott the store until they stop carrying unrated and restricted movies."

"Sure Callie, I'll take a look at that," Twanda said, stuffing the postcard in her pocket. "You have a nice day, now."

She edged around Callie to the return slot, then headed back to her car.

"Thanks for standing up for our community, Twanda!" Callie called after her.

Twanda didn't seem to hear.

Callie hoped Suzanne might've gotten bored and left, but the older woman was still standing there. Worse yet, she was quiet. A quiet Suzanne generally meant some advice was about to come your way.

"Callie," she said, "how much longer you gonna keep this up? You've been out here for months."

Callie shrugged, uncomfortable.

"Are you going to picket all winter long? It's gonna get mighty cold out here."

"I don't know. Maybe so. The Lord's work takes time."

"That it does, that it does," Suzanne said, nodding.

Callie knew her to be a person of faith. She'd sent her postcard in right away.

"But Callie, no one wants to see you get frostbitten over this," Suzanne said. "It's all well and fine to worry about others, but when it comes right down to it, it's their responsibility what movies they rent. If they want trash, they're going to get their hands on it one way or another, what with everything on the internet."

Callie shrugged again and looked down at her boots. They were all slushy, so she stamped them on the sidewalk.

She didn't want to get in an argument with Suzanne, but she just didn't agree. Maybe most people could make good decisions for themselves. Or make bad ones and be held accountable for them. But there were those who were vulnerable, who needed help. They should be protected. You don't turn your back on people like that. They're asking you for help, even if they don't know they're doing it.

Suzanne sighed. "Well, you take care, Callie. Bring some cocoa with you tomorrow, okay? It'll keep you warm, maybe put some meat on those bones."

"Good idea, Suzanne. I'll do that."

Suzanne smiled and headed into the CVS drugstore next door.

Callie watched her go, then turned. Another person was approaching Big Screen Video.

"Hi there, Mr. Cooper! Have you had a chance to look at that literature I gave you last week?"

Johnny Cooper shot her an annoyed look and hurried into the store.

Callie sighed and turned back to her card table.

I'll give it one more hour, she thought. Then she'd need to start her patrol. The pale winter sun was already high overhead, and she preferred not to search for demons after dark.

———————— • ————————

Callie spent the afternoon patrolling Frederick, which was the next town over to the west. She checked on the five demons she knew to be living in the area and managed to find three of them.

She also kept her eyes peeled for any new arrivals. About halfway through her patrol, she found one. Its true form resembled an elephant, but tiny—no bigger than a Shetland pony. It had disguised itself as a short, fat man with a cigar and a big boxy suitcase. A salesman, maybe. The disguise was only a half-working, so she could see both it and the demon's real body occupying the same space.

Years and years ago, when she'd first started seeing through demons' illusions, she'd found the double-vision disconcerting. She'd long since gotten used to it.

How many years has it been?

She watched the demon hurry down Frederick's main street and into an Italian restaurant.

More than a decade, certainly. Could it be as many as fifteen? *Yes*, she thought, counting back, *fifteen years and four months*. She remembered that first seeing-through all too well. It had been the beginning of a very bad time.

Once the elephant-demon had disappeared from view, she drove by the place to get the address. Then she pulled over and texted Theo Duff the demon's description and location.

Maybe he'd send someone to kill it, maybe not.

Callie never could quite understand why so many demons were allowed to walk the Earth for so long. Some of the ones in Frederick had been there for years. It didn't seem right to her.

She knew the organization didn't have infinite resources. Only one in a hundred thousand people were like her—blessed with the sight—and most of the blessed weren't fighters. That meant prioritizing. Making tough decisions.

Theo's predecessor, Graham, had explained this to her, and Theo said the same: sometimes there weren't enough people to handle it all.

Especially if there really *was* a war going on.

She'd heard that rumor, but she was skeptical. Surely the Lord wouldn't allow this precious world to be the demons' battleground.

Then again, the tsunami that hit the Gulf Coast—that had been strange. Very strange.

Callie shook her head. At least Dorf was free of demons for the time being. That was something.

The sun was setting by the time Callie turned left on Church Street and headed north toward her neighborhood. The shadow of St. Mary's solid red-brick bulk lay across the road, and a flock of crows was coming to roost in the church cemetery's biggest pine. Callie reached down to flip on her headlights.

As she did so, something caught her eye.

There was someone in the cemetery.

She was immediately suspicious. Until recently, a demon had lived in that cemetery. It had been a particularly frightening one—huge and furry, with horns and claws and big, sharp teeth. She'd been reporting it for years. John Williams had finally taken care of it in the spring. But perhaps another had come to take over the empty spot.

She slowed down a bit and studied the figure. It was at the north end of the church property, standing in the tall grass and small trees that separated the cemetery from Gil Jensen's farm. The figure was small and dark, but she couldn't make out more than that.

Callie drove on past, then pulled over, placed her field guide to North American birds prominently on the dashboard, and raised her binoculars.

It was a child. A child in an oversized dark coat.

Callie lowered her binoculars, quite surprised. What was a child doing out in a cemetery at twilight? It didn't seem right. She opened her senses. No sign of a working—whatever she was looking at, it hadn't shape-shifted to disguise itself.

163

So, it was just a child—one that was out too late, in her opinion, but that was neither here nor there. Parents will do what parents will do. She set her binoculars down.

Suddenly, that special place in her consciousness flexed, and Callie understood that she needed to get involved in this situation. She was a bit perplexed but shrugged it off—her blessing had dealt her much bigger surprises in the past.

"Lord, thank you for your guidance," she murmured and got out of her car.

The child was engrossed in something in the trees and didn't see Callie until she stepped off the sidewalk and her boots crunched in the old, crystallized snow. At the noise, the small figure wheeled around and bolted across the cemetery.

"Wait!" Callie called. "I won't hurt you!"

Without stopping, the child glanced back. Callie glimpsed a pale, frightened female face. Then the child tripped over a low grave marker and sprawled in the snow.

When Callie got to her, the girl was folded over her right leg, trembling. She was hurt and trying not to cry.

Callie knelt in the snow next to her. "I'm so sorry. Are you all right?"

"I think I hurt myself," the girl said shakily.

"Can I take a look?"

The girl wasn't well dressed, Callie noticed. She had the big parka, but no mittens. Instead of winter boots, she was wearing sneakers. Her jeans were soaked through with melted snow. It was much too cold for an outfit like that.

"What's your name?" she asked.

The girl didn't say anything.

Moving slowly, she straightened the girl's leg and began to roll up her sodden pants.

"Are you afraid you'll get in trouble?"

The girl sniffled and nodded.

"I promise not to tell," Callie said.

The girl studied her face but said nothing.

Callie smiled at her, then continued working the pant leg up. The girl's skin looked very red. She was on her way to frostbite.

"There's a cut—see? But not too bad. Mostly it's bruised."

Gently, she touched the girl's skin next to the injury, then froze. Callie could feel the girl's ability to work essence. And the girl could clearly feel Callie's. She jerked away and scrambled up, backing away.

"I didn't do anything," she said, looking panicked. "I haven't told anyone." A terrified sob escaped.

"Hush, child. No one sent me. I live here, just up in Pinecrest. I saw you while I was driving home. I didn't know you were one of the blessed."

The girl stood there, terrified but also clearly hesitant to leave. She looked lost and very alone.

What an astonishing thing, Callie thought. The blessed were so few. That tiny little Dorf should produce Beth Ryder and this child, as well... it was so unlikely.

An idea came to Callie. One that made her stomach lurch.

"Is Justine Ryder your mother?"

The girl hesitated for a long moment, then nodded.

Callie sat back on her heels, angry at herself. Why hadn't she thought of examining Justine's offspring before now? Justine was Beth's sister-in-law. She'd also turned out to be a demon. Any child she'd borne would be half-demon.

The child wasn't blessed. She was cursed.

Callie stood and began backing away, heart racing. She had no way to defend herself.

"Well, you'd best run along home," she said, trying to keep her voice even. "It's getting late."

The girl looked confused. Then despair flashed across her face, brief but profound. She turned and limped off through the snow, hands stuffed in her coat pockets.

Callie watched until the girl reached the southern end of the graveyard, turned right, and was hidden by the church building.

She swung around and hurried back toward her car. The cemetery suddenly felt alien and threatening. She knew she wouldn't really be safe until she was home, behind the protective barrier John had built for her.

———— • ————

Callie stood in her bathroom, wrapped in a thick white bathrobe. She'd gotten home and immediately showered. Her encounter in the graveyard had left her feeling cold and tainted.

She bent closer to the mirror and examined herself. She thought she could see every one of her thirty-four years. Her face had always been thin, but it was beginning to look a little drawn. Her hair was pale enough that the gray was hard to see, but it was there. There were dark smudges under her eyes.

She didn't sleep well. Bad dreams, probably. She didn't usually remember them, but she often woke up in the night with an uneasy feeling and couldn't get back to sleep.

Oh well, she thought, looking away from her reflection. *So I'm getting older. It won't do to be vain.*

She headed into the kitchen and heated up some tomato soup. As she ate, she thought about the Ryder crossbreed. Obviously, the situation had to be dealt with, but Callie really had no idea what to do.

The organization must be aware that Justine Ryder had a child, but no one had asked Callie to check up on it. Perhaps they didn't think the girl was old enough to be a threat.

Callie tried to remember how many children Justine had. More than one, she thought, but she wasn't sure. They attended different churches, so Callie had only met her a few times in passing.

Well, she would have to find out. Technically, it should be easy enough: so far as the residents of Dorf knew, Ben Ryder had been abandoned by his wife and was struggling to raise a family on his own. Calling on and offering help to someone in that situation was perfectly normal.

On the other hand, the thought of going into a house with multiple half-demon offspring terrified her. Callie knew that, among the blessed, she was considered extremely strong, but her gift wasn't useful for physical protection. She was defenseless.

She decided she'd better call Theo and ask for advice, so she finished up her soup and retired to the den.

He picked up on the first ring.

Callie liked Theo. He wasn't as strong as Graham, the last regional overseer, had been, but he seemed more trustworthy. She hoped he lasted a while.

After some initial pleasantries, Callie described her encounter in the cemetery and explained her concerns about how many half-demons Justine might have spawned.

After she finished talking, Theo was silent for a few seconds.

When he spoke, his voice was sad and quiet.

"Callie, these are children you're talking about."

"Yes, I know. I thought this one might've been ten or eleven."

"Twelve. Tiffany's twelve."

"Oh, okay."

Callie waited, suddenly unsure of herself. Finally, Theo spoke again.

"I sent Tiffany a birthday present in October. I knew Beth would want her to have something. I sent her a little silver locket with Beth's picture inside."

Then Callie understood. "You want to let the girl alone because she's Beth's niece."

"No," said Theo, sounding impatient, "I want to let her alone because she hasn't committed any crimes, and there's nothing wrong with her."

"She's a demon. Well, half, anyway."

"Callie, you know the rest of us don't think of the other world in religious terms."

She did know that. She'd heard the others talking often enough. She also knew, in her heart of hearts, that they were wrong. The other world was Hell, and its inhabitants were evil.

That the others misperceived things didn't bother her much. Whatever they thought they were doing, they were good people doing the Lord's work. Good people came in all types and had all kinds of beliefs. What mattered was what they did, how they acted in the world.

She didn't think it would be tactful to get into all that with Theo, so instead she said, "Yes, I know," and hoped her tone got across the fact that she continued to disagree.

Theo got it. "I tell you what," he said in a conciliatory tone, "why don't you do some closer surveillance of the family. Find out how many children there are and how much of their mother's difference they may have inherited."

"Is that safe?"

"You touched Tiffany. How much strength does she have?"

Callie thought back. "Not a great deal, I don't think. Less than you or Kara. Like Zion, maybe."

"Okay, so that's moderate strength. She's young, so she's still coming into it and won't have learned any workings. Unless she has a highly-focused offensive gift, I think you're pretty safe. She may not even have manifested a gift yet."

"How can I be sure, though?"

"I guess you can't. But you do want to do something about the situation, right?"

Callie recognized the attempt at manipulation and resented it. At the same time, Theo was right—she'd called him because she thought something should be done. But did it really have to be her?

"Don't do anything you're not comfortable with, Callie. The situation will keep until I can get up there."

"When are you coming?"

"Definitely not 'til after Christmas. Maybe mid-January."

More than a month. That was surprising.

Maybe the rumors of war were true. Something like that might keep Theo tied up.

It'd be dangerous for him too.

"All right," she said. "I'll think about it. I can at least keep an eye on them from a distance."

They said their goodbyes, and Callie hung up.

The call left her unsettled. She thought a nice happy movie might take her mind off things and rooted through her DVDs, but nothing caught her eye. So she puttered around the house for a while, then got in bed.

Sleep was a long time coming.

---- • ----

"You done with your holiday decorating yet, Callie?"

Callie turned around, hands full of pamphlets. It was Suzanne.

"Oh, yes. I don't do a whole lot, since it's only me."

"Well, I'm on my own these days too, but I can't seem to break the habit," Suzanne said.

"Won't you be visiting your son's family for Christmas?"

"Yes, but only for a few days. The rest of the time it's just me and my plastic Santas."

Suzanne did favor Christmas lawn ornaments. She had at least a dozen out in her front yard this year, not to mention the glowing reindeer team and sled up on the roof. Her house was Christmas central for all the children in her neighborhood.

"I think your decorations are very nice," Callie said truthfully. She would not have wanted to draw so much attention herself, but she loved seeing people get into the Christmas spirit.

"Thank you, dear, that's very sweet. Speaking of decorations, did you hear that someone stole all the lights off the hedge in front of Dr. Nielson's office Monday night? I heard Chief Michalski saying that community service..."

Callie's attention drifted to the minivan that had pulled into the lot. It parked in front of the drugstore, and Ben Ryder got out. Callie hadn't been able to call his face up in her mind, but now that she saw him, she recognized him. He actually looked quite a bit like Beth. Even from a distance, she could see he had the same strikingly pale gray eyes.

Ben opened the minivan's side door, and children began to emerge—first Tiffany, then one, two, three more. The youngest didn't even look kindergarten age.

Callie found herself shaking her head at the thought of the poor man trying to take care of so many young children on his own. Then she remembered they weren't really children.

"Such a shame," Suzanne said, turning to follow Callie's line of sight. "Fine man like that, struggling alone. Not that I'm surprised, mind you. That Justine was no good. I know Betty was worried about her when she disappeared, but my money's on her running off with another man. Women like that, motherhood's too much for them. It's all about the hair and the nails and the clothes. One day it's one dirty diaper too many."

Callie nodded, only half listening. She was watching Ben trying to shepherd the girls into the CVS. Tiffany was standing off to the side. She was studying the ground with her hands stuffed in her pockets. Her father called her, and she looked up, catching Callie's eye.

168

Callie saw a flash of recognition cross Tiffany's face, but the girl didn't otherwise react. She simply stared at Callie for a moment, then looked away. Her face seemed empty.

Suzanne cleared her throat, and Callie startled and turned her attention back to the older woman. Suzanne was studying her with a sharp eye.

"Yes, he's a fine man," she said, as though Callie had asked her opinion. "Took good care of Betty after their mother passed. Always coming over to check on her, even with that Justine harping on him every minute. A good son, good brother, good father. I daresay he'll make a better woman a good husband one of these days."

There was no missing what Suzanne was getting at. Callie felt herself turning bright red from the base of her throat to the roots of her hair.

As soon as Suzanne stopped talking, Callie stammered out an apology and began packing away her pamphlets. The Big Screen boycott was important, yes, but it had suddenly become a lot more important not to be standing there when Ben came out of the CVS.

Suzanne good-naturedly helped her pack up. Callie could hear her chuckling to herself.

————————— • —————————

As Christmas approached, the days slowed to a crawl.

Callie thought of herself as fortunate. She was safe and well provided for, which freed her to spend her time trying to make her little corner of the world a better place.

But Christmas was always difficult. Old faces began to show up around town—Dorf's erstwhile sons and daughters returning to spend time with their families, all aglow with their exciting lives in the larger world. The stores and restaurants up and down Center Street played carols relentlessly. J.T.'s went so far as to pipe Christmas tunes out onto the sidewalk. People walked through the musical cheer with smiles on their faces as they shopped for their loved ones. The schools closed for winter break, and public areas teemed with happy children.

It made for too many reminders of past losses and of the gaps in the life she now led. As the days ticked off, Callie found it harder and harder to get a good night's sleep. Every morning she looked in the mirror and saw herself looking more pale and tired.

It was on such a morning that Theo called to say he was being sent to Atlanta for a month or two to help with a crisis. He wouldn't be able to come up to Dorf after all.

Callie wished him luck, then went back to the cookbook she was paging through. She generally tried to get her shopping done on weekday mornings, when the supermarket was quiet. But first she needed to plan meals. Meatloaf and... yes, corn chowder.

She jotted down the ingredients she'd need, then paged on through the book absentmindedly, sipping her coffee. Eventually she found herself looking at a recipe for "Sweet-'n'-Salty Rudolphs"—chocolate-flavored Christmas cookies shaped like a deer's face, with chocolate-chip eyes, Red Hot cinnamon candy noses, and antlers made out of pretzel pieces.

Looking at the picture in the cookbook, Callie felt that special place in her consciousness spasm, then twist hard. She was swept into an unusually rich and specific vision: Tiffany Ryder was biting into a Sweet-'n'-Salty Rudolph. Callie could hear the sound of the girl's teeth going through the chewy cookie, see the look of pleasure on her face as she tasted it, and feel her own face breaking into a smile in response.

The immediacy of the image faded. Callie was left with the sense that this was something that should happen, *needed* to happen.

Fear shot through her. The thought of going into Ben Ryder's house and interacting with his half-human offspring frightened her profoundly.

But one does not argue with a blessing. Callie took a deep breath and tried to let go of the fear.

She bowed her head and murmured a prayer of thanks for God's guidance. Then she picked up her pen and added chocolate chips and Red Hots to her shopping list.

———— • ————

"Hi. I'm Callie McCallister. I'm a friend of your sister's. I went on a cookie-making spree and thought your children might enjoy..."

No, "spree" wasn't right. "Spree" was for shopping. And shootings.

Maybe "bender"? No, that was entirely the wrong connotation. She'd just say, "I've been making a lot of cookies."

Callie sighed and shifted the platter of still-warm Rudolphs from her right hand to her left. She reached up to knock on the Ryders' front door, then thought better of it. "I've been making a lot of cookies" made her sound obsessive, didn't it?

"Hi. I'm Callie McCallister. I'm a friend of your sister's. I thought your family might enjoy some cookies at this special time of year."

That sounded like a commercial.

"Hi. I'm Callie McCallister—"

The front door swung open, revealing Ben Ryder. He looked her up and down and said, "Can I help you?"

Callie opened her mouth, but nothing came out. She felt herself blush scarlet.

After what felt like an eternity, she managed to say, "Cookies?"

Ben looked from her down to the platter.

"You made cookies for me?"

"Yes. No. For your children."

"Oh."

They stood there awkwardly. Callie had never been so embarrassed in her life. Only the knowledge that she had to see Tiffany eat one of those cookies kept her from thrusting the platter at Ben and running off.

Finally Ben seemed to realize that she wasn't going to hand the cookies over and leave.

"Would you like to come in? The girls have just had lunch. I'm sure they'd love some cookies."

Callie didn't trust her voice, so she simply nodded. Ben stepped back and gestured for her to come in.

"You're Callie, right?"

Callie nodded again.

"I don't think we've actually met," Ben said, turning and walking back toward the kitchen, "but I've seen you out in front of Big Screen. And other places."

He pushed some clutter back to make room for the Rudolphs on the kitchen counter.

"Is this a church project—making cookies for people?"

She set the platter down.

"Sort of," she said and smiled. Why hadn't she thought of that excuse?

"Good to know the whole town's concerned about me," Ben said. He sounded a little bitter, but mostly tired.

"Oh, it's not like that," Callie said. "Not at all." The second wave of acute embarrassment made her eyes sting, and she blinked fast.

"Hey, don't worry about it. I'm...uh...you know. Really, the girls will be thrilled."

Ben walked out of the kitchen. Callie heard him shout up the stairs that everyone should come get cookies. Then he came back and opened the fridge. He pulled out a milk jug, but there was only a swallow left in the bottom.

He frowned. "Damn."

The littlest girl was the first one down the stairs.

"Cookies? I want five!" She looked up at Callie. "Hi, pretty lady. I want five 'cause I'm five. Almost."

An older girl walked in. "Madisyn, you're not even four and a half. Jeez."

Madisyn's little face scrunched up, and she ran out of the kitchen.

"Jazzy," Ben said, sounding very annoyed.

"Whatevs," the older girl said, and rolled her eyes as she reached for a cookie.

Tiffany walked in. She was carrying the fourth child, who looked to be a bit older than Madisyn. Callie was surprised Tiffany could carry her.

The little one saw Callie and buried her face in her big sister's shoulder. Tiffany stopped short and stood there staring at Callie, clearly afraid.

Callie, in turn, was very afraid of her. Her hands found the edge of the countertop she was leaning against, and squeezed. She hadn't stood face-to-face with a demon in a long time. It was hard not to edge away.

"Tiff," Ben said, rooting around in the fridge. "Are we out of milk?"

Tiffany glanced at her Dad. "Yeah. I told you yesterday."

Ben exhaled in annoyance. "Miss Callie made us some cookies. Everyone can have one. Sorry about the no milk."

"Two," the little one said into Tiffany's shoulder. The word was muffled, but still distinguishable.

"All right, Lia," Ben said. "Two cookies. But that's it."

Lia peeled herself away from Tiffany's shoulder and reached for the cookies. Rather than coming closer, Tiffany set her down. Lia ran up and grabbed two. She looked down at them for several seconds, then smiled up at Callie.

"Rudolph!"

"That's right," Callie said. It was hard not to smile back.

Lia ran out of the kitchen with her treats. After a few seconds, Madisyn came back in, sniffling.

"I want some," she said, as though she'd been denied them.

"You can have two, Madisyn," Ben said.

Madisyn's lower lip trembled, and Callie waited for the call for five to be renewed. But after a few seconds, the child collected herself and came forward. She took two cookies, biting into one immediately, then stood there chewing and looking up at Callie with big eyes.

"Yummy," she declared, sprinkling the floor with crumbs, and left the kitchen.

Jazzy wandered out after her, leaving Callie alone with Ben and Tiffany. Callie stared at Tiffany, and the girl stared back.

"Can I get you something to drink, Callie?" said Ben.

"Um, no. I mean, yes. Uhh...some water, please."

"You sure? I just made coffee."

"Oh. Okay, if you have enough. Thanks."

Ben went to pour a cup.

Callie looked back at Tiffany and gathered her courage. "Would you like a cookie?"

Tiffany shook her head. Callie had the sense that if she so much as twitched the wrong way, the girl would bolt. She carefully looked away.

Ben set her coffee down on the counter, then sat down on one of the tall kitchen stools. He gestured for Callie to sit as well and pushed the milk over to her.

She would've taken some sugar, too, but didn't say anything.

"So you go to St. John's?" he asked.

"No, Calvary Lutheran."

"Ah." Ben looked a bit confused, but let it go.

An awkward silence passed.

"How's the boycott going?"

Callie shrugged. "All right, I guess. Fewer people have gone in this month than last."

Ben nodded. He looked down and stirred his coffee. Callie found herself watching his hands, which were large and calloused. Suzanne had told her he ran Gene's Building Supply and Lumberyard. She'd never been in the place, but she imagined working there meant handling tools and stone and wood and other rough things, even if you were a manager.

Ben glanced up at her. His hands looked strong and capable, but in his eyes, he looked lost.

Callie understood that.

"It does get better," she said quietly.

Surprise crossed his face, then something verging on anger. He studied her for several long seconds. With relief, Callie saw him decide not to take offence.

"You lost someone?" he asked.

"Not 'lost,' exactly. It was more…" This was difficult to talk about. "It was more that I escaped from him."

Ben was watching her intently.

She shrugged, uncomfortable. "You don't get over it, exactly. I guess you learn to live with it. Build a life that fits around the fact that it happened."

He continued to look at her. She found she couldn't look away. Finally he shifted his gaze and nodded.

"You don't think she's going to come back," Tiffany said from across the kitchen.

Ben and Callie both jumped. They'd forgotten the girl was there.

"I don't know that," Callie said carefully.

"What about Beth?"

"I don't know."

Strictly speaking, it wasn't a lie. She didn't *know* about Beth—not truly. But Callie didn't think people came back from Hell. Not even good people like Beth.

Tiffany saw it in her face. She turned and left the kitchen. Callie heard her going up the stairs.

"I'm sorry about that," Ben said. "She's really struggling with everything that's happened."

Callie nodded.

Tiffany hadn't eaten a cookie. Maybe she'd eat one later. But no—in the vision, Callie had very clearly been present. She'd felt herself smiling.

With an unfamiliar mixture of fear and excitement, she realized she might need to visit the Ryder home again.

———————— • ————————

As sometimes happens after you meet someone, Callie ran into Ben and his family several times in the coming days. The grocery store, the gas station, Center Street—they seemed to be moving through Dorf on the same schedule.

Every time they met up, Madisyn would grab Callie's hand and start talking to her about some funny little-kid something or other. Lia would smile shyly and hold up a doll or other toy for Callie to see. And Ben would watch them and smile his sad, proud, overwhelmed smile.

Soon she was finding it difficult to think of the girls as anything other than ordinary children. From Madisyn's sensitivity to Jazzy's obnoxiousness, they were so relentlessly normal. She prayed on it but received no new guidance, only repeated flashes of what she'd already seen: Tiffany eating a Sweet-'n'-Salty Rudolph.

So Callie kept making cookies. Unfortunately, the time never seemed right to show up on Ben's doorstep with another batch. Instead, every pastor in town got a box of Rudolphs. It was a good thing, Callie reflected, that Dorf had a lot of churches.

By Christmas Eve, Callie was starting to worry. The vision had begun to fade from her mind. That never happened. Things she saw that way, as a fully-formed sensory experience—they always came true. It disturbed her to think she had somehow disrupted the order of things by not letting the vision play out in reality.

As the evening drew on, Callie made herself some dinner and turned on the TV. *Miracle on 34th Street* was on, as it was most years. She settled down to watch but couldn't relax into it. Things felt troubled, wrong. In the end, she turned off the TV and went on patrol. Demon activity was the most likely explanation for her antsy feeling.

She drove around town, looking through windows, down alleys, and behind dumpsters. She saw nothing. The town was calm and quiet. People were doing what you'd expect: spending time at home with their families.

By the time Callie headed home, it was quite late. In fact, it was probably Christmas Day.

She felt tired and oddly empty. Patrolling on Christmas wasn't a good experience. Driving by house after house and thinking about the people inside spending time with their loved ones—it made her feel more alone.

She turned onto Church Street and was surprised by the knot of cars around St. Mary's. Then she remembered that Catholics celebrate a midnight mass on Christmas Eve. She slowed and edged past the parked cars that had overflowed from the church's small parking lot onto the surrounding streets. The church itself was aglow from within. It was, she realized with a pang, just another home—God's home—where people had congregated with their families.

She drove on, passing the graveyard behind the church.

Once again, there was something at the northern end of the property—a small, dark figure.

Tiffany, she thought. *Maybe I should tell Ben she's sneaking out at night.*

Oddly, she didn't feel afraid. Perhaps you couldn't remain afraid of someone when you constantly associate them, in your mind's eye, with Christmas cookies.

She drove past the church and pulled over on the shoulder beside the Jensen farm. She reached under the seat for her flashlight, but when she got out of the car, she found she didn't really need it. The moon was waxing toward full, and the fresh snow that had fallen that morning reflected its light over everything.

Callie pocketed the flashlight and walked back to the cemetery.

Tiffany was still there. Once again, she was standing in the tall grass and trees that formed a boundary between the farm and the graveyard.

Like a wall of life, holding in all that death, Callie thought, then dismissed the idea as rather silly. It was December, after all, so most everything on the Jensen farm was dead too.

"Hi Tiffany."

The girl didn't react. Once again, she was underdressed. Callie was going to have to get all the Ryder girls some long underwear and boots.

"You okay? It's awfully late to be out by yourself. Awfully cold, too."

After a long beat, Tiffany said, "I think he's dead."

Callie was mystified. Then she realized the girl wasn't ignoring her. She was looking up at something. Callie followed her line of sight and saw a thing up in the branches. It looked like a sack—one of those canvas shopping bags.

"He always comes out when I call, but now he's not moving," Tiffany said.

Alarm washed over Callie.

"Is something in that bag? A…a creature of some kind?"

Tiffany nodded. "I found him in the fall. I could feel it from my house—that there was something here that was like us. So I came and looked for it. At first he ran away, but after he got to know me, he liked me. Maybe just 'cause I bring him mealworms." The girl patted the pocket of her huge parka. "But I guess the cold got him."

She sounded calm and rational, but when she finally turned to look at Callie, her face was wet with tears.

"Could you check? Could you see if he's alive?"

Callie looked from Tiffany to the sack. Reaching up and touching that thing was about the last thing she wanted to do, much less open it and look inside. But she felt she should. Someone was asking for help, and she was the only one there who could give it.

She licked her lips. Immediately the dry air sucked the moisture away, leaving the thin skin tight and ready to split.

Tiffany was looking at her.

"Okay," Callie said. "Okay, let me see if I can reach it."

She stretched up and touched the sack. There was no reaction. She put her hand on it more firmly. When nothing moved inside, she began to pull the sack off the branch it was hanging on. It didn't come easily. A dozen little twigs seemed to reach out and snag it on purpose.

"Did you put this up yourself?"

"Yeah," Tiffany said, "in October. I could see he was getting cold, so I put a bunch of old scarves and mittens and dry grass in there and hung it up."

Callie worked the sack slowly off the end of the branch, then lowered it. She wanted more than anything to hand it to Tiffany, but that didn't seem right. Tiffany was only a child.

She stood there holding the bag, so frightened that she thought she truly wouldn't be able to make herself open it. But in the end, she opened it and looked in.

She couldn't see anything. The inside was full of darkness.

Callie looked up at Tiffany, but the girl just stared back at her, her face a horrible mixture of grief and hope.

She couldn't do it, Callie realized. Tiffany couldn't be the one to reach into the bag and touch the dead body of the little friend she'd made.

So Callie did it.

If you asked her, years later, what the bravest thing was she'd ever done, reaching into that bag would be the thing that popped into her mind but went unsaid because it sounded so silly.

She felt fur, soft and dense. She was touching some small, fluffy animal, like a rabbit.

It felt cold.

"Tiffany—"

It moved a little. Callie jerked her hand out of the bag with a yelp.

"Is he alive? Did he bite you?"

"Yes. No. Hold on."

Callie reached back into the bag. The creature again moved a little when she touched it. Slowly, she slid her hand under it and pulled it out of the bag.

It wasn't a rabbit. Callie wasn't sure what it was. A small monkey, maybe, or some kind of 'possum. It was curled up in a ball, its feet and face all tucked in together under its body. It shifted slightly and sighed, as though in pain. Something small and wet touched her hand. It had licked her.

Without even thinking about it, she unzipped her down coat and tucked the little animal inside.

"Come on. We have to get it out of the cold."

She headed back to her car. Tiffany grabbed the fallen bag and followed her, asking over and over if the creature was going to be okay.

———— • ————

Callie turned away from the stove, leaving the pan of milk on a low heat.

Tiffany was sitting at her kitchen table. The creature was curled up in a box in front of her with a heating pad and a thick shawl. It was starting to move sleepily and make little chirruping sounds. Its fur was a strange silvery color that seemed almost to glow under the kitchen's fluorescent lights.

"What do you think it is, Tiffany?"

"Some kind of lemur. I looked online when I found it. See how he has such big eyes? That's for seeing in the dark. And he has fingers too, just like us."

The creature did indeed have fingers. Very long, thin, creepy fingers.

"They're for catching bugs," Tiffany said.

At that moment the animal opened its eyes. They were a brilliant shade of lime green and improbably large, like golf balls. In the bright light of the kitchen, its pupils shrank down to the size of poppy seeds.

The creature looked up at Tiffany and made a soft chirring sound. She reached into the box and started petting it.

"It's from the other world," Tiffany said.

"Are you sure?" Callie said. "It could be an escaped pet."

Tiffany shook her head. "Its essence feels like it came from far away."

So the girl was a tracker, like Zion.

"How do you think it got here? Through the strait that was open in the spring?" Callie suddenly realized she was talking to the child as though she were one of the blessed. "Um...do you know about that?"

"Yeah. Beth told me. Something came throughthat was hunting my mom, and that's why she has to stay in New York for now."

Callie blinked. Beth had told the girl quite a bit.

"I think Fluffy belonged to Bob," Tiffany continued, "that big white gorilla thing that used to live in the cemetery. I think Fluffy was his pet. Bob was furry enough to keep him warm in the winter."

"Fluffy?"

Tiffany shrugged. "That's what I call him. Anyway, I guess Bob left him behind, for some reason."

Callie contemplated the incongruous idea of demons having pets. She wondered what, if anything, the demon lemur could do. She hadn't felt any essence-working capacity in it when she touched it, so the answer was probably nothing.

She heard the milk on the stove approach boiling. She got up and made two cups of cocoa, then set them on the table.

Fluffy had nestled down against the heating pad and gone back to sleep. Tiffany sipped her cocoa with one hand and petted him with the other. A comfortable near-silence filled the kitchen.

After a few minutes, Callie remembered. She got up and lifted the latest batch of Rudolphs down from atop the fridge, pulled off the plastic wrap, and set them on the table. She sat back down and, after a moment, took two cookies for herself.

Tiffany took one as well.

"These are really cute," she said.

"Thanks."

"Are they always chocolate?"

"They don't have to be. You could leave out the cocoa powder. Then they'd be more like sugar cookies. Would you like that?"

"Yeah," Tiffany said. "But these look really good, too."

She turned the cookie over in her hands.

"Callie," she said hesitantly, "do you think you could keep Fluffy over the winter? So he doesn't freeze?" She glanced up and then quickly lowered her eyes again. "He's not loud or messy. And I can bring you these to feed him."

She pulled a puffy plastic bag of yellowish mealworms out of her coat pocket and set it on the table.

Callie looked at the worms, which were wiggling sluggishly.

Then she looked at Fluffy. His fingers were balled up into little fists, and his nose was tucked between them. He was snoring very softly.

Finally, she looked at Tiffany. The girl's head was bowed, so all Callie could see was her roughly parted dark-blond hair.

"Yes," Callie said. "I can do that. I'd be happy to."

For the first time, Tiffany smiled. "Thank you."

Then she ate her Rudolph, every last crumb.

About The Author

Becca Mills doesn't want to write about what she knows. That gets enough coverage in real life. Instead, she focuses on what she doesn't know, because our information is always incomplete and it is folly to think otherwise. The lines between knowledge and conjecture are blurry, so Becca prefers to embrace the teeming void of "I don't know." She challenges us all to think deeply, and to ask "What if?" Because by making new worlds, we can reimagine the one we have. Come on. Let's get our imaginations on.

For more information, visit the-active-voice.com.

The Red Flame of Death

Van Allen Plexico

Editor's Note: Written in the same high style as the adventure serials it celebrates, this story takes us to yet another of the rich milieus of fantasy history: the treasure filled desert wastes that lie east of the Mediterranean. A fitting place for any righteous demon hunter to track his ungodly prey.

In May of the Year of Our Lord 1693 the puritan soldier Gideon Cain left his family and home in Salem, Massachusetts on a mission from God. He left behind a town and colony shattered by accusations of witchcraft and by the execution of his neighbors.

After the witch trials, Cain had come to believe a demon of the ancient world dwelt among the people of Salem, subtly tempting mortal men and women and influencing their decisions and their judgment. He later claimed that, upon discovery, the demon fled from his holy wrath.

Over the next seven years he traversed the globe on a self-appointed–he would have claimed divinely appointed–mission, seeking the biblical demon Azazel, its agents and mortal pawns.

Cain's dogged pursuit of Azazel carried him from the Atlantic coast of the American Colonies to the far corners of the world. By mid-1697 Cain's epic chase across half the world brought him at last to the forgotten desolation of legendary Dudael in the deserts of the Middle East. Scholars may yet argue over the exact location of the scriptural prison of the demon Azazel but few will review the account of Cain's visit there without a shudder...

———— • ————

The hellish, burning sun had long since set, and now a baleful moon stared down cold and hard on the trackless wastes of the Middle East. Beneath that pitiless, star-pocked sky sat a group of four men of diverse origins and appearances, their blanket-swaddled forms huddled about a lone campfire.

Each of the men kept to himself and an eerie silence reigned—until at last one of them cast off his blanket and stood, stretching his lean form. The tallest of the four, he was clad in plain, somber garments that included a long, dark-stained suede buff coat of apparent military origin and matching slouch hat. His motions revealed a sheathed blade at his side, the hilt fashioned in the form of an English mortuary sword.

"Tell us again, effendi," called one of the rugged men at the fire—the leader, called Aqhar. "What wants an Englishman here in Mesopotamia?"

"My business is my own," the tall man answered brusquely. "And I hail not from England, but from America."

The questioner shrugged. "It is all as one to me, Puritan," he replied. "Still, you must have a reason for hiring three guides such as Faruq, Aziz, and myself, and paying us to bring you here—to the middle of nowhere."

"Indeed I do," Gideon Cain replied, "and those who love God and despise the Devil would do well to follow my lead and otherwise remain silent!"

Whether the man thought to react verbally or physically to the puritan's stark warning, Cain would never learn. For scarcely a moment had passed after he had uttered those words before a monstrous, batlike shape swooped down upon the group. Its leathery wings beat against the cool night air and its unearthly shriek chilled the very blood of those there who heard it, each of whom pressed flat to the ground in shock and terror. Each, that is, save the tall, dour puritan, who instantly drew his sword and swung it in a long arc in the direction of the attacker.

A furious hissing sound greeted his efforts, and the bat creature struck again, talons lashing out and catching Cain on the side of his head. His dark slouch hat tumbled to the ground, and he felt fortunate his head was not still inside it. Quickly then, before the monstrous, only half-glimpsed beast could come at him again from the stygian sky, he whipped one of his flintlock pistols free from his belt and attempted to aim.

The wings beat again. The shriek sounded, making his skin crawl in revulsion.

He fired the pistol. Its report added one more layer of deafening sound to that which now drenched the heretofore silent desert.

Whether his shot struck home he could not say—but, in any case, the creature swooped down again, razor-sharp talons slashing. Casting his pistol aside angrily, Cain drew its twin from his belt, then waited until the horrifying visage was mere feet away, closing fast. He fired.

The pistol's flash revealed a frozen and horrific image of the bat-thing bearing down on him, shrieking its fury all the while, before darkness enveloped them again. The shot seemed to Cain to have struck the beast, and yet it continued on unimpeded, and only a frantic dive to one side prevented Cain from being torn to ribbons.

The guides were scrambling here and there in terror, shouting and cursing in Arabic, but Cain paid them no mind. He stumbled backwards over the rough, rocky ground, the creature moving in and out of his vision as it fluttered through the inky darkness. His spent second pistol had joined the first on the ground, and now he stood armed only with his sword.

A second passed. Two. The bat creature did not strike; it was lost to him somewhere in the darkness.

"Silence!" he cried to his guides, who instantly quieted their frantic jabbering. Then, cocking his head to one side, he listened.

The bat creature came down at him in a rush from behind, its wings pulled back as it plunged with great speed toward his back. It made so little sound he barely heard it at all. Just before it could reach him, however, those leathery wings fluttered a mere tad—and Cain whirled, the mortuary sword flashing in the firelight, its blade lashing out in a curving arc.

Another unearthly shriek, this one cut dramatically short, changing midway to a hideous gurgling sound.

Cain stepped forward and struck again, seeing his target revealed now, fluttering madly before him, silhouetted against the firelight. A mighty downward blow served to lop the thing's head from its body. With a final, demonic screech, both parts tumbled to the ground.

The native guides climbed to their feet and rushed over, eyes wide and mouths hanging open. As they stared down at the ruined body where it lay on the rocky surface, it caught fire in a dozen places and began to burn.

"Your death awaits you soon, Gideon Cain," croaked the severed head nearby. "My master is with you always, even as you dog his steps and track him ceaselessly across the globe. He is closer than you know, now, fool of a man. Soon…"

Cain plunged the silvery sword blade through the bat-thing's forehead. The awful voice ceased instantly and then the head, too, began to burn.

"Get thee back to Satan," Cain breathed, his face twisted with revulsion. "Tell him thus would Gideon Cain treat with any of his ilk who dare oppose my righteous mission."

The guides prayed silently while Cain looked on, jaw firm and eyes reflecting the blaze. Soon enough, nothing remained of the creature but ashes. One of the Arabs kicked at them quizzically as Cain walked back to the fire and seated himself, as if nothing unusual had happened.

"What in God's name was that thing?" asked Aqhar as he dropped to the ground beside the puritan, nervously running his still-shaking hands through his thick beard and tugging at his gray turban.

"Some creature of the Devil, surely," Cain muttered, retrieving his hat and wiping methodically at his sword. "I know not. But it is a good sign."

The guide stared at him, incredulous. "A good sign?"

"Yes. It means we draw nearer to our goal."

Aqhar appeared to consider this for a few seconds but did not reply. He merely gazed into the campfire as the other two men returned to their spots. They cast sullen glances his way, clearly discomfited by what they had witnessed, but they said nothing.

Cain stared up at the full moon rising, its form all too similar to a skull lost amid the stars. A sort of chill moved through his gaunt frame. Grunting, he reloaded his pistols and then continued wiping down his sword. When he was finished he cast the cloth aside. The flames flickered off the polished silver blade as he turned it this way and that, examining its fine, two-edged surface.

The man nearest him, Faruq, leaned in and gasped, his eyes widening. He exclaimed a few words in his native tongue and Aqhar translated.

"He says that your sword, Puritan, has some sort of writing carved into it."

Indeed, from hilt to tip, the sword blade sported an etched design consisting of long, curving forms of an almost Arabic design, punctuated by odd, individual shapes that resembled nothing so much as Icelandic runes. The shapes appeared to sparkle and dance in the cold moonlight.

"Faruq wonders if this, too, is the work of the Devil."

"God curse any who would suggest such a thing," Cain growled.

The others moved in closer and studied the fine engraving work in amazement.

"I have some acquaintance with the blades of the world, Puritan," Aqhar stated, flexing his muscular shoulders as if to drive home his words. "And I have seen the likes of yours only once before—in the hands of a veteran of Oliver Cromwell's wars in England."

Cain said nothing by way of reply.

"So—were you a soldier for Cromwell, then?" asked Aqhar, his bushy black eyebrows extending out past his tattered hood. "What was it called, that army?"

"The New Model Army," Cain whispered.

"Yes, yes," Aqhar nodded. Beside him the third guide, dark-skinned Aziz, continued to gaze in silence at the sword, seemingly hypnotized. "You were a part of that?"

"I did not serve the Protector," Cain replied coldly. "I was but a boy when his bold experiment—the Puritan Commonwealth—ended in failure. My parents took ship to America—to the Massachusetts Colony. I hail from Salem Town."

Aqhar took this in and nodded slowly.

"Salem," the Arab replied. "I have heard strange tidings of the events that transpired there—"

"I will not speak of it," Cain muttered.

Aqhar made a placating gesture with one hand and then turned his attention to the blade once more, a subject about which Cain appeared slightly less reticent.

"The etching—it appears to be writing of some sort, but I cannot read it. It is not English, certainly, but neither is it Arabic, nor Farsi—all languages with which I as a guide have at least a passing familiarity." He pursed his lips. "Parts appear to be similar to those languages, though."

"'Tis no language you would recognize," Cain replied cryptically, "for God and His angels alone speak it. Though," he added, "there is one other for whom it has a...special meaning. And I aim to acquaint him with it very soon."

With that, he slid the blade back into its scabbard and lay down to sleep, pulling his dark slouch hat over his face. The three guides stared at him in puzzlement for some time afterward, but kept their further questions to themselves that night.

———— • ————

With the morning light, Cain was up and on his feet, urging the three guides to wakefulness and exhorting them to hurriedly pack up camp and get moving.

As they made ready to move on, Faruq approached the leader, Aqhar, and nervously whispered something to him. Aqhar shushed him quickly, casting nervous glances Cain's way.

"What troubles your man?" Cain asked as he tucked his pistols safely into his belt.

"Faruq thought he heard something moving out beyond the fire during the night," Aqhar replied. "But I told him to pay such things no heed. He is merely nervous and shaken from the attack of that creature last night."

Cain appeared to consider the words. Then he said, "I am well aware that something tracks us," he told them brusquely. "Something more dangerous, I believe, than the bat-thing. If it values its life, it would do well to keep its distance from me, and not interfere with my holy mission."

"You are either very brave, effendi," Aqhar said to him by way of reply, "or very foolish."

"Which would you suppose?"

"It is not my place to judge, Puritan. But after last night, I feel we are at least on the side of God."

"Never doubt it," Cain breathed, and the little group set out across the rocky wastes.

On they marched, as the sun climbed the sky and the oppressive heat increased. After a few hours they moved at last out of the flatlands and into a rugged, ravine-filled region covered in light scrub. Cain strode quickly, his long legs propelling him at an almost unnatural and untiring pace. Aqhar and Faruq managed to keep up, though they occasionally had to slow in order to accommodate the tall, slender Aziz, who carried a large, heavy pack on his back.

The sun rode high in the sky by the time they entered a particularly tall and narrow canyon, its sides mercifully blocking out much of the light.

Cain removed his hat and mopped his brow for a moment, then searched about the dim and rocky terrain with his eyes.

"We are close now, yes? To the cave we spoke of?"

"Close, yes," Aqhar nodded. "Though—as I have told you more than once—why you should wish to go there I cannot fathom. There is nothing

183

of value there."

"I believe you are wrong," Cain replied. "The texts pointed me there, and thrice since departing Constantinople have I dreamed of the location. God means for me to find it—else how would I even know of it?"

Aqhar could only shake his head in wonder. "God does as God wills," he answered, "and you will do as you will—though I am not so sure the two are one and the same, in this case. But so long as my friends and I are paid..."

"You will be paid, I assure you of that. Now blaspheme no more and lead on," Cain demanded coldly.

The sun had reached its height in the sky, standing clear of the steep canyon walls and beating down mercilessly, by the time the band reached their destination. Aqhar stood with hands on hips, regarding the sheer stone wall for a long while, taking in its nearly blank features with a studied, scholarly air, before nodding at last and beginning to work his way laterally along the formation. Meanwhile, his two assistants looked on in silence. Aziz dropped the heavy pack from his shoulders and seated himself, waiting.

Cain pulled his hat down to shield his eyes further and hooked his thumbs in his plain leather belt. He could make out nothing special about the cliff wall, but the anxiousness burning within his breast compelled him to await some indication from his hired man.

At last, after much searching, Aqhar returned and nodded to Cain, pointing in the direction from which he had come. "This way," he told them, and then he strode confidently to his left, his brown robes flaring behind him. The others followed.

"It is there," he said, pointing down the curving slope of the ravine floor to another seemingly blank segment of rock wall. "You see?"

"I see naught but cold stone," Cain replied, "but you were hired to lead me to this place, so I have no choice but to trust you."

"Your trust is well placed, effendi," Aqhar stated firmly as the group started to move forward. "For I have not failed you."

"Why could you not find it more easily?" Cain asked, picking his way over the rough terrain. "You told me you have been there before."

"Well," Aqhar began with some reluctance, "I must admit I was last here many years ago, effendi... And something about this area has changed. I do not pretend to understand it, but..."

Cain regarded the man with skepticism but nonetheless continued onward, his pace now faster than before. Within minutes all four men stood before the spot Aqhar had indicated.

In answer to Cain's unspoken query, Aqhar moved to his left and pointed around behind an outward-jutting rock formation. Cain realized at that moment that the formation had blended perfectly into the background, such that he had not realized it was there. He stepped past the three guides and around it—and the narrow mouth of a cave loomed before him.

"Yes," Cain muttered almost inaudibly. "Light the torches," he ordered his guides, who scrambled to obey. And then, drawing his mortuary sword and holding it aloft before him, he led them into the darkness.

His confidence reigning supreme, Cain did not deign to glance back and assure himself that the three men were following him. Had he done so, he might have noticed the torch flames reflected in the eyes of his guides—and the bizarre, crimson light that flickered in the eyes of one, out of synch with the torch he carried.

———— • ————

The group reached the back of the narrow, low-ceilinged cave in short order, and to Cain's puzzled expression Aqhar could only shrug.

"You asked me to lead you to the hidden cave in these hills, effendi, and that is what I have done. And you will see that it is just as I told you—hidden, yes, but not worth the trouble of finding it."

"No," Cain breathed, his eyes narrowing and his mouth drawn into a tight line. "No, this cannot be."

Raising his sword high in his right hand and a torch in the other, he strode to the very rear of the cave and studied the bare walls, misery creeping over him.

"Too far," he said tiredly. "Too far have I traveled to lose the trail thusly. All the signs pointed to this being the location of fabled Dudael. It must be here. It must!"

In a fit of anger he struck the sword blade against the pale rock face. The resulting sound echoed back—and echoed, and echoed, as if coming from a far larger space than the one they currently occupied.

"What devilry is this?" Cain demanded, moving forward again and raising a booted foot to kick out at the wall. On his third kick as he moved steadily to his right his boot appeared to pass through the stone and he fell forward, his sword and torch tumbling from his grasp.

Righting himself quickly, he snatched up his sword and whirled to see the three guides coming up behind him, each of them emerging, ghostlike, from the blank wall. They looked at least as disturbed by this as they had been by the bat-creature.

"Some sort of illusion," he reasoned. "Or an ancient spell, protecting this —this what?"

He turned again and regarded the area he had fallen into.

What had once been a natural cavern, much larger than the first, had been worked by many hands over long years into a vast, imposing circular space perhaps a hundred feet in height at its center and twice that in diameter. At the far side, carved and incorporated into the sheer rock wall of the chamber, stood the stone façade of what looked to be some strange and bizarre temple, complete with altar and eerie, twisted statues of angels and devils set into recessed sconces at various levels. Columns formed from gray stone struck through with veins of dark red and black towered high up to the room's ceiling.

Cain started forward, then hesitated as he looked down. At first he had taken the uneven nature of the floor of the chamber to be the result of broken and fallen stones alone. A closer inspection revealed that innumerable human skeletons in various stages of final decay lay scattered everywhere.

"Name of the Devil," Cain cursed as he regarded a particularly disturbing skull nearby that peered sightlessly back at him. Slowly he picked his way across the rugged stone floor, past the human remains and over and around jutting stones upset from their former positions during the long ages of the temple's existence. The guides all gaped as they stumbled along behind him, torches held aloft.

"Truly is this the work of Satan himself," Cain pronounced as he arrived at the far side and looked from the horrific floor to the loathsome and demonic carvings set into the stone walls and columns. Some of the repulsive forms appeared to cavort in the flickering light of the torches.

"Al-Shaytan, indeed," muttered Aqhar, his bearded face twisted with disgust. He spat upon the shattered floor.

Cain wasted no more time in conversation. He held his torch aloft and moved rapidly along the front of the temple façade, studying the structure carefully.

The other three men joined him, but confused glances between them prompted Aqhar to ask, "What, exactly, are we looking for, effendi?"

"Something...more," was all Cain could say. "There has to be more than just this. There must be more."

After thirty minutes that felt more like two hours, Aqhar and Faruq had given up and sat wearily on a large piece of stone debris, torches resting to one side. Aziz, meanwhile, continued to search the temple front with the same quiet determination Cain was demonstrating. Nonetheless, after another half hour, even Cain himself was near despair of ever finding anything useful when suddenly a grinding sound echoed throughout the chamber and Aziz cried out in Arabic.

The other three men rushed to where he stood, finding him staring down a narrow passageway that had been completely hidden previously. He motioned to indicate that he had pressed a small gargoyle statue and caused the panel to slide open somehow.

"Yes," Cain breathed. Holding his torch before him, he stepped cautiously through the opening.

The room in which he now stood was much, much smaller than the one he'd exited. Its stale air smelled of great age, as though the door had not been opened in a millennium or more. The light of the torch revealed smooth, unadorned white marble walls curving upward to a point at the center of the ceiling, as if the room were the inside of a dome.

"Ah," Cain said to himself, stepping forward. "This would appear promising."

The puritan stood before a huge block of red granite. Its smooth, polished surface glinted in the light. About eight feet long, it stood perhaps four feet high with an equal width.

"This—this could not have been brought through the door," Aqhar gasped as he came up behind Cain and peered at the granite block. "How—how could it have been brought into this cavern?"

"I do not question the works of the Devil," Cain growled by way of response. "I smite them."

But instead of striking the huge granite block with fist or blade, as Aqhar half-expected him to do, Cain instead bent down and began pushing hard at the side of it.

The other two guides had entered the chamber, and Aqhar glanced back at them in bewilderment. Then he said, "You cannot possibly hope to move such an object."

"With God on my side, I hope to accomplish greater feats than that," Cain grunted, his face darkening with strain.

The guides looked at one another, shrugged, and all three of them bent down beside Cain and pushed.

The great granite stone creaked and then gave way all at once, sliding smoothly on hidden rollers. It moved until it encountered the far wall, where it was brought up short with a resounding thud.

Cain and the others gazed down at what had been revealed underneath the spot it had occupied.

A gaping opening, filled with darkness, stared back at them.

Cain's face expressed a wild mixture of exultation and determination. The torch aloft and ahead of him once more, he found the edge of a narrow, black, wrought-iron stairway twisting down into the bowels of the earth, and he set his foot upon it.

"I do not ask for you to accompany me further," he told the three guides after he had disappeared halfway into the opening. "You need only wait here for my return."

Aqhar shrugged. "And suppose you do not return? No, I believe I at least will accompany you to the end of this mad journey, Puritan."

Cain's eyes met the Arab's for a long moment, then he nodded silently and continued down the stairs.

Stepping off the foot of the metal stairs, Cain breathed deep of the air that filled the underground chamber. It was much fresher than that which he'd left above. This fact troubled him deeply.

"Is there another way in—or out?" he whispered to himself.

Turning this way and that, he brandished the torch and studied his surroundings. Moments later, the light grew brighter as first Aqhar, then Faruq and Aziz wound their way down the steps and joined him.

"There," Aqhar said, pointing up to the chamber's dark ceiling.

Cain looked where the guide was indicating, and saw holes—open spaces —amidst the blocks of the ceiling.

"Air passages," the guide explained. "I have seen such things before, such as in the pyramids of Egypt."

Cain nodded, pleased that this might mean no other way of entrance into the chamber existed, and losing interest now that a possible natural explanation had been found.

Quickly the men turned their attention to the central object in the room. Another huge, stone block, it appeared at first glance very similar to the one they so recently had moved to uncover the stairs. A closer look revealed that it was of a sort of black marble rather than granite, and that it was not made of one huge block but two—though the blocks had been fitted together so cunningly, so skillfully, that the horizontal seam which divided the two, one block on the bottom and one on top, was almost invisible to the naked eye.

"This is a sarcophagus," Aqhar muttered. "But—whose?"

Cain ignored the question and kept his sword held aloft, even as he continued to stare intently at the black marble. It looked as if he were attempting to read some hidden writing carved into its surface. After a moment, with the torch light playing on it, the face of the sarcophagus did indeed begin to shift and change, the pattern within the mottled marble swimming subtly before their eyes.

Seconds later it had changed sufficiently to reveal a strange, narrow, curving script in red that covered the lid from one end to the other.

"That writing—if writing it is—it matches what is inscribed on your blade," Aqhar murmured.

To this, Cain only nodded.

"Can you read it?"

"I know what it says," Cain replied in a flat tone, his sword now held tightly in his outstretched right hand. "Thank your heathen god you cannot read it."

Aqhar glared at him a moment but then whispered a prayer and waited, curious what the puritan would do next.

As if in reply, Cain moved his sword blade down and touched it to the black marble. Instantly the scripting seemed to catch fire, the words on the stone blazing up with foot-high flames. The guides gasped and stumbled backward, but Cain didn't budge.

Even as the fire atop the sarcophagus continued to burn, the ground began to shake. Gently at first, the earthquake grew stronger by the moment.

"Effendi," Aqhar exclaimed, "we must leave—now!"

Before Cain could reply, the walls crumbled all around. But instead of falling, they merely slid down into the floor. And what lay revealed behind them caused the three guides to forget caution entirely and cry out with joy.

"Treasures!" Aqhar gasped. "More treasure than I've seen—or heard of!"

All around them, set into spaces carved deep into the rock, lay piles of gold and silver and sparkling gems beyond count. Golden plates and silver goblets and statues of all sizes, with eyes of ruby and emerald and diamond, glinted in the half-revealed recesses.

The three guides stumbled across the room and dipped their hands into the treasure, then began shoveling it into their bags. Meanwhile, the ground continued to shake.

Cain ignored all of this. His eyes had never left the lid of the sarcophagus, nor the flaming words that burned on its surface.

"Hear me, Azazel," he hissed. "I know that your body lies within yon tomb. I mean to destroy it now, before ever you can reclaim it, and wreak still greater evil upon this world."

And with that strange pronouncement, Cain laid his hands upon the black marble and shoved.

Nothing happened.

Cain glared at the sarcophagus, then whirled about and realized for the first time what his guides were doing. He peered at the piles of treasure, then frowned deeply and held his sword aloft, edge-on, between his eyes and the newly-revealed riches.

The treasure vanished—at least to his sight. In its place lay a scattered few ancient iron implements—swords and knives, bowls and pots. To one side stood a tall mirror in a black metal frame, its glass surface covered in layers of ancient dust.

Lowering his sword, the treasure returned to view.

"Ignore these worldly temptations!" he shouted at the guides. "They are but illusion, sent by the Evil One, meant to weaken your resolve!"

The guides ignored him.

Furious, he strode to the nearest one—Faruq—and grasped the man by the arm, pulling at him.

"Cannot you discern the work of the Devil, man?"

Faruq shoved him away and continued to fill his packs with gold.

"Aqhar! Order your men to obey!"

The leader of the guides glanced up at Cain, wild-eyed, then back at the gold, as if weighing his options. His resolve wavered and his hands shook.

"Effendi—such treasure! Even a man such as yourself must have need of —"

"I have no need for the works of Satan! Now gather your wits—I require the assistance of all of you."

Cain looked over to the other guides, only to see the one called Aziz bent at Faruq's side and whispering something in his ear, even as he pointed —directly at Cain.

"So, you mean to betray me, do you? And for naught but a fool's treasure."

The puritan brandished his blade and stood ready, his eyes shifting from one guide to the next. The ground beneath his feet shook still harder, and now tiny bits of stone rained down like hail all about.

Faruq straightened suddenly and, with a mad cry, rushed at Cain. The puritan waited until the last moment before pivoting and striking the guide with the pommel of his sword hilt, sending the man crashing to the stone floor.

"What madness overtakes you?" Cain demanded, staring down at his stricken guide, now his foe.

Aqhar rushed to Aziz's side and spoke loudly and rapidly in Arabic. The tall, slender man replied in soft but intense tones, and Aqhar's eyes began to narrow as he listened.

Cain had bent down to help Faruq to his feet when Aqhar suddenly rushed at him, slamming into his back. The three men all sprawled across the ground. The torches each had dropped tumbled here and there, causing the shadows to dance madly on the crumbling stone walls.

"Curse you all!" cried the puritan as he struggled to his feet, snatching up his sword where he had dropped it and positioning it smoothly between himself and the two attackers.

Faruq and Aqhar wasted no time. Even as the ground shook still harder and debris rained down, the two guides dove at Cain, one aiming for his legs and the other for his torso. Cain slashed out with his sword, not wishing truly to harm the obviously bewitched men but desperately anxious to finish his business here and depart swiftly, lest he and the others be crushed or entombed alive.

Cain was able to fend the two attackers off for several seconds, during which time larger chunks of stone began tumbling down from the fractured ceiling. One of them struck Faruq and knocked the man momentarily senseless, but Aqhar merely attacked once again, his voice now ragged and his words incomprehensible. Coming in low and with the strength and stamina of a man possessed, he took Cain's legs out from under him. The two wrestled on the ground for a few moments before Cain managed to free one of his pistols. Just as he fired it, Aqhar's hand lashed out and struck it—and the shot fired directly into the now-revived Faruq as he had leapt over a piece of rubble at Cain. The shot caught him full in the chest, and the man was dead before he struck the floor.

The sound of the shot seemed to startle Aqhar, who stumbled about in a daze. Meanwhile Cain whirled about, suddenly very aware that the third guide, Aziz—the one who had appeared to be poisoning the others against him—had vanished.

"Aziz! Show yourself!"

And then he realized what was happening: Aziz was leaning against the far side of the black marble sarcophagus, pushing with both hands.

And the lid was sliding slowly open.

The light of the fallen torches caused Cain's shadows to twist and flicker madly as he leapt atop the sarcophagus and rushed toward Aziz. His sword lashed out—but the guide was already gone. He moved like lightning, casting himself to one side, rolling to a halt, and then springing to his feet in one smooth motion.

Cain ignored the performance and leapt forward again, his sword singing and his other pistol now in hand.

Aziz sidestepped the attack and brought his hand down in a savage blow —one that felt much more powerful than the wiry guide should have been able to generate. Cain stumbled back, crashing into the piles of treasure with a shattering sound.

"No," Cain gasped, "not treasure."

The sword held before his eyes once more, Cain saw that he had impacted not piles of gold and silver, but instead the ancient, dusty mirror that had stood in its metal frame. Now long, jagged shards of glass lay littered about the stone floor. Moving the sword away and back into a defensive position, Cain realized that, for whatever reason, the spell upon his eyes had broken. He could see the contents of the chamber clearly now, even without the sword to aid him.

Aziz struck out at him viciously, newly-taloned fingers lashing out. Cain punched him in the face, to no real result. And now, as the two struggled at close quarters, for the first time Cain saw the blazing red light dancing in the depths of the man's eyes.

"You!" he cried.

Aziz struck hard and the sword tumbled from Cain's nerveless fingers. Before the puritan could retrieve it, a huge stone slab—the largest yet—fell from the ceiling and smashed down upon the sword, covering it and crushing it.

"No—no!"

In vain did Cain attempt to move the stone, but it was far too large and heavy.

Aziz watched this performance and laughed, deeply and long. His voice sounded different now, and his face had twisted beyond recognition. Now when Cain looked back up at him, all he could see of the man's face was the merest trace of human features, all washed out by the bright glare of red light that spilled—flooded—from his eyes. With a wordless grunt, Aziz sprang upon him and wrapped his long fingers around Cain's throat, leaning in close.

"Too long have you dogged my steps, human fool," breathed Aziz—or that which possessed Aziz. "Now, I believe it is time that I—"

Cain's coat sleeve had been pushed back, revealing the edge of a black line tattooed into his lower arm. Something about it caused Aziz to glance down —and he cried out in surprise and dismay. With a shout of fury, he shoved Cain away.

Cain saw instantly what had happened, and he shoved his sleeve up, revealing the full tattoo on the inside of his arm. It was a rune, four inches in length, and exactly matching one of the signs etched into his sword blade.

"This hurts you, does it not, demon?"

Aziz hissed at him; it was a guttural sound, a sound that did not come naturally from the throat of any human who had ever lived.

Cain ripped open his buff coat and revealed his bare chest, upon which a series of much larger runes had been burned.

"My body is beyond you, demon! God and his precious works protect me from your evil!"

Aziz stumbled back, clawlike hands held defensively before his burning eyes. Then he reached down and grasped a chunk of stone from the floor, hurtling it with blinding speed at Cain.

The puritan was unable to completely dodge the missile in time. The jagged stone sliced out a line across his temple as he ducked, and Cain cried out in pain and righteous fury. Before he could recover, Aziz leapt at him and kicked him hard in the chin, sending him sprawling.

Quickly Aziz pointed to Aqhar and snapped his fingers, at the same time growling words in a hideous language unknown to human ears. In response, the now ensorcelled man strode forward and began to shove at the lid of the sarcophagus as Aziz looked on.

Cain uttered a curse and struggled to his feet once more, but now found that Aziz was ignoring him. Instead the possessed man had leapt atop the half-opened sarcophagus and was staring down into it.

Cain leveled his pistol and fired.

The shot struck Aziz in the ribs and knocked him from the sarcophagus, off the far side.

Cain rushed forward and first looked for Aziz, but he had disappeared.

Then he turned and gazed into the depths of the sarcophagus.

A body lay within. At first, Cain would have sworn it was a monstrous, depraved shape, all twisted and wrong somehow, with a sense of pure evil hanging about it like a cloud. But then, as he stared down at it, the body appeared to subtly change. Even as he watched, the demonic shape flowed into a far more pleasing form—though whether this represented the demon's true likeness or the illusion it preferred to affect, he could not say.

Cain brought himself out of the near-trance and cursed, turning away just in time to see Aziz rearing up, a huge stone clutched between his hands. He was only partially able to dodge the blow; the possessed man smashed the block into the side of Cain's face, sending the puritan crashing backwards, tumbling limply away.

Aziz cast the rock aside and regarded the body in the sarcophagus once more, a smile slowly spreading across his repulsive face.

"At last!"

He leaned down, and the hellish red light appeared to flow from his twisted features, from his body itself, down into the form that lay within the stone box. Like a liquid it gushed down, beginning to fill that shape and abandoning the body of the guide.

"Never!" cried Gideon Cain—and suddenly the still-possessed Aziz felt a jagged piece of glass striking and penetrating his back.

The demonic creature started to laugh.

"Surely, Puritan, you cannot expect that—"

His words died out, his expression changing from one of triumph to wonder and then to horror.

From a short distance away, Cain hurled another long sliver of broken glass, this one lodging squarely in Aziz's chest as he turned about to confront Cain. Then another, this one slicing into his stomach.

Aziz lurched forward, shards of dusty glass protruding from his body. But not entirely dusty, no. For upon the nearly opaque surfaces, Cain had quickly and frantically traced copies of the runes that covered his body and his sword.

The holy runes that Cain claimed God had revealed to him in dreams. The holy runes that brought pain and death to creatures such as this.

"You will not have your own physical form back, Azazel," Cain cried, readying another shard. "You will not walk this earth in your full power and horror again!"

The demon Azazel, still inhabiting the body of the poor guide Aziz, glared at Cain in fury and in obvious agony.

"Damn you, Puritan! Your interference has grown intolerable!"

The blood-drenched guide lurched toward Cain, his features now twisted beyond human recognition and his eyes in full crimson blaze. The talons that had been his hands reached out for the puritan, and his mouth split open in a mind-numbing wail of horror.

Gideon Cain did not move, did not retreat. He stood hard and still, his dark eyes narrow slits, his mouth a tight line of defiance and righteous determination.

"You are finished, Azazel," he pronounced coldly. "Your reign of terror ends here—now!"

And with that, as the demon grasped for him, Cain struck out with the largest shard yet—a jagged piece of glass he had covered with a dozen hastily-drawn runes. The glass sheared through Aziz's neck and sent the guide's head tumbling to the floor.

Blood gushing, the unfortunate guide's body collapsed and lay unmoving on the dusty floor. Cain stood over it, his expression now one of equal parts satisfaction and disgust. He did not allow the pity he felt for what had been the man Aziz to temper his sense of justice dealt to a great evil.

"In the name of God, man," the chief guide, Aqhar, cried out as he finally came to his senses and hurried over. He gazed down at his former friend and comrade in shock. "What have you done?"

"That which I had to do," Cain replied coldly, allowing the dripping glass shard to fall from his fingers and shatter on the floor.

The ground now shook more violently than ever, and massive pieces of stone dropped to the floor, each of them taller than a man and some larger even than the sarcophagus. One landed directly on top of that marble box, obscuring it entirely from view.

"We must leave—now!" cried the sole surviving guide. "The roof will be down at any moment!"

Cain cast one last look back, first at the space where the sarcophagus had rested, then at the stone that covered his now-lost sword. And then he hurried after Aqhar up the spiral stairway and back into the upper chamber. Behind them, the ceiling collapsed and the space of the crypt vanished forever.

Cain and Aqhar emerged from the hidden upper room back into the cave that held the temple façade. It, too, was shaking and crumbling, and masonry rained down all about. They pressed on, across the skeleton-littered floor, and thus out through the hidden passage and into the cave. Massive slabs of rock fell behind them, sealing off the chamber forever.

A few more hurried steps and the two men were back out into the desert.

"Yet more devilry" Aqhar exclaimed. For now, in place of the noon sun they had left behind scarcely two hours earlier, the moon hung high overhead, and it looked to be close to midnight.

Cain took this in stride and merely sat, dusting himself off and refastening his buff coat with its ties that his people preferred over the more ostentatious buttons.

"Which way back to our camp?" he asked the bewildered guide.

———— • ————

Days later: that same pale moon stared down cold and hard on the two men who huddled about the campfire. One of them gnawed at a bit of food while the other hunched over something he held in his lap.

"I pray for my friends," Aqhar said softly as he ate. "They did not deserve such a fate."

"None do, yet thus will demons and devils ever treat with Man, until we defeat their master utterly and cast him into the darkness forever."

The Arab considered this and nodded sadly.

"There at the end," Aqhar said, "before we departed the crypt, I saw that there was no treasure. I do not understand it, other than to believe a jinn cast some spell upon my eyes."

"You have the main of it," Cain replied, nodding once.

"Yes. Bewitched, we were. I believed we were surrounded by treasure—and Aziz, he convinced me in only a few words that you meant to take it all and leave us stranded in the tomb. I believe he did the same to Faruq."

"It was not Aziz," Cain replied, glancing up at the guide. "Not truly. He had been possessed by the demon Azazel, whom I have pursued from my homeland to yours, and across many miles in between. He worked his mischief upon the Witch Trials of my native Salem, causing terrible harm to come from them, rather than the simple and honest justice that God demanded and that we expected." Cain's eyes were cold. "I know not whether he survived our recent struggle, but I suspect he will return—though where this time, I cannot say."

"Surely he could not have survived the collapse of the crypt?"

"He has survived many clashes and catastrophes over the past two years that I have pursued him," Cain said, his gaze level. "But so have I. And I will not be thrown from his trail quite so easily. I will never stop seeking him until I have finally cast him down and ended his evil forever."

Aqhar listened but said nothing at first. The moon shone down cold and pale, and a stiffening breeze swept across the desert. Then he said, "We will reach Baghdad tomorrow. At that point my services for you will be complete. I hope, effendi, that you remain safe after we part."

"I will feel safer when I am once again sufficiently armed," Cain muttered.

"Armed? But you purchased both pistols and a new sword from the caravan we passed yesterday. You are as well-armed now as you were when we met."

"Hardly," Cain replied, before bending back over the naked sword and resuming the task he had been working on for the past two nights: carefully etching the same holy runes into it that had covered his old blade. "But soon I shall be."

"Then we part on fair terms," Aqhar replied. "May your journey end in success."

"It will," Cain replied, all of his attention focused squarely on his labors.

The two parted the next day, and only much later did Cain learn that his demonic quarry had once again been within his grasp—and had once again slipped through his fingers.

Azazel had not been trapped in the crypt, Cain discovered, but had found yet another host to carry his vile essence away. And with that knowledge, the puritan could imagine the signs he in his single-minded focus upon his sword had missed that final night in the desert.

He remembered Aqhar offering words of encouragement before turning away from him, away from the campfire, and facing the darkness of the deep wasteland.

How that darkness must have been illuminated, Cain realized. How it must have veritably danced with the dim light of the campfire—and with the baleful red flames of death that cavorted madly behind Aqhar's eyes.

About The Author

Van Allen Plexico won the 2015 Pulp Factory Awards for both Novel of the Year and Anthology of the Year. He is the bestselling author of more than a dozen novels and numerous short stories, novellas, nonfiction books and essays from a variety of publishers. He is considered one of the founding fathers of the New Pulp movement and is proud to help revive the classic pulp writing style for modern action/adventure fiction.

For more information, visit www.whiterocketbooks.com.

The Blue Breeze

Regina Richards

Editor's Note: Easily the most fantastical of the worlds presented in this collection, this one reignited the sense of beauty and wonder I remember as a child when I first began reading about worlds of the strange and fantastic.

The kissama tree ruffled its bark with peevish insistence, scraping the portions of Lāākē's flesh not protected by his leather boots and breeches. He lifted his bare chest a little away from the massive branch on which he lay and pulled a dead rodent from his pamu-hide satchel. The kissama rubbed its upper branches in anticipation and the bark smoothed.

A knothole yawned wide. Lāākē dropped the rodent into the toothless maw. Its tail flicked as the knothole sucked it in, then sealed over the tip with a final smooching sound.

That small an offering would buy him no more than a few moments. Kissamas were the most tolerant of the trees within the Hell Hollows, but even they would not tolerate a visitor who did not pay generously and often. Fortunately, this morning his traps had been full. If need be, he had enough in his satchel to buy hours more. And if necessary, he'd spend it gladly and let his belly growl.

Lāākē scooted out on the limb until his head was no more than an arm's length from the light. He'd chosen the kissama not only because it accepted paying visitors, but because of all the plants in the Hell Hollows, it was one of the few that dared grow to the very edge of the Cleaving.

A flash of blue to his right caught Lāākē's eye. "Go away," he said with amiable tolerance. Instead the Blue Breeze whirled out of the bushes, its morpheus mist twirling gleefully in the small clearing beneath the tree. It was almost indigo today, which meant it had probably already been the length of the valley and back, tormenting all it encountered.

"Go away," Lāākē repeated, more sharply. "I've no patience for you today."

But the wispy blue demonkin remained, though it slowed its whirling dance and its edges evened and rounded, hovering, curious. Then it shot upward into the tree, stinging over Lāākē's naked back like a horde of tiny insects.

"Stop, you mannerless twist of Hell hurl." Lāākē gripped the branch with his thighs to avoid being knocked to the ground and yanked an arrow from his quiver. He gyrated the tip through the Blue as if mixing board stain, tearing glistening silver swathes through its misty mass. The Blue retreated to the ground below, reforming to slither-dance in sparkling, offended aqua.

Lāākē returned his attention to the world just past the kissama's leafy branches, the one so different from his own. *Her* world. The world beyond the Cleaving.

The barrier the Wasobi people called the Cleaving was in truth two cleavings, each encircling the base of one of the twin mountains. The mountains, situated a half day's walk from one another, erupted like radiant volcanos from the shadowy Hell Hollow valleys that surrounded them. Their slopes rose with unhurried grace through sunshine-bathed meadows and richly gardened terraces, growing gradually steeper through the lush alpine forests and sheer rock cliffs, until the white-capped peaks scraped mighty slashes through passing clouds.

At the base of the southern mountain, Lāākē's side of the Cleaving was as different from the dazzling mountain realm as mud from music. The murky world of the Hell Hollows was a dense tangle of lethal forests where plants, animals, and men were locked in constant battle. The Cleaving divided these two worlds as cleanly as the razor tongue of a phantel might cleave a man in two.

Lāākē adjusted his position on the branch and gazed at the verdant meadow just across the Cleaving. Chiseled gray stones as tall as trees stood edge to edge in the sunshine, creating a smooth-walled semicircle that abutted the Cleaving at either end. At the precise pinnacle of the semicircle's arc, directly across from the Cleaving, a wide, gateless entrance gave access to the meadow. The enclosed space could easily host two hundred people. But this morning it was empty, save for short grasses and delicate wildflowers growing tranquil beneath the ring-shaped sun.

Cerreleans, the people of the southern mountain, called this place the Cup of Justice. Although the Cleaving cut it precisely at its diameter, making it more a half-cup of justice. It was a place with a purpose.

Twice a year the Cerreleans came here to blow their trumpets and cast their condemned into the darkness. More often, their youths came to picnic amongst the wildflowers and play shrieking games of dare-and-dash near the Cleaving wall. It was safe enough fun. Unless a skirt or tailcoat penetrated the wall, and something quick and hungry waited in the darkness.

The kissama raised its bark, scraping Lāākē's bare chest. He dropped another rodent into a knothole, his attention on the Cup's entrance.

Something was wrong.

The ring sun had been up for an hour and its stronger brother, the disk sun, was beginning to rise. Soon, the suns would favor the mountains with nourishing sunshine, and withhold much of that same light from the Hell Hollows. In the days since he'd first seen her, the blue-skinned goddess had never been late. Always she appeared with the soft light of the ring sun to stand among the gentle flowers and temperate grasses of the southern mountain and stare at the Cleaving. He knew she could not see into the Hell Hollows. None of them could. Not the people of the southern mountain. Nor the people of the northern. They saw only their own hazy reflections on a wall of polished onyx.

And yet on that first morning, she'd stared directly at the place where he'd stood, wrestling fruit from a xsaxsa bush. And though she could not possibly have seen him, her gaze, so different from the disgusted glares of the Wasobi people, had been balm on his hate-charred soul. The shock of it had drawn him to the very edge of the Cleaving, pulled him so strongly he'd almost stepped through the barrier into the certain death of the light. He'd stopped short only because she turned and hurried away, following the call of an unseen female from beyond the semicircle of chiseled stones.

Aleesha, the voice had called. And every day since, Lāākē had waited at this same spot. And every day Aleesha had come to gaze into the darkness. And he had gazed back, his hunger growing.

It was a waste of time. Time better spent hunting. Though he could see clearly to her side, he could never go there; not without being burnt to ashes. But if she ever ventured near enough, he might be tempted to accept the loss of a hand or perhaps an arm to snatch her into the darkness, to look into her eyes and know for certain she saw him. *Him.* Lāākē, the shunned.

Had it been like this for his green-skinned father?

But his father had been no half-breed. His father had been a respected Wasobi warrior. Well seen. A merciless killer. And yet, when his blue-skinned mother had been cast into the Hell Hollows by her own people, condemned to be consumed by the dwellers in darkness, his father had not slit her throat and mounted her blue-eyed, black-haired head on his lodge wall. He'd hidden her. And when he could no longer hide her, he'd companioned her. Though doing so had cost him everything: his lodge, his people, and a significant slice of his rancid soul.

The people of the Hell Hollows could see into the light, but never go there. The people of the mountains, north and south, could enter the darkness, but from their side never see into it. Green and blue were not meant to be together. Yet his parents had been. And they'd been happy. So too had he, while they lived.

The whipping tail of the Blue Breeze curled around Lāākē, brickbatting his despised cyan flesh, stinging his unnatural turquoise eyes. Then the Blue passed on, moving through the Cleaving, shedding both its color and its wickedness as easily as a phantel might sluff its scales on a hot day. Changed, the breeze skimmed tenderly over the sun-kissed grasses to flutter the delicate pink fabric of Aleesha's skirts.

She was here. Finally.

Lāākē's heart stuttered. He sidled along the branch, closer to the Cleaving wall. Her blue-white skin shone radiant beneath the morning suns. Tendrils of long black hair tickled her smooth cheeks, catching on generous pink lips. She brushed them aside with casual elegance. Today her forearms were painted with pink swirls to match the small pink stone she always wore suspended above her breasts on two silver chains. She was well-curved but slim. And tall. Taller than most Cerrelean women he'd observed through the barrier. Taller still than most Cerrelean men. But not as tall as he. The top of her head would tuck neatly beneath his chin. It was easy to imagine the Blue Breeze had gentled itself just for her, turning from bitter to sweet.

She crossed the grassy field with smooth grace, her eyes fixed on the wall at precisely the place where the kissama grew. The kissama ruffled a payment demand, but Lāākē's flesh barely registered the scrapes. The tree tilted the branch beneath him, threatening to slide him into the sunlight. Lāākē hastily paid with the largest rodent in his satchel.

The female voice he'd heard that first day called from behind the boulders. Aleesha frowned and headed back to the entrance. Lāākē's chin jutted forward. She'd never left so soon. With a single backward glance she exited the Cup. Lāākē almost called after her. She would have heard him. Like the Blue Breeze, sound passed easily through the barrier. But the words died on his tongue. What would he say? *Come, Goddess of Light, draw near to my darkness so that I might... what?*

No, that would only frighten her and she might never return. He would be patient and perhaps some incautious day she might—

"You can't run away from me, Aleesha." A man's voice rang from behind the boulders.

Aleesha appeared again at the entrance, her cheeks flushed violet, her breath fast and shallow. Alarmed blue eyes darted over the meadow, searching for a place to hide. There was none. Two guards in yellow uniforms hurried through the entrance behind her. She spun to face them. They paused, and then slowly advanced as she backed away.

The burlier of the two grinned. "I've chased many women, but none as swift as this one."

His fellow, thinner and with a bulbous scar where his left ear should have been, laughed. "The faster they run, the louder they scream."

Lāākē's jaw tightened. Beneath his chest the kissama gave its branch an insistent shake. Lāākē ignored it. He scooted farther out, recklessly close to the Cleaving.

Aleesha drew an ornately carved dagger from a waist sheath. Lāākē's shoulders tensed. She held it as if preparing to stab an unsuspecting victim, rather than wielding it like an experienced fighter.

"Stay back," she warned the Cerrelean guards.

A man as bald as a pamu's butt and twice as ugly strode into the Cup of Justice. He spread the voluminous sleeves of his yellow and purple robes in a fatherly gesture.

"Ah, there she is." He smiled, revealing wide-spaced teeth. "A knife?" He tsked. "My dear, I realize you are unwell, but—"

"I am not unwell," Aleesha said. "I've only pretended to eat at your table this past week. I will not miss the Choosing again. I will take the Path. I will wear a blue stone."

For an instant the man's mask of amiability slipped, revealing a glimpse of something hard and vicious. Then he smiled again, his tone reproving. "You speak as if the fact that you still wear the pink is my fault. Four years ago you were a mere child of fifteen, too young to choose well. Yet did I not put my own misgivings aside and order the servants to prepare the procession? Have I not done the same this very week? It is not my fault both times you have fallen sick.

"I am not sick this time. And if I must starve until the suns align and burn a passage between the southern and northern mountains, this time I will travel the Path." Aleesha retreated farther.

Two more steps and Lāākē could easily slip the end of his bow over her neck and pull her into the darkness. He would not, of course. He had no need of a blue-eyed trophy for his lodge wall, and no life to offer a companion, especially a blue-skinned one. And yet...

"You can travel the Path in another four years. You will still be young, an exquisite flower. You will still have your choice of companions. Trust me in this. Haven't I always done what is best for you?"

Aleesha raised her dagger. "You do only what is best for yourself, Eeloos."

"Uncle Eeloos." He moved toward her. "Sweet child, how you do test my heart."

"Stay back, *Uncle*," she ordered. "Or I will test your heart with my blade."

Lāākē shook his head slowly. Courageous words, but she was no match for Cerrelean guards. And with her back to the Cleaving wall, she'd no place to run.

Beneath Lāākē the kissama's knotholes snapped in irritation. He fumbled with his satchel, seeking another rodent. Distracted and in haste to appease the restless tree, he unintentionally turned the satchel upside down. The remaining rodents tumbled to the ground below. The kissama rattled its displeasure. Lāākē clamped his thighs to the quaking branch, but his eyes never left Aleesha.

"Take her," Eeloos commanded. The guards advanced. Aleesha's dagger flashed, but found only air. The men wrested it from her with ease. One-ear pinned her arms. The burly guard lifted her legs from the ground. They held her suspended and struggling between them. Lāākē's blood heated.

"She's not screaming." The burly guard's grin rounded into an *umph* of pain as Aleesha's foot slammed into his crotch. He stumbled, but didn't release her.

"Yet. But perhaps some parts of you are." One-ear laughed.

"Bring her," Eeloos commanded. "And do not bruise her overmuch."

Lāākē yanked his bow from his back. Among the Wasobi it was forbidden to loose weapons across the Cleaving. Any kill was not retrievable, and pleasure-killing wasn't worth the loss of a good weapon. But like sound and the Blue Breeze, objects without life could travel unharmed into the light. No, the Wasobi never loosed a weapon across the barrier. But as they reminded him often, he was not Wasobi.

Lāākē's half-breed soul growled in anticipation. He loaded arrow to bow.

The kissama went suddenly still. Lāākē's mind registered the wrongness of that, but there was no time to ponder it. He sent the arrow from darkness into light. The burly Cerrelean holding Aleesha's legs cried out. His knees hit the ground, a bright red stain forming on his yellow-clad buttocks.

Fear lit Eeloos's eyes. He spun, searching the grassy meadow for the source of the assault. He motioned frantically at the one-eared guard.

"Bring her!" Eeloos fled the Cup of Justice, leaving the wounded guard sprawled on the ground moaning and One-ear fighting alone to subdue a ferociously struggling Aleesha.

Lāākē pulled a second arrow from his quiver. The kissama shuddered a giggle. Too late Lāākē realized his danger. Something clamped his ankle, pinning it to the tree. Lāākē's flesh went cold.

Wrapper.

The one predator feared by every animal, large or small. The one predator welcomed by every hungry plant.

Like living ropes they crept through the Hell Hollows, hunting in packs, ambushing the unwary. Stealthy rather than quick, they used their thumb-thick, short-rope bodies to tie their victims to whatever was handy, extending their length as needed by knotting themselves together. And while they could be sliced, pulling at them only made them constrict more tightly around their prey. Once they'd secured their victim, they simply waited. Waited for starvation or other predators to kill for them. And when the creature was dead, they waited still. Waited for insects to lay their eggs in the decaying corpse; waited for the eggs to develop into larvae. Then, finally, they feasted.

Even among the extraordinary variety of deaths waiting at every turn within the Hell Hollows, a wrapper death was a singular horror.

The kissama snapped its knotholes in anticipation. Wrappers were paying guests.

Lāākē kicked his free leg, sending an unsecured wrapper flying through the charcoal air. He rolled from the branch, twisting as he went to avoid breaking the ankle already bound fast to the tree. They could still wrap him, truss him like hung meat. But with most of his body away from the tree at least he'd have a fighting chance.

He kept his knee bent as he fell, but his spine still jerked. Arrows dumped from his quiver to click-clack together on the ground below. Blood rushed to his brain. For an instant he swung wildly, a full body length above the ground, a pendulum suspended by one ankle. He tapped his free foot to the branch above to still the worst of the sway, then bent it well away from the tree. Wrappers didn't fly. They crawled. Already one was winding slowly down his leg.

The only weapons remaining to him were the knife sheathed at his thigh, a single arrow in one hand, and his bow in the other. He used the bow to flick a wrapper toward the Cleaving. It sizzled as it passed into the quick death of the light. But more came. If they reached his arms, they would wrap him inescapably. He needed to cut the one at his ankle and hope the head-first fall wouldn't break his neck. With the end of his bow he sent a second and a third to fry in the light. Still more came.

Beyond the Cleaving a man screamed. Aleesha had sunk her teeth into One-ear's shoulder. He slapped her, knocking her to the ground. The blood pooling and pounding in Lāākē's head turned icy hot. Aleesha scrambled on hands and knees, closer to the Cleaving. A wrapper wound past Lāākē's knee. Lāākē pressed his lips, narrowed his eyes and nocked arrow to bow.

The shaft streaked over smoking wrappers and found its mark in One-ear's shoulder. He screamed but didn't fall.

Aleesha's brow knit, her eyes on the arrow. With dawning understanding she turned to the darkness. And though it was impossible, Lāākē felt seen.

A wrapper wriggled over his chest. The tip of his bow launched the creature and three of its brothers to a fiery death. Aleesha gasped and jumped to her feet as one landed close and burst into flame.

Eeloos re-entered the Cup, shielded behind a new guard. "Who's there?" he demanded of the darkness.

One-ear wrenched the arrow from his shoulder and flung it aside. Blood bubbled from the wound. His face puckered with rage. He lunged at Aleesha, knocking them both to the ground. They breached the Cleaving, landing with their legs in the mountain light, their heads and shoulders in Hell Hollow darkness.

The third guard ran to grab One-ear's ankles. Lāākē sent several more wrappers through the Cleaving. They rained around the third guard, their bodies popping and sizzling as they ignited.

"Leave him. Save her!" Eeloos ordered. He fled to the safety of the entrance and pressed himself to the side of the opening.

Aleesha lay on her back beside One-ear, her eyes closed, her long hair splayed over the emerald moss like a dark fan. She'd breached the wall. Was she unconscious or simply waiting to die?

Death moved toward her.

Hissing with pleasure, it lumbered out of the forest.

The phantel had probably been following the wrappers at a safe distance, waiting for them to bind and settle, to present it with an easy meal. Now it saw a new opportunity. The six-legged lizard, five paces wide and ten from snout to tail, headed toward One-ear. And Aleesha.

"No!" Arrows gone, Lāākē hurled his bow at the massive lizard, and watched it bounce harmlessly off the phantel's horned head.

Perhaps his voice awakened her, or perhaps she suddenly realized she'd survived the fall through the barrier. Aleesha opened her eyes. Blue blinked up at turquoise, and didn't look away.

Even as a wrapper bound his left arm to his waist, Lāākē felt *seen*.

The phantel's razor tongue whipped from its green-scaled snout and severed One-ear's head at exactly the same moment the third guard yanked his fellow back into the light. Blood fountained from the neck stub, spraying both the Hell Hollows forest and the gentle mountain grasses red. The guard dropped the dead man's legs and turned to run.

"Not him, you idiot. Her! Save her!" Eeloos screeched from the entrance.

Lāākē drew his only remaining weapon from his thigh sheath and held his arm clear of his body. Multiple wrappers bound his legs. More crawled to help the one trapping his left arm.

"Sit up! Now!" he shouted. "Run!"

Her eyes left his. She saw the creature moving toward her. All blue tone drained for her face and the high-pitched, horror-whoosh of breath she pulled in nearly burst Lāākē's heart.

The phantel's long green tongue licked out to curl around One-ear's severed head and draw it into its mouth. Skull crunched. Brain splurted. Still Aleesha didn't move.

The lizard swung its long snout toward her. Lāākē aimed for the creature's eye and let his knife fly. But fortune favored the phantel. It blinked and the same scale-armored hide that protected its massive body sent Lāākē's knife thudding harmlessly to the ground. The phantel advanced on Aleesha.

"No!" Lāākē shouted and struggled to keep his final arm free. The lizard's tongue whipped out. Lāākē felt his heart would explode. But the creature didn't sever Aleesha's head. The razor edges of its tongue folded inward, transforming it into a flat, blunt-edged appendage. With fluid dexterity the phantel gathered Aleesha's splayed hair and wound it into a leash.

Curved horns rose in two parallel rows down either side of the lizard's back and between the rows its spine sunk. Above the bowl created by the caved spine, the horns arched and bent inward, coming together at their apex like steepled claws.

Lāākē released a rattling breath. Like his own death, Aleesha's would not be swift or merciful. The phantel was female.

Aleesha's legs kicked in the mountain sunshine as the creature dragged her through the Cleaving and fully into the darkness. She twisted and flailed, digging her heels deep into the moist soil. Her hands clawed frantically at the ground. Anything she could grasp—rock, stick, plant—she threw at the creature. As she passed beneath the kissama tree her hand closed on Lāākē's knife.

"Go for the eyes," Lāākē shouted. But it was too late.

The phantel released her hair. Its tongue encircled her waist. The horns steepled on its back opened like a pair of hideous jaws. With an effortless flick of its tongue the lizard tossed Aleesha into the bowl on its back. The horn steeple snapped closed.

Aleesha scrambled to her knees, stabbing and lashing at the creature with the knife. But the walls of her scale and horn prison were impervious to the blade. The phantel ignored her, stopping to lap One-ear's blood from a bush.

Lääkë shook a wrapper from his free arm. "Use the knife on yourself," he said quietly, his voice hoarse, as if he'd been shouting for hours.

She gazed up at where he hung from the tree. Turquoise eyes held blue.

"She will take you to her den. Feed you alive to her young. Use the knife on yourself."

Aleesha's gaze left his to dart around her. To the carnage across the Cleaving wall. To the dead rodents, bow, and arrows littering the ground beneath the tree. To him, tethered upside down, wrappers trussing him like curing meat. The phantel turned to leave. Aleesha looked at the knife, and then again at the bow and arrows. Her eyes met his and she bobbed her chin once in acknowledgement.

Her arm extended out from between the horn bars of her prison. With a grim smile, she flung the knife upwards.

He caught it. The blade flashed with savage swiftness. Wrapper bodies rained from the kissama as the phantel's spiked tail disappeared into the forest tangle.

On the other side of the barrier, Eeloos shoved his guard toward the Cleaving wall. "Go. Get her back."

But the guard's fear of the Hell Hollows was greater than his fear of his master. He backed away, shaking his head and muttering beneath his breath. Eeloos's face turned indigo with rage. He charged the guard, boxing his nose. "You worthless imbecile. Post men around the mountain. If she comes back, deliver her to me. Immediately."

"No one has ever come back." The guard pressed one hand to his bloody nose.

Eeloos snatched up the arrow One-ear had ripped from his shoulder before he died and shook it at the man. "No one has ever had help."

The guard dragged One-ear's headless body from the Cup. The burly guard, arrow still protruding from his buttocks like a feathered tail, crawled after them.

Lääkë sliced the last wrapper free of his ankle and rolled as he hit the ground. He took no more than the space of a breath to find his feet before gathering arrows and rodents.

His bow had fallen across the Cleaving just as Aleesha had, half in the darkness, half in the light. Eeloos stood near the bow, his jowly cheek not quite pressed to the wall.

"Aleesha?" the bald man called slyly. "You are there. Alive. I know it. Come back, child. We are family, are we not? I am yours. You are mine."

Lāākē stooped to retrieve the bow. As he straightened his face passed breath-close to Eeloos's.

"No, old man," he whispered from the darkness. "Now, she is mine."

———————————— • ————————————

Lāākē tracked the phantel as closely as he dared, occasionally catching a brief glimpse of Aleesha, her hands gripping the horn bars, her expression grim. And yet despite the desperateness of her situation there was nothing defeated in the set of her shoulders, in the way she studied her surroundings, looking for an opportunity.

It became clear that they were near the lizard's den. The reptile was more cautious, stopping frequently to sniff the air with her flickering tongue. Lāākē was forced to hang farther and farther back to avoid detection.

At a place where the ground turned rocky, the phantel's trail disappeared with a suddenness that told Lāākē she was home. Aleesha had been safe enough while riding caged, but once inside the creature's den her time would be short. Urgency pounded in Lāākē's temples. He forced a deep breath.

Phantels were burrowing reptiles, but there would be no obvious opening to the lizard's den. They hid the entrance using their sharp-edged tongues to fell and weave sturdy saplings into trapdoors, then covered those doors with thick sod flats. Their precision made the door nearly indistinguishable from the surrounding ground.

Lāākē began in a clearing close to the last lizard track. Working swiftly but methodically, he moved out from the center in a tight spiral, dragging the toe of his soft-boot along the ground. His foot bumped over an uneven spot. Yes, the ridge ran for some distance beneath the underbrush. He dropped to his knees, scrambling to find the corner. One man would not have the strength to lift a phantel door alone. Certainly not from the outside. But massive lizards began as lizardlings. There would be a smaller trapdoor built along the edge of the larger, a door within a door. One through which a lizardling could come and go. One through which a man might also pass.

The thought of Aleesha, a woman of mountain sunshine, buried in a stinking lizard hole caused sweat to bead on Lāākē's bare chest. The detached attitude he normally maintained while hunting threatened to slip. His fingers grew increasingly frantic. There. Finally. The small door opened. Lāākē slid from dusky daylight into a disconcertingly bright tunnel.

Blue stones, larger versions of the ones exchanged at Cerrelean Choosing ceremonies, protruded from the walls, giving off a hazy glow. Wasobis claimed one could judge the age and depth of a phantel warren by the number of blue stones within. If that were true, this one had seen many hundreds of years and was probably as deep as a lightning lake. Five men could easily have walked the tunnel entry abreast, and just half the stones embedded in the walls could have lit a Wasobi village for generations.

Lāākē nocked an arrow to his bow and sprinted through the tunnel, following his nose. The sloping passage took him deeper and deeper into the earth. He passed blue-lit chambers of a size comparable to those of the grandest Cerrelean castles. Not that Lāākē had ever seen a Cerrelean castle. No Wasobi had. But they heard tales of many Cerrelean wonders, told by blue-skinned captives whose heads eventually decorated Wasobi lodges. And in Lāākē's case, told by his own mother.

The passage ended in a modest chamber which branched into four new tunnels. A single sniff of the first two told Lāākē they'd not been used for some time. He started toward the third. A gut-wrenching sound made him pivot and dash for the fourth. He would find Aleesha there. He need only follow her screams.

He raced through a maze of tunnels, skidding to a stop at the entrance of a large chamber. Discarded scales and old white bones littered the floor, gleaming in the unearthly blue light of a thousand wall stones. The phantel sprawled on one side of the room, scratching her belly with her middle legs, her indulgent attention on her lizardlings.

On the other side of the room, three lizardlings, each the size of a man, crept toward their next meal, tongues flicking with anticipation. From behind a waist-high pile of bones, Aleesha screamed and hurled skulls and scales, bones and blue stones, whatever she could lay her hands on. They bounced harmlessly off the trio's armor-like bodies. Each time a lizardling moved within striking distance, mother phantel's tongue reached out to lift her offspring, repositioning it to begin stalking again. She was training them.

Relying on Aleesha's screams to cover the sound of his movements, her scent to mask his, Lāākē clamped two arrows between his teeth. Any hope of leaving this chamber alive rested on disposing of the adult first. Using the blue stones set in the wall as foot and hand holds, Lāākē climbed with reckless speed. At any moment the phantels might tire of stalking practice and begin striking drills. Their bladed tongues would cut and carve, sever and segment, careful not to kill. Not completely. Lizardlings preferred to eat their meals alive.

Climbing the wall was relatively easy. The ceiling was a different matter. Bracing soft-boots and hands, Lāākē moved with muscle-burning strength. Sweat beaded on his face and dripped onto the glittering scales of the phantel's back. Lāākē held his breath, but she seemed not to notice. The going was slow and difficult. He was still short of his target when his feet slipped, leaving him dangling, clench-fingered from a knobby stone.

Aleesha's screams turned hoarse and weak. But as long as she was still screaming, she was alive. Lāākē clamped his teeth tight on the arrows. He'd only get one chance. The instant he fell on the phantel, she would know, and her tongue was faster than he would ever be.

He cocked his body up with his elbows and swung, releasing his hands, then snatching the arrows from his mouth as he fell. He landed, legs splayed around the lizard's neck, each fist jamming an arrow through an eye socket. Her piercing shriek filled the chamber. Her head thrashed, launching Lāākē across the room. The razor edge of her tongue missed his cheek as it sliced past.

He crashed atop the wall of Aleesha's bone and stone fortress, silencing her mid-scream. Her expression incredulous, she grabbed him beneath his arms and yanked him in. A lizardling's tongue ripped through the air where he'd just been. Lāākē found his feet and pulled his bow from his back. He reached for his arrows. He found only one. The rest lay strewn amongst the bones on the chamber floor.

The trio crept forward, tongues whipping. Lāākē nocked his bow and shot the nearest. It collapsed in a tail-whipping seizure that sent bones and scales skittering.

Aleesha lifted a leg bone half her own size, holding it like a fighting staff. Lāākē slung his bow on his back and did the same. The remaining lizardlings—one black, one brown—hissed, their middle legs pounding the ground, their jaws snapping. The black's tongue shot out, ripped the bone staff from Aleesha's grasp, and threw it across the chamber with such force it shattered against a wall. Lāākē leapt in front of her and the juvenile's tongue sliced through his bone staff as if it were a blade of grass.

From behind Lāākē a storm of bones and blue stones flew as Aleesha pummeled the brown lizardling, stalling his attack.

Lāākē dropped half his split staff. The black's tongue shot out again and wrapped the remaining long stub. But before the lizardling could rip it from his grasp, Lāākē lunged forward. Wielding the bone in club-like fashion, he rolled up more tongue with a twirling loop. Then he shoved full force, cramming the tongue-tied bone down the creature's throat, wedging it deep. The lizardling stumbled and staggered, wheezing and heaving. It reared on its four back legs, its front legs clawing at the bone.

Aleesha had deserted her bone fortress to draw the brown away from Lāākē with a relentless barrage of bones and stones. Lāākē drew his knife. He sprinted across the room and leapt onto the remaining lizardling's back.

"Run!" he shouted to Aleesha.

She didn't.

Legs choking the brown's neck, knife gripped in both hands, Lāākē aimed for an eye and stabbed with all his strength. The blade missed, deflected by impenetrable scales. The brown bucked, sending Lāākē skidding across the bone-strewn chamber. He rolled and the lizardling's spiked tail missed him. Aleesha rushed to pull him to his feet and shove something into his hands.

Bow and arrow.

Lāākē's arrow pierced the lizardling's brain and it fell, tongue lolling. Across the room its siblings thrashed and jerked in the final spasms of death. Lāākē and Aleesha started for the chamber exit, then froze.

The female phantel blocked the exit. Her tongue flicked from one dead lizardling to another, sniffing. She lifted her snout in an ear-piercing shriek of rage, blood gushing from the arrows embedded in her eyes. Lāākē's spine iced.

He'd failed. His arrows hadn't reached her brain. She was blind, but not dead. Her tongue lashed out, searching.

Lāākē grabbed Aleesha's hand. They fled across the room to a small opening in the wall, not much wider than a man's shoulders.

"Where are we going?" Aleesha asked as he picked her up and shoved her in feet first.

"No place good," Lāākē said and followed. The tip of the phantel's tongue nicked the back of his shoulder as he fell through the chute.

There were no blue stones; just darkness worn smooth by centuries of blood and bone. They accelerated down the steep angle of the chute, faster and faster. The shock of cold air told Lāākē when they neared the bottom.

"Curl and roll!" he shouted repeatedly, and she must have, because she appeared unharmed when he tumbled out to land beside her among dozens of frozen, half-eaten carcasses.

"Where are we?" Her words puffed white in the cramped blue-lit chamber.

"The larder." He pulled her to her feet. "This is where what isn't eaten, up there, is sent for storage."

Aleesha's brow furrowed and she touched a gentle finger to the place where the phantel's tongue had nicked his shoulder. Lāākē winced. Not because the wound was deep or painful. It wasn't. But though the lizard was blind, that brief tongue-touch had told it as much as its eyes might have.

"We must get out of here fast," he said. "She knows where we went. She's coming."

They scrambled through the ankle-threatening maze of body parts, moving quickly into a cold, steeply-sloping tunnel. There were few blue wall stones to light the way, but it didn't matter. Larders were built below the permafrost, buried as deep as the bottom of a lightning lake. Between the larder and the main warren there would be no other chambers, no forks leading to other tunnels. It was a long way up, and if the phantel entered this tunnel before they made it out, there'd be nowhere to go. They'd be trapped.

So they ran. And Lāākē's mind ran ahead of them, planning their escape.

The number of blue stones increased. The air warmed. An entrance arch appeared ahead. Hope expanded Lāākē's chest and he urged Aleesha to greater speed. The main tunnels and chambers of the warren would still be a good distance, but this was what he'd hoped for. They entered a room so foul his throat and eyes burned.

Aleesha leaned against a wall, pressing her side, gasping for breath. Then her nose wrinkled.

Lāākē dropped his knife, quiver, and bow. "Take off your gown."

"What?"

"Take off your gown. Hurry." He began stripping off his breeches.

"Why?" she asked, but she kicked off her shoes and began to undo her gown, her eyes still on the knife.

Now wearing nothing but a loincloth and boots, he stuffed his breeches into his satchel. He jammed her shoes in as well and held the satchel open to receive her gown. She stood before him in her own loincloth and breast bindings, arms folded over her chest.

"The people of the mountains are not entirely ignorant of the ways of your people." Beneath exhaustion and still trembling terror, dignity threaded her voice. "We know our heads are desired trophies. But I see no reason why I must undress."

While she spoke he'd knelt to remove his boots.

She dove for his knife, and then held it before her in that silly overhand manner. He stood, tapped her head with one hand to distract her, and took the knife with the other.

He knelt again, laid the knife back where it had been, and resumed removing his boots.

"Do you think I would follow you into a phantel's den for your head?" he asked. But she wasn't wrong to be suspicious. Some foolish warriors would. The Wasobi assigned great prestige to a blue head trophy. "I do not want your head on my wall."

Lāākē stuffed his boots into his satchel. Then he shoved the satchel deep into a pile of excrement. He rubbed more over his body as he spoke. "The clothing holds the filth too far from the body and increases the chance she will pick up our scent." He scooped a handful of excrement and plopped it into her hand, motioning for her to spread it over herself.

He sighed with frustration when she just looked it. He scooped another handful and rubbed it over her legs. Reluctantly she began to do the same to her arms and stomach.

A scratching sent a jolt through his body. He snatched up his knife and dove at her, knocking her from her feet, knocking them both deep into a pile of feces. His finger pressed her lips in warning. The phantel filled the doorway, blood seeping from its eyes. For too many heartbeats, the lizard's tongue tested the air.

Then it moved on.

Aleesha stood and looked at the feces covering the pink painted swirls on her forearms. Then she looked at him. "Today I've been thrown into darkness, imprisoned and almost eaten by lizards, and now I stand nearly naked and covered in lizard filth before a complete stranger. I'm Aleesha, and I think it's time I knew *your* name."

Her words brought his chin up, but it was the blue eyes staring so candidly into his that made his mouth go dry. *Seen.*

"I am Lāākē." He retrieved his satchel and they left the lizards' latrine, cyan skin and blue now equally brown.

Lāākē moved swiftly upward through the tunnels. Aleesha kept pace. With only one tunnel and one larder to check, the phantel would soon discover they'd gotten past her. She would return. And she knew this warren well. Even blind, she would find them.

"Do these tunnels ever end?" The exhaustion and frustration in Aleesha's voice matched his own. They'd encountered two dead ends and been forced to retrace their steps.

"All warrens have at least two entrances, the main and an escape," Lāākē said. "Both are at the surface. If we keep going up, we'll eventually find one or the other."

Unless it finds us first. The unspoken thought hung in the air between them. Lāākē wished he'd marked the trail when he'd entered the warren, but there'd been no time. The tunnel they'd been following ended in a modest chamber with four entrances. Lāākē stopped.

"What is it?" Aleesha asked. He grinned.

"I've been here before. One of these will lead us out." He chose the most upwardly sloping tunnel and they hurried on.

When they turned a bend in the tunnel Aleesha made a sound like a child offered a sweet. Her eyes twinkled like blue stars above her dung-smeared cheeks. Before them, the tunnel ended. Not in another chamber, but in a trapdoor.

They ran toward it. Their feet slowed, stopped.

The trapdoor cracked open. A long tongue snaked through from above. Lāākē and Aleesha rushed back to the place where the tunnel curved. Pressed flat to the wall, they watched as the trapdoor opened fully, and *it* entered.

Daddy was home.

Lāākē and Aleesha fled back to the four-tunnel chamber, halting abruptly dead center. The blind phantel blocked one entrance, bellowing for her mate. From the tunnel behind them came an answering roar and the scrabble of rushing claws.

They dashed down one of the remaining entrances and quickly realized their mistake. The tunnel sloped at an angle nearly as steep as the larder chute. And like the chute, there were no branching tunnels, no chamber entrances. Deeper and deeper they ran, the sounds of pursuit growing eerily more distant. Lāākē suspected the creatures knew they could take their time. This was a dead end.

When they were easily as deep as the larder or more, the tunnel floor leveled. They entered a chamber large enough to host a thousand men, different from any they'd seen before.

As in the warren above, stones decorated the walls, but they were uniformly small, no larger than might fit in a child's palm. Stranger still, they'd not been placed at random. Instead, pink joined blue to form patterns; some decorative geometrics, others telling lively stories of hunts, births, and battles.

The chamber ceiling was different as well. Glowing pink stone arched in stunning magnificence over a small paradise of white sand beach, crystal clear water and blue-stone lake bottom. Skillfully chiseled statues of various sizes stood in the sand facing the water. Made of the same gray stone as the Cup of Justice, they depicted fierce warriors, beautiful youths, and menacing water creatures.

Aleesha circled a particularly brutish warrior. "I recognize this one. In Cerrelea he's called—"

A hiss from the chamber entry frizzled through Lāākē's bones and sent them both reeling back to the edge of the water. The male phantel stepped onto the white sand with odd caution, head swinging from side to side, tongue poised ready between open jaws. His blind mate remained in the tunnel, visible but timid.

The male's tongue reeled out, testing the distance to his prey. He'd need only take four or five steps to be within kill distance. Yet he hesitated.

Lāākē's already rushing blood began to pound in his veins like Wasobi war drums. What could frighten a phantel?

He glanced at the water behind him. Blue pebbles beneath sparkling crystal.

The phantel took a tentative step forward.

Aleesha's hand slipped into Lāākē's. They backed into cool, startlingly refreshing water. Brown lizard dung fizzed from their feet, staining and then vanishing into the crystal water. Tingling energy wove up Lāākē's exhausted legs, renewing and reviving every muscle in his body. Beside him, Aleesha's breathing calmed, her back straightened.

This was a lightning lake. Its pleasant waters lured the unwary, reviving and relaxing them, enticing them to linger. Perfect bait for the creatures that dwelt beneath its waves: beasts whose touch could strike a man dead with the force of a lightning bolt; monsters large enough to swallow a phantel in a single gulp.

A faint churning stirred the water behind them. Suddenly the dung fizzing away from their legs felt like blood in the water. The hair at the nape of Lāākē's neck tingled a warning. He scanned the water. Nothing.

Cautiously the phantel advanced, giving Lāākē and Aleesha no choice but to retreat. Dung fizzed away from knees, thighs, hips.

Aleesha released Lāākē's hand and ducked beneath the water, coming up with handfuls of stones, polished smooth by a thousand years of waves. When she held them out, he almost smiled. These would do no more than annoy a phantel. Which was why they were perfect. He sheathed his knife and accepted the stones.

"You gather, I'll throw," he said. She nodded her agreement.

The phantel was nearly to the water's edge. Its tongue lashed out, whipping close to Lāākē's jaw. Hastily he backpedalled, shoving Aleesha behind him, forcing her to tread water.

The churning increased, moving to Lāākē's right and he prayed whatever waited there, blending in with the blue-stone bottom, preferred fat phantel to cyan and blue.

Water swirled dung from his chest. Lāākē threw a fistful of stones. They thudded harmlessly on the lizard's snout, but he bellowed with rage and stomped forward, his front feet entering the water. Echoing his bellow, the female left the chamber entryway, moving to stand by his side, her tongue whipping blindly.

Lāākē backed up, shoulder deep. Again and again Aleesha plunged beneath the surface, bringing up handfuls of stones. Lāākē pelted the phantels with them relentlessly. Their enraged bellows echoed through the chamber and they sploshed farther into the water, the tips of their tongues lashing air, the tips of their tails thrashing sand.

Aleesha continued to dive and deliver, Lāākē to barrage. The water to their right churned. The lizard's middle and back feet entered the lake.

An eel-like leviathan with pebbled flesh as blue as the lake bottom sprung from the water, massive jaws gaping. Its long neck shot forward. White sand exploded with the impact of its strike.

Aleesha screamed. The male phantel fled. The leviathan's body snaked rapidly from side to side as a punching bulge rippled down its throat. Then the monstrous creature sunk slowly back beneath the rippling waves. The female lizard was gone.

Aleesha swam for the beach, but Lāākē caught her and held her tight against his chest.

"That way is sure death," he said gently against her ear. Her gaze whipped from beach to blue-pebbled lake and back to the beach again. She stopped struggling in his arms, but her heart continued to pound against his chest.

The male phantel settled, huffing, at the chamber entrance, clearly determined to wait for them to come ashore or for the lake to dispose of them.

Aleesha's eyes searched the seemingly empty waters. "It has fed, so perhaps it's gone," she said, her voice reedy with hope.

"We must go before it returns," Lāākē said.

"There's nowhere to go."

"There is if we have the courage. A thing that large doesn't live in a place this small." Lāākē knew of only one lightning lake near where they'd entered the phantel burrow. It would be deep. All lightning lakes were. But the geyser at its center was strong. If this chamber was not too far above the lake bottom, they might have a chance to make it there and ride the geyser to the surface.

Eyes never leaving the hissing phantel, Lāākē held Aleesha closer than was necessary and spoke careful instructions. Then he looked at the phantel. There would be worse creatures swimming in these waters. But they had little choice.

It took three dives to find the tunnel entrance on the chamber floor. On the third one, Lāākē was certain he felt the water churning. Perhaps Aleesha felt it too. She came up clutching a blue stone in her fist.

"We may need light," she said.

He knew they wouldn't. But her knuckles were seized white around the stone, so he simply took her other hand in his. "Take a deep breath and don't let go."

They swam out of the chamber and into a wide stone-speckled tunnel. Twice Lāākē felt the wake of something large pass them and once saw a creature so fearsomely spiked a dozen men could have been impaled on its tail alone. But they were allowed to pass unmolested, and quickly emerged from the tunnel.

When Lāākē headed down rather than up Aleesha resisted, but he firmly pulled her on, and she came. The beach chamber had been deep. Too deep to swim the distance up with held breath. They would drown before they reached the surface. The only way out was to ride.

Among the Wasobi, lightning lakes were celebrated for many things: crystal clear water; their energy-boosting properties; and the cool, effervescent geysers that spewed from the bottom of the lake to the top with enough force to create fountains at the surface. It would be a rough ride, but it was their only chance.

Lāākē followed the muted pound of the rushing water, ignoring the distressed insistence of his lungs for air. By the time they reached the geyser's base his lungs were ready to burst. The silent panic on Aleesha's face told him she too was near her limit.

He motioned for her to curl into a tight ball as he'd instructed earlier, then towed her as close as the force of the geyser allowed and propelled her into it. She vanished upward in a rush of white water. He moved to join her. And went nowhere.

Where there had been nothing but rocky lake bottom, a plant now squatted, its spikey yellow foliage wrapping his ankle. All around him similar plants scuttled across the lake bottom, speeding toward him. Lungs screaming for air, vision blurring, Lāākē pulled his knife and slashed the foliage pinning his ankle. He sheathed his knife, flattened his feet against the bottom, and bent his knees in a deep squat. His vision went black, his lungs screamed for air. With his last shred of consciousness he thrust upward, somersaulting into the blasting white water.

He was floating. A warm arm encircled his chest. Sweet charcoal air stung his lungs. His heels furrowed mud. And then he was lying on his back, looking up at the dusky afternoon sky, with Aleesha, collapsed and panting, beside him.

An hour later, scrubbed clean and re-vitalized by the lightning lake, Aleesha and Lāākē sat in the afternoon dusk. They'd spread their clothes to dry and Lāākē had plucked them each a popie fruit. They ate in silence, save for the low moans of pleasure the popie made as it was consumed.

"Why do the Wasobi want Cerrelean heads?" Aleesha asked when the quiet between them had stretched too long. "What harm have we done them?"

"Why do the Wasobi live in the Hell Hollows where even the plants try constantly to kill them? Why do the people of the mountains live where, if they bend to inhale the fragrance of a flower, they need not fear it will bite their noses off?"

"I don't know why our lands are so different."

"Nor do the Wasobi. But they do know that you may enter their lands, while they die if they enter yours. So perhaps they feel entitled to your heads if you trespass."

Aleesha finished her popie. She picked up the blue stone that had survived the ride up the geyser clutched in her fist. It was a stone of unusual clarity and depth of color, teardrop shaped and polished smooth by the lightning lake. She took her pink stone from around her neck and removed one of the two chains before returning the pink, now on a single chain.

Silver glinted in the light of the twin suns—one a disk, the smaller a ring —as she began bending the pendant wire attached to the remaining chain so that it caged the blue stone. Lāākē watched her work and something lumped in his chest.

She was ripe to go. To choose. The curve of her waist, the flare of her hips, even the fading pink swirls painted on the creamy blue-white skin of her forearms declared it. She was of an age to be companioned. In a few hours, when the ring sun aligned before the disk sun, a path would burn through the Hell Hollows. By tomorrow morning the ash would be cool enough to allow passage. Then the people of the northern and southern mountains would be free to travel without fear of the terrors waiting within the Hell Hollows. Free to do commerce, to visit loved ones, and—for those who were Ripe and uncompanioned—to choose and be chosen, to exchange pink and blue. Lāākē stood and cast his unfinished popie into the forest. It smacked hard on a distant trunk.

"Before—" He took a deep breath and willed his voice calm. "Before, when you stood on your side of the Cleaving...did you see me?"

Her eyes were on the blue stone, now securely attached to the silver chain. "I did not," she said slowly. "But...I can't explain it. I think I sensed you."

She moved to stand squarely before him, so close that though she did not touch him, the warmth of her was like a caress. He breathed in her delicate, soul-searing scent. Lifting the chain with its blue pendant high, she placed it around his neck. For an instant the stone felt cold against his bare chest. Then she pressed her palm to it, and both he and the stone warmed.

"I must go soon." It sounded like an apology. Her hand dropped away from his chest.

He closed his eyes just long enough to allow himself to step back from her. "Get dressed. We will go and watch the Burning."

Their clothes, still damp when they put them on, were dry by the time they reached the chick-chick tree. It was the only chick-chick near his lodge, and Lāākē had been feeding it regularly since he was a child. They would be well-tolerated guests.

He climbed the tree ahead of Aleesha, showing her the best hand and foot holds. She exclaimed repeatedly over the mammoth branches and purple elephantine leaves sturdy enough to build a lodge on. Of course the chick-chick would never allow such an intrusion.

By the time they neared the top, they were well above the forest canopy, and wonder and anxiety were alternating in Aleesha's eyes. Lāākē settled them on a flat leaf facing the line of the Path and they sat gazing out over the bleak forest.

"Are there others in the trees? Watching?" she asked.

"Multitudes," Lāākē said. Few could afford a chick-chick, but secreted among the lower trees the whole of the Wasobi people would be waiting with varying degrees of anticipation and bitterness.

They wouldn't have long to wait. Already the yellow disk of the larger sun hung above the northern mountain, bathing it in golden light. That light skipped across the Hell Hollows without illuminating them, twisted away by the vast energies? magics? of the Cleaving, but lovingly bathing the southern mountain in that same golden glow. Already the smaller, ring-shaped sun had begun its eclipse of the larger. When it reached the center, the rays of the larger would pass through the ring's center, and the forest would ignite.

Lāākē leaned back on his elbows and crossed his boots, but his shoulders tensed. Beside him Aleesha's hand encircled her pink stone.

"Why does your uncle wish to prevent you from choosing?" Lāākē asked.

Aleesha's eyes remained on the skyline. "My parents are dead. I was their only child. Eeloos is my guardian. He controls all that is my birthright. Until I wear the blue."

"Why does he not kill you and take what is yours?" Lāākē's voice ticked with alarm.

"He is not of my blood. He is the Chosen of my mother's sister. He has no direct claim. If he kills me, all I own will pass to a cousin."

216

"So to control your wealth, he must keep you alive. And a prisoner." Lāākē wished one of the arrows he'd loosed across the Cleaving that morning had found her uncle's heart.

"Alive and uncompanioned. When I take the Path tomorrow and attend the Choosing, when I exchange my pink for blue, I will be free of his guardianship."

"And what if he simply kills the man you choose, the one who gives you a blue stone?" Lāākē's hand rested momentarily on the hilt of his knife.

"There would be no point. Even if my Chosen were to take only a single breath wearing my pink and I his blue, Eeloos would still lose all he now controls."

"A single breath and you are free?"

She nodded.

"And what your uncle controls? Is it so important to you?" He looked at the fine fabric of her pink gown, a dress fit for a princess, not a lodge in the Hell Hollows. The lump in his chest returned.

"It's my birthright. All that remains of my parents. Protecting it is what kept me moving forward when I lost them. Without it and the connection it brings to them, I am lost, alone." Again there was soft apology in her voice, and melancholy as well.

He nodded as the first scent of life burning wafted over the tree canopy. The eclipse was total, the small ring centered on the larger sun. A broad line of incandescent orange cut through the Hell Hollows, slashing a path from the base of the northern mountain to the base of the southern. At the very center of the path, midway between the mountain-islands, a larger circle burned like a fiery ball balanced at the center of a blazing stick. A mournful chant rose, Wasobi voices accompanying the pop and sizzle of trees and animals incinerating.

When it was over, only gray ash and steaming mist remained. And a silence pregnant with malice. Somehow, once again, Aleesha's hand rested in Lāākē's.

The climb down the chick-chick was somber. Aleesha followed patiently as Lāākē checked nearby traps before heading for the lodge. Neither spoke.

Dusky daylight was giving way to twilight when they approached a grove of sentinel bushes growing so close together that even the thinnest wrapper could not have passed between. Aleesha exclaimed at the sweet fragrance and beauty of the red flowers covering them and reached to pluck one. Lāākē caught her hand.

"They are not friendly to strangers," he said. From his satchel, he pulled several of the rodents he'd taken from his traps. The entire grove shimmied in anticipation, perfuming the air with the scents of fruit and flowers. He tossed several rodents into the foliage and the branches parted to reveal an ornate wooden door.

They entered and he hung back a little, grinning at Aleesha's coo of pleasure as she saw his home. The gray stone lodge was three stories high and built in a pleasing style that combined the best of Wasobi strength and Cerrelean elegance. Balconies graced the second and third floors, and the glass windows were lit by bluestone lamps. To one side of the house was a garden. Filled with medicinal plants and vegetables in well-tended rows, a stone path through them led to a smokehouse and kitchen rooms. On the other side of the house an elegant stone bench was surrounded by peaceful flowers and greenery. And visible above the wooden fence that enclosed the house and yard rose the green foliage and red flowers of the defending sentinel grove.

"You built this?" Aleesha asked, and his chest expanded at her tone.

"My parents and I did, while they were still alive."

He was still smiling when she yelped and began to dance wildly, engulfed in a whirling blue cloud. He reached in to grab her hand, and the demonkin that had descended without warning from the open air above bit at him as well. Lāākē laughed as it chased them to the front door, swirling around them, nipping and stinging until they slammed the door on it. Through a window, they watched as it dervish-danced about the garden. Then it leapt into the air and spun away.

"What was that?" Aleesha rubbed her arms, looking for bite marks. There were none.

"A demonkin, a minor demon, called the Blue Breeze." Lāākē smiled. "It has touched you before."

"No. I would remember."

"I watched it ruffle your skirts just this morning." He lifted a dark lock of her hair and laughed at her expression. "It only stings here in the Hell Hollows. In the light of your mountain it gentles and becomes..." He hadn't realized he'd moved too close until his hand caressed her cheek and desire surged. He stepped back.

"It felt alive." Her cheeks had blushed violet. "Like it was biting me intentionally."

"It is alive. And it was."

She frowned. "But you said it crossed into the light this morning. I thought nothing living here could cross the Cleaving.

"Nothing in the Hell Hollows that has life: animals, plants, rocks—"

"Rocks?" She looked with alarm at the walls of the stone lodge.

"Not these," he grinned and his gesture took in their surroundings. "But some."

"But if the Blue Breeze is alive and nothing that lives in your land can cross into mine, then how?"

"The Blue Breeze is the exception. No one is certain why. Some say it's because the breeze belongs to neither the light nor the darkness. Others say it's because it belongs to both."

He moved across the room, stilling the temptation to touch her again.

———————— • ————————

They spent what remained of the Hell Hollows twilight in the garden picking vegetables which they roasted in a stone stove in the kitchen building. When they returned to the house, he led her to the bedrooms on the second floor, pausing overlong before a door carved with graceful Cerrelean dancers. When he would finally have opened it, she stayed his hand.

"Your parents' room?"

"I haven't disturbed it since they disappeared. Everything is exactly as they left it."

"Then let it remain that way." Her voice was gentle. "If my uncle had allowed it, I would have done the same with my parents' things." They moved on.

There were no beds in two of the remaining rooms. There'd never been any need of them. So he took her to his bedroom and remained in the doorway as she entered.

"You will find sleeping shirts in the drawers," he said.

"You own shirts?" Her teasing smile almost brought him out of the doorway.

"Mother made Father and I drawers full. We never understood the need."

They stood awkwardly for a time, until finally he said, "If there is anything you need, I will be nearby. Sleep well, Aleesha." He started to close the door.

"Wait," she said, though her exhaustion was obvious. "We haven't discussed tomorrow."

"We have." He watched her from the doorway, every instinct within him wanting to keep her here. Not to mount her head on his wall, but to bring life to this lodge, to him. "You say you must go to the Choosing."

"I must," she said. Did he imagine the mournful note in her voice?

"I will leave at first light," she said.

"We will leave at first light," he agreed. And with a thousand times more will than it had taken to enter the phantel's burrow, he closed the door between them. He sank to the floor and leaned against the wall. Exhaustion as great as any he'd ever known claimed his body, but it could not quiet his restless heart.

In every corner of the Hell Hollows tonight men and beasts, agitated by the burning, would be on the prowl. Tomorrow they would watch the mountain people parade through their land, displaying their prosperity and happiness. And when the people of the northern and southern mountains met at the reflective stone near the center of the Path, a thousand felonious eyes would peer at them from the darkness, and watch the Choosing with simmering fury.

Lāākē had watched the spectacle many times. But tomorrow would be different. Tomorrow his heart would not be burning with curiosity, anger, or envy. Tomorrow, as tonight, it would be breaking.

He stretched out on the floor outside the door to his bedroom. There were more comfortable places to sleep in the lodge, but none close enough to her.

It was more of a dreamy murmur than a cry that brought him to his feet, knife drawn. He entered the bedroom on stealthy feet.

Aleesha's pink gown hung on a wall peg. The half-cover had been placed on the bluestone lamp beside the bed, but the dim light was enough to prove the room was free of danger, Aleesha safe.

She lay on her side atop the tumble of furs and silks on his bed, one hand beneath her cheek. Despite being engulfed from chin to knee in one of his sleepshirts, his eyes could trace every feminine curve of her: breast, waist, hip, thigh. She looked tempting, and a little cold. He spread a fur over her. Then he simply stood gazing at her, knowing he should go back to the floor in the hall, but not able to leave.

"Do you plan to stare at me all night?" she asked softly as she opened her eyes.

He snatched back the hand that had somehow been poised to trace the fading pink swirls on her forearm.

"Lie down," she said

He turned to leave and she caught his wrist. "Here, with me."

He must have looked surprised and perhaps a little overeager because she shook her head. "I am offering you nothing but a place on your own soft mattress. We must be clear on that. Nothing."

"Nothing," he agreed. But as he settled beside her, her sweet scent enveloping him, her warm body touching his, he knew this was so much more than nothing. For him, Lāākē, the shunned, a man who had not known the caring touch or true presence of another human being in years, to lie beside her in the quiet darkness of his own lodge was so much more than nothing.

There was no future for them. She did not belong in his world and he could not live in hers. Any child of hers born in the Hell Hollows would be shunned. And any child of his born in the Cerrelean sunshine would burn to ash before it took a second breath.

They lay quiet for a long time, her back nestled perfectly against his bare chest, before she spoke. "Why are you not companioned?"

"No Wasobi woman would accept me," he said simply.

She turned her profile toward him, disbelief threading her voice. "Surely there must be dozens begging to wear your blue stone."

"The exchange of stones isn't how it's done in the Hell Hollows. And if it were, no Wasobi woman would accept mine. The blue in my skin offends them."

"Tell me about it," she said softly, and as they lay together in the darkness, he did. All of it; every humbling, humiliating detail. She didn't interrupt and she didn't argue.

When he finally fell silent, she cuddled her back more firmly against his chest, pulled his arm over her waist, and hooked her foot over his ankle, drawing him in in a way that was more comforting, more affirming than any words could have been.

Tomorrow he would return her to her own kind, and he feared the silence of this place without her. But tomorrow could wait for tomorrow. Tonight he would lie beside her, listening to her even breathing as she slept, and for a short time he would no longer be alone.

———————— • ————————

He slept little and woke in the black hour before the shadowy Hell Hollow dawn. She was curled against him, her breath warming his chest. If he had his way, he would never move, but the Cerreleans would begin their parade between the mountains at first light and if Aleesha was to join them, it would be best to get her safely to the Cleaving before the Wasobi gathered to watch the violation of their lands by blue skins.

He left her sleeping to prepare: gathering bow and arrows, sharpening his knife, packing his satchel with enough rodents to buy their way safely through the trees. She was awake and dressed when he returned carrying a pair of his mother's boots, a slim dagger, and a calf sheath. His fingers were clumsy as he fitted the boots for her. She lifted her skirts just enough for him to attach the calf sheath. Her breath caught on a muted sigh as his fingers traced a slow path of longing from the back of her knee to her ankle. He settled her skirts back in their proper place and left the room.

They shared a somber breakfast in the garden as dawn arrived. Then, with an ache a hundred years in a lightning lake could not have soothed, Lāākē gathered his weapons. Aleesha followed him to the sentinel bushes, waiting silently as the branches parted to allow them to pass out of the compound. But when he passed through, she remained behind looking at him through the entry.

The sight of her framed by greenery, his home behind her, set fire to Laaake's already burning heart, turning it to ashes. As he'd been all his life, he was on the outside looking in at what he could never have. And as painful as that had always been, his perpetual shunning, this—being forever separated from Aleesha—would be a wound from which he would never recover.

"Come," he said. "If we are to return you to your people in time for the Choosing, we must go now."

He held his hand out to her. She took it, but when he started again toward the forest, she gently resisted, pulling him back into the archway, pulling him slowly to her until his body pressed the length of hers.

She tilted her head up and her sweet breath puffed against his lips as she spoke. "I think your parents' room has been empty long enough."

Her kiss was feather light and for long moments his matched that tenderness, that intense innocent exploration. But soon his kisses turned greedy, and hot, and worshipping. Her arms encircled his neck. She pressed herself closer.

"This is your Choosing?" he asked.

"This is my Choosing." She lifted the pink stone from her neck and placed it around his. With sacred deliberation he placed the blue stone she'd made for him around hers. It nestled above the blue-white mounds of her breasts.

With a joyous growl, Lāākē lifted her in his arms and carried her out of the archway. The bushes perfumed the air sweetly as they sealed the entrance behind them.

About The Author

Regina Richards spent much of her childhood with her nose in a book. At night, when darkness and responsible parents forced her to set her books aside, she'd lie in bed and create stories in her mind's eye of daring adventures, cunning escapes, and improbable feats of heroism on alien planets. Today Regina lives in Texas with her husband and three children. She still tells herself a story each night before she sleeps, but now she also tells one to the computer during the day. Not the same one of course. Her bedtime stories are her own private world.

For more information, visit reginarichards.net.

The Rakam

Karpov Kinrade

Editor's Note: Some stories are small, encompassing only the characters involved and the events depicted, while others seem a gateway into an entire world filled with mythic adventure. This is one of those gateway stories.

The evening sun sets low in the sky as the maiden moon begins her slow crawl into the impending twilight. Her sisters, the matron moon and crone moon, won't join her for some hours yet. I breathe in the scent of the sea as brackish waves crash against the underbelly of the great kiasheen who glides effortlessly through it all, as if the giant shells packed with humans on its back matter little. I stand at the rostrum, peering over the great whale's head as it moves us toward our next port two days north, where jewels will trade hands for spices and cloths, and the rich will get richer.

But I am not here for riches. For wealth. For the temporary haze of half-felt happiness those earthly pleasures offer.

"Sev!" A stern voice calls to me with a name that is not my given, and I turn to see Captain Kanen eyeing me with distrust. "Do ye not sleep, lad?"

"The moons keep me awake," I tell him truthfully. It might be the only true thing I've said in my entire time with his crew.

"The moons, the sun, the waves. Ye be drowning in ye own haze if ye don't lay yer head soon," he says, crossing heavily-muscled arms over his broad chest. He is a man of the sea, hailing from one of the lesser families of the Shattered Islands. Hints of blue and turquoise in his hair, eyes and nails show his meager abilities to wield the island water stones, but he doesn't need them to captain. He was a man born to make love to the sea; you can see it in the way they peer at each other at night, when he thinks no one is looking. His face is weathered, lined with the sun and salt of a life on water, his body hardened from years of labor on the kiasheen whale-ships. His crew trusts him, that I've seen clearly. It is not just the scars that occupy half his face and neck... the scars he earned at the sharp end of a rakam. His survival is a thing of legends in itself, and makes a man such as him a god in the eyes of his crew. And they do not follow him out of greed or fear, though that would certainly be enough motivation for some. They follow him because they see in him the sea-song that anyone drawn to this life craves.

It is why I chose him, chose his whale-ship, for this journey. "Whether I drown in my haze or not, you've gotten your pay."

He nods gruffly. "Aye, that I have. Not many men willingly part with that many stones for a trip like this. Makes my men nervous, it does. Yer secrets. Yer skulking."

He peers at me with dark eyes streaked with light blue.

My own eyes have none of their original darkness left. It is the one trait I cannot change, the startling blue of my eyes. I am a dark-haired man with too-blue eyes and too many secrets for his liking, but wealth often trumps suspicion, I've found, at least for a time.

"We will part ways at the next dock," I assure him. *Barring any delays*, I think, but I don't put that thought to words. No need to make him more restless.

His head jerks forward once, like a spasm at his neck. "See that we do, and all is well."

Sea folk are a superstitious lot, more so than most of the Shattered Islands. They spend their lives out here on the waters and they forget how to live within normal society. They are too much surrounded by monsters and waves and a world beyond their control.

The captain whistles and shouts commands at someone above me. I look up to the shell that rides atop ropes of kelp, its small passenger staring intently at the waters. She looks down from her perch as a young man climbs up the kelp to relieve her of her duty for the night. She shimmies down, giving the shelled seat to him, landing on bare feet slapping against the great shell, loose-fitting bamboo-knit pants flapping against her skinny legs. Her hair is black, her eyes slashed with sapphire, so she must have touched the stone once, and I wonder how she came upon such a rare gem. Her arms are thick and muscled, the arms of one who leads a kiasheen, pulling upon the heavy reins that guide the beast by its nostrils.

"I'm free till sunrise if ye be looking for something… or someone, to do." She winks at me and saunters off, not waiting for my response, making her way within the great shell to her quarters.

The first night I arrived on board, Calla cozied up to me during dinner and didn't take it personally when I wasn't interested. Since then she flirts lightly, as a young woman who has had many lovers and isn't concerned with where the next one comes from.

I don't mind, but I don't reciprocate. I'm not here to find a new lover.

Captain Kanen glares at me when he sees Calla's wink. I maintain eye contact with him, not aggressively, but not passively either. He averts his eyes first, and I turn and make my way inside the shell to my own cabin.

I've seen enough of this night, and the captain was right about one thing. I will fall into the haze if I don't try to sleep.

I climb down the alabaster stairs to the small shell, that odd space between the great shell and the kiasheen where the whoosh of the ocean and the simmering sounds of the great beast's belly collide into a strange kind of music that is both beautiful and terrifying. My generous offerings bought me a private cabin toward the fluke, so I walk through the narrow shell halls until I reach the end of the tunnel. I'm about to open the door to my cabin when I pause and still my breath.

My gloved hand is soundless as it turns the shell knob and pushes the door in.

The man standing over my trunk does not see or hear me as I approach him from behind.

I can smell his stink as I reach for his arm and twist it behind his back, pulling his bulk against my chest as I hiss into his ear. "You'll kindly keep your grimy fingers off my belongings, or you won't be leaving with your hands."

———— • ————

The man stiffens in my arms, fear and panic warring with indignant anger over his face. But he is more coward than fighter and he slumps against me, sniveling. "I just be looking is all. No harm meant."

I glance over his shoulder and see my trunk open, my few belongings stinking of his sweaty palms. "What were you looking for?" I ask, twisting him around and pinning him against the shell wall, my forearm crossing over his windpipe to keep him in place.

"Yer so much to yerself, me mates and I had a wager on what treasures ye keep hidden."

I nearly gag at the liquor on his breath. The sea swill they drink in these parts has a particularly fishy odor. "You're the one they call Clam, yes?"

He nods.

"And did you find hidden treasure?" I ask, knowing the answer.

He shakes his head, shells and bits of bone clanking together in his long, weedy beard and locks of hair.

"And will you be intruding on my space again, Clam?"

He shakes his head again and I bore into him with my eyes, with my purpose, until I smell the piss running down his legs. I let him go and push him toward the door of my cabin. "Tell your *mates* I like my privacy, and if any of you are found in here again, you'll soon find yourself rakam bait."

His eyes widen and he taps three fingers on his chest three times, a super-stitious sign to ward off evil, and then trips over himself to escape my room. I hope my warning keeps him and his friends away. I hope it doesn't push them to more violent action.

I close the door behind him after he leaves, latching a small shell to a strip of kelp to keep it locked from inside, then I move with one long stride back to my trunk. I shove aside the clothing and feel for the small lever that pops open the floorboard compartment. I take out a long bundle wrapped in kelp and cloth to reveal a black obsidian box. I breathe a sigh of relief as I feel the heat emanating from it, sending sparks through my fingers even while still closed.

Securing it and the kelp bundle back in place, I seal the compartment and fold my clothes neatly, returning them to their rightful place, before spreading myself over the hanging stretch of stitched kelp covered in swatches of bamboo cloth. Kelp is deceptively strong and holds my tall body and heavy muscle, suspending me in comfort as I attempt to sleep.

My eyes flutter closed, but sleep eludes me, as it always does. Instead I see her face. Hear her voice. Smell the sun and sand on her skin as her turquoise eyes crinkle with laughter.

Her hand reaches for me and my eyes flash open, my breathing coming too fast. I slip out of the sleeping net and leave my cabin in search of distraction.

I find it within the great shell, in the large mainroom where the crew eats and drinks together. Most are away, either on shift or resting between shifts, but a few men and one woman occupy a shelled table in the corner, their drinks clinking together as they toast the sea goddess and drink one—or more—for their fickle deity.

I find the bar and pour myself the sea swill I normally can't stand, clutching the shelled cup as I find a seat alone and away from the others. It's a bitter brew, with a fishy aftertaste that's acquired more than enjoyed, but it's strong and it bites my insides and burns me to the core, filling my blood with the song of the sea, a sweet, far away floating that none other can match. This is why people drink the brew. Not for the taste—for the forgetting.

Garen, a large man two heads taller than me, finger bones clanking in his black beard, raises his voice to tell a story to those around him. He fills their ears with tales of legends, of those who rode rakam and lived to tell of it. But when he moves on to the legend of Dak'Ra, I look up, curious.

It is a version of the tale I have heard many times—of the legendary warrior of the famed Ra family from Ra'Kia'Ruu Island who fell in love with the beautiful daughter of the Kia clan. They defied custom to be together, to make a new family separate from their first, and so they were banished to the sea. And there, under the three moons, they were taken by the depths into the warm embrace of the Deep Mother.

His big voice fills the room. "They say Dak'Ra and Sa'Kia still haunt the seas, searching for one another, two halves of one soul," Garen finishes.

I down the last of the swill until I can no longer feel my lips and my head is numb. "Her name was La'Kia," I say softly.

Garen looks over at me. "Ye deaf? It was Sa'Kia."

I meet his eyes. He's in a haze over his drink and looking for a fight. I'm not. Not with him, at any rate. "You're right," I say, raising my cup. "I might be misremembering. Maybe it was Sa'Kia."

He narrows his eyes. There's a stillness in the room, as if everyone is holding their breath, then the big man raises his cup and laughs heartily. "Aye, maybe it was."

I smile at the man whose face shifted with his smile, from menacing to jovial. "Thank you for the tale," I say, grinning.

I'm walking back to the bar for a refill when an awful sound fills all the empty space around us. It's a loud whine followed by a shriek of pain. I have only a fraction of a moment to react before the entire great shell is tipped to its side like a cup being knocked over, its contents spilled across the floor, the sound of teeth scraping against shell creating a discordant and frightening harmony with the cries of the great whale.

The bar crashes into my legs, swill staining my beige bamboo pants, turning them red as blood.

The crew members who were drinking are now shouting orders, scurrying up and out of the shell to find out what happened.

But I know what happened. I knew at the first loud whine.

The rakam have come.

———— • ————

The crew know. You can see the truth on their normally dark, fierce faces, now drained of color, their eyes, blends of browns with some light blues, all wide and hyper-focused. Some scramble over the great shell, pulling on cords of kelp, tying things down, as others grab long spears made of the very creatures they now fight. Long poles of bamboo with the deadly chiseled swords that make the rakam so dangerous. They are fierce creatures of medium to large build, made for fast swimming and lethal hunting, with long protruding faces that come out like a sword with teeth. They are nearly unbreakable, those mouths, and make excellent weapons, if you're lucky enough to kill one before it kills you.

Taking on one rakam is doable, if you have a team working together. But they rarely hunt alone. And when they come in a swarm, feeding on the full belly of the kiasheen, that's when you know you're in trouble.

If our kiasheen dies, we all fall in the water. And in the depths, where the rakam are faster and stronger, they do not worry about killing. They eat their prey alive.

I have seen a fallen ship once, heard the bone chill screams and swum in the blood red water. It was enough death for three lifetimes.

I take in the scene around me: Calla thrusts a spear into the depths, hitting a rakam in the belly as it snaps at the kiasheen's wing. Kanen shouts for someone to fetch the nets. Clam fires precious arrows into the waves. Garen, the storyteller from the mainroom who is by far the biggest of the crew, howls and jumps onto a rakam, drives a spear into its head, and jumps back onto the shell, laughing. The man is insane.

Something doesn't make sense. I grab the arm of someone scurrying by, stopping him. "Why didn't we fly over this section?" I ask. The kiasheen can fly. Not high and not for long stretches, but that is the beauty of their breed. They can fly over dangerous waters—rakam-infested waters—and land their crew in safety.

The man looks at me wild-eyed. "There ain't been no rakam in these parts in over two hundred years. We ain't ne'er had to fly over these waters. It don't make sense. The goddess is angry. She has cursed us." He taps three fingers on his chest and pulls out of my grip, running off with spear in hand.

In the distance, amongst the dark clouds, I see a shadow drift over us. It could mean the death of the rakam, but no. Not now. I can't reveal myself just yet.

Instead, I find my own spear and aid in the best way I know how.

By killing.

The kiasheen is crying into the night, its dark blood seeping into the water, attracting more and more deadly rakam.

Their fins break the surface of the choppy water as they surround us, dozens of them hungry, their sword mouths tearing at the flesh of the gentle whale who cannot defend itself against the onslaught. Who is trapped by shell and humans and the very girth of its body.

We are its only defense.

The spears, too precious a resource to be squandered, have a strand of tightly wound kelp at the end of them. I tie it around my wrist as the sky opens up, drowning us in the freshwater of rain even as the ocean swells up to swallow us.

I squint through the night, the crone moon now full in the sky. I take a breath, my vision focusing, my heart rate slowing, and I aim. A rakam sinks into the ocean, and I use the kelp to yank the spear out of the body and bring it back to my side. Again and again I aim, throw, kill.

I never miss. If anyone were to notice, I would be questioned—suspected of being more than I claim. But no one is paying attention to the mysterious stranger on their boat. They are all fighting to survive. As long as I don't hinder their survival, I am free to be myself—at least for now.

And so I continue my slaughter, killing one after another after another.

I hear a scream that is too human to ignore and see one of the crew members fly overboard, his spear not pulling free of the rakam in time. Before anyone can react, he is devoured by the great beasts, their long sharp mouths crunching into bone and flesh, making a quick meal out of the big man until his screams are only echoes in the sea, lost forever to his goddess.

I don't let that break my concentration. If the tide doesn't turn in our favor soon, I will have to reveal myself, and all my efforts, all my planning, will be for naught.

But none of that will matter if I am dead.

I am close to revealing myself, but I do not. I throw my spear, again and again. Then a young man of no more than sixteen years stumbles into the water, and the rakam impale him in the gut, spilling his intestines into the murky water even as he still lives.

His suffering does not end until they tear the limbs from his body. He then falls silent, sinking into the Deep Mother's embrace at last as the rakam feed on his remains.

I break. I need to rush back to my room, back to the box within my chest. As more of the crew fall to their death, as the kiasheen is torn apart, piece by piece, floating into the dark waters, as the storm hits us harder, as if the heavens themselves are in collusion with the rakam... I cannot let more die.

But before I can move, before I can act on my new plan, another ship enters my line of sight. Their kiasheen is enormous, at least three times bigger than ours. The night sky lights up with brightly-lit torches as spears shoot out from their whale-ship, impaling the remaining rakam and leaving the sea suddenly silent save for the low moaning of the still-injured kiasheen we ride atop.

Calla is already mustering a crew to administer healing to the kiasheen as the other ship approaches. They show the flags of the Great House of Ruu—a red volcano framed by a white, cloudless sky—marking them as one of the three Great Families of the Shattered Islands. My heart trips over itself when I see those flags, and I peer into their great shell, trying to identify their leader, to see if I recognize him. Or more importantly, to see if he will recognize me.

There is a pause in the flurry of movement as Captain Kanen assesses our new allies.

"Permission to come aboard!" A voice calls from the larger whale-ship.

The captain looks around, seeing the injury and toll this attack has taken on his crew. Those not killed were injured or exhausted in a fight that felt hours but lasted no more than minutes.

"We have supplies we will gladly share!" The voice calls again.

"Permission granted," the captain shouts back, gesturing with a nod of his head for a member of his crew, who scrambles to untie the kelp that holds the bridge shell up.

As the bridge falls to the side of the ship, the other boat latches itself onto us and stabilizes in the water, and three members of its crew walk across the shelled planks to greet our captain.

The man in the lead is tall, with strong streaks of blue in his hair, nails and eyes. His eyes are sharp as he takes in the state of our ship. "I am Han'Ruu, of the Great Family, captain of this ship. We were traveling to a nearby port for trade when we heard the cries of your kiasheen."

He looks around, noting the injuries, the blood splashing against the great shell. "We have supplies, food, healers. We are happy to help if you'd like to take sanctuary on our ship while you make repairs and heal your kiasheen."

Captain Kanen nods a head. "Yer generosity and the generosity of yer great family will be remembered," he says.

It doesn't take long to move most of the crew to the larger ship while the healthiest members of the crew stay behind to make repairs. Han'Ruu sends his own men and women to help.

I stay to the side, observing, noticing. When Han'Ruu's eyes land on mine, I nod as a submissive to a greater house, and he acknowledges, giving a half nod. "You do not look like crew," he says.

"Just a passenger," I say.

"And yet you speared the rakam like one born with a blade in his hand," he observes.

Why was this man paying so much attention to me, I wonder. "I come from one of the lesser houses of the Shattered Islands, trained as a hunter. It comes in handy."

He studies me, then nods. "Fair enough, brother. I hope you will enjoy the comforts of our ship until yours is seaworthy again."

"Of course."

He speaks as one of the Ruu, his accent faint, sophisticated, but I don't recognize him. It's been many years since I last set foot in the Shattered Islands. Much has changed, it seems.

I disappear onto the Ruu ship, nodding to their crew, who are well-kept and well organized. They wear the ornaments of traders, beads and shells that clank and clatter on their clothing, suggesting wealth and haggling abilities. I can smell the spices they have stored within the shell, cinnamon and nutmeg and more exotic flavors floating on the wet wind. The rain has stopped, and the damp world picks up the secondary scents more strongly now, with the cleansing of the clean water.

Another scent tickles my nose as I make my way deeper into the ship. I raise an eyebrow, intrigued, before I'm pulled into the mainroom where food and sea swill are being handed out liberally. I take my plate and cup from a burly woman with a thin mustache over her broad lips, and find a seat alone.

I eat slowly, quietly, watching as the crews from the two ships mix and mingle. Some have just returned from having wounds bandaged and are slugging down the swill as if they haven't drank in months. Others are inhaling their food like it's the last they might ever see. There's a rush that fills the blood after a life-threatening experience, and I see it playing out around me. People who held on too tightly are now letting loose, relieved that they don't have to be in charge, that someone else is here to fix things so they can stop shaking and find a way to breathe again.

I never stopped breathing, myself, until the woman walks in, her long white and blue dress teasing at her bare ankles. I catch a small design on her right ankle, made with pigments of red, before her dress moves to cover it once again. She fills a tray with clams, steamed fish and fried seaweed, and fills a large mug with sea swill, her eyes darting around as she works. Her long black hair is streaked with light strands of blue and piled high in a bun on her head. When she looks up, our eyes meet. Hers are striking, deep blue—almost turquoise—and so sad. She reminds me of the woman in my dreams, but only for a moment. Her eyes are too sad, her body too pulled into itself as she averts her face, grabs the tray and scurries out of the room before anyone can speak to her.

But as she closes the door behind her, she glances at me one more time, briefly, and I feel a voice form between us. A message. A plea.

I stand and slip out of the room, leaving my food and drink on the table.

I don't know where I'm going or why. I know only one thing.

I must speak to the woman with the blue eyes.

When I enter the side shell, the woman is gone.

I walk through halls, past doors to private cabins, the eyes of the local crew regarding me with suspicion as I continue my search with a casual non-chalance I don't feel but must fake. By the time I give up looking for her, I have traversed most of the ship, including the armory and a rare bathing room. This kiasheen and crew must be at least three times the size of the one I commissioned. Their gear is of top quality: thrice-thickened nets, stone-tipped arrows, and even an iron pot in the kitchen. This is the opulence that comes with being part of a great family. I do not care for it, but I find myself wondering if they have any pillows.

I have not found the woman, nor the pillows, when I'm deep in the belly of the shell, and I hear a scraping sound coming from a deck below me. I follow the noise and find a set of stairs protruding from the wall, part of the shell, part of the original carved design. I take them down and reach a door that does not lead to a private cabin or deck. It is guarded by two crew members playing a popular game, Shells and Stones. It's a betting game, and they have a small pot of coppers piling up between them as they toss their shells and stones and pray for luck to guide them.

The bushy-haired thin man looks up when I approach. He has a long goatee growing from the center of his pointed chin, the rest of his cheeks smooth as a child's. Bits of colored cloth are woven into his dark beard, with matching bits tied into his hair. He raises an eyebrow when he sees me. "You from the other ship." It's a statement, not a question.

I nod. "I think I got myself turned around looking for a place to piss."

The small round man with him guffaws and looks to his partner. "Man's got to piss, Mal'Ruu?" He turns back to me. "Ain't you ever heard of pissing off the side of the ship?"

His words are slurred, as if he's had too much sea swill while on duty.

"I'm a private man," I tell him.

"There be a latrine near the fluke," Mal'Ruu offers. "If you can't wait, there's a bucket in the kitchen. Tel'Ruu here just took a dump in it, so it be nice and fresh for you."

Neither man has moved from his seat, but I feel the tension in the air thicken when I don't immediately leave. "What's behind the door?"

Tel'Ruu sighs, seemingly annoyed, but Mal'Ruu smiles and leans forward. "We recently came upon a nest of drakruu," he says quietly. "Caught us a young'in."

My eyes grow wide like a child's on drowning day. The blue shadow, the sapphire scale, the winged reptile that, when fully grown, can carry a man or woman over the seas, lies behind that door. They are born black, but once they feed on the sapphires deep within the ocean their scales begin to turn blue. A merchant once told me the beasts cost more than a small island, and only a few have ever seen one up close. Seen one and lived, that is.

I grin, sheepishly. "You think I can—"

"Sorry," says Mal'Ruu, raising a hand to his bearded chin. "But no one goes in. Not even us. You understand."

I nod and turn to leave.

"Hey," says the tall man. "Mind keeping this to yourself? Some men feel the gold calling when they hear of drakruu, yes?"

I think of people like Clam and nod again. "Be at ease, searunner. I shall tell no one as I search for that bucket."

The men chuckle and return to their game as I drift back down the hall I came from, my hope of finding the mysterious woman with blue eyes lost for the time being.

But knowing there are drakruu on board piques my curiosity. This crew is like me. We are both full of secrets, and we are both lying.

———————— • ————————

When I return to the great shell, I'm not surprised to find a section of the surface covered with dead rakam. In life they are fierce, deadly, terrifying. They do not lose their awe in death. If anything, they are more terrifying, their ever unblinking, unclosing white eyes still staring at you as if the fight isn't finished and they will prevail.

They are brutal hunters, first impaling their victim with the tip of their spear-like mouths, usually in the gut. As their victim bleeds out, releasing intestines in the process, they begin to feed, slowly. Some say, you die from the pain before the wounds.

But this time, the rakam are the dead ones, lying in small pools of water as crew members from both ships strip the beasts of their skins and mouths for use in weaponry and clothing. The meat is saved for rare stews and broths —said to give a man a pair of fighting balls if eaten raw—and the useless bits are tossed back into the sea as food for other species.

The smell is strong, the stench carrying with the winds. I step away, letting my eyes fall back to the injured kiasheen. It's resting peacefully in the water, the healers doing their work to give the great whale its strength back as they use ancient balms and seaweed strips to close the wounds. I find the captain of my own ship supervising the process.

He looks up and grunts when he sees me. "If yer here to ask for those stones back, yer wasting yer breath. I told ye when we started this trip, once a man sets sail on these waters, his fate be in the hands of the goddess."

I shrug idly, never having intended to ask for compensation. It says much about the captain and the people he's dealt with that he thought I would. "We were lucky the Ruu ship came when it did," I say, eyeing the grizzled old man.

He glares at me from the side of his eyes, his scar twisting over the clenched muscles of his jaw and neck. "I taught them, you know," he says, glancing back at the healers. "Taught every one of them."

I raise an eyebrow. "You were a healer?"

"Still smell the healing sap on my hands." He takes a swig from his flask. "Back then all I wanted was to be captain, but now, I think that was a simpler time. A better time." He smiles and points at the working crew. "See how they apply the balm in layers, not all at once like those big island folk? That's the right way." His words focus on the healers, but I see his mind is elsewhere. I see it in his stone heavy shoulders, in the way his smile never reaches his eyes, in the way his hands cradle his flask like a lover. His mind is yet to forget. His mind is yet to forgive.

"Any idea when we'll be back on the water?" I ask.

"If all goes well, two suns' time."

I mentally calculate all that could happen in two suns' time.

Too much.

For a moment, we sit silently in the darkness. Before I leave, I grip the captain's shoulder and use my softest voice, the one I learned from my mother. "You led your men well," I say. "No other captain would have saved as many." Then I walk away swiftly, for it is a rare thing to hear words of kindness and know that no words are needed in return.

I spend the rest of the afternoon exploring this new ship, talking to the crew, getting to know as many of them as I can. My cover as "Sev," a lower-family cast off, stands. No one questions why my eyes are so bright, why I wear gloves to hide my nails, why I'm on this trip at all.

And so both crews settle into a rhythm that is focused and efficient. When the final repairs are made and our whale is deemed seaworthy once more, Han'Ruu invites everyone for a final celebratory dinner to cement our friendship and say our goodbyes before we set sail the next morning.

The dinner takes place on the larger whale-ship, atop the great shell, with everyone in attendance. It's a grand affair for a ship, with multiple courses of complex meals—including of course, roasted rakam—different flavors of wines and liquors, and several choices of desserts. The alcohol flows freely and there isn't a sober man or woman left by the time the crone moon is high in the sky.

I am sitting at the edge of the shell, watching the festivities from afar, cradling a wine cup in my hands, when Calla saunters over to me. She runs a long finger down my chest as she puckers her lips. "Such a waste these last few days have been," she says, grinning mischievously. "You and I could have had so much fun, if you'd wanted." She leans into my shoulder and whispers into my ear, her breath hot on my neck. "They have beds, ye know. And the moon is still high. There is time."

"Perhaps in another life," I say, gently pushing her away. As I do, she opens her lips and brushes the side of my face with her hand, but there is no part of me that responds to her touch. That part of me belongs to another.

Seeing my lack of excitement, she shakes her head and settles into the chair next to mine, clutching her cup close to her. She eyes the bundle tied with kelp that hangs from the side of my chair. "Tell me a secret tonight. Just one." Her eyes are bright and glossy from the drink, but also from unshed tears of those recently lost.

"I have no secrets worth sharing."

She laughs loudly. "That is the boldest lie ye've told so far. Come on, play along for just one night."

I hold eyes with her for a moment, and a genuine smile crosses my lips. "Fair enough." I lean in conspiratorially, whispering. "I really, really, really hate roasted rakam. Anything made of rakam makes me sick."

I lean back against my chair and she swats at my arm, but she laughs, as I'd hoped. "Truth?" she asks.

I hold three fingers over my heart. "Goddess sworn," I say. "Now your turn."

She nods, and her eyes take on a faraway look, her smile lost to something sadder. "I always wished I'd been born a man," she says after a moment.

I raise an eyebrow in honest surprise. "Why? Women have all the power on the islands."

She shakes her head. "That power, yes, it's real. It's there, but it's also its own prison, too. Men get to set sail their whole lives, without worry of childbirth and rulership. We have the power, but not the freedom."

"Men don't have freedom to stay," I remind her. "They are expendable, useful for hunting, for trading, maybe for leading crews, but they cannot choose their woman, claim and raise their own children, choose the life of their own desires."

She tilts her cup into her mouth and swallows what's left of her swill. "Ye speak truth. I suppose we are all trapped in our cages, some are just more gilded than others."

She stands then, her smile back. "I still have time, before I'm called back to bear children and take my place in society. I will make every moment count." She leans in, her breasts close to my face. "Ye should do the same."

She saunters away, her offer unspoken as she walks back to the great table at the middle of the shell, joining Clam and Garen in a game of Shells and Stones. Though I have always rejected her advances, she has never acted bitter, never cruel or spiteful. She even treats Clam well, though no one else does. Hers is a kind soul, one that, if things had been different, I could find happiness with. But there is another woman in my dreams, and her voice is the one I heed tonight.

Hours pass, and as the maiden moon begins to fade, Han'Ruu begins a game of Shells and Stones with a few of his men. I walk over to his side at the head of the great table. "May I join you?" I ask.

"Of course, brother. Of course. Sit down, have more wine." He snaps his fingers and the woman with the blue eyes refills my cup. I look at her, but she does not look at me as she finishes her duties and steps back behind Han'Ruu's chair.

"What shall we bet tonight, brothers?" asks Han'Ruu.

Mal'Ruu throws a dozen stones on the table and Tel'Ruu tosses an iron ring into the pile. I unfurl my bundle of kelp and lay a gleaming sword before them.

Their eyes grow wide. Their mouths curl in greedy smiles. The blade is carved from a pale blue rakam head. The guard and grip are forged from precious steel. But it is the pommel that draws their gaze. There, under the silver moonlight, glitters a deep blue sapphire.

Han'Ruu speaks softly. "What would you have me wager?"

I think it over, my eyes flashing to the woman. "Her," I say.

"But she is—"

"She is a slave, is she not?"

The captain's smile fades. Tel'Ruu watches us, his hand sliding below the table. I pay him little mind as I lock eyes with Han'Ruu, my words firm. "I will have her, and nothing else for this sword."

He looks to his men, then smiles. "Very well. Let us begin."

Tel'Ruu hands each of us a cup filled with three stones and three shells. No one else plays, for it is clear no one else has anything to match my wager. Han'Ruu and I shake our cups and place them face down upon the black table. I peek under my cup, counting the amount of shells with the ridges up and the stones showing three lines. Han'Ruu does the same. We both proclaim our points. We do not have to be honest.

"Two shells, two stones," says Han'Ruu. Tel'Ruu records four points, then a bonus two for the pair, writing with charcoal on a stone slate.

I shrug. "Three shells, one stone."

At this point, either player can challenge the other, and if Han'Ruu was to challenge me now, I would lift my cup and reveal my one shell. He would see that I lied, and I would lose. However, he must be sure, for if he is wrong, and I am being honest, then I am the winner.

There is no challenge, and we play three more rounds, adding up our points. I have nineteen. He has twenty-three. The first to reach thirty, or to win a challenge, wins the game.

I pat my gloves and clean my side of the table. We shake our cups and peek at our stones and shells. "One shell, two stones," says Han'Ruu, grinning. He is almost certain to win next round.

I shrug, keeping my face calm. "Three stones, three shells." Nine points. Enough for me to win. Those who have followed along, grow still.

Han'Ruu snickers. "Challenge, brother."

I lift my cup. Three stones. Three shells.

"Inspect them," says Han'Ruu, and Tel'Ruu checks my stones to see if they are marked on only one side. They are. He tosses them three times to see if they are weighed evenly. They are. He does not notice the black powder on my gloves, the one I spread over my side of the table, the one that covers the second marks on my stones.

Han'Ruu laughs. "What a game, brother, what a game. You may have her tomorrow—"

"Tonight."

The crew chuckles.

"Tonight then," says Han'Ruu, with a smile. "Feel free to use my cabin, brother."

I nod and stand and take my sword by the hilt and the blue-eyed woman by the arm. Calla catches my gaze as we leave the mainroom and smiles, clearly pleased I'm exercising my carnal rights, even if not with her.

My hand tightens on the blue-eyed woman's arm, and I escort her to the captain's quarters. Once inside, I secure the door and sit down, not on the bed, but on the floor, and motion for her to sit across from me. She remains standing, her eyes stabbing at me like rakam knives. She thought I was one thing, and now she thinks I am another. If, when her eyes pleaded with me earlier, she had any hope of escape, I have crushed it.

Now that I am within arm's length of her, I see where her beauty has been marred by bruises and scars, and the inked mark of the slave on her ankle. She is not as flawless as she seemed from a distance, but in her wounds she is made even more beautiful, like a broken bird who has almost forgotten how to fly.

"What is your name?" I ask.

"Vasa."

"Vasa, tonight, you must stay in this room," I say. "You must bar the door. You must not let anyone in until the sun has risen. Do you understand?"

Her eyes are confused, her lips trembling. "Why?"

"Because the men outside must pay."

She is quiet for a long moment, and then her voice turns harsh. "Fool, all of you will be asleep soon."

"We will not," I say. "My crew knows about the wine."

She blinks, then frowns, challenging me. "How?"

"Do not worry how," I say. "Will you stay in this room, Vasa?"

She nods.

I sigh with relief. "Then it begins." I take three deep breaths and exit the room. I lift the necklace around my neck and place the whistle to my lips. I blow.

And a roar rips through the skies.

———— • ————

The drakruu descends like shadow, like death. She glides around the ship, the beat of her wings a steady thrum amidst the shouts and screams as all look to the skies.

I walk forward, my sword flashing in the moonlight. "Drakruu," yells the man who calls himself Mal'Ruu, as he grabs a spear from the side of the ship. I step forward and slice open his calf. He sprays blood over the shell as he crumbles, cursing and spitting.

The crew rushes to fetch spears and arrows, and the man who calls himself Tel'Ruu notices my blade and draws his own. We exchange three moves, and then he falls, his sword hand cut from his arm. Han'Ruu yells for his men to fetch nets, yells of the stones a drakruu is worth, and then his eyes meet mine. They see the bloody men in my path, and they grow wide with fear.

He tells one of his crew, a women larger than me, to stop me. She charges, yelling, rakam-tipped spear pointed at my chest. She makes it three steps, and then she is pulled into the sky. My drakruu carries her high, shredding her body with sharp teeth, and once she no longer screams and jerks, she falls into the water like a bloody rock casting red ripples over the dark sea.

"Everyone to me," yells Han'Ruu. "To me." His crew rallies around their captain, and that is when my crew draws their daggers, surrounding Han'Ruu and his men. My drakruu lands behind me, her sapphire scales catching the moonlight as she roars.

"How?" asks Han'Ruu. "The wine—"

"We changed the cask," I say.

"But how did you know? We had the ship of a Great Family. We knew their customs and their speech."

"Even the greatest of Ruu ships do not carry thrice-thickened nets, nor stone- tipped arrows. They are traders, not warriors. That is for the Ra."

"How would you know this? Who are you?"

My eyes drift to the rest of Han'Ruu's crew. "I am the one who has taken this ship. I am your captain now."

Some of the men and women glance at the bodies behind me. "What if we join you?" someone calls. "What then?"

"Then your lives will be spared."

Han'Ruu spits. "Spared only to be branded traitors and tied to a rock by the sea." His crew look to him, they look to me. Their faces shift from fear to anger, to curiosity and fear again, fitful as the wind.

"He is not wrong," I say. "Those who surrender will be given to the Ruu. You have dishonored them and done far worse, and they will deal with you as they see fit."

The crew recoils, and in their frightened eyes I see that I have lost them. Better to have a chance at life here than a promised death soon after. They begin to shuffle forward, but I will not let them. There will be no glorious battle, no triumphant last stand. I have let too many die for my cause already.

I pull the sapphire, the one I kept in my box, from my pocket, palming it in my grip. It is almost too big to grasp. I put the thread that holds it over my neck, and the stone gleams and burns against my skin. I remove my gloves, revealing my bright azure nails, and I draw the heat of the sapphire within. My black hair turns blue, my eyes glow in the night.

Both crews stare at me with shock and wonder. Stormborn, they call me. Stonebearer, they whisper.

One of Han'Ruu's men breaks from the group and runs to the side shell. I do not follow. Instead I sprint to the edge of the kiasheen and dive into the sea.

There is no splash, no cold shock, no dampness as I hit the water. I slice through the waves, the sapphire burning against my chest, allowing me to move through water easier than I move through air, allowing me to speed up faster and faster with nothing to stop me. I glide under the kiasheen faster than a rakam, faster than an arrow, and I burst out from the water toward the fluke of the ship. I fly through the sky, a trail of water still following me as I curve around onto the ship, and smash myself into the fleeing man. He crashes into the ground as I land on my feet, my breath steady, my clothes dry.

Women scream. Men cry. The false crew drops their weapons. Han'Ruu runs.

He is on the other side of the ship now, so I jump into the water, spiraling under the kiasheen's belly. The sapphire burns but it is no longer as hot as before. It must bathe in the sun and absorb its rays to be of use to a Stonebearer, and the more it is used the more heat and light are drained, until the stone must be charged once more.

I explode from the water and curve myself to follow Han'Ruu as he reaches the door of the great shell. Someone—Calla—attempts to fight him off. They exchange a blow, but Calla's blade slips, and Han'Ruu's finds purchase in flesh.

Calla falls, her hands covering her bleeding chest, color draining from her face. She will not live from such a wound. She glances up, her gaze meeting mine for a brief moment. She smiles a bloody smile before the light in her eyes fades forever.

I take a breath, letting the rage burn and grow inside me, and then I fly through the door into the great shell, following Han'Ruu. Before I can catch him, my momentum runs out and I land running. Here, within the bowels of my ship, my sapphire will not aid me, my drakruu cannot help me.

I follow Han'Ruu deeper and deeper into the ship, letting my anger grow hotter, preparing myself for what is about to come.

I find him at the bottom of the ship, in a room that protrudes outward from the kiasheen and over the water. This room was locked before. It is locked no longer.

Han'Ruu stands over the pool of water at the base of the shell, over the wild rakam thrashing there, their teeth scraping against the walls of their prison. His back is turned to me, his voice is soft. "I am of the Ruu," he says.

"I know," I say, taking a step forward, my blade lowered. "Why did they banish you?"

"I loved a woman," he says, turning his face to me, his eyes red and weary. "All we wanted was a home together, a family. Children we could call our own. You understand, don't you, Dak'Ra?"

I pause at the sound of my true name. "You know who I am," I say, the fire cooling within me. I think of Calla and let it rage once more. "Then you know I cannot allow this."

"Why not? We were both banished," he roars. "We were both thrown to the seas, left to scavenge and scrape to survive. This was my ship, and I took it back after my first mother said I was no son of Ruu. Now I take what I must, not because I wish to, but because they made me so. The Ra family did the same to you. You search for La'Kia because of them. You lost her because of them."

My mind drifts to La'Kia, to the sound of her laughter and the smell of her hair, and I imagine her warm embrace, her tender lips, and the way we lay atop the great mountain and talked of the children we would have and the dreams we would make real.

I take a breath, and let the image fade. I will not think of La'Kia when I do what comes next. I take a step forward. "We are not the same."

Han'Ruu sighs, and the weariness leaves his face, like a man who has had a great weight lifted, like a man who has been told he may come home. We exchange twelve moves, our blades ringing as shouts grow closer, as the rakam twist and snap and splash. Han'Ruu is fast, skilled in his way of Ratat, but I am faster, and on the thirteenth move, I pierce his belly. He falls to his knees, groaning and whimpering. The pain makes a boy out of man. "Sa'Ra," he mutters, voicing the name of his love. "Moon of my heart. The waves bring me home." He looks up at me. "Give me the quick death, brother."

I raise my blade to his neck. I could end it now, but Calla's bloody smile flashes in my mind.

I raise my foot and kick him backwards into the water.

In the depths, where the rakam are faster and stronger, they do not worry about killing. They eat their prey alive. Some say, you die from the pain before the wounds.

———— • ————

After a battle, when the blood rush fades, you are left with the ghosts of those you have killed. For me, it is harder than the killing—there is too much blood lust and battle cry to think on such things then, but in the end, when the calm returns and humanity settles back into you... in the end, you remember that you are alone in your mind, and you must live with what you have done.

I should not have given Han'Ruu to the rakam, but he had killed Calla and enslaved Vasa and so many others. I wanted him to suffer. A part of me hopes he suffers still, deep in the Deep Mother's embrace.

Kanen's crew killed the rakam hidden in the bowels of the larger ship; their heads and skins and meat will fetch a nice price at trade.

The crew cleaned themselves and the decks of blood. Those who were injured received medical care, often in the form of strong sea swill.

Many songs were sung and many tears were shed and many toasts were shared over clinking cups.

I saved my tears for Calla, whose friendship extended to so many, who died with that contagious smile frozen on her lips. Captain Kanen gave me leave to honor her in my own way, so I took her body upon my drakruu, and together we flew over moonlit waves until we reached sapphire blue waters. There, I kissed her forehead and whispered the old words of my people. And when the crone moon set, I sent Calla into the waves, where she will once again smile and laugh in the company of those she loves.

———— • ————

The rakam will come. The blood in the water draws them. So I tell Garen, who now steers the Ruu kiasheen under my command, to take us skyward. He pulls hard upon the reins, and with a great moan the giant beast tilts its head upwards and flaps its wings. We fly higher, drifting on the water. We fly higher, the wings barely touching waves. We fly higher, and we are free of the sea.

I look down upon the shimmering waves and up at the glowing sun. There is a peace in the sky that is not found in the sea. Here you feel as if you have found something man was never meant to find, a secret paradise away from the depths below. I remember La'Kia. I remember taking her flying on my drakruu, and the kisses and whispers we shared with no one around to hear. I told her then that it was in the water I was strong, but it was in the sky I was free. How foolish I was.

A loud moan breaks me from my haze. Kanen follows us in his ship with half his crew, his kiasheen drifting beside mine. The blue skin of the whales is like dancing waves in the light. The shells are like gleaming pearls. The smaller kiasheen opens its mouth wide, and I know it's feeding on the small creatures that live in the sky, just as it feeds on the small creatures in the water during long voyages. The beasts are calm and peaceful. I wish I could be like them.

"You are Dak'Ra," says Vasa, standing behind me at the rostrum. She is the first to confront me, but I have heard the crew's whispers, and I know they have all guessed who I am.

"And you are of the Ra family as well," I say, turning to face her.

She nods, startled. "Yes. I have a sister back on Ra'Kia'Ruu. Three years ago, I was on a ship near the rakam teeth, training to be a Stonebearer, when this ship took me and mine. They were all sold in a week. I..."

"I understand," I say kindly. She need not relive the horrors Han'Ruu forced upon her for my sake. But there is one thing that puzzles me. "How is it that you walked without chains? That you moved about the ship freely?"

Her blue eyes flash with ferocity. "Han'Ruu knew I would not reveal his schemes. If he had threatened me with my death, I would have spoken in a stone's throw. But he threatened pain and the deaths of any I told. I would not trade the chance of freedom for the lives of others."

I nod and place a hand on her shoulder.

She recoils, startling both of us. "I'm sorry," she says.

"Don't be."

241

She bites her lip and turns to leave, but there is one more question I must ask. One I have already asked of the false crew locked within the shells below. "Have you seen a black kiasheen?"

She pauses. "That is the ship that took your lover?"

"It took us both," I say softly. "Later, I was sold to a family of land, she to a ship much like this."

"That is why you ride the kiasheen," she says. "You search for crews who wreck and steal like this."

I nod.

She turns her face to the side so I cannot see her blue eyes. "I have not seen the black ship," she says.

Hours pass, and when the sun is beginning to set, the kiasheen land. We tie our ships and set up planks between the shells to easily cross from one to another. On the great shell of the large kiasheen, Captain Kanen hands me a cup of swill and holds his up for a toast. "I owe you my life and the life of my crew and ship."

"You owe me nothing," I say, "but I do have one request."

"Name it and it be yers."

"Make sure the men and women below are given over to the Ruu, and make sure Vasa'Ra is returned to her family."

My drakruu roars amongst the clouds, and we hear the splash as she dives deep into the sea to catch her dinner.

"You won't be staying with us, then?" asks Captain Kanen.

I shake my head.

"Yer woman?"

I nod.

"Then may the goddess guide your way, and feel well knowing I will honor yer request. I swear it by the Deep Mother." I grasp his forearm as he does mine. "And if ever ye need help," he says, grinning, "remember ye have friends here."

I turn to leave, and Garen grabs me in a giant hug, lifting me, cracking my spine. "So it was La'Kia after all," he says. "I'll be getting that tale right from now on, brother. You best know I'll be getting that tale right and spreading it wide and far. Dak'Ra still rides the waves."

He chuckles, rattling the bones in his beard as he puts me down. I gasp for breath melodramatically and grin. "Thank you," I say, turning to the great shell and the rest of the crew. "It has been a pleasure to ride the waves with you, brothers and sisters, but there is one more thing I ask of you," I yell. "Tell all you see that Dak'Ra still lives. Tell them he comes for the black kiasheen."

It is late when I stand on the rostrum with my drakruu, tightening the saddle she wears on her back. Most of the crew is asleep, and even the kiasheen slumbers, when Vasa'Ra approaches me, her white dress billowing in the wind. "May I?" she asks, raising her hand to my drakruu.

I nod. "Here, behind me, away from the head."

She stands to my side and touches the blue scales below the wing. "What's its name?"

"Her name is Rin, but I call her Rakam Eater."

Vasa'Ra giggles, and I realize it's the first time I've seen her laugh. It is short-lived as her grin fades.

"I have seen the black ship," she says, her voice trembling, "and the man who leads it. He is the one who killed my first mother when my sister and I were but children. He is the one who took three Ra ships with one. Do not go to him," she pleads, touching my hand.

"If it was my life, I would stay. But my life is no longer mine. It belongs to another, and she waits amongst the waves." I push Vasa'Ra's hand away and mount Rin. I pull something from my pocket and toss it to the blue-eyed woman.

"No, you can't—"

"Keep it," I say.

Her eyes dazzle at the sapphire in her hands. "But why?"

"Because a man once did the same for me," I say, grinning as I pull on the reins and lift into the sky toward the maiden moon.

As I drift through the pale blue clouds, I think of that man who gave me my first sapphire.

He is the one who rides the black kiasheen.

About The Author

Karpov Kinrade is the pen name for the husband and wife writing duo of USA TODAY bestselling, award-winning authors Lux Kinrade and Dmytry Karpov. Together, they write fantasy and science fiction. Look for more from Karpov Kinrade in The Nightfall Chronicles, Shattered Islands, and The Forbidden Trilogy. They live with three little girls who think they're ninja princesses with super powers, and who are also showing a propensity for telling tall tales and using the written word to weave stories of wonder and magic.

For more information, visit KarpovKinrade.com.

Afterword

Did you like these stories? Then you might be interested in following the daily reviews at ImmerseOrDie (immerseordie.com)—the site that scours the indie marketplace to find great new authors, and then promotes them to the world.

Whether it's short story anthologies like the one in your hand, StoryBundles of full-length novels like this (storybundle.com/indie), or some program we haven't dreamed up yet, ImmerseOrDie is committed to celebrating the best of indie genre publishing. Tough love for a tough market.

Or maybe you're an author yourself and you think your work will stand up to our test. If so, then why not send it in and maybe get a little of this promotional action for yourself? Guidelines are available right here (creativityhacker.ca/iod-submissions). All you need is the guts.

So no matter what brought you here, don't be shy. Get in touch. And by all the holy floating baubles in all the worlds, please feel free to give this book to your friends, or send them a link (creativityhacker.ca/shiny) and let them download it for themselves.

Help us share the awesome, and we'll keep bringing you more.

www.ingramcontent.com/pod-product-compliance
Lightning Source LLC
Chambersburg PA
CBHW061613170626
46811CB00001B/412